Contents

The Mutiny

A Novel

JULIAN RATHBONE

ABACUS

First published in Great Britain in 2007 by Little, Brown
This paperback edition published in 2008 by Abacus
Reprinted 2008 (twice)

A CIP catalogue record for this book
is available from the British Library.

ISBN 978-0-349-11932-8

Map by Russ Billington

Typeset in Goudy by M Rules
Printed and bound in Great Britain by
Clays Ltd, St Ives plc

Papers used by Abacus are natural, renewable and recyclable
products made from wood grown in sustainable forests and certified
in accordance with the rules of the Forest Stewardship Council.

Mixed Sources
Product group from well-managed
forests and other controlled sources
www.fsc.org Cert no. SGS-COC-004081
© 1996 Forest Stewardship Council
FSC

Abacus
An imprint of
Little, Brown Book Group
100 Victoria Embankment
London EC4Y 0DY

An Hachette Livre UK Company
www.hachettelivre.co.uk

www.littlebrown.co.uk

Julian Rathbone is the author of many books, including the bestselling *The Last English King* and the Booker-shortlisted *Joseph*, as well as the hugely acclaimed *A Very English Agent*. He is married with two children and lives in Hampshire.

Praise for *The Mutiny*

'Although the story of the mutiny has been told many times, it is fascinating to revisit it in such intelligent company ... ambitious, sweeping ... The British, with their quaint slang, and casual, unthinking racism, are very convincingly drawn. Rathbone also elicits great sympathy for the Indian mutineers, with their complex, often contradictory, motives'
Sunday Telegraph

'A gripping read ... keeps the reader glued to the pages'
The Hindu

'Enjoyable and exciting to read ... Rathbone reveals himself to be a novelist of skill, compassion and imagination'
TLS

'The fierce drama, complexity and enigma of the Indian Mutiny make it the most compelling of historical settings'
Waterstone's Book Quarterly

I should like to dedicate this book to all who have helped me write it or contributed to whatever good is in it. The list is far too long to include here – but you know who you are

Author's Note

This book is a novel, a fiction. Most of it relates the imagined adventures of people I have invented, although historical personalities do appear with the names and characteristics by which they were known. Both at the time and since, contradictory judgements have been made about some of these people. Where this has meant that I was faced with a choice, I have been guided by what I perceived would best suit the fictional story I am trying to tell.

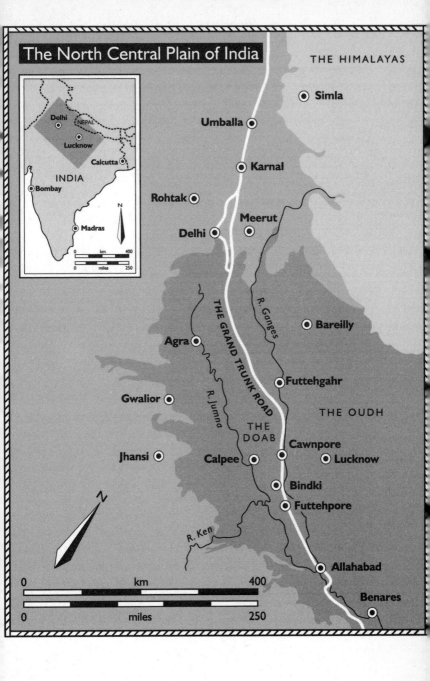

The North Central Plain of India

THE HIMALAYAS

Simla

Umballa

Karnal

Rohtak

Meerut

Delhi

THE GRAND TRUNK ROAD

R. Ganges

Bareilly

Agra

R. Jumna

Futtehgahr

Gwalior

THE DOAB

THE OUDH

Jhansi

Calpee

Cawnpore

Lucknow

Bindki

Futtehpore

R. Ken

Allahabad

Benares

INDIA

Delhi

NEPAL

Lucknow

Calcutta

Bombay

Madras

N

0   km   400
0   miles   250

0   km   400
0   miles   250

People rise up, that's a fact, and that's how subjectivity (the subjectivity of anyone) becomes part of history and breathes life into it. A delinquent weighs up his life against excessive punishment; a madman has enough of being locked away and dispossessed; a people rejects the regime that oppresses it. This doesn't make the first one innocent, cure the second, or guarantee the third the future it seeks . . . Nobody is obliged to find these muddled voices sing better than any others or that they speak the deepest of truths. That they exist, and that against them is everything that strains relentlessly to silence them, are enough for it to make sense to listen to them and to seek to understand what they are trying to say.

Michel Foucault, *Dits et écrits*, III (Gallimard, translated by Alayne Pullen)

One of the keys to understanding the sudden darkening of the horizon, is Marx's conception of 'primitive accumulation' – the earth-shaking use of force to create or restore the social conditions of profitability.

Retort, *Afflicted Powers* (London and New York, 2005) (as quoted in the *New Left Review* 36, November–December 2005). The group Retort was commenting on the Iraq crisis

In actual history it is notorious that conquest, enslavement, robbery, murder, briefly force, play the great part . . . As a matter of fact, the methods of primitive accumulation are anything but idyllic.

Karl Marx, *Capital I*, Chapter XXVI, The Secret of Primitive Accumulation

PART I

The English

1

Sophie Hardcastle, eighteen years old, not yet used to being Mrs Hardcastle, still thinking of herself as Sophie Chapman, called goodbye to her husband Tom and closed the front door of their substantial bungalow. Shaking out and hoisting her parasol she crossed the small garden to the latched gate in the picket fence. A large and heavily mustachioed sepoy in white uniform with red facings and red turban came somewhat perfunctorily to attention and offered her an open smile.

Perhaps too open.

'Mem!' he said, and saluted – somewhat sloppily she thought.

He wasn't armed and she didn't see how he was much use, except to keep pedlars and beggars at bay. And that smile – not so much open as knowing. She allowed herself a slightly irritated shrug and set her face to the long gravelled ramp that would take her through a hairpin and on to the Upper Mall.

The hillside dropped steeply away beneath evergreen oaks, quite unlike any she had seen before, and the more elegantly horizontal fronds of the deodar cedars. These she liked. Though etiolated, they put her in mind of the big cedar on her father's lawn, just in front of the ha-ha, back in Dorset. Crows, more obviously hooded than jackdaws, bustled busily through the spaces at her eye level, black kites swung above them, and an even higher buzzard rode the thermals with almost no movement at all. A red-faced monkey bared quite vicious looking canines in an unwelcoming snarl and swung into the

3

first crotch of what it clearly believed was its personal tree. Beyond it all a spur of a real mountain, still clinging to the last rags of a snowy shawl, floated, sun-tinged with gold.

And this, she thought, is supposed to be the part of India that is most like England – outside the cantonments of Calcutta where they had stopped for a week before taking a steamer up the Ganges to Allahabad and then a smaller one to Cawnpore. After that it had been elephants, a novel and terrifying experience, especially on the narrow hairpinning track which had climbed the last twenty miles. She shrugged off a pang of cold loneliness that had become more familiar than she had thought likely during the three months since she had turned from her mother's clinging embrace and allowed her new husband to hand her up into the coach that would take them to Plymouth.

The Upper Mall, divided between a gravelled path and a sandy track that echoed Hyde Park's Rotten Row, was busy. Between her and the white-towered church nearly half a mile away, dedicated to the Christ and therefore called Christchurch, gentlemen in tall top-pers, with ladies on their arms whose bulging dresses were supported inside by domes of crinoline, cruised like passing ships. They saluted each other with raised hats or inclinations of ringleted, bonneted heads, only occasionally heaving-to to exchange a greeting, gossip or news. Some rode, on lively chestnut Arabs for the most part, though a couple of swells from one of the Queen's cavalry regiments made a race of it for a furlong or so, the hooves of their handsome black chargers throwing up the coarse sand and gravel.

Those who had been introduced to Sophie during the previous fortnight included her in these acknowledgements and perhaps their heads turned for a moment after she had passed. Again, this irritated her. She knew she was good-looking, had a good figure which fitted the hour-glass fashion without undue constriction, but she did not like to be in any way an object of more than perfunctory attention from slight acquaintances. Consequently she held her beaded reticule across her lower stomach at all times, though as yet there was nothing at all to be noticed.

It was a relief then to hear a quickened footstep behind, and sense before she saw the presence of Catherine Dixon, falling in somewhat breathlessly behind her.

'Mrs Hardcastle? May I walk with you?'

'Oh, please call me Sophie.' She stopped and turned, waiting for her new acquaintance to catch up. 'I am still quite likely to look around me for this Mrs Hardcastle person when she is addressed in my presence.'

'Sophie, then, and you must call me Catherine. Mind your step – monkey poo, such a nuisance. If we get on I shall allow you Cathy.' Mrs Dixon looked to be about twenty-five though her manner was of someone younger than that, while her figure was a touch more matronly. 'You are on your way to Lady Blackstock's?'

'Yes. And you too?'

'Of course. As you are no doubt aware we are the West Country–Meerut Contingent. The wives anyway. I expect you've realised that that's the common factor. At the beginning of every summer, a week or so after we have gathered here again, she gets us together, those of us who have spent the cooler months in Meerut, or used the place as a staging post. And then we meet again in September before going back down again. It's quite a jolly idea, really. Helps the new faces, like you – there are always some – to get to know us all, that sort of thing. And when we get in the dumps there's always someone to talk to who knows Wells or Yeovil or Sherborne, whatever.' All this said in a rush. Mrs Dixon always spoke in a rush not moderated by the roundness of her West Country vowels and the ripple of her 'r's. But even she had to take a breath and Sophie seized the moment.

'I welcome her good intentions,' she interjected. 'But I confess I am somewhat in awe of Lady Blackstock.'

'Oh, she's a good stick, believe me. A bark yes, but no bite. And she stood by me when most thought I had behaved somewhat wantonly.'

Sophie reflected that 'old stick' would not have been her choice of words to describe Lady Blackstock. Massive, lightning-blasted oak, perhaps, and a very English one at that.

'How was that then?'

'Have you not heard? It was quite a subject of conversation and even judgement a year ago, but has blown over since then. One scandal drives out another, don't you think? And there have been several since. There, on our right is the Gaiety,' she indicated a building with a rococo frontage, set in the hillside just below the Mall, so it was actually below them though entered from where they were; 'we have such fun with our productions. A *Midsummer Night's Dream* is spoken of for this season and I shall read for the part of Hermia . . .' she paused to glance up at Sophie. 'You could be Helena, you know? I'm sure you'll hear all about it sooner or later.'

They walked on past the church and the lending library into a more residential area where the houses were houses not bungalows, much like substantial suburban villas back home, with extensive lawns and gardens. Catherine guided them down a short drive planted with rhododendron, to a quite modern house, gabled, with a small tower at one end and a glazed lantern in the middle of the roof. She pulled the polished bell-knob while Sophie furled her parasol.

An elderly Sikh in a white turban, white single-breasted jacket buttoned at the neck, white pantaloons and black shoes that were ever so slightly curled at the toes, pushed open the double door from inside and stood aside for them to enter. She could not but notice that his left hand had suffered some accident – all but the two outside fingers were missing.

'Mrs James Dixon,' he murmured, 'and . . .?'

'Mrs . . . Hardcastle,' Sophie muttered and then, aware of rising colour, said too loudly, 'Mrs Sophie Hardcastle.'

The Sikh bowed very slightly and announced them in a quite gentle voice which yet had enough weight to be heard by anyone interested enough to pay attention.

'You should say Mrs Tom Hardcastle, you know. Until you are a widow,' Catherine murmured.

'I am Sophie, not Tom,' Sophie replied.

'Of course.'

'And I have no intention of being a widow.'

'Indeed, I should hope not.'

This exchange was conducted *sotto voce* and with covert smiles as they progressed across a parquet floor beneath the large glass and wrought-iron lantern, set like a dome in the moulded ceiling, to the far end of the big room where Lady Blackstock held court. Behind her a huge heavy silk punkah was kept unnecessarily in motion by a young lad whose skin was exceedingly dark. Unnecessary because even in the last week of May the mountain air was cool enough – that was the point of being there, six thousand feet above the plains. The boy's skin was much darker than the Sikh's – virtually, Sophie thought, a nigger, though there was nothing Negroid about the cast of his features which were, to her Caucasian eye, attractive, with a well-shaped nose set between darkly luminous eyes.

But now Lady Blackstock was greeting her with a large, plump, gloved hand, whose plumper wrist disappeared first into a foam of lace and then a quite startling turquoise satin. Sophie took the hand briefly and contrived a motion of her body that was not quite obsequious enough to be taken for a curtsey, but was more than a mere bob. Truly she found her hostess overpowering. She was very big, with a huge embonpoint that provided a worthy cushion for a cascade of emeralds and diamonds. This flowed over her Rubenesque shoulders from under a lacy mobcap that sat on the back of her head, pinned to dyed black hair which tumbled about her cheeks in springy ringlets. Her face, which was broad and must once have been handsome, was rouged and powdered, the lips painted.

'Such a pretty gel,' she boomed. 'Young Tom Hardcastle should be a very happy man. How did he find you?'

Young? But he was, at thirty-three, fifteen years older than Sophie. Not that she minded. As her mother had said, he could be expected, being a mild man as well as older, to treat her carefully, as something to be treasured. Older husbands were always so much more attentive than younger ones. She supposed though that it was all a matter of where you stood. Lady Blackstock was well into her fifties.

'Tom's father, and his father before him, have been our solicitors in Blandford Forum for a hundred years perhaps. Our marriage was the most natural thing in the world.'

'Your family are litigious? Need the services of a lawyer awfen?'

'Not at all, madam. The connection was far more social than professional, the professional side being confined to conveyancing when a property was bought or sold, setting up marriage settlements, executing wills. Nothing more exciting than that, I assure you.'

'I meant no offence, dear. Now run along and enjoy yourself. The tea is Indian, of course, so much more robust than the China stuff I was brought up on, almond gaufres, some orange jelly I believe, and so forth.' She turned to the older woman at her side but did not drop her voice. 'She's eating for two, you know. Married three or four months, healthy girl like that . . .'

With four older brothers who paid her little attention, Sophie had spent much of her pre-pubescent years in her father's stables, where her companions had been grooms. Even now, occasionally, out of extreme provocation and never out loud, she resorted to the vocabulary she had picked up from them. 'Bitch,' she muttered.

Seeing that Catherine had turned to the left away from her ladyship, she turned right, not wishing to appear clinging to her only real acquaintance in the room. The room was nearly circular apart from the one straight side that housed the main entrance. There were five arched alcoves whose inner walls were filled with flush doors decorated with grisaille paintings depicting aspects of the sub-continent. The first she came to was of an almond-eyed rajah on an elephant. Meanwhile, a pretty Native girl in a yellow saree handed her a small teacup and saucer, blue and white with gold-leaf rims (which Sophie recognised was Spode willow pattern, like her grandmother's back in Shaftesbury) and indicated a three-tiered cake stand set on a small table with a walnut veneer. Sophie took a bright yellow tart whose base was very flaky pastry; it was sweet and yet eggy too. She didn't like it, but the tea was all right.

She continued to move clockwise round the room and was soon chatting with the other guests, all women, all married, and several of them not much older than she, about fifteen altogether. For the most part they had a lot in common. They were all from the West Country, occasionally shared acquaintances back home, and all, apart from Sophie herself, well acquainted with each other. What did become apparent though was that the reasons they, or rather their husbands, were in India covered a wide range of occupations. Sophie had expected that they would all be the wives of officers, but two were married respectively to a supervisory railway engineer and a surveyor for the telegraph; two had district magistrates for spouses and the husband of another, a Mr Andrews, was a deputy collector.

'What of?' Sophie asked, with enthusiasm. 'Geological specimens? Native flora?'

'Taxes,' was Mrs Andrews' answer. 'What else? In a little principality a long way south from here, called Jhansi. We usually stop off at Meerut on the way out and on the way back, since we have a large acquaintance at the station there.'

But the husbands of most, and in one case a brother, were officers in one of the Queen's regiments or one of those raised by the Company.

'And what does your husband do?' was the inevitable follow-up.

'Tom is an assistant advocate general,' she replied, and rather

8

hoped that the matter would stop there. She really had very little idea of what his duties consisted, except that he seemed to spend a lot of time at his desk in his study, surrounded by shelves of leather-bound law books.

Presently one lady, a lean woman with a pointed nose, a white but freckled face and bright red hair, took her elbow and guided her back into one of the alcoves.

'So you are young Tom Hardcastle's wife,' she began. Her voice was high, sharpish, but at this moment moderated to something like a whisper.

'I am. But not for the first time surprised to hear him described as young. He is so much older than I am.'

'Unattached gentlemen of whatever age are always young to the rest of us. In the hill stations at all events. Unless, my dear, they are evangelical Christians of whom we have recently had far too many. Evangelicals are almost always old far beyond their years, don't you think?'

'I don't think my Tom is at all an evangelical.'

'Indeed not. Serious, hard-working perhaps, but then, being not the brightest pin in the cushion, he has to keep on top of his job. So my husband says.'

'Your husband?'

'Of course, I must introduce myself. He is Captain Arthur Fetherstonhaugh and commands a troop in the Queen's 9th Lancers. He comes from Frome in Somerset which is why I am a guest of Lady Blackstock, though I have never been to the place. I am from Waterford, my mother a Beresford.' This was said with a touch of condescension and Sophie realised she was in the presence of a person with pretensions. Indeed the fact that she had made the point that the 9th Lancers were a British regiment, rather than a Native one with English officers, was already an indication.

Mrs Fetherstonhaugh went on, her voice even quieter than before. Without the acerbity of her usual speaking voice a trace of an Irish lilt was apparent but entirely of the Ascendancy, not a hint of your ordinary Irish person.

'I could not help noticing that you arrived with Catherine Dixon. Is she a friend of yours?'

'I hope she may be. But our acquaintance so far is limited to two rather formal meetings.'

'You are not aware, then, of what she did a year or so ago?'

'No, and if what you are about to say does her discredit, then I would prefer not to be.'

'Hear of it you will, my dear, if not from me then from the next gossip you meet. However, it is a matter of personal judgement rather than a moral issue and I will leave you to come to your own conclusions. But I think it only fair that you should know before you get in too deep with her.'

Sophie was now torn between a desire to know more and a growing dislike for this lady from Ireland. At all events she allowed Mrs Fetherstonhaugh to put yet more pressure on her elbow and move her further into the alcove whose monochrome painting this time depicted a dancing god with a high crown that resembled the heaped-up pinnacles of a Hindu temple and whose performance was enhanced by the fact that he boasted six limbs rather than the usual four.

'Mrs Dixon is in the grip of two passions which she indulges to excess and which occasionally come into conflict. The first is for her husband, the second for her four children, with a fifth on the way.'

'These seem worthy feelings to me.'

'So we all thought. Yet it was also supposed that when her eldest son reached the age of seven she would find it a relief to have him shipped back to England to the care of a grandmother and the ministrations of a good boarding school. The whole family went back to make the arrangements but when the time came to return here, Mrs Dixon refused to go. She said her place was with Adam, the seven-year-old son, and she would not part from him but arrange instead to remain in Dorchester—'

'Sherborne.'

'Wherever. Where she would see to his education while continuing to look after his three younger siblings, two of whom are girls. Poor Dixon was at his wits' end but perforce had to return without her or resign his commission. This he could not do as he has very little money of his own and no talent beyond that of riding very fast over difficult ground and persuading others to follow him. So he came back on his own.'

'And . . .?' Sophie's interest was now aroused. Would infidelity prove to be the climax of the story? But she had forgotten its beginning.

'There followed a long and passionate correspondence between the two from which it became apparent that Mrs Dixon could no more support the absence of her husband that she could that of her eldest child. The consequence was that six months ago she brought them all back and vowed she and her children would remain at her husband's side for ever.'

'Is that so terrible? It seems natural, indeed admirable, to me.'

'But it's awful! How can you say such a thing? His colonel summed it up well enough. What would it be like if all the wives did the same? Imagine. A regiment with say forty officers, with forty wives, and maybe, in the due course of time, two hundred children? But there is nothing in the Company's Regulations which expressly forbids the arrangement so there was nothing to be done. And anyway it was soon made clear to the senior officers that very few wives would countenance any such arrangement and that almost all of us are profoundly relieved to have our children off our hands once they are old enough to be a nuisance, that is once they are too old to be left solely in the care of a Native ayah. Indeed, it has become quite the thing to send them home at the age of five or younger. Pardon me, but I have just noticed Pamela Courteney is here and I must have a word with her about the evening at whist she is planning. She has to keep these evenings a secret from her husband who is a most evangelical sort of person and absolutely dead against card-playing.'

But really, Mrs Fetherstonhaugh had registered the approach of Catherine Dixon and clearly any further comment on the latter's idiosyncracies would be out of place in her hearing.

'I suppose that woman has been prattling about me?'

'In a manner of speaking. But she said nothing about you that makes me think any the less of you. I find your regard for your children and your husband admirable and needing no defence.'

'Really?' Mrs Dixon's blue eyes, suddenly dark with feeling, held hers for a moment. Then she smiled. 'I can see we will get on. We must arrange for you to meet my brood as soon as possible. But now let me tell you about some of the others who are here. We all have our little peccadilloes, our oddities, but none, I assure you, of any great consequence; just enough to give us something to talk about behind each other's backs. Now, without appearing to stare, take a look at the apparently Native lady who has just arrived, not, you will notice, by the outer door but from one of the inner rooms.'

The woman in question was, Sophie decided, a vision. Not above five feet in height but perfectly proportioned, she was wearing, but not so that it covered her head, a pale buttercup-yellow saree, shot with silver. Her long black hair was tied back with a matching silk scarf. Gold flashed on her dark fingers and bracelets chimed on her bare forearms. She had her palms together in the posture of the standard Native greeting which she repeated to the two ladies who had been standing in front of the door she had come through. In this case the grisaille depicted a prone female tiger, nursing her cubs. For all her poise and charm she was not, Sophie decided, more than sixteen years old, perhaps younger. Her skin was a shade darker than 'wheaten', the word the Natives used to describe the palest, most Aryan of their race.

'Who is she?' Sophie whispered. Then, 'I think I can guess. I have been told about her if she is who I think she is.'

'I'm sure you have. She is Uma Blackstock, Sir Charles's daughter by his first marriage. Her mother was a cousin of the Ranee of Aligarh and a renowned beauty. Charles Blackstock fell for her when he was a subaltern and in hospital following a wound received on the north-west frontier. It was not at all uncommon in those days for officers to marry high-born Native women, though of course the reverse hardly ever happened. The arrival of us memsahibs put a stop to all that, but that did not get under way until a decade later . . .' Catherine at last drew breath and Sophie, out of a desire to show polite interest rather than any real thirst for knowledge, managed to interrupt the flood with what she hoped might be a pertinent query.

'And how do such alliances work out? Not well, one presumes. One has heard so much spoken against miscegenation.' She faltered on the last word, wished she had said 'marriages between whites and blacks' instead.

'Rubbish! All of it.' Catherine lowered her voice. 'The fact of it is that Native women are taught to be submissive and biddable everywhere except in the bedroom. There they have the reputation of possessing skills modesty must leave to your imagination. The combination is apparently irresistible.' A quick glance directed beyond Sophie's shoulder. '*Parlons d'autres choses . . .*'

Sophie ignored the warning note.

'And the present Lady Blackstock? How did Sir Charles acquire her?'

12

A voice boomed in her ear.

'Acquired her, my dear? I assure you I acquired him. At the Salisbury Races in '45 to be precise. I am sure Mrs Dixon will be able to provide you with a garbled version.' And the galleon, borne on lavender-scented zephyrs, passed on after tapping a small fan on Catherine's shoulder in a gently reproving way.

'Oh my gosh,' murmured Catherine and steered Sophie away from her hostess.

'Well?' asked Sophie.

'Well, what?'

'The garbled version, if you please.'

'Sir Charles, as he already was, having been honoured with the red ribbon for the way he led a division in the Battle of Chillianwallah in the Second Sikh War, his brigadier having lost his head to a two pound shot . . .'

'Red ribbon?'

'The Bath . . . and suffering from a recurrence of remittent jungle fever, resolved to spend a season at Cheltenham Spa and, by the way as it were, have himself invested with the insignia from the very hand of a grateful sovereign at Windsor. Having gone through with both of these he paid a visit to his elder brother, Lord Ludgershall, who entertained him by taking him to Salisbury Races. There, in the members' enclosure, he met Mrs Betty Corbett, the extremely wealthy widow of a corn factor. In his estimation, and, I would add, in that of all of us who know her, her good humour, strength of character and robust health far outweigh her lack of social graces. She loves the life in India, and will not think of returning to Dorchester where she fears she will be ostracised both by the gentry and her former acquaintance. She considers herself a worthy stepmother to Uma, and she is a surrogate mother to us all.' At last Catherine paused for breath then her shoulders drooped. 'There,' she sighed. 'There we are. That's Lady Blackstock for you.'

She lifted her head and her now slightly misted eyes seemed for a moment to lack focus. She shrugged, turned the restored sharpness of her gaze to meet Sophie's.

'I shall leave soon. I become fatigued quite easily.' She glanced down at her stomach. 'Dear Dixon. He is so in love with me. As I say, you must meet my brood. Do please call tomorrow, at eleven o'clock, say. Have tiffin with us? We are usually more or less visitable by then.'

'I'll come with you.'

'Certainly not. There are other ladies here as well as I whom you should meet. That is the purpose of our being here.'

And Catherine Dixon walked away from her towards the front door which the Sikh held open for her. Sophie could not help remarking that her gait now seemed weary, that of a woman much older. But at the door she straightened, looked around the room with a bright smile, and was gone.

That evening, after a light supper of rogan josh (Tom Hardcastle subscribed to one of several Simla mutton clubs whereby families bought the carcase of a sheep or two and divided them between them), dahl, chappatis, followed by the first of the season's mangoes, they walked out on to the rear verandah of their small compound so that he could smoke his cheroot and she could watch the still fascinating, tiny fireflies.

'There are so many more of them than when we came,' she murmured.

'They'll be gone with the first night-time frost. And so shall we. But that's a long way off yet. Five months.' He squeezed her elbow affectionately, protectively, and then put his hand on her further shoulder. Tall though she was, he was taller by a head and, though thin, he sometimes felt frighteningly solid to her; at other times this solidity was a comfort. He worked hard, his eye sockets were often grey with tiredness and occasionally his work left ink stains on the inside of his right index finger. Although he was an officer attached to one of the Queen's regiments of foot, he was a lawyer first, with divisional responsibilities. She admired him, felt as safe as she could in this strange and awful country with him at her side. Almost, she loved him, and, at this early moment in their marriage, was prepared to learn to.

A little light from the lamp inside fell across the yard but did not reach the three huts below them at the back of the property where most of their servants lived, but still the whitewashed cow-dung bricks caught a glow from the fading sky beneath the plate-like tiles which were made from the same ubiquitous material. Charcoal beneath the pots their meal had been cooked in glowed intermittently as a slight chill breeze caught it. A saffron saree seemed to float for a moment behind them, and a dark child in a white shirt ran

14

across to it with a little subdued but cheerful cry. Below the rear fence the hillside dropped steeply beneath tall thin deodars to the hidden abyss beyond. An owl squawked and was answered from a distance.

'They always seem to do that at this time of year.'

'And not all through the winter?' She was thinking of the woods that bordered the Stour near Blandford. 'At least until Christmas?'

'I've no idea,' Tom laughed. 'I've never been here in the winter.'

'Of course not. Silly me. But we come back every May?'

'You do.' He had explained this to her often but showed no irritation at having to do it again. He understood the insecurity she must feel. 'Whether or not I do will depend on what is happening in the plains.'

'I hope you do. I hope you do come back with me. I shall be awfully lonely without you.'

'Believe me, you'll fry if you don't. Even by May it's pretty unbearable. Not good for young ladies.'

Silence. He sensed there was something unsaid in the air. Then she took a very deep breath and squeezed his hand more tightly.

'And not good either for very young babies,' she said, and then was instantly embarrassed as he took both her hands in his and, kissing them, went down on his knees.

'Oh thank you, my darling, thank you, thank you, thank you, thank you.'

Which surprised her, as she felt she had had very little to do with it.

15

2

Meerut. Last Sunday before Advent, November 1853

Meerut was a military station forty miles north-east of Delhi. It suffered somewhat by comparison with Umballa, which was further to the north, closer to the Himalayan foothills and much larger.

For Sophie, pregnant as she was, the less demanding atmosphere of Meerut was congenial enough. It was normally the base of two or three Native Infantry regiments and Native Cavalry, led from the rank of lieutenant and up by British officers trained at the Company's establishment at Addiscombe near Croydon, with some British NCOs. Usually there were also units of the Queen's Army, bringing the whole establishment up to the strength of a brigade.

Sophie calculated that she had conceived towards the end of March, on board ship from Aden to Madras, during a storm which had frightened her and led her to seek comfort in her husband's bunk, a move which he had misconstrued. Lovemaking was something of an embarrassment to both of them since neither really knew what to do and were not prepared to talk about it, but it was almost always initiated by Sophie, following advice given to her by her mother.

'You have to do it,' she had said, on the night before the actual wedding, 'since men expect it and even the nicer ones can get very melancholic if it is denied them. The less nice may resort to violence. I am sure Tom will not do that. However, he will expect it. The thing to do though is to make it clear to him that you will decide when it

16

happens and, I have to say, at your age it is quite natural for you yourself to look for satisfaction in the act, and you may find that you are happy to indulge in it quite often once you are used to it. But start as you mean to go on.'

The consequence of this was that the marriage night, spent in a coaching inn on the Plymouth road, had been passed playing backgammon until Sophie declared herself quite worn out with the excitements of the day and went to sleep.

But that had been February, the Saturday before Ash Wednesday, and in spite of all and thanks to that storm, towards the end of March she was pregnant and due to give birth somewhere between Christmas and New Year.

Meerut suited her. The army had been there since 1804 and a tradition of politeness, even decorum, had grown up over the half-century. This was mirrored by the neat lines of bungalows occupied by the English officers of the Native regiments. Set in avenues of mast trees and a forest-size variety of fig, each had its neat plot planted to emulate English cottage gardens. The unpretentious officers' messes suggested neo-classicism with their white pillars. The European units were stationed in equally neat cantonments to the north and it was in this area, not far from the church, that the Hardcastles had their rented bungalow. Sophie, after suffering one scornful rebuke from Catherine Dixon, had quickly learnt to lengthen the 'o' of 'cantonment' into 'cantoonment'. To the south there was the Mall (any station of any size had both a mall and a racecourse) where you could promenade or take the evening air in a carriage or on horseback.

Beyond the Mall were the Indian lines and the Suddee Bazaar which served the whole garrison with all it could need from basic foods and spices to cottons and silks; there were too dressmakers, jewellers, harness makers, wheelwrights and manufacturers of artefacts from lines of ebony elephants to bronze Shivas doing the cosmic dance. Finally, beyond the bazaars, lay the small country town that gave the station its name.

And best of all, facing the main parade ground, was St John's, the garrison church. Although it had been built in the 1820s it was a simplified version of early eighteenth-century English churches, with its three-tiered spire and its rows of plain and arched windows piercing smooth stuccoed walls washed with a pale primrose yellow. Inside

17

there was a semicircular domed apse at the east end and then a nave supported by tall and elegant unfluted Ionic columns which, as well as bearing the weight of the roof, carried deep-stepped galleries on both sides and a steeper one, with pews, over the west end. This interior was painted white apart from the pews and well lit by its large, clear windows. All in all, larger though it was, it put her immediately in mind of the church of St Peter and St Paul in Blandford Forum.

The services were conducted by the Reverend John Ewart Rotton in the old-style, strict Church of England, none of the Oxford Movement's bells and smells, no ranting evangelicalism either. In short it seemed to her, and, apart from the evangelically minded gentlemen in some of the regiments, to everyone she knew, an entirely proper and decent place, a place you could learn to love and to which no one could possibly take exception.

To the surrounding populace and most of the sepoys too it was as alien as a large Hindu temple, or a mosque with two minarets, would have been in, say, Salisbury Cathedral Close. Sophie, along with all her acquaintance, had not the slightest understanding of how the Natives resented it. And feared it too. The sepoys especially sensed the extent to which many of their rulers subscribed wholeheartedly to the great project of the time – the conversion of India to Christianity.

Every Sunday, Lady Blackstock and her flock of West Country fowl, along with most of their race, attended, as a matter of course, divine service. Glowing in the evening light, they floated in their white dresses, like white hens or geese, attended by crows or scarlet macaws, into their allotted pews (those who had them), or found places nearer the back. They took off their gloves and laid them with their tiny bags on the shelves in front of them, knelt for a moment on hassocks tapestried by their sisters in years gone by, and said a quick prayer before sitting up straight and finding the first hymn to be sung from the book in front of them. A clatter of boots and fifty tall men from a grenadier company, clutching their muskets, climbed up into the west end gallery where each place had its slot beside it for the butt of their weapon and a notch in the shelf for its barrel. Silence at last, then the two-manual portative organ on the south side of the chancel wheezed, took a breath. All stood . . .

Lands of the East, awake,
  Soon shall your lands be free;
The sleep of ages break,
  And rise to liberty.
On your far hills, long cold and grey,
Has dawned the everlasting day.

It is not easy to assess the quality or depth of the congregation's devotion which no doubt varied from person to person. Outside church they rarely prayed and only under extreme stress. They took Communion on the first Sunday of the month, and found the experience slightly embarrassing. Evensong was their preferred service.

Almighty and most merciful father; we have erred and strayed from thy ways like lost sheep. We have followed too much the devices and desires of our own hearts . . . For my eyes have seen: thy salvation, Which thou hast prepared: before the face of all people; to be a light to lighten the Gentiles: and to be the glory of thy people Israel.

Then the collect for the last Sunday before Advent . . .

Stir up, we beseech thee, O lord, the wills of thy faithful people, that they plenteously bringing forth the fruit of good works, may of thee be plenteously rewarded . . .

'Oh my gosh,' Sophie remarked, but silently, 'today must be "Stir-up Sunday", and back home Mama will be stirring up the plum pudding for Christmas . . .'

Never mind. Tomorrow would do . . . But would she manage without her mother at her side?

So be it, Lord; thy throne shall never,
Like earth's proud empires, pass away;
Thy kingdom stands, and grows for ever,
Till all thy creatures own thy sway.

Sophie's heart was full. Transported back to the village church of her childhood, some five miles from Blandford, she felt she could smell again the stone dust, the ancient wood, the beeswax on the woodwork. St John's, Meerut, might be different, a bit brash, a bit new, the workmanship not yet smoothed by centuries of polish and care, but it was identifiably the same thing; the words were the same, the responses and the singing, some lusty and confident, some little

19

more than an ardent whisper, echoing in the high-vaulted rafters above.

And there was a pride there too. Here she was, thousands of miles away, surrounded by an alien people, contributing just a little to the history that had brought this rightness, this news, this perfection of understanding, this civilisation and love of God to a benighted land, torn with religious dissension as it had been, chaotic, anarchic. It was a noble calling, a noble company she was part of. Earth's proud empires might indeed pass away, like those of Alexander, Rome and the Mughals, but this one, being the empire of God as well as Queen Victoria, would not. On it, with God's blessing, she thought, recalling a phrase her father had pointed out to her in the *Edinburgh Review*, the sun would never set.

3

But Sophie was not prone to such enthusiasm in more than an intermittent, superficial way. She was a practical girl, with practical everyday problems and concerns and these moments were only indulged once a week, in Evensong, in the church of St John. Feeling a wave of tiredness as she opened her parasol in the church's porch and slipped her free hand into the crook of her husband's elbow, her mind went back to the coming festival and she reflected that, while Prince Albert was clearly a wonderful consort, his introduction of the German Christmas was not such a wonderful idea at all.

The quickest way to their bungalow took them through the cemetery to the north-west of the church, but just as they were approaching the gate a six-foot, turbanned and heavily mustachioed havildar, a sergeant in one of the Company regiments, walking briskly, came up with them, stamped himself to a halt and snapped a smart salute.

'Captain Hardcastle, SAH?'

Tom gently unhitched Sophie's hand from his elbow and touched a finger to his brimless cap.

'Sergeant?'

'Beg leave to deliver a request from Colonel Carmichael-Smyth that you attend him at HQ to offer advice on an important matter, sah!'

Tom turned to his wife.

21

'I'd better go,' he said. 'Will you be all right? We're less than ten minutes walk from home.'

'You go on. I'll be all right.'

She watched the two of them walking briskly down the little avenue, her husband in front trying not to look as if he were marching, which made her smile a little, then turned, crossed the road and went through the arched cemetery gate. There was a little lodge which a retired Native soldier, old enough to remember Tipoo Sahib, looked after. Two of his mates sat on the step and chewed betel. One of them was missing an eye and flies buzzed round the socket. She wondered if she should give them some annas but decided against it: if everyone who came to the cemetery did so they'd soon be rich, well, rich enough to take bhang instead of betel.

The cemetery was large, and, at least within a hundred yards or so of the central gravelled path, full on both sides. The tombs and graves were varied, from structures ten feet tall with black domes, through shapes like vaulted coffins, to small boxes. Few of them were carved stone apart from the memorial tablets: flaking stucco on one or two of the older ones revealed thin bricks beneath. All were set on what had clearly been planned as a green sward, an English lawn, planted with trees with a suitably dark foliage, but now, in late November, the effect of sun on rain-soaked soil was already producing a riot of every shade of green wherever weeds could get a hold, in the angles between tombs and grass, along the shallow ditches that had been cut to carry the water away, and up through the gravel. Perhaps, she thought, the Hindoos have a point: inhumation is not the best way of disposing of bodies in this climate.

But there were birds, and they pleased her: a purple sunbird hovering among the branches of a flowering quince, a brahminy myna, not unlike a Dorset nuthatch, and a flock of shrill green long-tailed parakeets playing catch-me-if-you-can through the tree tops. She wondered if they were from the broods just fledging from nests in the high eaves of the church. Dogs barked in the background and, some way off, a sepoy company, untrammelled by sabbatarian considerations, was on rifle practice. The clear sky beyond was shifting from the pure blue of day to something approaching turquoise, and purple shadows lengthened across the graves.

Tom and she had already walked down these paths several times, but this was the first time on her own, the first time she had paused to look at the inscriptions.

She had expected most to record the deaths of soldiers, and there were many, and the dates clustered round those of the many small wars in the north-west, but soldiers who died in battle or on campaign in those days were almost always buried, or burnt, where they fell. Some clearly, though, made it back to the cantonments before succumbing. But what she had not reckoned on was the number of women and children.

> *Sacred to the memory of Annie, eldest daughter of Major*
> *John J M Hewson, Paymaster, 35th Royal Sussex Regiment,*
> *born at Kandy on 19th January 1836, died at Meerut . . .*

She had been only sixteen, two years younger than Sophie.

> *Sacred to the memory of George, aged three, and*
> *Charlotte aged 2, who were taken by cholera on . . .*

> *Sacred to the memory of Jane Fitzpatrick, aged twenty-three,*
> *wife of Captain James . . . of the Royal . . .*

Tears began to form in Sophie's eyes and she felt a great heaviness, a foreboding almost, in her womb. Let's face it, she said to herself, is a Christian Empire, on which the sun does not set, worth all this . . .?

'I say, no need to look so down, even if you are in a boneyard.'

Because she had followed a turfed alley between the graves, she had not marked his approach coming from behind her. She turned now and faced him. He continued:

'If you're lost, or whatever, I might be able to help but if I am intruding on some private grief . . .'

'No, no. Not at all. I am neither lost nor grieving, just a little overcome by . . . thoughts of mortality, I suppose.'

She took him in, head to toe and back again. He was, she knew, an officer in a Highland regiment. For Sunday service he had put on the full fig, fore and aft cap with black forked tails behind and black and white check border, red coat with buff facings, kilt. He was tall, had bright red hair and a luxuriant beard and moustache to match which made him look older than he probably was. She reckoned him to be in his mid-twenties, and already knew he was a lieutenant and from the brass buckle on his chest his regiment was the 75th Highlanders. Actually, she knew a fair bit more about him because he had been a subject of some gossip. Seconded from his regiment which was still in Persia under the command of Brigadier General Henry Havelock, but which was expected to return to India in the natural course of events, Bruce Farquhar was in Meerut to learn the local native languages and customs, assess the performance of the sepoy regiments, and get to know the topography and character of the north-west plains. In short, he was emulating Havelock's own self-education at the same age.

But there was something else as well. She was almost sure she had met him some three years earlier at one of the very first assemblies she had been allowed to attend. But the young subaltern he reminded her of had not had a beard so she was less than certain that they were the same person. His regiment, on its way to Plymouth before embarking for the East, had been briefly camped on Blandford racecourse, known as Blandford Camp because it had been used as such during the Napoleonic Wars. There had been races in which the local gentry took on the officers, and she remembered how Farquhar's ginger head had been carried into third place in a two-mile steeplechase. Then there had been a ball of sorts in the Blandford Forum Assembly Rooms, and this same young man had been very attentive to her, almost too attentive, pestering for dances for which she had already engaged herself elsewhere.

He was tall, lean, his complexion sun-tanned to a leathery red, his eyes, beneath sandy lashes, a very bright blue, one might almost say forget-me-not blue were it not inappropriate to ally such delicate flowers with a rather obviously tough young man. His legs and knees, seen in the small gap between kilt and stockings, were hazed with yellow hair that looked almost downy. But they were bony and muscular too, the knees indeed almost knobbly. Sophie blushed as she realised that she had actually noticed this detail.

'"Thoughts that do often lie too deep for tears"?' he suggested.

His accent, just as she remembered it, was that of a gentleman but still carried a regional note. Irish? Scottish? She really was not sure.

'Well, yes,' she replied, then, pleased to recognise the quotation and even more pleased to be able to cap it, 'but those you mention surely belong to Intimations of Immortality, do they not?'

24

He laughed, took a step nearer so he could touch her arm.

'It's getting dark,' he said. 'May I see you to your home?'

'Thank you. I believe you may.'

As they walked beneath the darkening trees she stumbled slightly and he used the opportunity to take her elbow.

'You must take care,' he said, alluding to the now very large bump she carried in front of her. Glad that he had provided a reasonable excuse for him to do so, she allowed him to continue supporting her arm.

She prattled in a conventional way through the five minutes it took to arrive at her bungalow. And he declared that he had passed through Simla in the summer and had he not seen her in *A Midsummer Night's Dream*? A splendid performance.

Arrived at the gate he declined her invitation to come in for refreshment, touched his cap and disappeared in the gathering gloaming. And she could not help wondering at the lightening of her mood as she set about the small preparations she should make for her husband's return, the lighting of lamps, putting out a whisky decanter and a bottle of soda water, finding his cheroot case and lucifers.

4

Meerut, Christmas 1853

Sophie had a son, Stephen, on 26 December, St Stephen's Day, 1853. In an odd sort of a way the labour was much eased and apparently shortened because almost everyone concerned, including Sophie herself, ascribed the inititial cramps to a goose inadequately cooked and eaten the day before. Ovens were not usually featured in the construction of the memsahibs' servants' kitchens and if the object of the cooks' attentions was too large to be accommodated in a pot and prepared as a pot roast, recourse was made to a Native baker's oven. Each bird, already rather high, having been hung for a fortnight in temperatures generally well in excess of those that pertain in a Dorset December, was dressed and stuffed and placed on a tray with a copper coin to act as marker, to distinguish it from the thirty or so other fowl that had to be cooked for other families during the same twenty-four hours. On Christmas Eve then, two of the kitchen wallahs carried it the mile or so through the sepoy lines to the bazaar and brought it back early in the afternoon of Christmas Day.

The Dixons were invited and a good time was had by all though Catherine still suffered mentally from the effects of the miscarriage she had undergone three months earlier. She cried a little, and when asked if anything in particular had distressed her replied that she had hoped that this Christmas would be enlivened, indeed sanctified, by the presence of a new baby. Meanwhile, she made much of little Robert who remained her youngest.

26

The husbands played the fool for the children while Catherine and Sophie put the finishing touches to the earlier courses of the meal, mock-turtle soup and a large carp taken from the Jumna. Adam Dixon quite noisily asserted he was too old for the hobby-horse his father had given him so Lieutenant James Dixon took it and galloped it round the small compound to the delight of all the servants and the younger of Adam's siblings. Tom Hardcastle took Adam to one side and, with the cricket bat which had been Sophie's and his gift to the lad, demonstrated the cover drive and the square cut. Miranda, Adam's elder sister, took the bowling hoop that had been one of her presents and contrived to make it swing round her waist, thus inventing the Hula-Hoop before its time. Tom found the motion put him in mind of nautch girls, the erotic dancers the regiments occasionally entertained themselves with, and told her to stop.

During all this, Sophie could not help contrasting Dixon's simple jollity, his readiness to create fun for the children and then appear to enjoy taking part in it himself, with her husband's aloofness, a certain sort of petulant shyness which she put down to his fear of making a fool of himself.

Later, after the prolonged meal, as dusk crept up and the temperature dropped, they left the verandah and sat or lay about the largest salon, decorated not with holly and ivy but such evergreens as were available among the rich profusion of fresh green that was rioting outside in what was the height of a late spring. A small sandalwood fire burnt in the fireplace and five or six candles were on the go by whose light they played word games. The party ended with Tom Hardcastle reading the last chapter of Mr Dickens's *A Christmas Carol* and then playing real carols on his squeeze box, since the Broadwood piano Sophie's parents had promised her for Christmas had not yet arrived. At about this time Sophie complained of cramps but, after the initial scare, accepted that she was suffering from indigestion brought on by undercooked goose. However, her waters broke shortly after midnight and Stephen was born eight hours later against a background of birdsong and a Vedic hymn sung on the far side of the compound. Within half an hour the servants had formed a line along the rear verandah, bearing garlands made from marigold flowers which they insisted on putting round the new parents' necks.

Sophie would have been happy to nurse Stephen herself but was told that the practice was considered unlady-like, even improper, in the European lines. No one could explain to her satisfaction why this should be. She decided for a time that maidenly modesty was at the root of it, but why? Maidens only very exceptionally produce babies. And the décolletage fashion then current for evening wear left more of the bosom exposed than a feeding baby does. Finally she decided that the embargo arose from two factors. First, the young female's breast was generally thought to be an object of attraction, even, not to put too fine a point on it, of sexual attraction. To expose it exercising its real function revealed the fetishism that lay behind the irrationality of idolising it for its power to promote aesthetic appreciation or inflame male lust. The second factor was even more unworthy. Feeding babies naturally was something the Native women did. To do so was to lower oneself in the eyes of one's acquaintance to the level of the Natives, the darkies, the – let's face it – the niggers.

From the three lactating women who presented themselves on the verandah before tiffin on Boxing Day she chose Lavanya, the youngest, a fourteen-year-old whose complexion was not really black at all, and whose almond-shaped eyes displayed intelligence and even a sense of fun, whose breasts were as round and as full as those of the temple goddesses Sophie had so far seen only in prints. Lavanya's husband, an incompetent mahout, had been sat on by his elephant in the fourth month of her pregnancy, a pregnancy that had precluded any talk of clandestine suttee. Her child was three weeks old, had not put on weight, was unnaturally pale and not expected to live, the weakness being ascribed to the shock Lavanya had suffered when her husband's crushed body gave up the ghost.

It all worked out very well. Stephen took to this source of goodness with a clear delight that promoted in Sophie feelings of envy which she suppressed; his foster sister, named Deepa, which means 'lamp', or Deepika, which means 'little lamp', took a turn for the better and began to thrive. Sophie took a liking to Lavanya and struggled to learn the dialect she spoke. One of the first things she learnt was that 'Lavanya' means 'variety' or 'beauty'. Lavanya, in her turn, learnt some English.

'Is she not too young for such important duties?' Hardcastle wondered.

'It's in her favour,' Sophie asserted. 'She will be biddable.'

The dead husband's family were happy to accept the price offered, about five pounds in English money; her own family had forgotten her almost as soon as she moved away from them.

Mrs Fetherstonhaugh (née Beresford) berated Sophie for being too familiar with her son's wet nurse and was given short shrift.

5

Simla, September 1854

'I wish,' said Sophie, doing her best to keep a plaintive whine out of her voice since it irritated her husband as much, she supposed, as it did her, 'instead of just saying that we don't have enough money for this or that you'd go through our expenses with me so I might properly understand why I am denied some of the things my friends seem able to afford.'

Tom Hardcastle looked up at her from the small desk he was working at. His hair, greying somewhat at the temple, was all anyhow, a sure sign he had hit a legal problem that was giving him trouble. His greyish-blue eyes looked tired and small in hollows exaggerated by the stark but not powerful light cast by his lamp, the bagginess beneath them exaggerated. The thin line of his upper lip above a rather sulky lower lip gave him the look of a middle-aged rabbit. He had taken off his jacket and the top buttons of his shirt were undone, the cuffs folded back over his forearms.

A cheroot smouldered in the brass saucer he used as an ashtray and the whisky and soda at the front of the desk was almost gone. A pad of legal stationery occupied one side of the desk, an open law book the other, and there were three more volumes, open or with pages marked, on the floor. He was actually studying Indian law, which was by now almost entirely Company law but with awkward little corners left by what had passed for legal systems under the Mughals. He had his career planned. After reaching the highest legal pinnacles the army could offer, full advocate general and possibly even judge advocate general, he aimed to transfer to a civil practice in Madras or Calcutta and in due time ascend the Indian Bench. All this had been thrust upon him since he was the youngest of five brothers all of whom were lawyers too and had staked their claims in the family law firm while he was still a schoolboy.

He looked up, blinked, no smile, but no unkindness there either.

'Dear Sophie,' he began, 'you have so much to do, so many responsibilities. I don't think I should add to your worries by trying to explain why this winter we can't afford to take the Broadwood to Meerut, which I imagine is the source of your present ill mood. I've looked into it and to be sure it is carried safely will cost all of eight pounds. I simply cannot afford that. On top of everything else.'

'It will be ruined if it stays here in the cold and damp.'

'Have you tried Reverend Collins, as I asked you? I'm sure he could find room in the church.'

'He's going home for the winter. He's leaving the church in the care of a Native curate who will probably not bother to open it between October and March. Why should he? Who will be here apart from that gaggle of old widows who can't afford to live in England? I'm told he goes to their houses for services and so forth and that they don't venture out at all once the snow comes.'

'The Blackstocks, then? I understand you are quite a favourite of Lady Blackstock.'

'Oh, come on, Tom. I get on very well with Lady Blackstock but I would not dream of imposing on her in the way you suggest. And in any case they are spending the winter months in Aligarh with the rajah. And their house here will be as damp and cold as ours.'

'I am sure they'll leave it occupied and heated.'

Sophie stamped her foot.

'Please, Tom, don't contradict or cap everything I try to say. Now please tell me why we cannot afford eight pounds' carriage for my piano.'

Hardcastle sighed, put down his pen, leant back, placed the palms of his hands behind his head with his elbows sticking out. Made him look like an elephant, Sophie thought.

'I hardly know where to begin, my dear.'

'Well, start with the servants. There seem to be a lot of them. Not far off as many as papa has at home if you don't count his outdoor ones.'

'Right then.' The front legs of the chair came down with a muted thud on the supposedly Turkey rug a carpet seller had persuaded them to buy in Port Said. Left hand in the air he began to pick off each finger in turn with the thumb of his right hand.

'First, my etwah and his wife, eight rupees each per month . . .'

Butler and chief cook, Sophie thought, though Tom referred to the etwah as his 'bearer'. He went on.

'Benjamin, the kitmutgar, seven rupees a month.'

Kitmutgar . . . in other words the real cook, the one who did the work. Benjamin was not his real name but it seemed to be what everyone called him.

'The bheestie, six rupees.' Bheestie meant the water carrier. Fine. At least he really did earn his keep: the nearest stand pump was nearly a quarter of a mile away opposite the post office on the Upper Mall.

'Sweeper, four rupees, my syce, groom that is, your syce, five rupees each, two grasscuts, three rupees each, and the dhobi wallah, five rupees. That's fifty-four rupees, about five pounds and ten shillings a month.'

'You've forgotten Lavanya.'

'Well, yes, dear. I've been meaning to talk to you about her. I do believe it's time to think of letting Lavanya go. Stephen is now nine months old and, so far as I understand such things, must surely be weaned shortly. Indeed the process is already under way, is it not? And perhaps it's not right for a girl of her age to go on feeding some-one else's child for so long . . .'

Sophie was momentarily overcome by a sudden surge of dislike for this man so intense that if she had ever nurtured in her bosom an emotion as strong as hate, that is what she would have called this feeling. A cold sweat broke out in her palms, she felt the colour drain from her face, though none of this, in the light of the candles and the lamp, was apparent to her husband who continued to witter on.

'The four rupees per mense we pay her,' he continued, 'may not seem much but it all adds up.' He stood, came round the desk. She knew he was going to touch her, put an arm on her shoulder perhaps, and she took a step back. Understanding the signal, he faced her instead, leant against the table with each hand on the surface behind him. 'Do listen to me, my dear. My normal pay is three hundred and sixty-five pounds a year which increases to four hundred if we are required to be on the march or off station. We have to rent two properties at seventy pounds per annum each, one here and one in Meerut. I have to provide my own uniform, horse and so forth, and then there are incidental expenses like the mutton club, mess bills when I use the mess. And there is your pony, and the barouche which we really do need if you and Stephen are to travel in comfort. Finally, cheap though food is, we are feeding more than ten people. All in all we live very close indeed to Mr Micawber's receipt for misery, which is, you will remember, annual income twenty pounds, annual expenditure twenty pounds and sixpence.'

Sophie took a grip on herself and the tiny handkerchief she was now twisting between her fingers. She made an effort to keep her voice low, and, she hoped, reasonable.

'Lavanya stays. She will be Stephen's ayah. Indeed, in effect, she already is. If necessary I will pay her out of my allowance. I shall find eight pounds for the transport of my piano from the same source.'

Was it possible? she asked herself. He allowed her forty pounds per annum out of which she was expected to dress herself well enough to appear in company without exciting comment, buy the very small amount of make-up she used and a little eau-de-cologne, presents at birthdays and Christmas, and provide tiny gratuities to the servants when they performed some service beyond their normal routine. Mrs Fetherstonhaugh probably spent almost as much for a single hat chosen from a fashion plate and sent by special delivery from Marshall and Snelgrove.

She had a final shot: she knew it would provoke but she could not resist it.

'One last thing. I don't know how much it costs to get all your law books down to Meerut, but I do think you might consider leaving some behind and perhaps use the saving to contribute to the carriage of my Broadwood. I don't see why you can have the table you are working at in Meerut while I can't have my piano. I'm sure we could buy a table in Meerut for a lot less than eight pounds.'

His expression shifted to one of condescension and sympathy, the sort one assumes when confronted by a totally unreasonable request from a child.

'My poor dear. How like a woman even to consider such a step.'

Reaching behind him he lifted the candlestick from the corner of his desk and used the flame to relight his cheroot.

'In the first place you used the word "work". I work with my books and at this table. Work is what I get paid for.'

He was speaking now very slowly, leaving a tiny gap between each word. If only, she thought, if only I had something I could throw at him. He went on.

'And what you call my table is, as you very well know, not a table at all, but a rather fine campaign secretaire. It can be taken apart and all the parts, legs and the drawers, are put inside the lid so it travels as a simple oblong box. As such its passage back to Meerut will cost no more than a few shillings.'

PART II

The Darkening Horizon

6

Bindki – one hundred miles from Allahabad to the south-east, thirty from Cawnpore to the north-west, sixty south of Lucknow. The Ganges flowed massively twelve miles away to the north, the Jumna scarcely further away to the south. The nearest town, Futtehpore, newly designated by the British the centre of a District, was eighteen miles up the the Grand Trunk Road that linked Calcutta with Delhi and passed between the village and the Ganges.

This is the centre of north India. Situated between two great rivers that never dry up, however disastrously the monsoon might fail, with soil as alluvially rich as millennia of flooding can make it, the land of the Doab is the best in India, in the world perhaps, for cultivation.

The great heat of summer, back in June, when dust swirled in clouds through the tamarinds and mangoes, when infants could die of heatstroke and the two wells got lower and lower, when the hens stopped laying and the cows gave no milk, when the buffaloes, rib-ridged grey hulks, their blackened tongues protruding like swollen adzes, panted themselves into exhaustion and lay in the almost dried-up pools and had to be dowsed with bucketfuls that the people could not find the energy to lift, when only the flies seemed to thrive beneath the brazen sun . . . all gave way at last to the monsoon.

And ten weeks of a different sort of hell. Grey mud clung like wet cement to everything it touched before thinning to a creamy soup a foot deep or more and the floodwater lay like broken mirrors across the fields. But the floods receded, leaving the soil of the vast plain moist and fecund, promoting a swift recovery through October and November, a steady burgeoning of growth. Over night green shoots carpeted the fields; fruit trees, varieties of plum (some small and sour and used in pickles), quince and pomegranate bloomed, white, pink and vermilion. With the new year lush vegetation shot up in uncultivated banks and reeds and rushes hedged the winding waterways. The birds returned: herons tiptoed through the long grasses and snow-white egrets perched on the backs of cattle; kingfishers, pied and white-breasted, skimmed the rivers; along the Grand Trunk Road green bee-eaters and blue rollers perched on the telegraph poles; flocks of emerald, long-tailed parakeets chased each other with their high cheery calls through the fresh-leafed mangoes. The ponds that the low dun or whitewashed huts circled remained filled up with water for the buffaloes to wallow in, and at the end of the village where the Untouchables lived, small dark coarse-haired pigs scurried and scavenged, squealed and littered.

And now it is January: think of a perfect April in England when life is not merely bearable but paradisiacal. The fields of marigold are starred with yellow buds, the mango trees are festooned with sprays of tiny white flowers, in the fields of opium poppies pearly white and mauve petals split the hairy green sepals, the wheat is four feet high and coming into ear, hay is tall and green and sugar cane too and their leaves are piled high on women's heads as they take huge bundles home to rethatch their houses or feed the cattle. Wild flowers fill the ditches and down on the Grand Trunk Road narcissi, wallflowers and tulips flourish round the post station set up by the English, the dâk bungalow with its Shropshire cherry tree in glorious bloom.

Women in bright sarees, saffron, vermilion, yellow, blue and green, line the streams thrashing the rocks with rolled up washing or spread it out across the fresh grass or bushes to steam and dry; men ride in buffalo-drawn carts, laden with roots and vegetables for Futtehpore market, indigo for the new factories. Children hoe rows sheeted with lilac and blue chickpea and lentil flowers, like tiny sweet peas, and butterflies glide and flutter around them.

Outside the village, set in a tope of hugely handsome mango trees, stand two small temples, white square structures, each wall pierced with an arch, the whole of each surmounted by a dome a mere ten feet or so from soil to top. Inside, each has a plinth with an image on it, crudely modelled and painted in primary colours, staring out from wide black-pupilled eyes set in white roundels, dressed in scraps of coloured cloth with shiny jewellery made from quartz, beads of polished nuts, and brass or copper rings. Decked with garlands they represent Rama and his bride Sita, but you'd need to be able to read the iconography to know. As far as the villagers are concerned this is where these two gods dwell. That is, in the sacred grove. They may be elsewhere too, that's a matter for others to decide, but certainly they are here. Outside saffron pennants flutter from long bamboo poles, gracefully bending to the breezes, the colour like gashes against the glossy green darkness of the mangoes.

In the mornings and evenings, carrying tiny lamps fuelled with ghee and silvery bells that chime, the villagers stroll out from the village to the temples with a cloud of children scattering around them. Chants begin in chorus and fade as one or another worshipper is inspired to sing a different song. If it's a festival day, and there are very many, they return to the village and dance and sing some more, beating their drums to drive on the old man who can make a single string fiddle, with a gourd for a sound box, scream and sigh, crow and laugh, for an hour or more beneath the moon. Paradisiacal? A summit of content and civil society? Enough to eat, the progression of seasons making each month a different challenge, a different blessing? Concord between women and men, children and adults? The cycle of birth, growth, reproduction, production and death and a belief in the return of the soul after death? The satisfactions, illusions, comforts and sanctions gained through dance and song, modelling, making and painting?

Well, not entirely.

The English out on the Grand Trunk Road are the latest of a long line going back to the Aryans themselves – all of whom, by force or legalistic chicanery, have expropriated the land these peasants farm.

Before the British there were the Mughals, the descendants of Tamburlaine. For four centuries they moved huge and costly armies to and fro across the sub-continent and fought wars against principalities within their own borders and against an empire as great as theirs to the west, that of the Persians. The Mughal Empire fell apart, and now its last representative, a babbling old man who writes poetry and cooks sweetmeats through a haze of bhang and opium, is not an emperor any more but merely King of Delhi, who rules not even Delhi but a corner of Delhi behind high red walls. But long before he succeeded scores who called themselves kings, princes, maharajahs and rajahs, who paid his ancestors allegiance and taxes, ruled their principalities on their own behalfs. They in turn were served by petty lords, talukdars, landholders rather than owners, each of whom might 'own' as many as a hundred villages or just a dozen or fewer. The talukdars took the surplus food from the villagers, and the rajahs take a good deal of that. Crops became commodities, and the people in the cities who built and lived in them, and the soldiers, priests, lawyers and craftsmen and artisans, had to make money to pay for them, and as often as not the rajah's tax collectors taxed that money as well.

Taxes were farmed out to moneylenders from Bombay and Calcutta, the princes withdrew into their palaces, and the talukdars were mortgaged beyond reason. There was still enough to keep them in luxury within their walled palaces, but beyond the palace gates law and order broke down. Bandits, gujars originally from Georgia, marauded across the countryside, and the bazaars of the small market towns were dominated by wild young men, the badmashes.

Into this anarchy, sucked in as if by a vacuum, came the Company, Johnny Company, the East India Company, first as a trading company with the power granted by Westminster to make commercial and political treaties. The princes were guaranteed status and wealth and the protection of the Company's sepoy army in exchange for tariffs and promises not to trade with any Europeans but the British. Bit by bit, over a hundred years, the princes lost more and more power in exchange for pensions and the British sahibs who had been Residents in their courts became Commissioners, *de facto* rulers. In 1833 the Company ceased to be a confederation of traders and became the arm of Westminster in India, was paid to run India in the Queen's name.

In the old days the surplus food and cash crops supported the emperors and rajahs in all their splendour, paid for their castles and palaces, their jewellery, fine clothes and gilded furniture, their hordes of servants and functionaries, and their armies. But now there is a new force in the land – one that is not so interested in conspicuous consumption, but needs an empire where it can invest its accumulated capital which in turn provides the surplus money to finance new enterprises, new industries, for only thus is the value of money maintained and profits increased, and not just in India but across the world. And of course there are still a navy and an army to be paid for too.

Yet, the Company is benevolent, or believes itself to be. And it is from Leadenhall Street in London that its senior functionaries run this Indian empire, this enterprise, and most of them have been no nearer India than Dover Beach.

Bindki. A half-mile outside Bindki, to the east, a lumpy column of black smoke is being pumped into the pure blue sky above the mangoes, the oaks and a stand of tall teak, left when the jungle was cleared. Under the trees a big black machine sighs and puffs and clanks. Its steel wheels run on steel rails that stretch back mile upon mile on a raised embankment perfectly straight, not a bend or deviation, all the way to a disappearing point on the horizon, to Allahabad and the Ganges where the steamboat connection back to Calcutta, the seat of government, is made. Behind it are five long low waggons loaded with more rails and sleepers cut laboriously from seasoned hardwoods. Beside the track there are pyramids of hard core, heavy gravel, each polygonal stone almost the size of a cricket ball, and, yes, the villagers do already know how big that is: the kids play cricket on the bare ground beyond the pond. A gang of dark workmen dressed only in dhotis, lean on shovels, waiting for the order to start, or hunker and chew and spit betel. The air shimmers round the machine and it smells of hot oil, hot water and, sulphurously, of burning coal, for the jungle is some way off and timber is scarce.

There are soldiers too, four tall Punjabis like Sophie Hardcastle's gatekeeper, in tunics faced with red and red turbans, who stand around smoking, leaning on their tall matchlocks, and, finally, five white men in the quite new domed, brimmed hats called sun helmets or sola topees, sola being the pith from which they are made, and topee meaning dome. They now walk purposefully towards but, following the direction of the rulered track, slightly north of the village, stopping occasionally to set up surveying instruments on tripods, and leaving markers.

They are attended by two neatly dressed young Natives – clearly, from their black tunics, white pantaloons and small skullcaps, Muslims, Bengalese, educated in Company schools to be 'writers', members of a huge underclass of clerks, many of them now Christian,

41

who record in words and figures every single operation the Company undertakes.

They all stop, a hundred yards short of the two temples set in their grove of mangoes. The oldest of the white men, hair cut quite long, goat beard, frock coat in spite of the heat which, by now – it is two o'clock in the afternoon – is balmy and pervasive, stoops over a theodolite that one of the younger men has carefully positioned for him. In the eyepiece, magnified and focused, the saffron pennants flutter.

He straightens, looks around him, walks away from the instrument, hands clasped behind his back, head held high, nose a predatory beak. This is Reginald Saunders, husband of Elizabeth, one of the many ladies whom Sophie Hardcastle met at Lady Blackstock's soirée in Simla nine months ago.

'They'll have to go,' he says. 'I'm not sorry. But we should tell them first. Ali, fetch me the headman from the village. Jackson, call up four of the men and tell them to bring picks and sledges. They're only mud brick or cow dung, it shouldn't take more than five minutes to clear them, but when they're gone we'll have to fell the trees. And, just in case, get the sepoys to stand to.'

The village headman, zemindar, arrives. He is tall, dark, with a pointed beard beneath moustaches and a white turban. He wears a voluminous white shawl above his dhoti, and he carries a thin staff of teak cut from the jungle a century earlier and polished with use. His name is Jiva and he is distantly related to the local talukdar, the man who 'owns' the land on behalf of the Rajah of Futtehpore. He stands like a heron, one foot off the ground resting against the staff, and does his best to understand Mr Saunders' painfully bad Hindi and the attempts of one of the Muslim clerks to put it into words he can understand. Eventually he believes he has the drift.

'It is not for me,' he replies, 'to grant you permission to do this thing, and if it were I would not give it. You must speak to Mohammed Khan, our talukdar. Or the Rajah himself.'

Mr Saunders tries again.

'Please make it clear to him that I am not asking him his permission. I have all the authority I need. We have bought the right to run the railway through this land. We are simply doing him the courtesy of telling him what is about to happen.'

Jiva listens. He says nothing. His dark eyes take in the sepoys and he allows himself a gentle sneer, which is almost concealed behind his moustaches. He doesn't move, he just stands, motionless, like a heron. At a sign from Saunders the coolies, Untouchables from Allahabad, move in with sledges and shovels. Quite quickly the temples and the vessels of purification within them become rubble. The coolies go to the rear waggon behind the engine and come back with big axes and a double-handed saw.

The villagers are arriving now, some from their cottages, some running down the paths between the fields, some still clutching their hoes and sickles, the women often with babies on their backs or toddlers held by their hands. They form a circle and watch as the coolies first pull up the bamboo canes and throw them clanging to the ground, their saffron pennants settling like an orange-tinged blood on the grass. The women pull their sarees across their faces and first wail, then settle into a dirge for the death of gods. The axes thud, the saw whinnies raucously, rhythmically, the first tree teeters as if on tiptoe like a wild old woman remembering the dances she used to do when she was young, but before this first one goes an old man, bent, with wispy white hair and not an ounce of spare flesh beneath his bronze skin, rushes into the white man's group with a howl on his lips, whirling his sickle above his head. The naik, corporal, of the sepoys whips out his tulwar and slashes him at the point where his neck joins his shoulder. The other three sepoys blow on their smouldering fuses and level their matchlocks. Writhing, jerking, choking on his blood, the old man expires and the women's chant rises into keening despair.

Saunders grumbles to himself, but not without quiet satisfaction as well. Yes, this will all mean a whole lot more pen-pushing, which the writers will do anyway, taking statements and so forth, but it won't stop the progress of the railway, the advance of civilisation, or the establishment of the true church.

7

Meerut, March 1854

Catherine Dixon and her brood remained Sophie's closest friends. The arrival of Stephen cheered Catherine up considerably and the infant soon found he was the centre of attention of not one mother but, with Lavanya, three. It became their custom to take short walks together after tiffin which, with the heat increasing daily, was now taken much earlier in the day. Because James Dixon's regiment was a Company one their bungalow was just north of the Native Infantry lines and that was where they all met up.

Two parasols led the procession down the Mall, like oriental or Chinese standards, borne by the two British women in front of a basketwork baby carriage, small but perched up waist high on a bamboo frame above small wheels. This Lavanya pushed, her bright saree, usually green or saffron, the only striking note of colour among all the spotless white. Deepa rode on her back in a sling. The Dixon children took up the rear, a regiment or at any rate a bodyguard to the King-Emperor in front of them. The three oldest were dressed as sailors with ribboned hats and navy blue scarfs folded to form triangles hanging on their backs above slips hooped in navy blue and white. Robert, the youngest at two and a half, still wore the skirts Victorians dressed even their boy infants in. They were saluted by other adults and children making the promenade, and once were given a shrill squeaky hunting-horn fanfare from Colonel Sir Charles Blackstock himself, riding by on a huge bay cob and wearing the hunt master's full fig.

On a hot day in the middle of March they had an adventure.

The Mall led nowhere; it simply ended at the end of the Native lines in front of a bridge across a shallow but still running stream called the Abu Nullah. Since there had been very little rain since October it had shrunk to a small channel running between cracked mud banks supporting etiolated rushes. Occasional litter fouled it – a broken chair, a shattered basket and the flyblown body of a pariah dog which, for some reason, the pariah vultures ignored. On the near side of the wooden bridge there was a blockhouse generally occupied by four or five sepoys who smoked, chewed betel, spat red juice, and showed off to the curious and idle who hung about them. Beyond was the bazaar. In the dusty space between the two was a flagstaff from which hung a rather tattered and very limp Union flag.

Sophie stopped, dabbed at the back of her neck with a kerchief from which the cologne had long since evaporated.

'I am parched,' she said, 'and I'm not going back without a drink. Lemonade for preference.'

Catherine looked doubtful, nodded towards the blockhouse.

'Perhaps the sepoys . . .?'

'No. The bazaar.' Sophie turned to Lavanya. 'Lavanya. Drink. Lemonade. Bazaar?'

Lavanya shrugged, not overenthusiastic, but '*Accha*,' she said.

'What does that mean?' Catherine asked.

'All right. She agrees.'

'Really? I thought she was sneezing.'

'Don't be silly.' And lifting her skirt above her ankles to step over a large plate-like but almost dry cowpat, Sophie moved forward, and the others followed, the children bunching up like threatened ducklings. She looked over her shoulders to make sure they were following.

'Actually,' she said, 'I've just remembered Tom telling me about a pop shop which the tommies use. Lemonade, ginger beer, that sort of thing.'

The planks of the bridge swayed and creaked beneath them – although it was frequently required to support bullock carts carrying provisions up into the lines, it was not well maintained.

'He had to sort out a fight over a last bottle of beer between an Irish squaddie and a Scot. They both ended up in gaol for a fortnight,' she added.

An alley opened up in front of them, bordered by two rows of stalls and shops; and, as the heat, already even in March almost unbearable at midday, began to diminish, it was filling up with crowds of shoppers, servants from the Civil Lines as well as the military, and, even at this end of the market, people from the town beyond.

Market? It was more than that. A warren of twisting alleyways, it was as big as Soho in London, and, to the uninitiated, even more confusing and frightening. The buildings themselves varied from one-roomed huts made from dried cow-dung to quite large wooden structures, some with a second floor. All had overhanging eaves behind big awnings which did not quite meet over the middle of the thoroughfare and were made from hemp sacking or rattan and supported by teak poles. This central line, occasionally touched by direct sunlight, was marked by an open sewer in which rotting vegetables, leaves, roots and fruit mingled with the excrement of cows, bullocks, monkeys, and, it has to be said, humans. All was washed out by the rains, but they had dried up five months earlier. Our tiny column therefore hugged the inner passage, which left them completely at the mercy of the vendors, and faced by a shifting wall of heaving humanity.

There was no immediate sign of either a pop shop or a lemonade seller. Sophie was ready to buy from a water seller with a big sombrero-like hat who carried a large gourd-shaped decorated vessel on his back and one small communal brass cup, but Catherine forbad her to touch it.

'It's not been boiled,' she cried, 'it's probably straight from the Abu Nullah.'

Actually it was relatively pure spring water, a fact she should have guessed since who would pay for water that was free fifty yards back?

They were now squeezed up together; the column had, you might say, formed a defensive square, with the baby carriage in the middle. The noise crescendoed around them as a variety of voices in a variety of versions of the mixed patois the Natives used with the English attempted to offer them crumbling cakes similar to the sweetest shortbread, grapes, jelly-like sweets made from milk and sugar, and when these failed, spices, sarees, belts, shoes, umbrellas, gaudily printed cottons, some of which had been spun and woven in Salford, and filigree silver jewellery. Every now and then a cow pushed up against them, not always the same one, with big sad eyes like a deer's and curved-up horns like those worn by the operatic gods in *Die Walküre* in Munich – Sophie had seen pictures of them in the *Illustrated London News*.

'Tell them we want lemonade,' Sophie shouted at Lavanya, and miraculously lemonade arrived, tiny tulip-shaped glasses of it, made from pure lemon juice and undissolved sugar so it tasted alternately brightly sour and sickly sweet and gritty. Still, it was refreshing enough, and she indicated they would repeat the dose, poured from a tall earthenware jug.

Then, inevitably, came the judgement.

'They want money,' Catherine shouted.

'I haven't brought any. Have you?'

'No.'

Impasse. Literally. No one was going to let them out until the vendor had been paid. The noise around them became puzzled, and then angry. When they tried to push back the way they had come they were met with solid bodies. They became more acutely aware of fresh garlic on the breath of those who shouted at them, of sour sweat as they got closer. A middle-aged but toothless woman, head shrouded by her saree, her face streaked with greying hair, seized Catherine's hand and began to pull at her wedding ring. Catherine screamed.

'We've got to give them something,' Sophie shouted.

'Not my wedding ring, we don't,' Catherine shouted back.

At this moment several things happened at once.

The woman without teeth gave Catherine a push in the stomach which would have floored her had not a man behind her caught her in her armpits and held her up. Very badly frightened now, suspecting that the strong grubby brown hands which almost met just beneath her breasts were poised for something worse than mere assault, she turned and, still in his arms, as it were, scratched his face. His hand went back behind his shoulder; clearly he intended a slap or a punch, but a voice barked an order behind him and he froze.

A younger man stepped round him and confronted the women. This one was tall, dressed in a tunic over baggy trousers, both spotlessly white. His hair was shoulder-length, black and very glossy and his moustaches were luxuriant, waxed and turned up. He too smelled, of patchouli, and behind him there were two more like him, but younger, so he was clearly the leader.

47

'Memsahib,' he began, in reasonably accurate though heavily accented English, 'the law of the market is demanding you pay.'

A near silence fell over the crowd.

Catherine took two deep breaths, and then, as was her habit, the words began to pour out.

'Of course. But we have been treated so badly, it is my intention to report the whole matter to the proper authorities, and yes, I'll pay, if you come with us to our bungalow. But I cannot allow this man who has laid hands on me to escape without . . .'

And at this point the glossy man reached round her, grabbed young Adam's arm, and pulled him away from the rest.

'He is staying here,' he shouted, 'while you are getting the money. Ten rupees. Minimum. Understand?'

Catherine would have none of that. She seized Adam's shoulders and began to pull; the Glossy One held on to his arms and pulled the other way, Lavanya began to wail and scream a mixture of pleading and cursing and attacked the would-be kidnapper as well, until the men behind her pulled her off. Sophie gathered the children around her and vowed to herself that she would die rather than let any harm come to them from these people who had suddenly become for her terrifying exemplars of all the stories she had been told since her arrival of the duplicity, rapacity and savagery the Natives could display when roused.

At this point yet another new arrival pushed his way through from behind, a quite different sort of a person altogether. He wore a big grubby turban above a heavily bearded, very dark, almost black face; from there he was naked to a big floppy, and again very grubby, dhoti which was his only other garment. He was tall, spare, but very fit looking, with muscles like knotted ropes over his almost skeletal limbs, and he carried a staff, a strong looking, roughly hewn stave of teak, six feet long. This he thrust between the Glossy One's legs and tipped him to the ground, then swung round with it, daring any of the Glossy One's followers to come to his aid.

A moment of near silence. Then the stranger delved into his dhoti, and came up with a coin which he handed to the lemonade vendor who took it, looked at it doubtfully, and then smiled broadly. Their rescuer then pointed with his staff over the heads of the crowd towards the open space beyond the bazaar, and uttered one word: 'Go.'

48

The crowd parted in front of them like the Red Sea in front of the Israelites, and, somewhat sheepishly, they went.

Back safely in the cantonment, the whole story was gone over again and again, until bit by bit their husbands' anger modulated into relief that after all they and the children had come to no harm, and explanations began to take the place of recriminations.

'The man you call the glossy fellow,' James Dixon asserted, puffing on his pipe, 'was almost certainly Balachandra. He's the leader of the bazaar badmashes.'

'And what are they?' asked Sophie.

'Young men, not married yet, with little money and no work, who are a nuisance in almost every town and market. They live by extortion, they foment trouble, and they never get locked up because no one will bear witness against them.'

'And our saviour?'

James grimaced, not liking her description.

'A fakir no doubt. Some of them cultivate their bodies to do strange feats of endurance through what they call yoga. The Natives take them for holy men until they catch them stealing and then they drive them out like the pariah dogs they really are, and they move on to the next town or bazaar. They are cheats, illusionists, basically mendicants.'

'And how come,' Sophie wondered, but not aloud, 'the coin he offered was a half-crown and he had blue eyes?'

She kept the question to herself because she knew the men would either insist she was mistaken or come up with some quite boring explanation. Indeed, she had herself done so. There were tribes from Cashmere among whom blue eyes were common, and anyone can pick up a dropped coin. She was also less than happy with her husband's reaction to the whole business. Tom had been angry when she felt he should have been solicitous, repetitively cautionary when she would have liked him to display a warmer relief that she and Stephen had come through it all unharmed, impractical when considering what steps should be taken to identify and punish the men who had assaulted them. All in all he measured up poorly in comparison with Dixon, not to mention their saviour, the mysterious fakir.

8

Shortly before the migration back to the plains in 1854 the Blackstocks entertained officers from a platoon of the 75th. They had been sent up from the not far distant station of Kussoolie to escort the convoy that would leave in two days' time for Umballa. The female guests were young ladies, mostly unattached, nieces and sisters rather than wives, chaperoned by older female relations. And, as was always the case, there were not enough to go round.

They used the large round room beneath its dome-like lantern, the one where Sophie had attended the tea for the West Country Contingent nearly eighteen months earlier. The tables and chairs had been pushed against the curved wall or into the alcoves and those of the guests who were young and sober enough to manage were dancing reels to an ad hoc band of four men from the regiment. Sir Charles and Lady Blackstock remained at the main table, Sir Charles sprawled in a large chair which, though upright and designed for dining, had a high back and substantial padded arms. Betty Blackstock kept her huge back, largely uncovered, towards him. She was dressed in off-the-shoulder red velvet, with rubies this time, among the diamonds of her necklace. Leaning on one elbow she gossiped to her neighbour, a Canon Rossiter up from Delhi to bless new colours that were to be presented to one of the Queen's regiments at Umballa. They were gossiping, as many people were at that time, about the fortunes of William Raikes Hodson. Hodson was esteemed as a daring and imaginative leader of cavalry, the best swordsman in the army, and – and this was not so much to his credit in Sir Charles's view – a clever chap, too clever by half.

'But not clever enough. All right, he suffers from terrible headaches, wears darkened glasses when afflicted, I'm told, and gets very irritable to the extent he is abusive and violent with the Natives, and rude to his colleagues. All that we can forgive, but embezzling from the regimental funds of the Corps of Guides, that's a different kettle of fish. Position of trust, don't you know.'

Rossiter leant forward so he could see the colonel beyond Lady Blackstock's enormous frontage.

'Nothing proved yet, I heard. More complicated than it first appeared. On account of the Corps being split up into numerous detachments and so forth—'

'Rubbish. Where money's concerned the man's a spendthrift and not to be trusted.'

On Sir Charles's right was a Mrs Anson, wife of a major of the 75th, obsessed it seemed with crochet and Christianity. She was not in the least interested in Hodson, but was in the grip of a monologue that had already been running for twenty minutes.

'You see, Sir Charles, and my husband approves every word I say, I firmly believe that the only justification for our presence in this lovely country is to woo the poor benighted Natives away from the horrid idols they worship and bestow upon them all the joy of Jesus Christ and his church. I'm sure you agree?'

'No, madam, I do not. The reason why we are here is so the coffers of City of London bankers and merchants can be filled with what they need to finance the building of ships like Brunel's *Great Britain* and railways both here and across Latin America. We are here to create and maintain a society where profits may be made. Any other reason anyone likes to offer is claptrap.'

'But, Sir Charles, I am not talking about *reason*. I am talking about *justification*.'

'Beg pardon, madam, that's what I mean by "claptrap". Sorry, got to leave you. Call of nature. The pork, you know?'

He let his grubby napkin drop into his plate along with the last of the flummery, pushed back his big chair and hauled himself to his feet. He looked down at Mrs Anson, a lady also fat but not so as to compete with Lady Blackstock, with dark hair, and round her podgy neck a black band supporting a cameo. By way of apology he offered her a smile which, twenty years earlier, had made attractive women feel faint. No longer. His face was jowly, the skin beneath his chin almost a dewlap, visible since he wore no beard but only big moustaches, white and swept up on to his cheeks. He gave them a push, first one side then the other.

'No offence intended, madam, I assure you,' and he pottered off through one of the alcove doors.

On her right, Victoria Marchant, the rather mannish wife of a captain of Native Cavalry, leant across the newly created space between them.

'I say,' she said, 'I heard the old boy mention the *Great Britain*. We saw her at anchor off Gibraltar on our way out in April. Stirring sight, I can tell you.'

The call of nature was an excuse. Sir Charles was tired of women and tired of the music. He pottered down the curving corridor and pushed open double doors into the billiard room. There was a foursome in progress, with three spectators, one of whom was acting as marker. They were young men, driven by the shortage of dance partners to their present pursuit, and very polite and respectful to the older man. They found him a chair, a glass of brandy, a cigar, and the two who had no occupation but that of spectators clustered around him. One of them was Lieutenant Bruce Farquhar.

'Interesting you should honour us with your company, sir, just at this point,' he began when all were settled again. 'We were just discussing the morale of the sepoy regiments. Seems there have been several cases of insurbordination and insolence recently, Johnnies going AWOL, the Hindoos being even more uppity than usual about caste, that sort of thing. What's your view of all this, sir?'

Sir Charles was too busy with the business of getting his cigar going to notice the sly little smiles two or three of these young men now exchanged. If he was aware he was being given a bunk up into the saddle of his favourite hobbyhorse, he didn't show it.

'Damn right there are,' he grunted. ' 'Course, I'm no longer in the thick of it, but I keep my eyes open, my ears close to the ground and I have a good idea of what's going on.' Puff, puff. 'For a start, Farquhar, you know damn well how the pay differential has grown in the last twenty years or so.'

'Indeed I do, sir, seven shillings a week, call it fifteen or so rupees for an English private in one of the Queen's regiments, ten for a sepoy but the sepoys' stoppages for uniform, services like laundry and so forth, are higher than your basic tommy's are. Both are just about what they were in 1815 but the value of money has dropped by half since then.'

James, a lieutenant with the sappers and engineers attached to one of the Native regiments, a big, coarse-looking man, unusually among the rest, apart from Sir George himself, wearing evening dress rather than dress uniform, came and stood in front of the audience, partly blocking their view of the table.

'Damn niggers,' he barked. 'Got no reason, if they know which side their bread is buttered, to get uppity.'

Sir Charles took a long, slow pull at his brandy, and then at his cigar. He blew smoke across the space between them.

'Young man,' he rumbled, 'you're a bloody fool.'

Silence, while James pondered what to do. Call his man out? Hardly. Argue the point? Almost as unthinkable. Suggest, in as dignified a way as possible, that the older man might like to tell him in what respects he was a bloody fool? Difficult to manage without losing face. Leave? Yes. He racked his cue and went.

'That young man, forgotten his name, sums up a lot of what has gone wrong with the Company army. When I came out, Company officers were gentlemen and one could get on with them. They were better paid than us and many had transferred. There was a tradition then of feeling bound to treat the men as decently as possible simply because they were Natives. Good strong discipline, of course, but fair, always fair. We remembered, when all was said and done, it was their country, their borders we were protecting, their internal squabbles and conflicts we were sorting out.' Puff, puff. 'Bankers and such were here for the loot, men of the cloth to make Christians of them, but we knew we were here to protect, keep order, establish the rule of law between states, just as the Native police force we set up were there to do the same within each state.'

The players had abandoned the game and were all now sitting or standing round the old man beneath a fog of smoke that swirled round the mounted heads on the walls. Two Bengal tigers, a black-buck and a giant nilgai reputed to be the largest ever shot. They were flattering him and he knew it, but why? He carried very little influence anywhere now. Or was it his daughter, Uma? To see her was to fall in love, one tipsy subaltern had croaked at him at the end of a ball where he had missed out on dancing with her. Whatever. Blackstock enjoyed the attention and played up to it.

'And now, sir?' Farquhar, egging him on, as if he needed it.

'You're all Queen's men, aren't you? Then I can speak freely. Most of the chaps that come through Addiscombe pass muster up to a point, but you know as well as I do a lot get here without training, just the examination. The specialists anyway, like the chap who just went. Not proper soldiers but exercising some skill.' Puff, puff. 'And who are they? Sons of shopkeepers and manufacturing people who have got some chinks together and want to go up in the world. People who've learnt all these new, what you call them, technologies. Take that young feller. Engineer he calls himself. He'll be designing machinery for manufactories in Bombay in a year or two, or building a railway. Half the time they're not where they should be at all. The other day I heard of two whole companies that had only one white officer among them. Whatever, they're not like the old Company officers.'

'And what were they like, sir?' Farquhar again.

'They were gentlemen. And as such they had respect for their men, were concerned for their welfare, the way a gentleman looks after his people. They could be jolly with the men. They'd put on nautches for them when they'd done well – no longer, the padres have seen to that. They mixed with the Native officers, joined in with cricket and football, even wrestling. You don't hear of any of that going on now. And they took some care of their men, over and above what regulations and the call of duty demand. Nothing of that now except from the Christianisers who are more interested in their men's souls than they are their stomachs.' He finished off his brandy, looked around, got to his feet. 'Ought to get back to base, I'll be ticked off if I don't do my duty. Give us a hand, there's a good chap.' He turned at the door. 'In the old days by and large the sepoys liked and respected their white officers and they respected their sepoys. Now they just shout at them, call them niggers and so forth and get dumb insolence in return.'

'So what would you do about it all, sir?'

'Lord knows. Gone too far I daresay. What we're seeing is just thunder over the horizon, mostly in the Oudh. If it boils up though, there'll be trouble. And, mark my words, thanks to this Crimea business we have too bloody few white regiments on the ground here to cope with it.'

*

54

As was often the case with Bruce Farquhar he had more than one agendum on the go. Chatting up Sir Charles in as discreetly flattering a way as possible was prompted not just by a wish to ingratiate himself with a possibly influential older man, but also by a much deeper desire to get closer to the old man's stepdaughter, Uma. Lieutenant Bruce Farquhar of the 75th was in love. Again. Following Lawrence Sterne, he believed that it had ever been one of the singular blessings of his life to be almost every hour of it miserably in love with someone. And now, some minutes later, he reflected, as he fell into line behind James the engineer at a sort of bar set in one of the alcoves, he was more miserable and blessed than he had ever been. Even more so than when, as an adolescent, he had fallen in a heap in front of young Sophie Chapman.

'Strathspey reel. You can do that. And there's a couple lost without us. Come o-o-on. Be a sport.'

'Mr Farquhar, I am not capable of being a sport. And I do not do Scottish. A polka, yes, a waltz too, even a military quickstep, but Scottish I do . . . not . . . do.'

'In that case, let me get you another glass of your father's very special champagne.'

'Not champagne, Mr Farquhar. But if you insist, some of my stepmother's bramble cordial with a soda would be nice.'

'I do wish you would call me Bruce, Miss Blackstock. Back in a moment.'

The bar was presided over by Ranjit Singh, havildar (or sergeant), retired. James took a glass of champagne, knocked it back, took another and moved away; Farquhar took his place.

'Ranjit, old chum, the lady wants a bramble cordial with soda.'

'That'll be the Miss Blackstock, then, sir. She likes it mixed four parts soda to one of the cordial.'

'I'm sure you know best, Ranjit.' Then as the small, rather tubby Sikh reached for the appropriate bottles, which he handled with a presdigitation truly extraordinary since one-half of his left hand had been shot away, leaving him with only the outer two fingers, Farquhar went on:

'Bramble cordial! Made, one imagines, from blackberries. Like bramble jelly. Does Lady Blackstock get it from England?'

'Indeed not, sir. The fruits ripen in thickets near the stream that runs below the house, in April or early May. Lady Blackstock organises an expedition to gather them of whomever will go with her just as soon as we return from the plains. And for you, sir?'

'Oh, chota peg, please.'

'Whisky, sir?' Eyeing the white stock, the black jacket, the kilt, the sporran and the dirk sheathed in his stocking.

'Actually, no. I think not. Brandy for heroes, the man said, and I rather feel I want to appear heroic. Make it two pegs, there's a good chap.'

He turned, with the two glasses in his hands. She was standing where he had left her, and alone. This, he thought, should have been remarkable, considering the perfection of her beauty, the open expression, almost a smile, on her face, the way the sheen on her dove-grey saree caught the light making her look like a caryatid or statue carved from twilight. But of course the problem was, as he began the walk through the prancing fours, that no one who did not know her well knew quite how to place her. Her mother had been a royal, but a Native royal. She was the daughter of a knighted colonel. It was odd, he thought. Most of the younger memsahibs could accept her as a sister, almost as one of them, but they were all on the floor or, the older ones, still at the table, and it seemed she was a problem to the men. Thirty years ago, when the colonel was a young man, you could marry women like Uma. Ten years ago, especially if the woman was just a little less obviously classy than Uma, you could invite her to manage your establishment, ask her to be your mistress. But the arrival of the memsahibs and the Christians had put a stop to all that.

'You are looking very thoughtful . . .'

Although she had learnt English as well as courtly Parsee at her mother's knee and later from an English ayah, there was more than a hint of the Native singsong in the way she spoke. He found it enormously attractive – melodic but rhythmic too in its rise and fall, like birdsong or a burn bubbling over pebbles. Girls back home whose first language was the Gaelic sometimes spoke English in much that way.

'. . . so I must give you an anna for your thoughts.'

'They are not worth so much,' he laughed and handed her her drink. She glanced at his.

'What are you drinking?'

'Brandy.'

'Such a large one. You will become drunk.'

'No. But I think I might want to.'

'Why?'

'Because once we have got you all safely to Umballa I shall rejoin my regiment at Kussoolie and I shall be heartbroken.'

'Lieutenant Farquhar, either you are drunk already or you are trying to flirt with me.'

'Princess, I am not flirting. I am making love to you.'

'You know very well that I am not a princess. And you cannot possibly be in love with me after two archery contests, two tea parties and this evening.'

'I was in love with you after one round of archery. After the very first shot I saw you take. Your pose . . . so statuesque, yet so full of chained-in energy as you drew the bow. Like Diana, the Goddess-Huntress . . . that was the first moment I saw you. Even before we had been introduced, I was in love with you.'

'You are mocking me. And it was not a good shot. The flight missed the gold by inches.'

'But that was what so captivated me—'

'That I am no good at the sport? That you might be able to beat me at it should I ever make the mistake of allowing you to shoot against me?'

'No. It was the excessively pretty way with which you expressed your annoyance. A little stamp of your foot, a smothered expletive perhaps, and then a laugh like a silver carillon.'

'There was no expletive, smothered or otherwise, I assure you. But I see my stepmother wants me to join her. Thank you for your company. You have been quite charming.' She turned, moved away, stopped and turned back.

'Mr Farquhar, Bruce . . .' – had the colour of her complexion deepened with a blush? – 'Mr Bruce Farquhar, I'm sure we shall see each other again on the way down to Umballa.'

Leaving him thus, she left him the most fortunate and most miserable man in the room.

Farquhar yawned, pulled out his watch. A minute of midnight. He took a nod from Lady Blackstock, and as it were passed it on to the band. The Strathspey died on the melancholic sigh of a literally expiring set of bagpipes which almost straight away were puffed up to scratch again.

The Queen.

Never sounds well on pipes – mercifully they kept it to one verse.

Farquhar went over to them.

'Nathan, George, and that's Sam, and Taff on the drums, yes? Well done, lads. I'm sure the colonel has seen you right, but you've been a credit to the regiment so here's a shilling for each of you, out of regimental funds. And I'm sure Ranjit over there will find you some beer.'

Black-bearded George folded down his pipes and managed to get a fart out of them as Farquhar moved away. The others chuckled.

'Och, he's a cumlie enow jock for a Sassenach, tha' Farquhar,' Nathan, who had lost his front teeth to a spent musket ball some five years earlier, whispered hoarsely, 'bu' I reckon I've 'ad me fill o' the gen'ry for one nich'. Let's see if yon nigger's go' ony whusky.' And he returned his fiddle to its case.

9

Dhondu Pant, the self-styled Maharajah of Bithur, known as the Nana Saheb, was more than a merely local prince. His history and origins dated back to the Third Maratha War of 1817. The Marathas were a confederation of principalities with the Marathi language in common, on the western side of the sub-continent, which, during the latter half of the eighteenth century, had wrested independence from the failing Mughal Empire. Their nominal leader was the King of Satara but the real boss was the Brahmin Peshwa, a hereditary chief minister, based in Poona. Between 1816 and 1818 the Marathas under Baji Rao II, the last Peshwa, rebelled against encroaching British influence. They were defeated and Baji Rao was exiled to a small town called Bithur, a few miles north of Cawnpore and a long way from Poona, and given a pension of eight lakhs of rupees a year 'to support him and his family'. Deprived of the title of Peshwa he was allowed to style himself Maharajah. A lakh was one hundred thousand, and a rupee was worth about two shillings. In short, he was receiving eighty thousand pounds a year.* This he enjoyed until January 1851, but died without leaving any blood issue.

Written into almost every treaty the Company made with nominally independent princes was a clause that stated they could only be succeeded by heirs of the blood. If there was no heir, the Company

---

* In so far as one can make any sort of meaningful comparison, this is about eight million pounds in modern money.

had the right to annex the territory. The justification for this was that in cases where no heir of the blood existed there was likely to be a disputed succession which could degenerate into civil war and anarchy. There was some truth in this – without strong and undisputed rulers many states did collapse into chaos. The Company's detractors, however, obviously judged this to be one of several means whereby the Company eventually expected to annex the whole of India.

Hindu custom sets great store on a male heir for, without one, how can a man be sure that his funeral rites will be properly carried out and his memory preserved as he would like it to be? Baji Rao had therefore adopted three brothers, the eldest of whom was the Nana Saheb, who, according to the Company's interpretation of the treaty, was now titleless and deprived of his adoptive father's pension. Some say he owned many villages in his own name and had inherited Baji Rao's considerable private fortune derived from the unspent surplus from his huge pension and increased by careful investment in Government bonds. Others say he had only thirty lakhs of rupees, in cash and chattels, and that was it. He wanted the pension. Indeed, to maintain any sort of state, he needed it, and, more than that, he hankered for the restoration of Bao's titles, including that of Peshwa of the Marathas.

In person the Nana was a nonentity. The view among the British was that he was 'an excessively uninteresting person. Between thirty and forty years of age, of middle height, stolid features and increasing stoutness, he might well have passed for the ordinary shopkeeper of the bazaar . . . He did not speak English, and his habits, if self-indulgent, had no tinge of poetry about them.' He lacked judgement and was prone to vacillation.

Following Bao's death the Nana pursued the usual paths to what he believed was his due. He appealed to the Government in Britain against the Government in India (the Company), to the Court of Directors, and finally, when all had failed, he sent his principal agent, or vakil, to London to plead his case directly. His agent? The fragrant, more than handsome, talented and charming Azimullah Khan.

Azimullah Khan was a fixer, a con artist, a philanderer. He was exceedingly good-looking and blessed with a natural charm which he cultivated and nurtured. He was never showy, always elegant and economical in his movements, whether dressed in the clothes of a European gent or in the formal but plain attire of a Mahometan functionary, not a swell, but someone of importance.

He was still an infant when he and his mother were picked up by charity workers during the famine of 1838. His mother, a strict Mahometan, would not allow him to be christened and so he was sent to the Cawnpore Free School where he became an assistant teacher while still in his early teens. He was given subsistence and an allowance of three rupees a month, about five or six shillings, while his mother worked as an ayah, or maidservant. As a waiter he moon-lighted in the same household. Later he was translator and interpreter for the then officer in charge of the Cawnpore Station, Brigadier Ashburnham, who sacked him for accepting bribes.

However, such were his gifts, both personal and intellectual, that he was, by his early twenties at the latest, not merely a gofer for Prince Dhondu Pant, known everywhere as the Nana Saheb, but his vakil – principal agent and adviser.

Azimullah Khan had a ball in London. Witty and quick, he was an adept at flattery. Men older and wiser than him would leave his company with the feeling that they were cleverer than they had supposed. An hour's *tête-à-tête* with him would convince women old enough to know better that the beauty and allure they had boasted ten or twenty years previously was still able to promote ardour in male breasts. They were also meltingly ready to protect him, feed him up (the slenderness of his figure fell short, but only just, of suggesting emaciation), and soothe the hidden pain they felt sure he suffered beneath a veneer of cheerful bravado – in short, they longed to mother him.

Supported by a small entourage, a writer or clerk, a barber, a valet, a cook and so forth, and known as the emissary of the adopted son of a man who had been one of the most powerful princes in India, he was accepted as if he were a prince himself. Charles Dickens counted him a friend. William Thackeray, not to be outdone by his rival, gave suppers at which Azimullah was the guest of honour. And the ladies . . . three years later, when the English sacked his master's palace, they came across letters he had kept. Lady So and So signed herself as his 'affectionate mother'. Miss Whatshername of Brighton wrote 'in the most lovable manner' and clearly expected to be mar-ried to him. But he failed to cut it with the Court of Directors and it was not long before most of the very considerable funds the Nana had given him for the prosecution of his case had been swallowed up by the Chancery lawyers. Dickens could have – maybe did – warn him about that. He decided to move on, but first he felt one last appeal might succeed where others had failed, or at least be answered by a clear exposition that he could take back to his master. Consequently, a chill day in early January found him standing on the pavement in Leadenhall Street looking across the road at a building as large and imposing as you would expect the seat of government of an empire should be – East India House.

Like all such grand, neo-classical buildings (it was built in the first decade of the nineteenth century and was roughly contemporary with the first Nash Terraces) it is depicted in prints in an idealised form. A massive portico of six Ionic columns dominated the centre beneath a pediment filled with suitably allegorical figures in various stages of undress. On each side five tall windows marked the piano nobile above five arched casements behind railings with gilded spear-heads. And, in these depictions, it is white. Pure white.

What Azimullah saw was a building streaked, in varying degrees of thickness and opacity, with black greasy soot, beneath a leaden canopy supported, it seemed, by fifty or so trunks of black sulphurous smoke that climbed from its partially hidden chimneys. And these were not alone, but merely part of a forest that stretched in every direction as far as the eye could see. What he could hear was not the crisp clip-clop of hooves on cobbles or the rich rumble of iron-shod wheels that you might expect from the elegant phaetons the prints depicted, but a slushy dull sound as tired horses dragged hooded carriages through a foot or so of horse shit and black snow. There was a road-crossing sweeper, a young lad, of whose efforts the Indian availed himself, picking his way across on a track where the muck was less thick. The lad attempted to blag a penny or a halfpenny from him but was overcome by a terrible racking cough which culminated in an oyster of yellow phlegm just as Azimullah reached the opposite pavement.

A brief letter from the influential husband of some lady he had charmed got him over the threshold and into a large colonnaded hall cluttered, in the way Victorians so liked such spaces to be, with what one might call *Indiana*: a large collection of paintings in heavy gilt frames that often flattered the mundane landscapes and portraits they imprisoned, and *objets* in cases and cabinets, from the extraordinary and valuable, a rajah's jewels, say, to the mundane and slightly whiffy – the head of a huge black nilgai buck, an elephant's foot – all lit in a gloomy sooty sort of a way by a high glass dome set in the roof.

The clerk who had let him in returned quite briskly.

'Mr Mill,' he said, 'will see you presently.'

Where an ordinary mortal might have shown boredom at this, irritation even, Azimullah flashed him a large open smile, slightly tinged with the sadness he almost always affected, and thus sent the clerk on his way thinking 'what a pleasant well-mannered young nigger we have here'.

Then, from somewhere behind him, within the northern colonnade, came a quite startling noise, somewhere between a wheeze, a cry, a roar. Somewhat gingerly Azimullah tiptoed towards its source and found, standing uncased on a plinth, a large lacquered tiger crouching full length over a prostrate redcoat, mauling the poor soldier's throat. Tipoo's Tiger. An automaton taken from the rebel Tipoo Sahib's palace some sixty years earlier. Press the right buttons and a small organ-like instrument in its belly activated and produced the sound Azimullah had heard. The smile on Azimullah's face, like that of the smile on the face of the tiger, was open now and uncluttered with *faux douleur*.

And beyond it, on the other side, a small, almost dwarfish old man, aproned and holding a broom, looked up at him. It was he who had activated the beast.

'Good, innit, sir?' he offered. 'Fawt you'd be tickled, on account of your skin is on the darker side of pale.' And he moved off, pushing his broom over the marble floor.

Footsteps, brisk and purposeful, across the same marble flags. He turned and was faced by a tall man, dressed in subfusc jacket and paler trousers. The top of his head was bald but the sides were wreathed, much as if by imperial laurel, with puffs of black hair. His face would have been handsome were it not severe of expression with a thin, turned-down mouth and swellings, carbuncles perhaps, on his forehead and left cheek. His dark, deep-set eyes were piercing. His beard, like his hair, was soft and fluffy and cut in the style known vulgarly as a Newgate fringe.

'Mr Azimullah? Mill is my name. I must apologise for keeping you waiting but I hope you have found our little collection interesting?' And he held out a hand, bony but strong. 'Do come to my den and let me offer you some refreshment. Tea perhaps? Yes? Charlie, do be so good as to bring a pot of tea to my room for Mr Azimullah, there's a good chap.'

A large door with ormulu furniture opened into a corridor lit by gas and decorated with more portraits and thence to a flight of stairs. At the top on the landing, Mr Mill pushed open another door and ushered his guest into the room beyond. Azimullah had just enough time to read the plaque set in the centre panel – *Examiner of India Correspondence* – and wonder what it meant. That it was a position of some importance was indicated by the fact that the 'den' was lit by one of the tall windows on the main floor and was next or next but one to the central portico. The walls were lined, like a lawyer's, with rows and rows of cabineted uniform leather-bound volumes from floor to ceiling, and for the most part titled in gilt tooling *Company Correspondence* with dates, rarely more than a couple of months to each volume. There was a large desk under the window covered with stacks of papers, many bound with treasury tape, quills, a small box of steel nibs, an ebony cylindrical rule, blotters and inkwells. A big chair behind it was placed so that the murky daylight fell over the occupant's shoulder. In front of it a low, octagonal table, also ebony, the sides of which were elaborately carved with elephants and trees, stood between two high-backed, winged armchairs upholstered in buttoned black leather and in front of a small but red-hot coalfire. The room was perfumed with a gentle but pervasive fragrance of sandalwood, leather and Mr Mill's cologne.

'Do sit down.' Mr Mill indicated one of the chairs in the middle of the room, and took the other himself, flipping the tails of his coat out from under him as he did so, like some lean mammal of the sea adjusting its tail.

'There was,' he said, with an open smile, 'no need for you to go to the trouble of obtaining a letter of introduction from Lord Brockenhurst: I was on the point of inviting you over anyway.' He leant back and his fingertips met beneath his smile and his chin. 'It has been on my mind for some days that we owed your master a more personal and complete explanation for the decision of the Court of Directors than was expressed in the actual judgement. I imagine that is what you have come for.'

Azimullah's smile was no less ingratiating.

'More than that, sir. I hope I might persuade you that justice should at least allow an appeal against the judgement.'

'Oh, I'm afraid there is no question of that. The Directors gave long and considered attention to your depositions and I am satisfied they came to a just and rational decision. I certainly could not advise them to spend any more time on the matter. You must realise that the Nana's petition was only one of many and, forgive me, not the most important or consequential. For instance, tomorrow we initiate the processes by which the government of the kingdom of Oudh will become our responsibility and already we have a pile of objections and complications to sort through even though, through our Resident in Lucknow, we have had effective charge of the kingdom for some months. What I can offer, however, is a full rationale of our decisions regarding the Nana and the Marathas.'

At this moment came a knock on the door, as obsequious as a knock can be, and in came the ancient dwarf who had been sweeping the hall, but this time carrying a brass tray furnished with everything that is needed to provide a single cup of tea. The tray arrived safely on the table, he busied himself with pot, cup and saucer (Wedgwood but Indian in spirit), sugar and tongs.

'Darjeeling to your liking, sir? Most Native gentlemen appreciate the Darjeeling. Sugar? No. Very wise, since I have heard it takes away the subtler characteristics of the brew. There we are then, sir.'

'That'll do, Charlie.'

'That will be all, sir?'

'That will be all, Charlie.'

Azimullah sipped his tea. It was all right, but nothing special.

'First,' the Examiner now began, 'there is the matter of the pension. Two points here. The original agreement with Baji Rao quite clearly stated that this was intended to be commensurate with the dignity of a man who had been an important prince and was designed to support him in some style and provide him with a retinue. None of this applies to the Nana. He has no official title and since he is not of the royal blood no claim to one either. We are aware that he has been left a private fortune worth thirty lakhs, which is about one hundred and fifty thousand pounds, together with disposable goods, chattels and land. Safely invested this will bring him an annual income of at least ten thousand pounds a year not including rents. It is not possible to be a pauper on ten thousand pounds a year.'

Azimullah shifted in his chair; the leather squeaked like a protesting mouse beneath him, and he cleared his throat.

'It is,' he murmured, 'if you have a hundred or so relatives and servants dependent on you and a personal bodyguard of some five hundred men who have to be paid, accoutred, mounted and properly armed. With a band.'

'But that is precisely my point. These things are the proper appendages of a feudal prince. But the Nana is not a prince. He is a commoner. An ordinary person. And, as such, a very wealthy one.'

'He will never accept that he is a commoner, as you call it.'

The Examiner allowed himself a dismissive shrug.

'Well, my advice to him is that he must accept the reality of his position. He may be brought before the courts, civil, military and criminal, and answer to them just as everyone in a rational society should, from the highest in the land to the lowest. But these things are all plainly set forth in the court's judgement. What I wished to explain to you – and it is to this end that I would have invited you here anyway – is what lies behind this and indeed all the measures we have taken and plan to take on behalf of your country and its peoples . . .'

At this point the Examiner stood and began to pace about the room, sometimes standing by the window, a gaunt silhouette against the dun light, sometimes in front of the fire, smiling down at his visitor, and once or twice running his finger along the backs of the leather-bound volumes as if he were about to have recourse to one or another of them to substantiate the point he was making.

'Your country is potentially enormously wealthy. Blessed with a variety of climates from eternal snow in the mountains to equatorial jungle, including huge alluvial plains, it can furnish in abundance almost every crop known to man. It has mines rich in every mineral from humble lead to gold and diamonds. It could feed itself twice over and export food to the needy of the world, it could develop modern industries on a scale to equal our own. All this, and yet, when my employers took over the administration, the majority of its population, a considerable majority, lived in need, in constant fear of starvation, and were subjected to the whims of potentates and warlords with no recourse to any proper system of law or justice. Its borders were constantly violated by invasions. Much of the land was dominated by bandits, private armies and the depradations of tribes of savages who descended on its villages from their mountain fastnesses.'

He turned away at this point and spoke more softly as if aware that what he was about to say might be construed as boasting.

'In a few decades we have done much to ameliorate all this. We have established recognised frontiers which are, since the last Punjab Wars, impermeable. We are abolishing tariffs and custom and excise duties between the old states and princedoms. We are developing, with the forceful and efficient methods employed by Lord Dalhousie, the present Governor General, a system of communications depending on railways, the electric telegraph and good, well-maintained roads free of bandits. Above all, we are rationalising and standardising the process of tax assessment and collection across the board. The actual burden carried by producers both agricultural and industrial will, and already does in places where the system operates, bear less heavily than it did under the rajahs. We are collecting less in the way of taxes than they did. That is a point not generally appreciated.'

He turned back to Azimullah and his voice took on a tone more severe and admonishing than before.

'It has not been easy to carry through these reforms. Two factors stood in our way like monstrous rocks diverting and corrupting the calm, clear and even flow of a mighty river. First, the collapse of the Mughal Empire into hundreds of states and statelets ruled by rajahs whose only interest has been their own aggrandisement and who have neglected the governance of their peoples so anarchy has everywhere prevailed, banditry in the fields, extortion and similar evils in the bazaars.

'But worse by far than the greed and incompetence of the princes is the effect of your two chief religions. I take it you, sir, are a Mahometan. To the basic tenets of your faith I take very little exception. If there are gods at all I should prefer there to be just the one. By and large the moral precepts of your Founder are not distasteful except in so far as they subject your women to even more in the way of lost liberty and domestic slavery than do those of the various Christian faiths. But there is an assumption of being the absolute holders of the incontrovertible truth that I find not merely distasteful but a negative influence on the way you conduct yourselves *vis-à-vis* other faiths. Many who share your beliefs exhibit a puritanical zeal beyond even that of the most calvinist of our Protestants.'

Here the Examiner returned to his chair and, leaning across the table, altering the tone of his voice yet again to one that communicated both absolute sincerity and a distaste so deep as to be construed as hate, he spoke more slowly, with even more decided emphasis.

'But this is nothing compared with the absurdities proclaimed and followed by the Hindoos. They surround themselves with taboos, ceremonies and customs that control almost every minute of their waking lives. Some of these, like suttee, are repulsive, indeed horrifying, to any person of rational and sensitive habit. Well, suttee we have dealt with, and recurrences of that vile practice are rarer and becoming more rare, but one universal barrier remains to hinder or prohibit almost any amelioration of the lot of peasants and workers alike, and the development of rational ways of thinking among the better off. I am speaking of the caste system. Take the army, the sepoy army, as an example. Most of our Hindoo soldiers are Rajputs, belonging to the second caste, that of rulers and soldiers, though some I believe are actual Brahmins, a caste which nominally demands of its members that they should be astrologers, teachers, priests and philosophers. These Brahmins and Rajputs consider themselves defiled by contact with lower castes, especially in the matter of food preparation, and they have to undergo elaborate and expensive ceremonies to regain their caste if they consider themselves to be polluted. They will not cross seas or oceans. None of this is exactly conducive to efficient soldiering.'

He shook his head, in sad but god-like wonder at the vagaries of human folly.

'Well, I need not preach to you, Mr Azimullah, you are aware of all this and I have allowed myself to be somewhat carried away . . . but you will perceive the dominant factors which continue to stand in the way of the development and progress of your country and to which I ascribe more than any other the misery and deprivation that plague the lives of most ordinary Indians . . .'

It crossed Azimullah's mind to suggest that the most rapacious presence in India, and therefore that which contributed most to the poverty of its people, was that of the Company, but he judged it convenient to maintain the expression of cheerful interest he had assumed. He was also puzzled, as almost all Indians were, by the assumption made by the Company and so trenchantly advanced by its representative at that moment in front of him that the subcontinent was one country, one entity, one nation. As far as he was concerned 'India' was a geographical term. It did not carry and never had carried, except perhaps in the minds of Alexander or the first Mughal emperors, a political or administrative connotation.

Here Mr Mill pulled a large handkerchief from his pocket and mopped his carbuncled and now glistening forehead. He stood up again and this time moved behind his desk so that, still with the light behind him, he seemed to preside almost like the image of a Hindoo god in his innermost sanctuary over not only his temple but a world beyond as well, albeit a world he had never seen.

'Let me conclude before I send you on your way, with this message for your master. Few governments, even under far more favourable circumstances than those supported by the Company, have attempted so much for the good of their subjects, or carried so many of their attempts to a beneficial issue. I should like him to consider the small sacrifice we are asking of him to be supported with this in mind – he has the opportunity to live out his time as a private gentleman of very considerable means, in the knowledge that by doing so he contributes to the greater happiness of the greater number of his fellow citizens.' The Examiner now lifted a small brass bell, brought from Benares but made in Birmingham, from his desk and gave it a shake. 'Charlie will show you the way out. Good day, sir, and my compliments to Mr Dhondu Pant.'

Having said which, our philosophising mandarin of mandarins resumed his seat without offering Azimullah his hand. Instead he folded a pair of wire-framed spectacles on to his nose and lifted a sheet of closely written foolscap from a pile placed on his right. No doubt the very latest piece of Correspondence to arrive there from India. At all events he now gave it the very closest of Examinations. Charlie, meanwhile, reappeared like a djinn and conducted the Nana's emissary back down the stairs and corridor, across the hall where Tipoo's Tiger again wheezed his triumph, and so to the front door. The dusk had deepened, more grey snow was falling, the urchin roadsweeper had packed it in for the day. At the far end of the street the gaslighter made his way from lamp to lamp, casting beneath each standard a pool of dim orange light whose glow never reached that of its nearest neighbour, leaving patches of deepest darkness between.

10

Enfield, January 1855; Istanbul and the Crimea, April 1855

Having failed to overturn the Court of Directors' decision Azimullah set out on an appraisal of the capability of the English army to put down an armed uprising. What follows is an encrypted report sent to the Nana and later found in Bithur, along with the other letters already alluded to.

There have been reports in the press of the successful launching of a new weapon in the Crimea, a rifle known as the Enfield P-53. P is short for 'pattern' and 53 refers to the year it was first designed. It was not difficult to uncover the fact that both the Horseguards and the Company have placed contracts with the manufactory for the equipping of regiments in both the Queen's army in India and the Company's. My visit to Enfield is worth recording in detail, not only because the rifle itself may turn out to be of considerable interest to us, but because in the course of an afternoon I witnessed how a manufactory of advanced weaponry may be most efficiently organised.

I took the East Counties Railway from its terminus in Shoreditch for twelve miles out into the countryside to a dreary looking station entitled Ordnance Factory. A signpost indicated I should cross the rails and follow a muddy lane running between flat meadows. The lane became the towpath of a canal, which I presently crossed at a lock, before entering a linked group of smoky buildings. Some had tall chimneys and some were flanked by pyramids of coal which were being added to from a string of barges. An odour, an infernal miasma, hung over everything. This was the Ordnance Factory, Enfield.

A moment of doubt as a Supervisor took some time making a meticulous examination of my document before passing me on to a Superintendent who proceeded to conduct me round the establishment.

This man, tall, wearing an old coat stained with oil and a rather flat, brimmed hat, always spoke briskly and to the point. He carried a pipe in his right hand which he puffed at when he was not talking, and used as a pointer when he was. Occasionally his chest was racked with a terrible cough no doubt aggravated by the noxious gases he was forced to breathe every day, yet he clearly shewed pride and a sense of achievement in what the whole concern was about. He told me his name was Mr Micklewight, Arnold Micklewight.

'How many parts make up the rifle?' I asked.

'Fifty-six, sir.'

'And how many rifles can you turn out in a week?'

'Working at what we call full capacity, fifteen hundred.'

This means that within a week they can equip a whole regiment of infantry.

I learnt that under the supervision of 'foremen' each piece starts in the 'rough' and is passed down avenues beneath a high girdered roof, from machine to machine, which perform in a moment tasks which in India would occupy skilled craftsmen for several hours or even days. Micklewight informed me that the machines save the company enormous sums of money: for instance, the exterior of the lock is shaped by an iron stamping hammer which is cheaper to use than individual labour by fifteen hundred pounds a week. Even something as simple as the trigger guard is filed by machinery at a saving of five guineas a week.

And the weapon that is the result of all this vulcanic endeavour? The Enfield P-53 is, with its bayonet, six feet and half an inch long, weighs nine pounds and eight ounces. It is sighted up to nine hundred yards by means of a calibrated sight that can be raised to increase the elevation of the muzzle but is effective beyond that. In the hands of a well-trained rifleman it is very accurate indeed up to five hundred yards. The bullet fired at one hundred yards will penetrate twelve half-inch planks.

Finally, a word about the cartridge. This is a heavy-duty paper tube with the bullet at one end and the powder filling the rest. To load, the rifleman bites off the paper above the powder and pours it into the barrel. He then places the still wrapped bullet in the muzzle, and rams the paper that housed the powder down on top. The paper ensures that the bullet will not fall out, but it is also quite heavily greased so it can be rammed down quickly and easily.

The grease can be a mixture of beeswax and mutton fat. These are, however, expensive, and a combination of other fatty substances can be used. Cow and pig fat were suggested. I can foresee, as no doubt your Excellency already has, a problem here. Our Hindoos will not touch cow fat and our Mahometans can't abide pig.

Excellency, there is no doubt in my mind at all that the Enfield P-53 is a very superior rifle, surpassing the French Minié in accuracy, range, lightness and penetration, and will remain the rifle of choice until the technology to make a breech-loader is developed. Its range and accuracy alone mean that a half-company of fifty men can destroy a battalion armed with the old Tower musket or even the Baker rifle before the latter are in effective range. Skilled marksmen will be able to pick off artillery men as they work their guns up to three-quarters of a mile away.

On leaving the Enfield factory I offered Mr Micklewight a silver threepenny piece for his trouble.

He would not take it but muttered, 'I ain't about to take no gratuity from a nigger.'

It is now my intention, since I do not think we can achieve anything more useful in England, to proceed to the Crimea where I hope to assess the potential of the British troops there and the effectivenes in the field of this new weapon.

I remain, dear Lord, your excellency's ever humble servant, desirous only as I am to forward the fortunes of your sublime benevolence . . .

Azimullah Khan

The ability to insert himself into the company of perfect strangers and achieve acceptance, however transitory, was not the least of Azimullah's gifts. His target in Istanbul was William Russell, the famed war correspondent of *The Times*, whose despatches to that paper had revealed a terrible tale of incompetence in the conduct of the war in the Crimea, but he had no letter of introduction, no one at hand who could vouch for him. His answer was to strike up an acquaintance with a certain Philip Henry Rathbone, a Liverpool businessman, philanthropist and politician of conscience, who had come out with the simple aim of seeing for himself how far Russell's criticisms were justified.

I followed the Liverpudlian to the great hammam designed by Sinan, on the hill above the Grand Bazaar, and through the long process of a Turkish bath he revealed that he too wished to see for himself the state of the allied armies. Together we went to Missirie's Hotel where Russell was known to stay, bought the journalist a good dinner, and persuaded him to use his influence to get us on the *Ottawa*, a supply ship due to leave for Balaclava.

Having disembarked, Russell took us over the hills to a point where we had a view of the battlefield. Below on our left, looking towards Balaclava, lay the scene of the cavalry charge of 25th October. On one side little patches of tents studded the fields as far as we could see. Around them spread the land which appeared to have

73

been partly cornfields and partly vineyards, but which is now strewn with the skeletons and carcases of horses. Above our heads a raven croaked hoarsely and in the distance the wind brought the booming of cannon.

On my request we went to see the camp of the Rifle Battalion which was at the top of the little hill to the right of Balaclava. Some were equipped with the new Enfield and I asked to see a demonstration of its capabilities. A lieutenant laid on a section of ten or so men who showed themselves capable of hitting man-shaped targets in the head or chest at over five hundred yards.

On our way back we were passed by Omar Pasha, General Carlobert and Sir Colin Campbell. Sir Colin it was who repulsed the Russian cavalry at Balaclava with his thin red line and the injunction: 'Remember, there is no retreat from here, you must die where you stand.' Russell told us that Campbell, as a very young man, a boy in fact, was in the Peninsula with Sir John Moore at Corunna and later in major campaigns under Wellington. He missed Waterloo because his regiment had been sent to America, but after that rose very slowly, because his origins were humble and he had no influence. In fact, he was the son of a carpenter and, in my opinion, no gentleman. He fought in several wars in India and China, and now at last, in his early sixties, is leading a division in the Crimea. He is not a big man, has abundant crisp, very curly grey hair, his habitual expression is one of penetration and enquiry but from an inner distance, though, as we passed, it was suddenly lit with a somewhat wicked smile and a brief bark of a laugh. His face is that of a sensitive man hardened by circumstance, deeply lined in a way Rathbone associated with overfrequent resort to spirits.

Everyone we spoke to abused the management of the army. A number of men declared they had become radicals in consequence of the present war, and even the officers were very sick of the whole thing. All in all I was left with the impression that the English army is

74

poorly led, the administrative side incompetent. The men are rebelliously minded and might, under greater stress, become mutinous. Apart from the Enfield rifle, which has so far reached only a few units of the Rifle regiments, they are no better equipped than they were at Waterloo. Apart from the rifle, I was impressed by nothing except perhaps Sir Colin Campbell. He indeed would be an enemy to be respected, even feared.

I remain, dear Lord, your excellency's ever humble servant, desirous only as I am to forward the fortunes of your sublime benevolence . . .

Azimullah Khan

11

The palace at Bithur, fourteen miles north of Cawnpore,
May 1855

' Azi, you have put me to some expense. A lakh, my treasurer
says, a lakh at least. And what have you brought back? Not
the title and emoluments of a Peshwa. Not even the honours and
income my father enjoyed in exile.'

The Nana leant back in his marble throne, its back a complicated
lattice of what looked like sugar candy, grasped the lion-head ends of
its arms and looked down at Azimullah who was sitting cross-legged
on crimson silk cushions, embroidered with gold. Suggestive though
they were of past glories the seams were parting and they were
stained here and there in a way typical of most of the furnishings in
the Nana's Bithur palace. They were what his adoptive father had
been able to get away with from his far larger and grander establis-
ment when the British took him out of Poona and dumped him
fourteen miles north of Cawnpore in what was little more than a
draughty, ill-appointed hunting lodge.

From the silver dish at his side the Nana took a cube of rose-water-
flavoured lokum and Azi salivated in response. It was he who had
brought the lokum all the way from Hadji Bekir's new shop between
Istanbul's Grand Bazaar and the spice market.

The would-be potentate dusted powdered sugar from his finger
and thumb, and then licked both. His was a plump, coarse-looking
figure with shaped eyebrows, black moustaches glossy and
immaculately curled, angel lips and a thick neck. The jewelled hilt of

a curved dagger or dirk peeped from a broad yellow cummerbund that conferred neatness on the dome of his tummy – the rest of his dress was brilliant in its plain whiteness apart from the heavy gold beads that hung round his neck and the rather odd-looking cloth of gold cap (it looked like a plate with a blancmange on it and was Parsee in origin) that he wore somewhat rakishly tilted over his left eye.

'So, Azi. What do we do now?' There was threat in his tone. Azimullah cleared his throat. He rather thought that even to contemplate the only course of action left would reduce the Nana to an indecisive, quivering wreck. Still, there is a tide in the affairs of men . . .

'Majesty . . . Rebellion, Revolution, a War of Independence, kick the bastards out.'

Definitely the Nana was taken aback. To say he was proud is to confer on him a moral stature he lacked; there was nothing of Aristotle's Great Spirited Man in his make-up. But he was arrogant, and deeply concerned not to lose face. He hoisted himself to his feet and, stumbling slightly on the step, wandered across to the ogee-arched gallery with its views west across a small town to the broad Ganges and the villages on the far side, villages which, he reminded himself through the turmoil in his head, would soon be paying rent, taxes, to the British Collector rather than to him.

Azimullah injected sweet reason into his tone.

'There is a precedent, you know?'

'There is?' The Nana could not keep a tremor of doubt out of his voice.

'The North Americans are now, already, perhaps the fifth or sixth most powerful country in the world although eighty years ago they were merely thirteen small English colonies on the Atlantic seaboard. And since then the Spanish republics in South America have achieved independence from their mother country. It can be done.'

The Nana struggled for a moment to remember just where the Americas were but decided that this was an irrelevance. The question was . . .

'How?'

A sort of silence settled over the wide and airy marble hall. A soft breeze, jasmine on its breath, caused a handful of rose petals to dance slowly across the floor. A big grandfather clock, the action European, the casing Indian, ticked apologetically as if it knew it was too loud. The Nana sighed, continued . . .

'I have been invited by the officers of the British cavalry to attend their horseraces in town,' he said. 'This evening we shall have a private divan. Just the two of us. And you will present to me a résumé of how a successful insurrection could be prepared for and put into action.'

The Nana returned from the races with very mixed but not powerful feelings about the day. Powerful feelings did not play a great part in his life. Boredom had become a habit and perhaps the strongest emotion he felt was a desire to shake it off. At all events he had been flattered by the small attentions the officers paid him, though these did not go beyond what they would have displayed to any invited guest. He had felt humiliated, as he always did, by the way they did not offer him the salutes they had made on similar occasions to his adoptive father. Their omission now was more than a slight: it was a demonstration that they were aware he had failed in his efforts to regain Baji Rao's titles and pension. However, he enjoyed the racing and was pleased when a three-year-old grey he had sold as a yearling to a young lieutenant won over a mile and a half, which, they told him, was the Derby distance. Nevertheless, he turned down an invitation to dine in the mess. He always did. He had the religious tolerance you would expect in a dull, bored man but, with the force almost of compulsive behaviour disorder, respected punctiliously the Hindoo practices of not drinking alcohol and having his food prepared and served according to the rituals appropriate to his caste. So, it was back at Bithur that he had a large evening meal of vegetable curries with a variety of unleavened breads, followed by two or three excessively sweet dishes, before making his way to his council chamber where Azimullah was already in attendance.

Here the seating was deeply upholstered and comfortable, though still carrying the signs of shabbiness that made homely most of what lay about the palace. The Nana spread himself across the largest of the chairs, a sort of ottoman, Azimullah sat in a far less comfortable upright on the further side of a large low table set between them. A servant brought the Nana his hookah and mint tea for both. Lokum, sugared almonds, coconut-flavoured creams appeared in small porcelain dishes. The hookah bubbled, smoke, mostly from dried apple and molasses, issued from between the Nana's lips. He removed the amber mouthpiece.

'Well?' he said.

He went to bed a changed man. His life had been given purpose, an aim . . . well, it had had those before, but as fantasies only, but now there was another factor – according to Azimullah he had the means, and that made all the difference. To have a dream is one thing, to have been shown that it is achievable is quite another. Azi had spoken well, to the point, had marshalled his facts and proposals into neat comprehensible packets. The theory, the method and the means became clear.

The Nana, high on it all, tossed and turned on his feather-filled pillows and bolsters, crumpled his embroidered satin sheets (and caught his toe briefly but irritatingly in a hole where the ancient material had worn thin) and strove to rehearse the main points, the main headings.

A successful insurrection needs a supportive populace – not necessarily active but in sympathy, ready to shelter fugitives, hide arms and other material, run messages, generally we are talking of the lower sort. Why? The better off you are the less you will look for change. Don't, in other words, expect much from the rajahs, not at any rate until you are winning. The peasants, though used to abuse and injustice from their indigenous masters, found the British even more arrogant, but also uncomprehending of local customs and practices, and, if marginally less rapacious over what they took, far more intransigent about getting it.

'You will be faced by an army and a police force,' Azimullah continued, with the urgency of a proselyte. 'These must be subverted or won to your cause . . .'

It was Azi's firm belief that the sepoy army could be tipped into mutiny. They had so many causes for discontent – one more big thing could push them over. 'The Enfields, the new rifles with greased cartridges. The grease. It could be pork or cow fat . . .'

'But what if it is not?'

'It doesn't matter, we tell them it is.'

'But when will they be issued in India?'

'Not until the Crimea business is over. Maybe as much as another year . . .' Azimullah, carried away by his vision, became even more excited. 'We need a year, we need a year at least. Two would be better.'

'Why, what for?'

'To be successful it must all go off at once, otherwise they will mop it up piecemeal. The sepoys must mutiny together at one time, in every barracks, cantonment, station across the country. From the battalions down to the sections guarding a district magistrate's court and bungalow. Every Britisher must be killed on the same day. Everywhere . . .'

He had then gone on to talk of secret cells, in every camp and station, of how they must not know who is involved outside their area, but must trust that they are not alone. How there must be means of communication between cells that yet know so little about each other they cannot betray each other. He concluded:

'This all takes time to set up, to recruit, to organise.'

The Nana recalled the English garrison at Cawnpore, the people he had spent the afternoon with.

'No sepoy army can win a field battle against the English,' he grumbled, almost a whine, as if he hated what he was saying.

Azimullah answered him.

'Because of the Crimea, Persia, Afghanistan and China, there are here ten sepoys to every British soldier. Even the British cannot win against such odds.'

'They'll reinforce. Especially if the Crimea is finished.'

'I have seen the troops in the Crimea. They are tired, ill, their numbers down, they are disheartened, they want to go home. If we start at the end of May they will die of sunstroke, camp fever and jungle fever, cholera.'

'Next May. May 1856?' The Nana's voice rose with almost breathless excitement.

'No,' answered Azimullah, hiding his impatience, 'we need more than a year. May 1857 is what we are talking about.'

Azimullah had remained in the council chamber, awake and in a more reflective mood after the Nana had left.

'Is it possible?' he asked himself in a dozen ways and found a dozen different answers. 'Can we do it?'

He had his doubts.

'There are two things we lack,' he said to himself at last. 'A belief in ourselves as a people, and a leader who, in a shadowy way, represents the people. The Americans had Washington and in the south Bolivar. They believed in themselves as nations fettered by foreigners. What have we got? The Nana? The King of Delhi, the last of the Mughals? An old man. An idiot. Worse than the Nana. What about India, Mother India?'

He uttered a short, pained laugh, got up and walked to the unglazed, uncurtained, arched casement. His fingers dragged his prayer beads, the Names of Allah, across his palm, then clenched on the tiny rope.

'No such . . . thing . . . exists. Every villager knows there are three or four more villages whose land borders their own and that is where their horizon, is – virtually next door. And the principalities and rajahs are much the same. And, like the villagers, they fight each other every now and then but they don't do that so much any more. Thanks, I may say, to the English. But India? Mother India? Forget it.'

He looked down at the beads.

'Cannot we make it a holy war, a jihad? And whatever the Hindoo equivalent is? Perhaps. Attacks on either religion stir them to the wildest excesses. And the Sikhs are worse. Adherents of all three will die and kill for their beliefs. But one is split into sects that don't mind killing each other, and the other into so many gods and goddesses it's hard to know why they call it one religion. No, we lack all cohesion except dislike and often hatred for our current rulers. And that is not enough.'

He looked up at the plum-coloured darkness above, filled with stars, the Milky Way a rooftree or a river spread across it.

'But if we manage to make them think that the ultimate aim underlying the whole British project is nothing less than the forced conversion of all to Christianity . . .? If they really believe that, and many do, they will rise, and not just the sepoys.'

He moved back into the divan, stopped to pick a last sweetmeat from a plate, first brushing away the green-backed fly that had settled on it.

'So, it'll be worth a try. And amusing too.' The laugh that bubbled up this time was fresher than the last, expressed a gleeful anticipation.

He popped the sticky sugary jelly into his mouth and through the

12

Bindki and Futtehpore, January 1856

The clever utilitarians in Leadenhall Street debated among themselves as to whether or not they should properly call themselves socialists. Mr Mill on the whole rather thought they should. Consider the tax system in the Oudh and the Doab. Before the Company took a hand the landholders, or talukdars, roughly equivalent to the squirearchy in England, extracted whatever the peasants could be made to produce surplus to their own basic needs, kept some of it for themselves and passed on the rest to the princes, rajahs, the feudal barons.

Enter the Company, Mr Mill and his 'socialists'. Where they had control of the land, through treaties and conquest, they relieved the rajahs (and, in the Oudh, the King) of much of their wealth, all their responsibilities, and in return gave them pensions. They then looked at the villages they had 'liberated' and found in each a headman, a zemindar, and him they appointed 'owner' of the village and the land it farmed. And it was on him that responsibility fell for getting together the contribution the village would be required to pay for the regulation and administration of the province, for a local police force and a more than local army, for improvements to the infrastructure such as roads, the telegraph and the post, and so on and so on, all the things the rajahs had neglected.

So far, perhaps so good. But then came the assessment and collection of what was due from each village, and here a brutal practicality asserted itself of which Leadenhall Street was not always fully aware.

Each village's liability was expressed in terms of cash based on current market prices, and the assessment on the records that had been kept for the previous five years. Although the amount actually arrived at for collection over the whole province was less than the old system had demanded there were areas that were grossly overassessed by overzealous collectors, or those who distrusted or misunderstood the records they had unearthed.

Finally, the new collection was to be run on the most rational utilitarian principles, but unfortunately with no regard at all for existing circumstances, social organisation, tradition or the feelings of important classes and individuals, nor of the upheaval caused by the takeover itself. And many of those appointed to administer it, though often old India hands, were arrogant and unbending, largely because their livelihoods depended on their being seen to be incorruptible and efficient.

Bindki. Assessors presented themselves to Jiva, the headman who had tried ineffectively to save his community's sacred grove. His first job was to commute the amount the village was expected to raise back from rupees into a volume of grain. In this he was helped by Nanak, a village elder who had been on a special course set up by the Company to train an accountant in each village. So how was it that their calculations seemed to show that they were being asked to give up 12 per cent more grain than they had in the previous year? And were they supposed to sell the grain themselves and hand over coin, or would the Collector accept grain? Threshed or not threshed? Ground into flour or as husked grain, attar? They'd have to go to Futtehpore and seek out the Collector, ask his advice, ask him to reduce the burden they were being asked to carry.

It was a trip Jiva made only rarely and was in fact, at eighteen miles, the furthest he had ever been from Bindki. Daunted by the prospect of facing the great man on his own, he decided to take Nanak with him. But how should they travel? On horseback, with some dignity, surely? But there were only two donkeys and one horse in the village and Nanak, conscious of his new dignity as village accountant, refused to ride on a donkey and clearly Jiva should have the horse. In a bullock cart? That would mean taking the driver, the owner of the bullocks, and at that time of the year cart and bullocks were needed elsewhere. On foot then? On foot, down the Grand Trunk Road.

It was not as crowded then as it would be fifty years later when a young lad called Kim, whose Native mother had been nursemaid to a colonel's family and his father an Irish sergeant turned railway worker, walked down it accompanied by a lama from the mountains. But the mix was no doubt much the same – the long-haired, whiffy Sansis with baskets of lizards and other unclean food on their backs (give them wide berth, for the Sansi is deep pollution); villagers returning from another village's festival, the lads chewing sugar cane, flashing cheap mirrors in each others' eyes, or haggling with sweetmeat sellers; a gang of changars perhaps, the big-bosomed, strong-limbed, blue-petticoated clan of female earth carriers hurrying to the next stretch in front of the railway to throw up the embankment; or a marriage procession with music and shouting, marigolds and jasmine, and a bride's carriage glittering with roses and tinsel. Certainly there would have been the grain and cotton waggons whose squealing axles Jiva could hear a mile away.

By eight o'clock, for they had started well before daybreak, the nearness of the town was heralded by more and more shanties along the roadside selling warm sweet masala milk served in tiny biscuit-fired cups which the users then broke, or lassi, or chappatis and dahl for travellers who had not eaten since setting out; there were tiny forges and farriers touting for custom with small red-hot charcoal furnaces, small anvils and, if they were lucky enough to get a customer, going at it, hammer and tongs, on a broken circle of fire, dong-didee-dong-didee-dong-dong. Others even more hopefully offered tinkered pans, corn dolls, bright scarves and saree lengths of flawed cotton, bottles of muddy Ganges water. At last a blockhouse occupied by a section of sepoys under a naik marked the town's boundary with, beyond it, a stranger sight – ten pillars, five on each side of the road, each inscribed, in Native alphabets as well as English, with . . . the Ten Commandments. These were new. Jiva stopped, scratched his neck below his turban and turned to Nanak.

'What are these all about then?' he asked.

'Christian stuff,' the old man replied, and spat. 'Thou shalt have none other gods but me. Thou shalt not make to thyself any graven image . . . thou shalt not bow down to them, nor worship them . . . Thou shalt not take the name of the lord thy god in vain . . . and so on.'

'Nothing bad about that. Why should anyone want to bow down

to any god but his own? Though I don't see why you shouldn't have a statue of her or him or a picture, if that helps you.'

'You're missing the point, Jiva. It's not your god they want you to bow down to, but theirs.'

'Oh. Why are they here? Who put them here?'

'How should I know?' But he turned and caught the sleeve of a passing water seller whose water bag must have been empty since he wasn't pestering them. He got an answer, turned back to Jiva.

'New judge. Tucker Sahib. Very Christian, he had them put up.'

But the water seller had more to say.

'There's a Christian priest, a Bengali called Gopinath Nandi. He preaches to all the people Tucker sends to prison, and six of them he's even given land to when they came out, so they could be farmers.'

'Why did he do that?'

'Because they pretended to have become Christian,' Nanak interposed. 'I know this Gopinath Nandi. He was one of my teachers when they taught me figures. He used the lessons they gave us in numbers to preach what he called the gospel and made us take a copy of their holy book home with us.'

Jiva suppressed an oath.

'Is this judge the one we have to see?'

Nanak shrugged. 'Maybe. But he is not the Collector, so maybe not.'

'I'm the wrong person for this,' Jiva muttered. 'If we want our taxes lowered, we should have sent someone who was ready to become a Christian.'

But at that time there was no magistrate-collector in town, the old one having retired back to England with jungle fever and the new one, a Mr Sherer, still not arrived. His duties were therefore taken on by Robert T. Tucker, the District Judge, a tall, large-boned man with a full and pleasant voice, who, though vivacious and social enough, was directed by the primitive piety of the early Puritans. Three days went by before Judge Tucker's clerk could find a space in the busy man's schedule for them, but on the fourth day, when they turned up just after sunrise at the court house, a large white bungalow with a verandah roof supported by Doric pillars, they were told they were third in line.

When their turn came they were taken to a large room, a somewhat cobbled-up version of an English judge's chambers. There was a portrait of the Queen above a *faux* fireplace and, serried behind locked meshes, law books bound in calfskin which seemed to sweat with the heat, the smell of which Jiva found nauseating. The judge's desk had a pot of wilting sweet peas on it whose sickly fragrance mixed ill with that of the leather. There was a big chair behind the desk and a plaque above it on which were inscribed the words 'Thou Seest me'.

'Who sees him?' Jiva whispered once Nanak had translated them for him.

'His god,' came the reply.

The only concession to India and its climate was a punkah in front of the open window, operated by a young boy wearing a neat white suit.

They sat on stools in front of the desk. In came Judge Tucker, and his lean wheaten-skinned Brahmin clerk, who told them to stand. They stood. Tucker sat. The clerk told them they could sit. They sat.

Judge Tucker, robust and rosy, fiddled with a sheaf of papers for a moment or two, murmured to the clerk, cleared his throat.

'You are Jiva Prasad, headman of Bindki.' His voice was full and pleasant, a joy to listen to, his acquaintance said, that is if you were in tune with his views or his judgements were favourable to you.

'Yes, sahib.'

'And you have a problem with the recent assessment made of your village's liability for taxes.'

'Yes, sahib.'

'In the last three weeks I have received three hundred and twenty-six similar applications. So far, out of the ninety-three I have looked at I have found only five errors and two of those were underestimated, not the other way about. The assessor explained to you how he had arrived at the figure?'

'Yes, sahib.'

Nanak cleared his throat.

'Your honour . . .' he began.

'And you are?'

'Bindki's village accountant, your honour.'

'Well, then?'

'Although the assessment is twelve per cent higher than the sum

87

we paid to our talukdar last year, it is the manner and time of collection that we would wish to question, your honour.'

Tucker, sensing a repetition of a plea he had heard many times before, sighed noisily. Nanak continued.

'It would be easier for us if the collection could be delayed until the whole harvest is in, by the end of June, when the monsoon comes . . .'

Jiva took up the tale.

'As it is, we will have to sell about two thirds of the grain we have set aside against a poor monsoon and to provide for the cool time that follows. If the second harvest fails we will not be able to buy back that grain and we will starve.'

Tucker's voice deepened in pitch and rose in volume.

'You will not starve. The Government will retain grain in case of famine and sufficient will be properly distributed if necessary. You know that.'

They had been told so. They also understood that such subventions would eventually have to be paid for and were in any case always inadequate. They also knew that the price would be set by rapacious Native grain merchants in Calcutta taking advantage of a surplus in one part of the world to profit from a shortage in another.

But Tucker had more to say.

'Meanwhile, if I let you keep your surplus you might do as others have done in the past, and either hide it or sell it and hide the money you get. Case dismissed. But before you go, let me give you one piece of advice. Accept Jesus as your lord and pray to his father, from whom all blessings flow, for deliverance from hunger, and if your hands and minds are clean of sin I am sure you will find your village will prosper.'

13

A Leap Year. Was that significant? No doubt an astrologer would have said so. A Hindu astrologer? Probably not. The Hindu year begins with the spring equinox, the back end of February is in the first week of the last month of the year which has thirty days, so Charles ('Carlo' to his intimates) John, Viscount Canning's arrival in Calcutta was not noted as astrologically important. A new Governor General was probably expected to have as little effect on the lives of ordinary Indians as does a new Prime Minister on our British lives today. Both are, were, at the mercy of historical forces whose instruments they were, but over whose activities they had almost no influence.

You would not have thought so if you had seen the fuss that was made as his ship, a steam-assisted packet called the *Feroze*, first dropped anchor in Garden Reach and was then warped to a landing stage whose simple, rough-hewn, and possibly rickety timbers, the sight of which, it had been judged, might cause a flutter in Lady Charlotte Canning's breast, were now draped in red, white and blue bunting, and over which an awning had been erected.

Much of this last stage of a four-month-long journey, which had taken them first to Paris to meet Napoleon III, and then to Luxor and the Valley of Kings, had been frankly squalid. The villages on the muddy banks were settlements of equally muddy fishermen who, nearly or actually naked, cast nets almost in front of the *Feroze*'s prow, and more than once, whether by design or not, defecated on

89

the riverbank well in view of anyone who might glance in their direction. Only yards away their women did their washing in the time-honoured way described later by Mark Twain as trying to break rocks with wet, rolled-up clouts. There was worse. The Hooghly, being the most westerly arm of the Ganges delta, bore with it, on its sluggish stream, all manner of refuse including kitchen detritus, faeces and dead female babies.

It had not all been like that. There were also groves of trees often laden with blossom, strange birds with bright plumage flying through and above them, and, in the uncultivated areas, crocodiles, antelopes and once, just once, the sight of a leopard draped along the thick lower bough of an acacia tree. At dusk, long single lines of pelicans cruised briskly, moving from one place to another, for who knew what reason. After an evening and a morning of this, the mud villages and the endless fields were broken first by an occasional large bungalow on the eastern, starboard side, most of them pillared in colonial style, then by more, and these more substantial, often with riverside frontages and gorgeous gardens planted round emerald lawns, and finally a long vista of pretty villas with green verandahs. English people at last, with white children, ran to the banks to see the great man's ship go by.

Eventually, lying just above the green line of the last of the jungle, they could make out the extensive ramparts of Fort William, a huge citadel built on the most up-to-date lines, not in the least medieval, but with scarps, glacis, bastions and redoubts. A telescope passed from hand to hand showed the Union flag on the one low tower, and as they drew nearer, surrounded now by a flotilla of small boats and with a Royal Navy steam pinnace as escort, a flash winked from the battlements and a cotton-wool ball of white smoke was followed by the thud of distant cannonfire.

Garden Reach at last and before they disembarked they had half a sight of the great port beyond. Ships powered by both steam and sail made a forest of masts, waiting their turn in front of the godowns and huge fenced yards filled with bales of raw cotton for Lancashire and jute for Dundee, sacks of rice, millet, wheat, tea and coffee or, in smaller volumes but yet more valuable, crates of indigo bars, sacks of spices and opium. There were timberyards and sawmills where teak, sandalwood and cedar were stacked to season. And incoming were all the products of the workshop of the world, metal goods from cheap tin trays and brass ornaments mass-produced in Birmingham to Indian designs to be sold upstream in the bazaars of Benares; knives, saws, tools of all sorts; handguns and field guns, howitzers and mortars; stacked railway track and huge wheels of coiled copper wire for the electric telegraph; agricultural tools and machinery and cotton again, spun, woven and printed, brought back to where it originally came from, all the way from Rochdale, Salford and Bolton, to be cut up for dhotis and sarees.

There was a band, 'God Save the Queen', 'Rule, Britannia!' and 'See, the Conquering Hero Comes' as Lord and Lady Canning crossed the richly carpeted boards, and then, as they set foot at last on the soil of India, much stamping of feet and presenting of arms. There was a carriage for each of them, to take them the short drive across the huge maidan, the vast parade ground that lay in front of Government House. This was, from the outside anyway, more splendid than Buckingham Palace, having not merely one portico but three, two fronting the large wings as well as the one that formed the main entrance. At the foot of the wide steps the Lieutenant Governor of Bengal welcomed them and conducted them to the top, where, between the two most central columns, Lord Dalhousie, thickset, clothed in formal black with a black stock, hands clasped beneath his tails, waited to greet them.

Which he did very prettily, wrote Carlo Canning in his diary that evening.

Canning. His grandmother, whose maiden name was Costello, had been a struggling actress and no better than she should be, his grandfather a hack who speculated unsuccessfully and died broke. Mary Costello then married a brute of an actor who beat everyone in sight, to the extent that young George, father of Charles, showed signs of turning into a rogue. Charles's great-uncle came to the rescue and procured George an education at Eton and Oxford, where he became part of the set that grew up to rule Britain during the Regency. Following Castlereagh's suicide he became a notable Foreign Secretary and briefly, in 1827, Prime Minister. Charles was the third of three sons but the only one who survived. On his mother's death he inherited the title of viscount, she, when widowed, having been allowed to inherit the title in her own right on account of the fact that her children were little more than babies and her husband had been PM when he died. Through the forties and fifties Charles showed himself to be a hardworking and efficient administrator as Postmaster General, and was known as a wit, a wag to his closest friends, but could appear cool and even aloof to others. He was of middling height, solid build and bald apart from a band of hair that circled the back of his head from ear to ear.

His wife, Charlotte, a daughter of the far nobbier Stuarts of Rothesay, was a treasure and had been married to him for twenty-one years. Though nearly forty she was still known for her wonderful looks, her wit and charm, and, as later became very apparent, her good sense and compassion. She had been a Lady of the Bedchamber to the Queen, who counted her a friend, and would send Her Majesty a full account of what was going on, with drawings, once every six weeks, throughout the Mutiny.

And how did they spend their first evening in the pile that was Government House? While the men went through the formalities of a regime change, Charlotte was given a tour and discovered that what had looked like a palace was huge, draughty yet too hot, a touch shabby and had no proper water closets – the drop between the house and the river not being enough to carry the waste away. The gardens were neat with, at the end of February, the flowers of an English summer – irises, delphiniums, hollyhocks and hedges of sweet peas.

In the council chamber Dalhousie took Canning through the ceremony of handing over the seals of office at the end of which a signal was sent, possibly by electric telegraph, across the maidan to Fort William where the Horse Artillery replied with a proper cannonade. The council chamber? Views over the maidan, a long polished table with upright armchairs beneath a huge chandelier whose drops needed cleaning, had a greyish sheen, and a huge silver something or other in the middle. Portraits of previous Governors General, life-size in heavy gilt frames, hung on all the walls, the gilt blackening in the corners because of the damp and heat; punkahs, but, on a February evening, no wallahs.

Over a glass or two of sherry, they had a chat.

'Obviously you'll be aware you're getting twenty-five thousand pounds a year.* Well, before I came out Lord Ellenborough told me I should be able to save a thousand a month. Rubbish, of course. In the eight years I've been here I've managed to pay off a big debt, buy a cotton mill, and I've got about seven thousand in the bank I didn't have before, but that's about it.'

Canning pulled his lips together in a *moue* which expressed surprise, sympathy and disappointment in equal measures. Dalhousie filled in some detail.

'Where did it all go? That chap Mill told me the Company pays the upkeep here and at the other residences, the household staff, the Queen's Birthday Banquet, and so forth. He asserted that the only people I would have to pay were our personal servants. Household staff, the Company pays, he told us. We thought a butler, a housekeeper, kitchen staff, some footmen and maids, gardeners, that sort of thing. One thing you'll find out about India is that a job that fills the time of one well-trained Englishman requires the attentions of at least six Natives, which doubles the expense. You might think these are household staff, but not so. What the Company means by household staff is not that at all, but turns out to be what one personally needs to run the show. Secretaries, clerks, "writers" is what we call them, archivists and so forth. They pay for all that, as they should.

'What else? This and that. The worst is the entertaining and there is a deuced lot of that, believe me. And so bloody dull, especially the Indians. I don't mean the Natives, I mean the families who were here before Clive and never go back apart from a bit of schooling and Oxford . . .'

They talked about the legacy Dalhousie was leaving. The departing Governor General reckoned he had done a pretty good job.

'Got things moving in all sorts of ways. Roads and canals, river transport, steamers and so forth, and we've made a good start on the railways. The telegraph and the postal system. I'm especially pleased with the latter, the dâk they call it. Hardly a village doesn't get the mail and there are dâk bungalows every twenty miles or so on all the

* £1.25 million in today's money: the thinking behind this was no doubt that, after the scandals of earlier GGs lining their pockets in not altogether honest ways, it was best to remove the occasion of temptation.

93

main roads. I've encouraged cash crops which makes tax collecting a lot easier, indigo, cotton, sugar, opium. Good tax earner, opium, though, as you know, we are still having trouble exporting it to China. Lot of investment coming in, shows chaps back in the City feel we're pretty stable now Nepal and the Punjab are in line. Have a cigar? No? Later perhaps. Persia and the Afghans are quiet at last, after the bloody noses we've handed out. The Russians, of course, could become a problem.'

The retiring Governor General moved over to one of the big windows that overlooked the maidan. A band was playing selections from opera and a regiment of foot were doing some pretty neat drill to the music. 'Main worry is lack of European troops. Thanks to this damned Crimea junket we're down to one British for every ten Native regiments and there's talk of sending another expeditionary force to China over this opium business so I don't suppose we'll get any more in the near future. And I don't like what I've been hearing about some of the Native units.'

'Is there going to be trouble?'

'Could be. Part of what's wrong is the sort of chaps the Company are sending out these days for officers. They're very heavy handed, some of them, at trying to Christianise the sepoys. I'm all for that in a general way. Part of our job. But they go about it wrong. If I were you, I'd badger everyone you can for some decent, well-tried Queen's regiments preferably led by gentlemen. Artillery and riflemen especially . . . If it comes to a scrap, and you can damage them at a distance, the sepoys'll run, they won't march into gunfire the way our chaps will, and they say this new rifle can kill at three times the distance of the old ones. But they're damn good at close quarters.'

'Do you think it might come to that?'

Dalhousie moved away from the window, pulled a chair out from the long table, sat in it, gestured to Canning that he should do likewise. Still then very much the man in charge, not quite ready, perhaps, to let go.

'Frankly, no. But I do get letters about it from the old hands. There's a colonel, Sir Charles Blackstock, on the retired list, who bangs on about it in an informed sort of way . . .'

'I've heard of him.'

'Did well in the First Punjab War. Anyway, I've asked him to go to Lucknow to advise our new chap there on military matters.'

'I've been wanting to ask you about that. The Oudh. It's just a fort-night ago, isn't it?'

'That was the formality. Whichever way the King decided to go it was bound to happen. We were all prepared for it, tax assessments in place, proper systems for collection, magistrates ready to take over. Should go like clockwork, though there has been a hiccup.'

'Yes?'

'Well, we had Sir James Outram there as Resident and he was to be Chief Commissioner. Good man, good general, good administra-tor. But poor health and he's had to pack it in, for the time being. Only man available is a civilian, Coverley Jackson. Again, a good administrator, but not an army man . . .'

'Which is why you've sent him Blackstock?'

'Exactly so. Not the soul of tact either, this Jackson fellow, so it will be up to you to find someone better as soon as you can.' Up to you. Handing over. He grunted, shifted in his seat, recrossed his legs. 'If I have a worry, it's not about the Oudh countryside but about Lucknow itself. The King had a private army of some seventy thou-sand that's been disbanded of course, and the court, which was corrupt, decadent to a degree, employed hundreds of artisans of all sorts from cooks to architects, and entertainers from nautch girls to courtesans. All these are now virtually on the streets and creating all sorts of trouble. The one thing they lack is a leader and it looks as though they might be getting one.'

'Tell me about him.'

'Her. Old Wajid has had several wives none of whom seems to have been able to produce an heir but then along came a lady, a cour-tesan, called Hazrat, who claims her son, now ten years old, called Birjis Qadr, is Wajid's son too. He believes her, well, I suppose he wanted to, and made her the boss wife, the Begum, and gave her the title Mahal. Now the main factions in Lucknow are apparently look-ing to persuade her to claim the throne for her son and act as regent. Which brings me to what I consider to be a much more dangerous grouping than the sepoys on their own can ever be. Begum Hazrat could well make common cause with two other so-called royalties who seem to think they've been hard done by. The Nana Saheb who thinks he ought to be Peshwa of the Marathas . . .'

'I know about him. His vakil, Azimullah Khan, made a nuisance of himself in London just over a year ago. And the other?'

'The Ranee of Jhansi. Same story as the Nana's. Her husband, older than her, had no blood offspring but there's an adopted infant son. She wants to rule Jhansi until he's old enough to succeed, but of course we don't allow adopted heirs. Got to be of the blood or we take over. So that's three of them. The Begum, the Nana and the Ranee don't amount to a lot separately, but if they make common cause they could be quite formidable. And we have had indications they are doing just that. Moreover, Azimullah has been to Delhi and had talks with the King there and even went up to Umballa, I believe, and looked in on Meerut on his way back . . .' Dalhousie paused, and quite suddenly passed both palms over his broad face.

'That's enough for now. More later, perhaps. Shall we go down? There are things about the establishment here Lady Canning should know about.'

On the sweep of the staircase he paused, looked back over his shoulder at his successor.

'It's been a long haul, you know. Eight years. Damned hard work and always a lot to worry about. And the climate! Wears you out.'

In four years he was dead, at only forty-eight.

They met Lady Canning and her ladies-in-waiting in the big entrance hall. She looked fresh, excited, almost gay in a slate-coloured silk dress she had found time to change into, with her very dark hair pulled back from a centre parting to expose delicate ears and discreet amethyst drop earrings.

'We've been in the gardens, Charles,' she said, 'very nice.' She turned to Dalhousie. 'You must have a good staff out there, James. But we disturbed quite a large mammal. As big as a fox would you say, Emily? You saw it better than I did.'

'Perhaps not quite so big, ma'am.'

'Sort of pepper and salt look, bushy tail, head like a weasel but bigger.'

'Ah, that'll be Aurangzeb, our mongoose. Take care of him.'

'Why should we do that?'

'He kills, and eats, the snakes, even the big ones like the king cobras.'

'We have snakes, James? In the garden? Well!'

96

PART III

The Darkness Deepens

14

Jhansi – Meerut, October and November 1856

On 10 November, in Meerut, the Fetherstonhaughs gave an informal supper party at which Bruce Farquhar was the chief guest. Once the food had been eaten, the main course being smoked salmon pickled in brine and transported by Fortnum & Mason in small barrels, they withdrew to the drawing room to drink tea and, in the men's case, whisky or India Pale Ale. There Bruce was invited to tell the story of his trip to Jhansi, which he had made at the request of no lesser person than the new Governor General himself.

The drawing room was panelled with oak brought from England, portraits of Beresfords and other members of the Anglo-Irish Ascendancy hung on the walls, the glass was Waterford, the service most definitely silver and not Sheffield plate, some of it indeed silver-gilt. The room was quite brightly lit by a small chandelier over the table, and, between the paintings, bracketed candelabra. These of course attracted the insects, giant moths and other more predatory and fearsome beasts which, battering themselves against the starched muslin which took the place of glass in the windows, filled in a burden of rumbling, clicking and a rhythmic buzzing.

In her meddlesome way, Mrs Fetherstonhaugh had placed Sophie opposite Bruce, having guessed that a flirtatious attraction existed between them, although it was generally supposed that Farquhar was on the point of engaging with Uma Blackstock.

Bruce took a long swallow from his glass of Bass, cleared his throat and began. 'Jhansi is a small town overlooked as so many such places are in Hindustan by a fort on a hill, quite a considerable one—'

'Is Jhansi not the place where Rose Andrews' husband is the Collector?' Victoria Marchant asked.

'He is,' Bruce replied. 'But at that time he was in Gwalior on Company business.' He continued where he had left off. 'The Ranee, however, does not live in the fort but in a palace set in extensive grounds and gardens nearby, between it and the main town. I was taken to a large tent, pitched beneath giant mango trees, elegantly fitted up and carpeted, where I was entertained by her chief minister, or vakil, who was a polite and learned old chap, rotund, small in stature, generally with a soft, kind smile on his face. The Ranee, so he informed me, had consulted with her Brahmins as to the most propitious hour for me to come to the purdah. The Brahmins told her that it must be between sunset and moonrise which, since the moon was nearly full, meant between half past five and half past six—'

'The Brahmins, pah!' Captain Fetherstonhaugh interjected. He was older than his wife and had been passed over for promotion on account, it was said, of a vile temper when in his cups. 'They use their confounded astrology to control everyone else.'

Bruce ignored him and went on.

'There was therefore a couple of hours to be got through. After five minutes or so the minister took me to one side and, making sure that none of the others present, other ministers, servants and so forth, could hear us, broached a somewhat embarrassing matter . . .'

His audience became even more attentive in response to Bruce's now lowered voice.

'Would I mind, he asked me, taking my boots off before entering the Ranee's presence?'

'What nonsense,' Mrs Fetherstonhaugh interrupted, 'I'm sure you did nothing of the sort!'

Bruce Farquhar ignored her too.

'I asked, did the Governor General's agent do so when he called? The minister replied that her highness has never allowed him or any other Englishman to come into her presence save a lawyer called John George Lang who represented her interests in Calcutta. And this Mr Lang, did he take off his shoes? I asked. On learning that he had I said I would do so too, but only if I might be allowed to keep on my hat. Please do, the minister replied, her highness will consider it an honour if you remain covered.

'I was then given a most magnificent meal which took us through to the appointed hour at which point I was conducted out of the tent to find a huge white elephant had arrived, caparisoned in red velvet, to carry me through the gardens to the palace. There, after a short wait, I was escorted through several rooms—'

'How did you get awn and awf the elephant?' a female voice on his right interrupted. This was Lady Tarrant, a daughter of the Northampton Bertram family, married to Sir George Tarrant who came from Devon and whose father had fought at Waterloo.

'Steps were provided, madam, and the beast was induced to go down on its knees.'

'Is that usual?'

'I believe so.'

'Such a relief. I shall look about me for steps, I assure you, should such an occasion be presented to me.'

Bruce took another swallow of IPA and resumed.

'I was led through several rooms, unfurnished save for carpets, chandeliers and paintings of Hindoo gods and goddesses on the walls—'

'Typical,' another voice came in, 'they always stuff their rooms with cartloads of junk or leave them entirely bare—'

'Please. Do let him get on. No more interruptions.'

'Oh, very well.' The problem was, few of those there could bear to remain unnoticed and unheard for more than five minutes at the most.

'At last we came to a larger door. The minister knocked and a female voice told him that I and I alone could be admitted. He indicated I should take off my boots. Well, this was a problem and it could not be solved until I had sat on the floor and allowed him to pull them off. Then, adjusting my hat, I was in full dress uniform but with trousers, not the kilt, my noble camel with my baggage having kept pace with me the whole way, I went in. In my stockinged feet.'

The hush deepened. To almost all there the mysteries of the purdah were unknown and the subject of much speculation.

'In the centre of the room, which was even more richly carpeted than the ones I had been through, was a large European armchair amid garlands of sweet-smelling flowers. Among those too exotic to name there were roses, honeysuckle, sweet-scented stock and sweet rocket . . .'

With a little lurch of her heart Sophie realised that she knew very few men – and her husband was certainly not one of them – who could name as many flowers.

'. . . all set in front of a richly embroidered curtain of muslin, the actual purdah itself, that hung like a mist, yet stirring in the draught from a punkah, between me and the other creatures in that room.

'From behind it came the sound of female voices urging a child to go to the sahib. Eventually he came through the gap in the curtain and I was satisfied by his jewelled costume, complete with turban sporting a peacock feather attached by a richly jewelled brooch, that here was the adopted son of the rajah, the rejected heir to the throne of Jhansi. He is now about eight years old, stocky in build, as many of the Marathas are. He welcomed me most courteously with a prepared speech, and then, in response to a call from beyond the curtain, slipped back through the gap. Now, by design I'm sure, this gave me a chance to see for myself, if only momentarily, the person of the Ranee herself . . .'

A muted gasp from several of his audience recognised that this was almost unheard of.

'She was half-seated, half-reclining on a mass of silk cushions and surrounded by her women, who, though themselves somewhat in the shadows, I perceived were mostly young and of a beauty that equalled that of their mistress —'

'She is thought to be a woman of considerable beauty, I understand. Did you—?' This time the questioner was a Mrs Dawson, invited because Mrs Fetherstonhaugh was under the impression that her husband was a surgeon. In fact he was the veterinary surgeon attached to the whole division.

Bruce held up a hand but maintained the suspense by taking another mouthful from his glass. He dabbed his mouth with his napkin and at last continued.

'The Ranee, whose name, incidentally, is Manikarnika, though she is now known as Lakshmi Bai, a name or title always given to the rajah's principal wife, is a woman of middle size – somewhat stout but not too stout. Her face must have been very handsome when she was younger and even now has many charms, though somewhat marked by the smallpox. Her eyes, which are particularly fine, express great intelligence, and her nose is delicately shaped. She is not fair-skinned but far from black. Her only finery was a pair of gold earrings, her dress being plain white muslin, but so fine in texture and drawn about her so tightly that the outline of her figure was plainly discernible – and a remarkably fine figure she had—'

'You seem to have been quite taken with her . . .?' This was Sophie, unable to restrain the consequences of a sudden though mild stab of jealousy.

'But if she has a fault it is her voice which is something between a whine and a croak. She was annoyed, or pretended to be, that I had had a full view of her, and expressed a hope that sight of her had not lessened my sympathy for her or for her cause. On the contrary, I replied, if the Governor General could only be as fortunate as I had been I was sure he would at once give Jhansi back to its beautiful queen. She returned the compliment in one way or another and then broached the subject of her claim. I told her that the Governor General would have to gain the support of the Directors, and that her best recourse was to petition the Throne and, meanwhile, take the pension offered. She replied energetically that she was not prepared to do this and repeated more than once *Main Jhansi nahin dengee* – I will not give up my Jhansi. I suggested that resistance from a small state like hers would soon be overcome, at which her voice became dark and passionate and she declared that there are others in the same position and that, if they all resisted the Doctrine of Lapse as one, the Company might find it had taken on more than it could handle. Finally, she urged me to advise Lord Canning that a sensible accommodation could surely be reached and that much possible bloodshed might therefore be avoided. I repeated that it was not in Lord Canning's power alone to make such accommodation. Nevertheless, we parted on very good terms and I returned to my tent in the palace grounds.'

A sort of shuffle and sigh went round Bruce's audience at this and it seemed general conversation might break out, but he held up a hand and continued.

'In the morning I was roused early, at daybreak, by the minister who urged me to accompany him to the maidan that lay on the other side of the palace. A section of this was enclosed by a low battlemented wall which, on the inside, had a gallery with fine stone lattice work of the sort that in such places is used to screen women spectators from what is going on below, but in this case the situation was reversed. We took our places on stone seats under the watchful eyes of two of the fearsome horsemen who had accompanied me on my jouney to Jhansi. They twiddled their moustaches, their eyes glittered in their dark faces, they fiddled with the hilts of their tulkars and the butts of their pistols. What they imagined I might do with a ten-foot drop below me and a stone curtain in front of me, they alone knew.

'There was a group of mounted horses at the far end of the maidan, milling about in a lively sort of way, their riders swathed in voluminous white cloaks and baggy trousers. Some carried lances, others carbines. A bugle sounded and with great precision they all came into a well-dressed line; the bugle sounded again and here they came, at full gallop across the sand which billowed behind them, right up to the wall we were esconced in. They pulled up, again with well-drilled precision, just as their leader, who held her reins in her teeth and a sabre in each hand, lifted the flashing blades in front of our eyes, and those that had carbines discharged them into the air. She – and yes it was she – though barely did I recognise her this time so lively and fierce was her expression with her cape thrown back and her hair cascading about her, let drop her reins and repeated in a shout her mantra – *Main Jhansi nahin dengee* – before using her thighs to turn her pony round and send it cantering behind her troop, who were all women, back whence they had come.'

Bruce paused, head lifted, eyes somewhat unfocused as if he were reliving still the experience he had described. Then he shook his head. 'It was a demonstration, of course. Of her determination to get or regain what she believes is her due.'

Silence fell round the room for a moment, then Mrs Fetherstonhaugh cleared her throat.

'I take it from your description that these harridans were riding like men. With men's saddles and so forth.'

'Of course.'

The pale, freckled, red-headed Anglo-Irish lady was not so much shocked as scornful.

'How disgusting,' she snapped.

Bruce shrugged, continued as if the interruption had not occurred.

'She gave me an elephant, a camel, a pair of greyhounds, silks and so on, the produce of Jhansi, and a pair of fine shawls. I tried to refuse them but my friend the vakil assured me she would be offended if I did. She also gave me a miniature of herself, done by a Native, a Hindoo.'

Sophie leant forward.

'You seem to have been quite taken with her,' she repeated.

'Well, yes. She excited in me an admiration I do not usually feel for persons of the gentler sex, that is the admiration I have felt for brave and determined men ...' his smile broadened and his eyes shone, 'but I have to confess too that she frightened me somewhat. Not in a personal way, you understand, but because of what I judge her to be capable of.' He fiddled for a moment with a nutcracker and some shards of shell on his plate, then looked back at Sophie.

'I have no use for the shawls she gave me and they are identical. Would you permit me to attend you tomorrow morning at your bungalow so that I might offer one of them to you?'

Sophie glanced at her husband, sought his approval by raising her eyebrows. He was thus forced to choose between compliance or appearing to be churlish. After a moment's consideration he chose compliance.

'I shall not be able to be present myself as I have to attend an enquiry into an alleged refusal to obey orders on the part of an enlisted man in the 60th Rifles. But I am sure Sophie will entertain you in an appropriate way.'

Sophie leant across the table again.

'Would ten o'clock suit you, Mr Farquhar?'

15

Meerut, 11 November 1857

Sophie had worked out the truth of the matter – that Farquhar knew beforehand that Hardcastle, as assistant advocate general, would be out of the house attending the court martial of the insubordinate soldier; consequently, to ensure she could not be compromised, she invited Catherine Dixon and her brood to join them for a mid-morning cup of tea with sweet mango-flavoured lassi for the children. However, at ten minutes to ten, too late to do anything about it, Catherine's syce arrived with a brief note that said that Emma had the colic and would not be left without her mother. It ended with an admonition '. . . keep Lavanya close and you will be all right'.

This irritated Sophie. The implication that she might not be able to look after herself was bad enough. That Catherine felt she could offer it doubled the offence. In the event the private patois she shared with Lavanya was sufficient to tell her that she wished to play the piano and read a little and would prefer not to be disturbed.

At five to ten Sophie sat on the stool in front of her Broadwood, spread her looped and flounced bronze shot-silk skirt over her crinolines and launched into a Mendelssohn Rondo Capriccioso, hoping that Farquhar would not be delayed to the point in the piece where she always went wrong. He arrived on time, the etwah let him in, but then of course as she rose to greet him, he begged she should continue and finish the piece. She duly fluffed.

'Bother,' she said. 'That's as far as I go.' She added the sort of lie young ladies are generally permitted without censure. 'It's less than a week since the music arrived. Hardcastle will be here presently,' she added, folding the score away beneath the lid of the stool. 'We'll have tea when he arrives.'

Bruce put a thin square package of brown paper tied with ribbon on the rosewood table, approached her, and took both her hands in his.

'Forgive me,' he said, and his blue eyes focused with considerable gravity on hers, 'but in that case I must come very urgently to the heart of what I have to tell you.'

Urgently . . . *heart* . . . What on earth might be coming next? A declaration? Her heart began to pound, her colour rose. Yet he released her hands almost immediately and took a turn round to the other side of the table.

'Mrs Hardcastle . . .' but said meditatively, not addressing her, 'you were Sophie Chapman when we first met, were you not?'

'I'm flattered and surprised you should remember my maiden name after so many years.'

'You should not be flattered nor surprised. You were an extremely fetching young lady and I fell instantly and passionately in love with you, the way only a very young man can who has never experienced the emotion before.'

'But, starved of my presence, the passion quickly faded.'

'Not at all. It lasted at least until Suez.'

'Where you fell in love with an Egyptian houri whom you mistook for Cleopatra.'

'Something like that,' he laughed, they were both laughing now, happy to make a lark of it all. 'But—'

'But? Something still lingers, like the odour of faded violets in a drawer of handkerchiefs.' Sophie's tastes were eclectic. She enjoyed romantic novels as much as she did Mendelssohn or Wordsworth.

'More than that. Let me come to the point.'

'Of course. I'm sorry.'

'No need to be. Mrs Hardcastle—'

'Sophie.'

'Sophie. Forgive me, if you can, for saying what I am about to say.' He paused and sighed.

'I should prefer it if you did not say anything which might require my forgiveness.'

107

'Perhaps I have said too much already.' He moved back to her side of the table and took her hands again. She hesitated. Should she not pull away? But sensing that she might he increased the pressure of his palms and she allowed her hands to remain where they were.

'Dearest Sophie, for despite the attractions of my Cleopatra, you do remain very dear to me, first love never dies, you know? I cannot but be conscious that you are no longer the very happy, lively, carefree girl I pursued so ardently in the Blandford Assembly Rooms.'

'The responsibilities of marriage, Mr Farquhar, an infant to look after, the vicissitudes of living in this strange and rather frightening country . . . The mere fact that I am several years older than I was then and have learnt much of the sorrows of this world—'

'Yet, Sophie, I do feel all these would be alleviated if you had the support of a husband—'

'I'll not hear a word against poor Tom—'

'There you are then. Poor Tom. Hardly a declaration of the mutual passion that should sustain marriage.'

He pulled her, ever so gently, a little closer, his voice throbbing a little with an emotion she told herself was no more than deep sympathy. Yet sympathy, an implied understanding of her situation, was just what she needed. She felt tears pricking, her vision blurred and a strange fluttering excitement composed of anxiety and anticipation filled her breast. This time it was she who moved closer so almost perforce he had to release her hands and fold her into a closer embrace with her cheek against his shoulder. For a moment he toyed with the strands of hair in the nape of her neck and then, as she lifted her face, kissed her on her lips and increased the pressure on her waist.

She had never before been kissed in this way. She had never before felt such a surge of physical longing.

She pulled back a little, looked up into his eyes.

'You must go,' she said.

'I suppose I must.'

'Tom will be back quite soon.' A thought occurred to her. 'I would not want to see you, hear you, sharing the platitudes of a morning visit with him, knowing as I watched you both—'

'I understand, dear Sophie, really I do.'

He kissed her once more, less fiercely, and went.

She watched him go and then turned back in to open the package.

The shawl was on the crimson side of the colour of blood, shot with gold thread and made from a very fine wool called *pashm*, the under-fur of Tibetan goats. She found herself in two minds about it. After all, it had been given to him by a Ranee whose attraction for him he had not attempted to hide. Nevertheless she hid it away before Hardcastle returned, in time for tiffin.

He was in a sad state, alternately almost tearfully morose and excessively irritable. It was evening before she persuaded him to tell her what the matter was.

'The young lad . . . enquiry, drumhead court martial. I doubt he was above seventeen. I was required to give my imprimatur to the punishment which was thirty lashes, and then I had to stay and count them, make sure the sentence was carried out. Damn near killed the poor boy . . .' At this he broke down properly at last. 'I'm a lawyer, I'm not a soldier, I am not a . . . beast,' he cried. 'I had no idea I'd be saddled with duties of this sort, and I don't think I can face much more of this sort of thing . . .'

He was in such a way that Sophie encouraged him into her bed that night, purely to comfort him as she would a child. After a time he thrust himself upon her; she tried to think of Bruce Farquhar, but it would not do, not at all. Nevertheless, he made her pregnant again.

A day later she told Catherine a little of what had happened.

'Is the man then a philanderer?' Catherine asked. 'After all, it is said he is pursuing Uma Blackstock. And he seemed from what you said to have been vulnerable to the Ranee's charms.'

Sophie did not answer immediately but gave the matter some thought.

Then, regretfully . . .

'Dear Cathy, I rather think maybe he is. Certainly a flirt.'

16

Delhi, December 1856

The Red Fort in Delhi, occupying behind its immense red walls the north-east corner of what is now Old Delhi, was a very different place in 1857 from what it is now. The main changes were carried out by the British military following the Mutiny. They drained and filled in a large tank* that lay in front of the Hall of Public Audiences, enlarged the spaces around it to make a vast maidan (now extensive lawns with some flowerbeds) by ripping out Islamic gardens that were said to rival those of the Alhambra in Spain. They also demolished a moderately undistinguished complex of buildings, erecting instead several rather ugly blocks of barracks for the Delhi garrison.

The administrative buildings they destroyed were those from which the Mughal Empire had been ruled. By 1856 they had already been reduced to a warren of apartments, rooms and even cupboards occupied by hundreds of what were basically mendicants – people claiming living room and survival in return for services performed by

---

* A 'tank' was a large man-made hole in the ground, usually not all that deep, lined to retain water, its surface either flush with the ground around or enclosed by a low parapet. It was functional, acting as a reservoir of water collected during the monsoon to take a community through the dry season, providing water to drink, to bathe in, to wash clothes in, and, if it was large enough, for irrigation. They were often beautified with surrounding flowerbeds, groves and fountains, and took on the appearance of ornamental lakes or ponds.

their ancestors decades or centuries earlier, or claiming blood links to the royal line so old that they were now of the order of cousins up to ten times removed. An overflow of claimants with less convincing credentials occupied thatched hovels in the corners, alleys, and up against the walls. A miasma of smoke from cooking fires hung over much of the whole fort which was haunted by hundreds of hooded crows, black kites and other scavengers.

It was from a room in one of these crowded buildings that Azimullah strove through more than a year to forge growing bitterness, resentment and hate for the British into a movement united and powerful enough to drive them into the sea.

Much had gone well. Cells had been formed throughout most of the Indian army, small tight groups of fanatics, Mahometans for the most part, though there were Hindoos too, especially in units where the most caste conscious of all, the Brahmins, had a presence. He had a network of messengers who often operated through drops, leaving their messages in hiding places rather than communicating directly with their co-conspirators, men who moved about the busy countryside as fakirs or maulvi, teachers of the law, because that was what most of them were. And what Azimullah was becoming increasingly aware of was an enthusiasm, a determination to get on with it, growing faster that he had expected. And he realised that once emotions and a readiness to rise and kill had reached a peak they could leak away in a fortnight, a week, if not acted upon.

Another factor bothered him too: the lack of a leader, a figurehead. There was only one possible candidate – the old wreck, drug abuser, cook and poet who still called himself King of Delhi, though he presided over no more than this one corner of the city, namely Bahadur Shah, the last of the Mughals, the last, apart from his sons, of a line that stretched back to Tamburlaine himself. For many of the vast population that peopled what had been his ancestors' realms he was their rightful ruler, betrayed, imprisoned, emasculated by the evil English. As such he would do, could be made to do. And then there were his three sons, wastrels, badmashes, but still young and ambitious enough, and reasonably presentable to a crowd or a mob, however much they were despised by the rajahs and princes.

With thoughts like these in the forefront of his mind Azimullah hurried down the side of the tank through the gardens to the pillars of the Diwan-I-Am whose steps close to the great canopied marble throne he climbed, and so into the Diwan-I-Khas, behind, the Hall of Private Audiences.

Although faced with fine marble and nicely proportioned to give the smaller room an aura almost as powerful as that of the Hall of Public Audiences, it had already lost most of its ability to impose and impress along with the Peacock Throne (only the pedestal remained) looted by the Persians, and its silver ceiling stolen by the Marathas. The raised area was filled with cushions, there were rich if moth-eaten hangings in the window embrasures, and ancient but still glowing carpets on the floor. The temperature was kept almost comfortable by a pair of charcoal-fuelled braziers. Some servants and guards stood around, but the dais was empty of people. Relieved, Azimullah took up a position near the entrance and struggled to breathe normally. Presently he heard a single held note, like a ship's hooter but blown on a long brass horn.

A procession was approaching down the long colonnade. Behind four guards carrying matchlocks six feet long and silver-mounted, with smouldering fuses in their left hands, the Nana Saheb with a small entourage of two or three secretaries and personal assistants came first. He was dressed with some splendour in a long heavily embroidered tunic, basically white, baggy trousers and jewelled slippers. His tilted Parsee headgear had a large ruby brooch over his right eye which winked and glittered as the light caught it. Behind him came Lakshmi Bai, the Ranee of Jhansi, swathed in a purple saree a corner of which she held across her face but not so that Azi could not see her eyes, dark but glowing with the light that dwells in mountain tarns, and the vertical tilak mark between her eyebrows. She was attended by three of her women, similarly veiled and wearing green sarees.

Next was Ramchandra Panduranga, known as Tatya Tope, and walking with him the most striking of all, Ahmed Ahmadullah Shah, the Maulvi of Faizabad. Tatya Tope was the son of a Brahmin counsellor of the Nana's adopted father who came to Bithur with him when he was exiled from Poona. He was thus brought up with the Nana and was an even more intimate friend and adviser than Azimullah. He was not, however, anything like as prepossessing. Of middling height his forehead was low, the nose broad, his teeth irregular and discoloured. To the English in Cawnpore he was known as 'Bennie'.

Ahmadullah Shah could not have been more different. He was very tall, very lean and muscular, had long hair that hung below his shoulders. His deep-set eyes were large, his nose high, genuinely eagle-like, his jaw square and strong . He wore sandals, a dhoti, had a cape or short cloak thrown over his shoulders against the unusual if seasonal temperature, and a turban. Since the annexation of the Oudh, nearly a year earlier, he had been travelling through the west of the province and into the Doab as far as Agra preaching revolt against the British and escaping arrest because the civil police refused to touch him.

Finally, after a suitable gap in the procession, there came a huge palanquin, its poles supported by four shaven-headed, castrated African giants. On it, beneath a big circular tasselled shade, also carried by a giant eunuch, an old man reclined. He was quite dark, like an olive just at the point when, on its way to blackness, it has ceased to be green. He wore a large white turban, voluminous and, you'd think, about to fall apart, but it never did. His robe, also white, was also very full, but he had not bothered to pull it over his thin shins. His face was narrow too, with wild yet vacant eyes in dark sockets beneath thick eyebrows, his nose more vulturish than aquiline above a mouth with lips still sensual. Thus, Bahadur Shah II, King of Delhi.

Those who had arrived ahead of him bowed and followed the palanquin into the Hall of Private Audiences, scarcely acknowledging the bowing and scraping of the servants already there. The King was helped, indeed almost carried, out of his palanquin and placed in the centre of the piled cushions. A hookah was brought, the coal already glowing, and the mouthpiece placed in his hand. He pulled himself around a bit, made himself comfortable, maybe allowed a short squeaky fart to escape, sucked on his comforter. The rose-water in the flask bubbled pleasantly and as he emitted smoke the wisp of a beatific smile flitted across his face. He took no part in the proceedings that followed, until the very end, the last item on the agenda. The rest disposed themselves on the cushions around him, save Azimullah who remained standing, and the Ranee who sat up very straight on a chair that had been placed for her as far from the men as she could get, with her ladies between her and them, creating a virtual purdah.

The discussion that followed was informal, though Tatya Tope acted as unofficial chair when necessary.

113

'Have we fixed on a date yet?' he began. His slightly sad but intelligent eyes settled on Azimullah who took a deep breath and came to a decision he had put off until that very moment.

'Yes,' he said. 'It should be the twentieth of May.'

The Maulvi of Faizabad cleared his throat and his pale brown eyes, that always seemed to be focused on a different, inner world, moved over them.

'No. It should be the twenty-third of June, the one hundredth anniversary of the Battle of Plassey. We have already gone to a lot of trouble propagating the idea that there have been prophecies delivered by sadhus and gurus that British rule will last for just one hundred years. By rising on that day the people will believe they are doing the will of Allah or Bramah, or whoever, and that therefore they cannot fail.'

Azimullah bowed with respect but his voice remained calm and decisive.

'It should be earlier, not so early as to deprive us of the benefit of the hot weather, but at least a month. Remember the monsoon will have arrived by the end of June—'

'Which will help you as much as the heat does.'

'Not so. The English like the rain. They are also richer than we are and will have more elephants and bullocks, carts and tumbrils. In the monsoon particularly they will be able to march and move impedimenta, stores, guns, more readily than we can—'

The Nana intervened, more out of a desire to have his voice heard than driven by any conviction that his contribution might be useful.

'Tell us, Azimullah, just what advantages does an earlier start confer.'

'We are working on both the villagers and the Native troops. We are exciting them, filling their heads with a sense of their own importance in the coming struggle. This excitement will, like a head of steam, reach an explosive point. If it is not allowed to explode it will seep away, our efforts will have diminishing returns, people will get bored waiting for something to happen, we'll lose it.'

The Ranee nodded her head in considered agreement, and Azimullah continued.

'There is another factor. The Enfield rifle. The first shipments are due. They will be issued to a British regiment, the 60th we believe, presently at Meerut but preparing to leave for China, and then to Native regiments in Bengal, at Barrackpore, Dum-Dum, that area, but in no great numbers. There will be a period of training during which detachments from all over the country will go east to learn how to use the thing. Meanwhile, the British regiments will be issued with the rifle. Now the situation we must avoid is one where the British have the rifle in substantial numbers while the Native Infantry have none or very few. That means rising either before the British are issued with them or after the whole Native Infantry has got them which may well not be for a year or more.'

The Maulvi's face had taken on a look of involvement, of a readiness to listen.

'There is another factor,' continued Azimullah. 'The thick paper of the cartridges is greased with cow and pig fat.'

Silence as the significance of this sank in. Then . . .

'Is that true?' murmured the Ranee. 'If it is, the sepoys will never touch them.'

'Probably not true. But because the sepoys are already so convinced of the perfidy of the British they will believe it. Indeed, they may even be persuaded that it is part of a plot to Christianise them.'

The possibilities inherent in all this were becoming clearer to Tatya Tope.

'If the English force the cartidges on them, they'll mutiny. How soon will the first cartridges with this fat be issued to Mahometans and Hindoos?'

'Training with them is scheduled to begin in May, I believe.'

'So what is your favoured date?'

'I have already spoken. The twentieth of May. At the latest.'

'Later. The anniversary of Plassey . . .' This from the Nana, who had felt a sudden coldness in his stomach as the reality of what they were proposing gripped him.

Bahadur Shah opened one eye, took the nargileh mouthpiece from his flaccid mouth.

'Let the astrologers decide,' he rasped. 'It's what I pay them for.'

He looked round at them all quite sharply for a few moments before sinking back into his narco-dream.

'Astrologers or not,' Azimullah insisted, 'we must be sure all rise at the same time. If it goes off piecemeal the English will destroy us piecemeal.'

A silence seemed to signal that there was no more to be said on the subject. Tatya Tope bowed his head and coughed.

'With your permission, my lord, there is still the question of legitimacy. You . . .' His gaze took in the Ranee, and the Nana, 'together with the Begum Hazrat in Lucknow, are all seeking to be restored to the rank, honour and, ah, wealth, your forbears enjoyed. The days when such things could simply be taken or seized are gone. They can only be conferred by a higher authority, a fountain of honour, as the British call it. We don't have one. Similarly, the sepoys and the people, the villagers too, may well rise to support, to restore, a local talukdar or rajah, but without an overall leader to inspire them, once they have achieved their local aim they will go home. If they do *not* achieve their local aim, they will go home. But if they believe they are fighting to restore a legitimate ruler, an emperor of us all, there is a chance they will rise with one voice, one immediate purpose.'

He turned to face Bahadur Shah and made a deep bow from the waist. The others struggled to their feet and did likewise.

'You, sir,' he continued, 'are the rightful Emperor of all the states of India and it is in your name we will seek to restore our independence under the benevolent rule of the Mughals.'

Silence again, then Bahadur Shah brought his eyes into focus and looked at each of them in turn.

'I am an old man,' he croaked, 'and a lot of good will it do me.' He grinned, whimsically, showing a limited number of discoloured teeth. 'My sons will be pleased though.'

He thrust the mouthpiece of his hookah away from him, and a servant took it. His giant eunuchs folded him into his palanquin and hoisted it on to their shoulders. A sweep of his long-fingered right hand concluded the audience and sent them on their way.

17

Here and there, January–March 1857

The date? The twenty-second of January. The place? Dum-Dum, the town, about twenty miles north-east of Calcutta, where factories clunked out arms and ammunition for the magazines of the Presidency Army. But where in Dum-Dum? Surely at the guarded gate or door of the workshops where the cartridges for the Enfield rifle were already in production. The time? Sunset, it must have been – when the assembly line was closed down for the night, time to go home, play a little, eat, sleep before turning up eight hours later for the next sixteen-hour shift. Where else, when else would a low-caste factory worker pass close enough to a high-caste sepoy, close enough to beg a drink from his special brass canteen?

This labourer, this khalasi, was he tall, thin, with deep-sunk eyes and a lantern jaw? Had he been taken on only days before, having come, he said, all the way from Delhi looking for employment? It's not impossible; it's even likely that he was the Maulvi of Faizabad.

The sun cast wavering black shadows through the blackness of the factory smoke, over the crude rawness of red brick, the churned-up dust of the rutted road that led to gates that would have disgraced a prison – the litter, refuse piles, piles even of human shit, the smell of gunpowder, tooled metal, raw wood and . . . animal fat? A half-dozen sepoys watched the hands emptying out through the gates, pulling out one or two at random to search for gunpowder being smuggled out or even finished cartridges.

One of the sepoys, a tall bull of a man, a Rajput, with the well-fed

117

look of someone who eats well but has enough physical exercise to keep him from going to fat, took little more than a controlled sip from a brass cup of water, a moistening for a mouth made dry by the dust stirred up by the labourers. Our tall khalasi paused in front of him.

'I am very thirsty,' he said. 'Let me share your water.'

'Get lost,' the sepoy replied, swilling the vessel round and pouring the water out on to the ground. 'It's been scoured. You'll defile it with your touch and I'll have to clean it all out and purify it again.'

The khalasi looked across the space between them: they were of a height but the one lean, thin almost to malnourishment, the other glossy, groomed.

'You make a big deal out of your caste, don't you?' said the khalasi. 'But in a short time your lords and masters will make you bite cartridges soaked in cow and pig fat, and what will become of your caste then?'

The sepoy reported the matter, but, when the police came out to arrest the khalasi he had gone. Steps were taken. Mutton or goat fat was insisted on from then on. No cartridges with cow or pig fat in them were ever issued. Yet ten days later sepoys at Barrackpore, a further five miles from Calcutta, who had been issued with the new cartridges, now complained that the paper was different, heavier, redder than the paper of the old cartridges. It was not the usual paper, imported from England. How can you be sure about anything at all to do with its manufacture? asked the tall, dark, thin man who moved around the camps, dropping a word here, a whisper there among the sepoys.

The Maulvi, with his knowledge of the people, prompted by the idea that they needed something simple, of everyday ordinariness, but which could be read as a symbol of something much bigger, hit on the idea of chappatis. Everybody, every day, ate chappatis.

He travelled back down the Grand Trunk Road from Barrackpore to Agra where he bought thirty-two of the small plate sized discs of unleavened bread. Next, he hired eight more or less reliable rogues and sent them out round the compass to the nearest eight villages. Each was to approach the village watchman, give him four chappatis and instruct him to bake three more to go with each of them. He was then to find four men who would take four chappatis each to the watchmen in each of the four nearest villages, and ask them to repeat the same procedure. By the end of the first week of February just about every village, and there were thousands, from Rohilkhand in the north, across the Oudh, as far as Benares in the east and Allahabad in the south, had received its four chappatis and sent out sixteen more.

No one knew what they meant, but they created disquiet at least in the minds of the Master Race, and lifted the spirits of the peasants in the fields and the women doing their washing on opposing sides of the rivers where they could call across to each other. The chappatis created a feeling of unity, of sharing the same lives, the same problems, with possibly the same solution (the annihilation of the English) and the same certainty that something was going to happen soon.

The question of the greased cartridges festered through February and into March. Small detachments of Native regiments from all over the north were sent to Umballa to train with the new cartridges. They fraternised, exchanged rumours and gossip, here and there small cabals of high-caste Hindu sepoys and Mahometan gentry, united by the common cause, came together, fanned the flames and brought regiments closer to open mutiny. When they found that the British disclaimers about the grease were making headway they reported back to the centre of the vast web, the small room in the Red Fort from which Azimullah continued to control the whole conspiracy, and back came the message: flour provided by millers employed by the Company, acting with the connivance of the British authorities, was contaminated with ground-up cow and pig bones. Cartloads of the stuff were tipped into the rivers and men went hungry. That it was all a plot to Christianise them was again the reason given though no one explained just how even serious loss of caste was going to achieve that.

Cases of insubordination, if not outright mutiny, multiplied. Buildings were burnt, including some in the railhead on the bank of the Ganges opposite Calcutta. A Queen's regiment had to be recalled from Rangoon to be on hand when a Native regiment, the 19th N.I., was disbanded for refusing to handle suspect cartridges. But the incident which became the most notorious occurred at Barrackpore on 29 March.

*

A young sepoy of the 34th N.I. was sitting alone in his tent eating small brown cakes. They had been given to him by a wandering pedlar, dressed only in a dhoti and turban, who had come down the lines selling them from a big wide tray. Seeing the lad was on his own, this pedlar entered his tent and engaged him in a long conversation designed to feed his most wildly absurd convictions. As dusk came on the pedlar left, having first given him cakes – which were filled with bhang.

This young lad's name was Mungal Pandy and the British were, according to the pedlar, responsible for almost everything wrong with his life. Only a few days earlier two friends, from a village close to his own, had been sentenced to fourteen years' hard labour for treasonable conspiracy. A Native lieutenant in his own regiment had been court-martialled and dismissed for denouncing the greased cartridge to his comrades. For the sake of their religion the whole of the 19th N.I. had forfeited everything a soldier values. Emotion began to swell in the young man's chest, the blood pounded in his ears, shadows thrown by the flame of an untended campfire lurched feverishly across the hemp wall of his tent. Madness exploded in his head.

Wearing his regimental jacket over a dhoti, he ran towards his company's bell of arms, a bell-shaped brick structure in which muskets, other weapons and ammunition were stored after each parade. Recalling it was padlocked, his bare heels skidded in the dust, he turned right, ran through the lines to the nearest forge, picked up a hammer and returned to knock the padlock off with a single blow. In a moment he was armed with a tulwar in one hand, a loaded musket in the other, and a handful of cartridges, the old sort, in his jacket pocket. He now marched to and fro in front of the bell of arms, screaming abuse at the British and swearing he would shoot the first white face he saw.

Mungal did not have to wait long. A Native corporal ran to the bungalow of the company's sergeant major, James Hewson. Hewson came as fast as he could and as soon as Mungal saw him he raised his musket and fired. He missed. Hewson ran behind the bell of arms and into the Quarter Guard guardhouse. The Native lieutenant commanding was called Issuree Pandy. Some say he was Mungal's elder brother, but as is the case with most Native patronyms Pandy was an exceedingly common name.

Hewson bellowed: 'Why in hell's name haven't you arrested the man?'

Issuree replied: 'What can I do? My corporal has gone to the adjutant, my sergeant has gone to the field officer. Am I to take him myself?'

Although nominally of lower rank than the Native officer, Hewson ordered him to fall in the guard and command them to load. Issuree passed on the order but the guard continued to puff on whatever it was they were smoking. Hewson went back out. At this moment the sound of hooves galloping through the dust announced the arrival of Lieutenant Henry Baugh.

'Where is he?' yelled Baugh.

'To your left, sir,' Hewson shouted. 'He'll kill you. Ride to your right for your life.'

Mungal fired and Baugh's horse crumpled beneath him. He grabbed for his saddle holster and ran at Mungal who was reloading. Mungal dropped his musket and ran; at twenty yards Baugh fired and missed. He drew his sword and ran at Mungal who drew his tulwar, cut and parry, and then Hewson too joined in, and at this point perhaps the most significant incident of the whole affair occurred, for Hewson was struck from behind by one of the Quarter Guard. He picked himself up and again went for Mungal, caught him by the collar and struck him several times with his sword, thereby saving Baugh's life since the lieutenant's left hand had already been smashed with a sword cut, and he had been severely gashed in the neck and on the back of his head. A loyal Muslim sepoy, Shaik Pultoo, now seized Mungal round the waist from behind and the two Englishmen were able to escape. Shaik Pultoo released Mungal only when attacked by other members of the Quarter Guard.

The regiment's commanding officer, Colonel Wheler, turned up. He was elderly, a God-fearing man who preached Christianity to his men, unpopular, incompetent. He was frequently to be seen arguing the case for his religion to Natives of all classes in the highways, cities, bazaars and villages, though not, he claimed, in the regimental lines. Canning himself thought Wheler was not fit to command a regiment. Wheler now ordered the Quarter Guard to arrest Mungal and they refused. Issuree Pandy said: 'They won't do it.'

Sepoys were now pouring out of their tents in various stages of undress and a riot if not a full-blooded mutiny seemed likely.

121

Fortunately Wheler was now supplanted by no less a person than Major General Sir John Hearsey, Commander in Chief of the Presidency Army, whose headquarters were nearby. He was accompanied by his two sons. Hearsey was everything that Wheler was not. He was popular with the army, and above all was determined and courageous in a crisis. He turned his horse towards Mungal and the Quarter Guard. Someone called out: 'His musket is loaded!'

'Damn his musket!'

In the guardhouse he found Issuree Pandy and twelve men.

'Follow me,' he ordered.

'He's loaded, he'll shoot us,' cried Issuree.

The major general pointed his revolver at the Native lieutenant who quickly responded that his men were just putting their percussion caps in place.

Hearsey led them out. One of his sons shouted: 'Father, he is taking aim at you, look out sharp!'

'If I fall, John, rush upon him and put him to death.'

At this moment a musket shot rang out. All froze. But the casualty was Mungal himself who, reversing his weapon, had attempted to shoot himself, using his toe to pull the trigger. However, he survived and was later hanged, as also was Issuree Pandy, who may or may not have been his brother.

Mungal Pandy has been elevated by many Indians to the status of a national martyr: there are statues, streets named after him, a postage stamp with his supposed likeness has been issued. Bollywood film stars have even been described as having the Mungal Pandy look, and a recent Bollywood film has canonised him.

18

Meerut, 24 April–8 May 1857

'You're lucky to be in the European lines.'

'Why do you say that?' Sophie looked up from old newspapers and a teacup of her best set of tableware, Spode, Chinese Rose.

'Safer, I suppose.'

'Safer from what?'

'Oh, I don't know. Riot, disturbance, mutiny.'

'Is it because you are nearer the bazaar that you say that?'

'Yes. Partly.'

'Partly?'

'Well, four of our neigbours have had the thatched roofs of their stabling and stores set on fire in the last two days. We all say it's bad-mashes from the bazaar . . . but that's because it's a matter of honour to say the men you command are the most loyal in the whole Bengal Army. But the servants swear they saw a man with a sergeant's stripes on his jacket among them.'

Sophie pushed a crumpled half-sheet of the *United Service Gazette* into the teacup, wrapped the cup in the rest of it, and laid it as carefully as if it were an egg in the corner of a half-filled tea chest. Then she looked up at her visitor, and did her best to produce a smile that was meant to be quietly reassuring.

Charlotte Chambers was a year or so older than Sophie, and a month further on in her pregnancy – the baby was due in June. She too was pretty, brunette but with blue eyes and a pale complexion, and, though her husband, the adjutant of the 11th Native Infantry,

123

was a Scot, she was from Hampshire. The officers of the Queen's regiments and their families did not mix much socially with those in the Company Native regiments, but these two had come together partly on account of their pregnancies. An unofficial sisterhood existed among the English women, one example being Lady Blackstock's circle of West Country women, the first object of which was to maintain their sanity through crises like the death of an infant or a first pregnancy due to come to term at the very height of the hot season. As far as the men were concerned, and the older and tougher of their spouses too, they were expected to conform to rigorous social norms, perform certain duties both domestic and public, from submitting to their husbands' marital rights to doing the flowers in the churches, organising small charities for those among the other ranks who needed them, and so forth. Private and personal needs, like coping with pregnancy, were meant to be just that – private and personal.

In short, a lady was allowed to get into a bit of a tizz over organising a large and formal dinner party, but expected to manage her own pregnancy, her children's teething or the death of a friend, with quiet, uncomplaining efficiency.

Sophie looked down at the plate in her hand. With a spray of three roses and foliage in the centre, red and green, it really was very pretty. It was meant, she knew, to be in some way oriental, and had been chosen by her parents because Spode said it was 'Indian' in style, but to her it was as quintessentially English as could be. She wished they could use it more often, but on Tom's instructions the service only came out when they had guests and the occasion was formal. She wrapped it and laid it to rest with the others.

'When do you leave?' Charlotte asked.

'In a week's time. Second of May. But the larger stuff goes on ahead. We have two elephants booked. Should be enough.'

'The piano go too?'

Sophie sighed.

'Oh yes. But Tom makes me pay the carriage out of my allowance.'

'He never does so!'

'OK 'Fraid so.'

Charlotte took a turn round the room, picked up a small porcelain bell, tinkled it, put it back.

'I'll miss you. Chambers says it will be the end of May, perhaps

124

later, before we can both get away and he won't hear of me going without him. It means I could have whatever's in here just at the hottest time of year and in one of the hottest places.' She ran both her palms over her bump.

Sophie, hearing the anxiety, fear even, at the back of this, put down the egg cup she was about to consign to the chest, came round the table and got her to sit on one of the upright dining chairs. She twisted another round so she was facing her, knees almost touching and, leaning forward, put her hands on Charlotte's shoulders.

'I'll get Tom to have a word with him. You need women around you, women you know, and most of us will be up at Simla by then. If nothing else can be done you can come with us, stay, live, with us until Chambers can get away.'

She suspected in her heart that this might be a false promise. The Simla bungalow was smaller than the one they were in, and she could easily see Tom declaring that the drama of two births within a month or so under his roof would be too much for his work.

'Who was there when you had Stephen? Did you have a midwife?'

'Yes. But Catherine was there too, Catherine Dixon, that is, and another friend, Victoria Marchant.'

'I know Mrs Marchant, of course. But I find her . . . Oh, a bit grand, that's all.'

'I know what you mean. But she's all right really.'

Charlotte pulled back a little, head on one side, a touch quizzical as well as tearful.

'The midwife . . . she was a . . . Native?'

'Of course. There is a Mrs Dolly McGuinness, a widow of one of the gunners, but she drinks and gives her clients raw gin if things go on too long. Anyway, she runs a brothel in the bazaar.' She glanced directly at Charlotte to check she had not found this offensive; apparently she had not. 'Most now prefer an Indian lady from the town. Mrs Chatterjee. She was all right with me. Competent and helpful and stayed in the background until she was needed. But I was lucky. It really wasn't that bad, whatever people say, and didn't last an unbearably long time.'

Charlotte uttered a huge sigh and then the words tumbled out.

'I really do not want a nigger with me. I don't want black hands to be the first to touch my baby.'

Sophie was taken aback, had to remind herself that, in the past,

125

she too had occasionally referred to the Natives as niggers. But since Stephen had arrived, and Lavanya had become almost part of the family, since she had had to deal with many more of them in the way of daily household arrangements, she had become more and more at ease with them – the women anyway.

'They're not so bad.'

'That's what I used to think, that's what I wanted to think. Because it was so near I even did my own shopping in the bazaar. I used to back home. We're not grand, you know, my father's the curate at Stockbridge and after my mother died I kept house for him, did the shopping and so on, everything. I thought I could carry on like that here . . .' She was sniffing now at every fifth word or so, but holding on. Clearly there was something she wanted to get out.

'Then one day, a month ago, I had to take a leg of pork back to the butcher. He's Hindoo, you know, and low-caste, so doesn't mind selling pork. Anyway, it was off and flyblown too, clusters of little yellow eggs. And his shop stank. Before then I had only ever been early in the morning when the meat is freshly butchered and everything clean and neat. By four o'clock in the afternoon it was awful. Blood everywhere, the smell, and flies so thick you could hardly see the odds and ends he still had left. I'm afraid I shouted at him, and he shouted back, and he banged his counter with his cleaver, and I thought he was going to come round the counter and use it on me. So I ran.' A sob caught her throat. 'Anyway, I told everyone I knew in the lines and they stopped buying off him . . . I think I can hear your husband, I'd better go.'

'You don't have to. Stay for tiffin.'

'Nice of you to offer, but Chambers will be expecting me. He's visiting the Dawsons. You know they've got the smallpox, but they seem to be pulling through all right.'

'Aren't you afraid your husband will catch it?'

'No. He had the cowpox when he was little. Most of us country people do.'

'I know. Me too,' Sophie commented.

Sophie took her to the gate, passing Tom on his way in. He paused to grunt what he took to be the right sort of things to say. Sophie's heart sank a little. Clearly he was in a bad mood; something had gone wrong.

Once at the gate the two women looked for a moment up and

down the narrow avenue. The acacias were already dropping leaves and their branches were black with long, bumpy seed pods. Midday and it was busy with men mostly on horseback returning home for tiffin, and Native servants, women in sarees with the occasional turban or brimless tribal cap bobbing among them, coming from the bazaar or moving back into their compounds from whatever task they had been set to do before the afternoon heat built up into the nineties.

Charlotte shuddered. Sophie looked at her.

'What's the matter?'

'There are so many of them. They're everywhere. We don't need so many. It's almost like a swarm. Or an ants' nest.'

'I can send someone with you.'

Charlotte gave her a wan smile.

'But don't you see, that would be just one more. One more black face.'

She had been right about Tom. He had gone straight into his study, on the other side of the hall from the dining room, and she could smell the cigarillo he had already lit. He was standing behind his desk and she knew he was waiting, waiting for someone on whom he could dump his woes, whatever they were.

'You might as well unpack all that china,' he began. 'Lord knows when we'll be allowed to leave.'

'What's gone wrong?'

'It's that fool Carmichael-Smyth.'

'Do I know him?'

'Must have been introduced.'

'Yes, dear. But there are what . . .? A hundred or more British officers on the station?'

'He's colonel of the 3rd Native Cavalry. Dixon's lot. And yesterday he ordered the ninety-odd skirmishers from the regiment to parade this morning, with their carbines, to be taught how to prepare and fire their cartridges by tearing off the paper to release the powder instead of biting it off . . .'

'Isn't this all rather difficult on the back of a horse?'

'No, you don't understand, my dear.' Nor had he until it had been explained to him. 'The skirmishers are the best shots in the regiment. Sometimes they are asked to act on their own, move to a position in

127

front of the rest, dismount, take cover and use their rifles at a distance, particularly picking off the enemy's skirmishers or their gun crews. For this reason they might be asked to carry the new Enfields instead of their carbines.'

'And they all think the Enfield cartridges are greased with pork or beef fat.'

'Precisely, my dear.' Touch of admiration in his voice now.

'Read about it in the paper.' The way you do when using old newspaper for packing. Sophie felt a short stab of discomfort low down in what she called her vitals, sat on the spare chair by the door but kept her head up, looking alert, interested, in spite of it.

'Well, his own officers thought he was being a fool since they're not likely to get Enfields for months yet and they all know how edgy the sowars are about anything to do with cartridges . . .'

'Sowars are . . .?'

'Cavalry, troopers.'

'Of course they are.'

'Sepoys are foot soldiers. So they went to him last night, I mean his officers, including, I imagine, your friend James Dixon . . .'

'Your friend too.'

Her husband shrugged, went on.

'. . . and asked him to cancel the parade. But the old fool refused. Said it would look like weakness if he did, that sort of thing, and anyway the cartridges they would be using, blanks of course, were the old ones, so who could possibly object?'

'But the . . . sowars wouldn't believe that, would they? What would be the point of training with the old cartridges?'

'That's exactly what they said.' He stubbed out the cigarillo, came round and stood in front of her, banging his right fist into his palm as he finished the story. 'All but five of them refused to handle the cartridges and the parade had to be broken. So now there has to be an official enquiry, the main purpose of which will be to decide whether a case for court martial exists. And that will be tomorrow, and I shall have to sit on it to make sure they follow the legal procedures correctly. And, inevitably, because direct refusal to obey a legitimate order is a court-martial offence, we'll find for a court martial. And it'll be another week at least before that's set up, maybe more since so many senior officers are absent for one reason or another, and I'll have to sit on that too. We'll be into the second week of May before we can get away . . .' he ended on something between a shout and a wail. 'You know what will happen, don't you, dear? I'll get prickly heat again. I will.'

And it won't do Stephen any good, Sophie thought. Nor me either.

Day succeeded day, as they do, but each was marked by the mercury as much as by the date on the calendar: Tom Hardcastle had a patent thermometer he had bought after seeing one at the Great Exhibition. The mercury pushed a little red dot up inside its calibrated tube and left it there as the temperature fell each night. But each night it left it a degree or so higher than the night before. Outside the geraniums that had looked so bright and brave (like little redcoats all in a row?) had shed their flowers and now their leaves were browning and shriv-elling, their stalks looked like old twisted twigs. The oleanders clung to a few withered flowers like so many grubby handkerchiefs, while the woody stalks of hollyhocks, Canterbury bells and other reminders of an English summer twittered and clicked in the hot gusts that stirred the fine grey soil into shifting devils across the yards and gar-dens. And it was still only the second week of May.

The convoy of elephants and bullock carts carrying the heavy stuff up into the hills left on the second, and after three days of trying to manage without his library, no spare chairs for guests and other inconveniences, Tom had accepted an invitation to move in with the Dixons for the week that he expected they would have to remain in Meerut. Oddly enough there was enough room, since, when the fourth Dixon child arrived and it was clear that there would in the due course of time be more, with none being shipped back out of the way to England, James Dixon had rented the bungalow next door to his and built a pleasant covered way linking them. It was this extrav-agance that had almost pauperised them for he was now spending his entire income as a private person on rent, leaving Catherine to manage the increasing household on a Company lieutenant's pay.

Although they had shed most of their own servants in this move, Tom agreed, after some argument (he called it 'discussion'), that Lavanya and her child should remain with them.

'I'll reconsider the matter in July,' he concluded. 'We will need a wet nurse then and I doubt we can afford that and an ayah.'

*

Although they had by then been married for more than three years Sophie still found her husband unfathomable. He was, she supposed, a competent lawyer and therefore rational if not clever: but he seemed to have a problem with the harsher aspects of the law, particularly when they involved hanging or flogging. She too could be upset by overlong contemplation of such things, but it never occurred to her to question them. Yet in other matters he could be harsh, overbearing, unduly authoritative and even violent – not, of course to the extent of hitting her or anything like that, but he had twice thrown books and once a glass in her general direction. His moods could shift from mawkish sentimentality to irritated anger, and – and above all this irritated her – he could change his mind for no obvious reason at all. She supposed she loved him, it was part of the marriage contract (Love, Honour and Obey) that she should, and for much of the time she valued his presence, his companionship, the way he shouldered all problems (except the most purely domestic, leaving them to her, as was proper), even though she often inwardly disagreed with the way he handled them.

It had been a mistake to promote his legal career through the army, for he was now discovering that he was not at ease as a soldier. Occasionally he hated it, but of course believed it unmanly to show this.

On Friday, 8 May, at eight o'clock, the four of them sat down to dinner in what Dixon jovially referred to as 'Dixon Bungalow Number One', south of the Mall but above the now almost completely dried-up Abu Nullah stream. The two men especially were tired and irritable: the interminable court martial had ended that day in stuffy, airless heat which three creaky punkahs had been unable to lift. It had been a draining experience and an emotional one too. It was Dixon's regiment that had been involved; Hardcastle had been in attendance as 'Superintending Officer'.

'Why the devil,' cried Dixon, spooning goat curry on to their plates to which Catherine added rice, 'did you allow it to go ahead with a court of Native officers?'

Hardcastle unfolded a damp linen napkin over his knees.

'We always do,' he said. 'You know that. Partly it's because we believe in the principle of men being tried by their own folk, partly because if they had been found guilty by an English court it would have been far too easy for the Natives to say the verdict was prejudiced.'

130

'But that's just the point, Tom. There, everybody got what they want? Pass the chutnees round, there's a good chap. If they'd been tried by British officers, they'd have been found not guilty or, more probably, guilty under extreme provocation leading to lenient sentences. But tried by their own lot, who are terrified of upsetting us, the poor bastards end up with ten years' hard labour . . .'

'James! Company!'

'Sorry, old bean, but we're all friends here, don't mind me if I lapse into the odd bit of French every now and then; I feel strongly about this. Damn it, fifteen of them were my own men and damn fine men, the best. They wouldn't have been skirmishers if they weren't.'

And so the meal went on: the women frightening themselves by repeating stories of pregnancies that had gone horribly wrong, the men bickering about the events of the day then boring each other with legal anecdotes from Tom and campaign reminiscences from James. At about half past nine there was a knocking at the front door which, since he had long ago decided to do without a footman, James went to answer. He came back ushering in behind him the station chaplain, the Reverend John Rotton.

'Come in, John, come in. You're most welcome, we were about to send the women off to the withdrawing room since they have no conversation but childbirth, but perhaps you'll find something else for them to talk about. Have a beer, why don't you?'

Rotton belonged to that newish breed in the Church of England – the Muscular Christians. He was big, with fair but thinning hair and a bushy ginger beard that reached his black cassock, which, and it was still unusual in those days, he wore almost all the time. He had a large family, mostly girls, played football and cricket with both officers and men with whom he was as popular as a chaplain who takes his duties very seriously is ever likely to be.

'Well, James, I'll stay as long as it takes to drink a beer, and certainly I'll talk to the ladies, for it is they I have come to see.'

He pulled a chair in beside Hardcastle.

'Budge up, old chap.'

And dug a pipe out from some hidden pocket in his robe. James pushed across a soft leather pouch with the badge of the 3rd Light Cavalry embroidered on it.

'Thanks all the same but I'll stick to m'own,' and out came a similar pouch but this time decorated with the arms of Wadham College,

Oxford. The room filled with smoke and Sophie began to wonder if she'd be able to stick it. Could these oafs have forgotten she was pregnant? The Reverend leant towards her.

'Won't beat about the bush. Fact is Lady Jane, George Tarrant's wife, you know? . . . pushed off nearly a week ago. She didn't tell me they were off so soon; I've only just found out, and I've got no one to do the flowers on Sunday. I'm just hoping that either or both of you can do them for me. What do y'say?'

As behoves wives when they are responding to a request or question they are not too bothered about, both women glanced at their husbands.

Who puffed assiduously for a moment or two and cast surreptitious glances at each other from behind the smokescreen they had created. James nodded almost imperceptibly, Tom cleared his throat.

'Seems fine to me. We were going to travel with the first lot but then this court martial got in the way. I still planned to try to catch them up by leaving tomorrow, but it might be as well to hang on until Wednesday and travel with the second lot. That is if Catherine and James are happy about it?'

Perfectly happy was the answer. Probably they would all be able to travel together. At any rate Catherine and her brood could go with the Hardcastles.

The Reverend finished his beer, stood.

'Bless you all. Wonderful to be reminded that I still live among Christian folk.'

And off he went.

132

19

Four o'clock. Daybreak, though you'd hardly notice. Grey storm clouds sat over the station; the air took on a grey thickness which gathered under the trees; smoke from cooking fires seemed to struggle to get above them. The regiments assembled on the European parade ground just below the church and the dust beneath their feet lifted and subsided in a soundless sigh.

First came the 6th Dragoon Guards, a Queen's regiment in khaki sun helmets, blue tunics or stable jackets, blue trousers with double white stripes, black strapping. They were armed with carbines and light cavalry sabres and the officers carried revolvers of their own or a pair of army issue pistols. The men in the rear files, newly arrived from England, looked very much paler than the rest. Some of their only partially broken horses were skittish and troublesome.

Then came the prisoners, the eighty-five skirmishers from the 3rd Light Native Cavalry, still in their uniforms of hussar tunics, light blue with silver facings, peaked round forage caps. Many of them wore campaign medals with battle honours. They were escorted by a troop of the Dragoon Guards and a company of the 60th (the King's Royal Rifle Corps) in white sun helmets, green jackets with red facings. Next came the 11th and 20th Native Infantry, the rest of the 3rd Light Native Cavalry, not mounted, and finally the rest of the rifle regiment and a troop of British gunners with two eighteen-pounder and four nine-pounder field cannon loaded with grape.

Flags were carried but drooped on their staffs: Union flags next to the regimental standards – the regimental standards white with the Union flag in the upper canton nearest the hoist, the regimental number in Roman numerals set within a laurel wreath in the centre and ribboned battle honours below. There were no bands for this solemn occasion, but there were drummers who kept up a marching beat while on the move and provided a drum roll before and after the sentences were read. All in all there were not far off four thousand men drawn up by the time they had all arrived, rather more, but not very many more, Native soldiers than British. The British of all arms carried live ammunition, the Native regiments did not.

It was a long business. First of all the sentences were read out and that involved reciting the name of every offender. A few were reduced from ten years' hard labour on grounds of age: these included both new recruits and old-timers coming to the end of their period of service. Then they were stripped of their uniform jackets and made to take their boots off so that the regimental smiths could rivet fetters on to their arms and legs. It all took getting on for three hours by which time the sun had brightened the eastern horizon and encarnadined the clouds above it. In spite of the clouds the heat was building. It ended with the prisoners being marched past the drawn-up regiments. As they passed their own, with Colonel Carmichael-Smyth and their British officers mounted in front of the colours, some of them shouted, cursed, and a few even flung the boots they were still carrying at their hated commanding officer. All were barefoot, all shackled, and they had to walk two miles to the new civil gaol on the east side of the town.

The parade broke up calmly enough, but the sepoys looked sullen and some shouted and even wept.

Half an hour or so earlier, at about eight o'clock, Sophie and Catherine set off towards the bazaar hoping to buy flowers. As they passed the Chambers' bungalow, Charlotte, supporting her bump with both hands, ran down the pathway to her gate.

'Where are you going? Can I come too?'

'To the bazaar, to buy flowers for the church.'

'Of course you can.'

'Chambers is on parade with all the others and I don't like being so much on my own.'

There was a small flower market of four stalls near the middle of

134

the bazaar which contrived to continue to produce lilies, both Madonna and arum, tea roses, carnations and pinks through to the end of May by dint of keeping them under awnings, watering them often, and even using boys as punkah wallahs through the heavy heat of the afternoons. Charlotte knew the way, so the other two were grateful to have her with them.

At first the bazaar was relatively quiet, but when they were still a hundred yards or more from the flower stalls an angry crowd of sepoys released from the parade, and townspeople who had been watching it, flooded in. The townspeople, particularly the badmashes led by Balachandra, accused the sepoys of cowardice: there had been more of them than of the British, hadn't there; hadn't this been the moment to break out and rescue their comrades; how could they bear to see such heroes shackled like felons . . .? and so forth. Scuffles broke out, iron-bound bludgeons appeared, knives. A group of gaudily dressed women came out on to a balcony of one of the larger buildings. Their faces were painted, they wore bangles, rings, gold chains, and the younger ones a muslin that did almost nothing to conceal what was under it. They too hurled abuse at the sepoys and even emptied slop buckets filled with urine or worse on them.

'Don't think of coming to Mrs Dolly's,' they screamed, 'we don't put out for cowards, give us real men with balls.'

The three English women ducked into a spice shop, squeezing between the small barrels of red, saffron, orange and yellow powders, but the owner and his son got hold of Sophie by the shoulders, turned her and pushed her back out into the alley. Catherine and Charlotte followed, quickly, angrily shrugging off the men's attempts to manhandle them in the same way. But Sophie, clutching her left breast, and white with anger, wanted to lead them back in. That childhood and early adolescence, spent in part hanging about her father's stables with the stable lads, reasserted itself.

'Bastard groped me! He got hold of my tit,' she screamed. The other two grabbed her arms and hustled her down the edge of the crowd, but not before she'd kicked over a barrel of turmeric which filled the air and stained parts of their dresses bright yellow.

Without much more in the way of incident they got back out on to the square of ground in front of the guardhouse and the bridge across the Abu Nullah. There were no sepoys in the guardhouse and they were just in time to see a small crowd of youths hauling down

135

the Union flag and setting fire to it. Again Sophie had to be restrained until the youths, still carrying the burning flag above their heads, ran off into the bazaar with it.

The three of them stood in the now more or less empty space and tried ineffectually to brush or shake the turmeric out of their skirts and get their breath back.

'Well, what do we do now?' Sophie asked. 'We still haven't got flowers for the church.'

'I'm not going back in there,' Catherine said firmly.

'Does it have to be garden flowers?' Charlotte asked. 'Grasses, rushes and suchlike can look very nice. If we walk half a mile down the river I know where we can find some.'

As they headed downstream the little waterway widened and deepened and puddles and little runnels of water appeared in the cracked grey mud. Vegetation still greened the banks, small rectangular fields of wheat stubble came to the edge and they saw a man with a team of two bullocks dragging a plough through it. The waterway ran straighter now, the banks built up to a height of a couple of feet and wide enough to walk on. Occasionally there were simple gates of iron or wood set in it, sluices to let the water into irrigation ditches, but all already dry although the earth looked moist and dark. There were trees dotted about the fields, including a giant mango, a perfect hemisphere of foliage and green and crimson fruit. Catherine, in her artless, chatty way, said it was a tamarind – Charlotte corrected her.

The nullah skirted a grove of more ordinary mangoes and here they found what they were looking for, clumps of bulrushes sceptred with dark brown seed clusters, teasels with heads already ochreish, reeds with tiny black pompom-like dried flowers seemingly stuck to their stems and a variety of grasses, some with drops, chandelier-like, of delicate oat-like grain. It took less than ten minutes to get an armful each. As they gathered them a couple of small black warblers flitted about them, or clung with feet insect-thin to the upright long stems, and sang.

They hoisted Charlotte back on to the bank and found three young women had arrived and were looking down at them.

'Please come have tiffin?' asked one, clearly the leader. They were wearing not sarees but white baggy trousers beneath long tunics and scarves over their heads, all brightly coloured so that against the burning sky they looked like small pillars of fire.

'Mahometans,' whispered Catherine. 'Look, there's a small minaret in the village.'

'Do you think we ought?' asked Charlotte – as usual her immediate reaction to Natives was hostile.

'Why not? I could certainly do with something to drink,' said Sophie. 'I'm parched.' She looked at the woman who had spoken. She was quite dark and very pretty, the prettiness enhanced by the way she wore the scarf over her head. 'That's very kind of you.'

'We kind to ladies full with baby.' She smiled, showing small, even and very white teeth.

'Everyone very kind to me, I had my little boy.' This came from one of the others who seemed more shy, hung back a bit.

And now they noticed that there was a tiny baby on her back, fast asleep and held there by a broad band of green cloth.

Still carrying their booty they followed the three Muslim girls into the village. The one street, made up of low square cottages or cabins, whitewashed beneath thatches of sugar cane leaves with similarly thatched awnings, twisted a little towards an open space, a village square. There was a tiny mosque with a low dome and squat minaret in front of a stone-flagged threshing floor and a covered well. Beyond it brown ducks swam in a large pool and a couple of big white geese scooped weed off the surface with orange bills; four water buffalo basked in the shallows. Hens scampered from side to side around them as they walked, pecking at the dry dusty pathway, and a cockerel crowed. The air carried a not unpleasant potpourri of cattle and their dung, spicy food cooking, and orange and lemon blossom from the trees that clustered in front of the mosque. Women, some nervously holding their scarves in front of their faces, and children came to doorways and watched them. Two boys and a girl in cotton trousers like the rest, still young enough to be a tomboy, did cartwheels in front of them, showing off.

The girl who had first spoken to them led them to one of the larger dwellings in the square and made them sit down on carpets some old women brought out. Catherine guessed she was probably the daughter of the village headman. There was a pause of five minutes or so during which the other two girls tried to talk to them in very strained and generally incomprehensible English, until the first returned with biscuit-fired clay cups of milk, very sweet and spiced. Then came a thin lentil dahl with chappatis and finally small squares of candy, almost pure sugar but flavoured with cardamom. There was lemonade too, also very sweet.

'Where are the men?' Charlotte asked.

'In the fields. In the camp.'

'Soldiers?'

'No, servants for the sahibs.'

The sun, now nearly above them, had burnt off the clouds. Even under the awning the English women were too hot. Charlotte began to sweat.

'We should go,' she said. 'I don't want to faint on you.'

On the edge of the village the leader of the girls touched Sophie's forearm.

'Stay home tonight. With your men soldiers. Trouble, big trouble . . .'

That was all she was prepared to say.

They set off the way they had come on the raised dyke above the fields and under the mango trees, three very English ladies in long white dresses, still spattered with turmeric, with touches of colour, a peach-coloured sash, a dove-grey ribbon. They held their heads high, two beneath sun helmets, one, Charlotte, wearing a black straw hat, wide-brimmed, fastened to the bun at the back of her head with two long pins. Sophie opened and hoisted her lace-fringed parasol. Catherine chattered on about everything that came their way including a cloud of yellow butterflies that rose in a cloud from a bush of marigold-like flowers. However, two columns of black smoke rose from the bazaar less than a mile away, and a third from the town beyond, possibly near the new gaol where the eighty-five mutineers had already been incarcerated. Occasionally there was a crackle of gunfire.

20

Up in Catherine's bungalow Lavanya was struggling to keep Stephen, the four Dixon children and her own girl, Deepa, under control. Adam, the oldest Dixon, the one who should, according to general custom and received wisdom, have been in England having some sense knocked into him at a proper school, was a real pain, often challenging her, trying to pick an argument with her in the grammarless mix of Hindi and English they both used. Occasionally he fell into the obtuse racism that stained all relations with the Natives, called her nigger, assuming that, child though he was, he was her better.

They were in Dixon Bungalow Two outside a large room at the rear, used as a nursery, whose doors and windows opened on to the yard. It was hot, almost midday, and the boy who acted as punkah wallah had gone back across the yard to join the other servants in the servants' compound. The Dixon servants, and especially their ayah, resented Lavanya's presence. All of the Hardcastle servants, apart from her, had either been dismissed or sent on ahead to Simla with the furniture and the piano. The Dixon lot had devised a strategy – when the memsahibs were out they left Lavanya on her own with all the children, knowing that she would not be able to manage and making it seem that whatever occurred was all Lavanya's fault.

By the time Catherine and Sophie returned bedlam had been achieved. Out in the yard Adam had used the last of the water from a big water jar. Out of the mud he created, his two younger sisters,

Miranda and Emma, were making mud pies, which they called chappatis, which Robert, the youngest Dixon, force-fed into Stephen who howled as far as he was able to. Deepa had already been treated in the same way on the grounds that, since she was a nigger, chappatis were what she'd like. Lavanya stood above them on the raised verandah holding Deepa in her arms, scowling angrily in an attempt to keep back the tears.

Catherine, seeing immediately how it was her children who were most at fault, took the initiative, putting the blame on Lavanya.

'How could you let them?' she shrieked and raised her hand to slap her. Sophie, in the act of pulling off her hat, rushed between them, putting an arm round Lavanya, who turned into her and burst into tears.

Although the afternoon heat prevented serious rowing, they all three, Sophie, Catherine and Lavanya, remained sullen and at odds with each other. The younger children slept, though Stephen fidgeted and occasionally whined with prickly heat. Adam played with his lead soldiers, firing dried chickpeas from a spring-powered cannon so that black-faced, turbanned warriors toppled over in front of it.

Dixon arrived and moaned and ranted for ten minutes or so about how one poor old man, with a dozen medals, had, within a year of getting his pension, lost everything. Then he took himself off to the drawing room in Bungalow One where he drank chota pegs and smoked until he fell asleep. Hardcastle sat in a spare room and wrote up his report of the court martial, the sentencing and incarceration of the prisoners. The women were still at loggerheads towards evening and Sophie, with an armful of rushes and grasses, more really than she could manage, went up to the church on her own.

St John's seemed immense; slanting blocks of fierce sunlight coming through the windows contrasted intensely with deep spaces of purplish darkness out of which the highly polished brass cross and candlesticks gleamed like gold from the altar in the shallow, semi-circular apse. Though hardly cool, it was less fiercely hot than the parade ground outside and in any case to be able to move in deep solid shade, instead of through air hot like a Turkish bath, was a relief. Sophie went straight to the back of the church, beneath the gallery, through the vestry and into a small pantry where various vases, copper, brass, and some in native-fired clay, were kept. Beyond the pantry was a small dark room, little more than a large cupboard, with a stone floor and small stand pump which, cranked, produced water for flowers, the font and cleaning the floors. The water drained from a rimmed circle of brick down a runnel and under a small door into the churchyard. It all had the musty, damp smell of wet stone and moss.

Sophie chose two small brass pots for the altar and two large terracottas to go on either side of the aisle, just in front of the chancel steps. Fortunately the brass ones were already clean and deeply shiny, good as gold – fortunately, since cleaning them meant using a noisome mixture of horse urine and wood ash that was kept in a glazed storage jar. An Irish washerwoman attached to the gunners was employed to do this chore, but sometimes she forgot.

Sophie made up the four arrangements in the pantry and then took them, one by one, the brass ones first, into the church. She put the second on the altar and then stood back to look at the pair; she did not quite like what she saw. It was all a little tatty, a little mean, and as she fiddled with them she began to wish she had Charlotte Chambers with her, since she seemed to know about this sort of thing. Eventually she decided she'd have to get some of the longer stems which she had put in the terracotta vases, cut them down, and use them to fill out the two on the altar. And if that left the big ones looking mean then she'd put all that was left in just one of the pots.

And as she turned away from the altar and began to walk back down the aisle between the double row of white columns she heard a new noise, the sound of the pump being cranked and with it the intermittent gush of water.

Who could it be? What should she do? She stopped by the font, rested her hand on it, became suddenly conscious of her heart beating, of sweat, tightness in her throat and the weight that bore down on the pit of her pelvis. Then she shrugged. This was silly. It must be a cleaner filling a bucket, something of that sort. Anyway, she couldn't leave her task unfinished, that would be stupid. She moved on towards the vestry, and was a little annoyed to find she was tiptoeing . . . yet, surely the pump had gone on without stopping for far too long to fill a bucket? From the door to the vestry she could see across the pantry to the cubicle which housed the pump. And at that moment the light tipping through the windows, the beams almost horizontal by now, dimmed, almost appeared to go out, and distant, deep-throated thunder rumbled.

There was a naked man at the pump. He was neither nigger nor white, but striped like a tiger, pale reds or orange – you couldn't call it pink – streaked with black. He had his back to her, was cranking the pump with his right hand, catching the gushing flow in one of the pots and when it was full tipping it over his head, the next over one shoulder, then, twisting so that he bent one knee and raised the ankle to make a pose like a statue of a Greek athlete, over the other.

Although she had been married for more than four years she had never before seen a naked man. Felt one in the dark, beneath a sheet and a nightshirt, yes, lying on her, pushing at her, but not actually seen. Indeed, come to that, she had seen very few unfigleafed statues. The compulsion to step back into the church fought with something deeper and she stayed where she was. Presently he stooped to pick up a cloth from outside the rim and, because the movement was unstudied and awkward, for a moment he looked quite ungainly and therefore vulnerable and on top of all the other intense feelings that were warring through her there came a stab of tenderness, so, as he began to rub down his shoulders and chest with the big rag she felt she ought to help him, help him clean up and dry himself.

All this in a moment or two only, a moment which brought his face round to look across his shoulder and see her. Lieutenant Bruce Farquhar.

She made as if to run for it but stopped at the door back into the church with one arm upflung and her hand on the doorjamb, then her arm dropped and she came back in. By now he was holding the cloth over his genitals.

'Mrs Hardcastle? Sophie. I . . . It would be best if you went. Perhaps you could stay in the church until I am clothed again and, um, able to explain myself to you.'

She tried to speak, to say that after what she had already seen there seemed no point in pretending that she hadn't . . . no, it was all a muddle. She said nothing. He shrugged, smiled a small private smile, turned to the pump and continued to wash himself down. She now knew that she really ought to do what he had said and go back into the church, but she wouldn't, couldn't, and the main reason why she couldn't was the memory of that one dark short moment of real passion she had felt when he had kissed her, after giving her the

Ranee's scarf. Above all, it had been a moment of intimacy, of bonding, however brief, and she felt that somehow it conferred on her the right to stay.

She realised he had been covered, completely, from the top of his head to his toes, in a sort of blackish-brownish ink or paint, which required scrubbing but which did come off with a little effort. A different memory asserted itself.

'Were you the fakir who rescued my friend and me and my maid? In the bazaar . . . two years ago?'

'Yes. That was me.' He turned away, resumed scrubbing, his left thigh and shin now. She could see everything. It all looked looser and perhaps larger than she imagined Hardcastle was. And his thighs, though thin, were smooth and rounded by the muscle below the skin, and the hair round *there* was reddish, but fairer on his legs, and yes, his knees still looked bumpy.

'You didn't quite fool me, you know? I sort of knew it was you.'

'Really?'

'Really. Are you a spy?'

'Sometimes. Today, definitely, yes. Brigadier Wilson asked me to go down to the bazaar and find out what the mood there is.'

She hardly paid attention to what he said; all she could do was look at him and revel in the wonderful lightness of feeling that flooded her as his body glowed and shifted in the gathering gloom. The thunder came again.

'Farquhar . . . Fakir!' she laughed.

He laughed too and stepped over the rim towards a pile of clothes in a corner. He pulled a shirt on over his head.

'And it's bad,' his voice serious again, 'very bad. The bazaar and the town might riot tonight, and the sepoys are talking of mutiny.' He went on clothing himself, the undress uniform of the 75th, slate-coloured jacket and trousers. He strapped a black belt with a revolver holster round his waist, over the jacket. Lastly he stuffed a turban and a dhoti into a shoulder bag.

'I'll see you back to your bungalow and from then on you must not go anywhere without at least four or five armed men. Understand? Oh, and don't tell anyone, not even Tom Hardcastle, about . . . all this.' He waved an arm over the pantry in a somewhat embarrassed gesture.

'Orders received and understood.' She bobbed him a mocking

curtsey, suddenly relieved as she was (and perhaps a little sad too) that their situation was becoming more normal, less exceptionable.

When they left the church it was dark, very dark except along the eastern edge of the sky where sheet lightning flared and lit the bellies of the clouds. Thunder continued to rumble. Occasional splashes of rain hit the leaves above them and the dust beneath their feet, bringing with it the smell of fixed nitrogen. Worst of all was the orange, ruby and gold of scattered fires and the rushing of invisible feet past them, in both directions. Sparks billowed and sometimes there were enough to light the smoke rolling over burning thatch and hayricks. The thatch crackled and occasionally there was the sharper report of a pistol or revolver. Farquhar held his revolver in front of him, and after she had stumbled held her hand with his free one. She relished, almost, yes, perhaps loved its hard dry strength. It was the hand of a man who rode a lot, not a pen-pusher's. She wondered what he was feeling, what his face would reveal, but it was so dark she could not make it out.

They reached the Dixon bungalows. And at the gate Farquhar kissed her, but gently, just enough to assert a memory of what had passed between them six months earlier. Then he handed her in to Hardcastle who was fuming with anxiety. He was brusque, showed no gratitude to Farquhar. When he had gone he turned on Sophie, and continued to berate her for staying up at the church until darkness fell.

'I came to no harm,' she reiterated. 'And with Mr Farquhar with me was not likely to.'

Hardcastle clutched her shoulders, held her at arm's length and delivered as dire a warning as Moses just down from the mountain to find the Israelites prancing round a golden calf might have done.

'Feller's got pale eyelashes,' he said. 'Never trust a feller with pale eyelashes.'

21

Meerut, Sunday 10 May 1857

In Meerut the mutiny lasted for two hours, two hours of almost complete darkness between sullen sunset and moonrise at the end of a day that had been more than usually hot and sultry even for the time of year. Once those who had attended matins at seven had got home for breakfast the English remained indoors, fanned by the continually moistened tatties or grass screens in their windows and doors and, in the larger establishments, by the motion of soaked punkahs. The men read their newspapers, the women sewed or read to the more biddable of the children, the less biddable squabbled in what shade they could find out of doors once they had decided it was too hot for cricket. Sunday roast was out of the question, and the men among their servants, especially those in the Native lines, told the women not to prepare the usual dinner of cold meats and summer puddings before they drifted away to the bazaar. No dinner? The feringhees, that is the Franks or foreigners, will all be dead by dinner-time.

Throughout the night before and now through the hottest part of the day Sophie was plagued with dreams and then recollections of what she had seen the day before, of Bruce Farquhar, unaware of her, at his ablutions. The memory occasionally made her feel dizzy, at times became almost obsessive, the tilt of his head and shoulders as he pulled the cloth across his back, the cleavage between his tight buttocks, the burnt ochre of his skin, and then those other parts . . . at times she allowed herself a small girl's almost playful shudder at their grossness, then compared them to those of the monkeys in Simla who were quite shameless. She even wondered what it would feel like to hold them in the palm of her hand, a thought that was guiltily smothered before it could properly form . . . And then came the worst fantasy of all. What if all had happened just as it did, but she not seven months pregnant? Would she have been able to resist him had he tried to embrace her? Naked as he was? In a *church*? Would she have hoisted up her skirt for him like some doxy in a Hogarth print? And at that point, she giggled. But to everyone else in the bungalows she was snappy, irritable.

Lavanya too would not stop grumbling. She had spent another difficult afternoon keeping the Dixon four from tormenting Stephen and Deepa. Adam, now eleven years old, was particularly nasty, chasing the little three-year-old round the compound, threatening him with a large black but dead scorpion. Later they played soldiers and Stephen was again picked on and designated a sepoy with a dishcloth turban and his face blacked up with boot polish. There was a row when this was discovered – the stuff wouldn't shift that easily and at about five o'clock Sophie declared that the children should not come to church. Lavanya was to clean them up and get them early to bed, with gruel only for supper. Lavanya tried to object: without an hour or so of no children, how would she be able to tidy things away? Sophie got sharp with her – it was on the tip of her tongue to tell her she might be dismissed before they left for Simla. Perhaps Hardcastle was right: there would be no Dixon children to look after and what would be needed in July was a wet nurse, not an ayah, for Stephen was growing to be a quiet lad, no trouble, always biddable and ready to amuse himself.

But at this point, at about half past five, a Native youth arrived at the front door with a note for her. She recognised him as one of Victoria Marchant's servants. The note was handed in, a half anna was passed over as a tip.

My Dear Mrs Hardcastle

Forgive me for intruding in a matter which is really none of my business. I had occasion this afternoon to visit our church where I discovered that one of the bulrushes in your very elegant display in front of the chancel steps has begun to shed its seeds which, I am

146

*sure you will be aware, have the characteristics of dandelion seeds
in that they open out like parasols and float over the countryside in
their thousands. I took the liberty of removing the head that had
begun to burst, but you may like to remove the others or at any
rate check that none is likely to perform in the same way.*

Your obed. etc

Victoria Marchant

'Oh shit,' said Sophie, but well under her breath. Then, out
loud, after passing the note to Catherine: 'Cathy, please come with
me. For I am sure neither of our fine men will do so, they are far
too busy. If we go now, we'll have time to get back to change for
the actual service. Thank God the Rev Rotton put the time back
to seven.'

They took the pony trap, which of course had to be got out and
the pony harnessed, but still made it to the church by six o'clock.

A second bulrush had indeed exploded and was filling the air with
its flighted seeds. These drifted down the aisle, across the pews, and
then, as the two women came through the door, the new current of
air sent them swirling up into the chancel. There were hundreds of
them, no, thousands.

'What can we do?' she wailed.

Catherine was practical.

'Get all the bulrushes outside before we have a worse disaster on
our hands . . .'

She was already at the terracotta jar, hauling the offending stalks
out. She rushed to the door and hurled them away so that they fell
beyond the gravel and under one of the mast trees, then she stood in
the doorway and looked south down the very slight rise across the
cantonments towards the bazaar. The sun, an angry red disc in a haze
that was almost brown in colour, dipped below the ceiling of cloud
towards the horizon to her right, and over the trees and roofs and
avenues in front of her darkness thickened like a lid, a darkness effec-
tively deepened by a sudden efflorescence of fires in the Native
lines . . . and this time, though she could not know it was so, it was
not just the thatched roofs of stores and stabling that were burning.
There was musket fire too, intense in short bursts, or crackling

147

sporadically, for it was at about this time that the sepoys of the 11th broke into their bells of arms and seized their muskets and ammunition, many of which they fired off into the air. She called back to Sophie.

'I think we should get back. There's trouble down in our lines, and it must be quite close to the children.'

'Oh, please. We've got to do something about this first,' Sophie wailed.

Catherine turned back in. Since all the windows faced either north or south the aisle and chancel were now in deep shadow, almost dark. Sophie had managed to find the chain which lowered the chancel light which was never allowed to go out and was manically trying to light candles from it. The seeds continued to swirl like tiny moths around her and occasionally one or two, caught in the updraught above the candles, flared and fell. At least if the church goes up in flames, Catherine thought as she ran back up the aisle, they'll blame the sepoys. Nevertheless she snuffed the candles, grabbed Sophie by the elbow and rushed her back to the door only to find it was filled by the silhouette of a big man in a long robe holding a revolver above his head. He fired it into the air and Sophie realised that what was required of her now was a faint. She let her knees go, Catherine caught her below the armpits and lowered her into a sitting position which allowed her unceremoniously to push Sophie's head down over her bump. The Reverend John Rotton hunkered beside her.

'I say, I am most fearfully sorry. I was on my way in to light the candles as I usually do before Evensong, and I'm afraid your clothes in the darkness lent you the appearance of Natives. The Natives are indeed rioting down by the bazaar and I understand that a large number of the 3rd Cavalry have gone to the gaol to release their colleagues.'

Sophie allowed herself to come to and raised her head.

'Cathy is right,' she cried, 'we must get back to our children.'

'You will do no such thing. And I shall do everything in my power to stop you. You will be killed or worse before you get there. I'm sure Dixon and Hardcastle are doing all that can be done to protect them. Meanwhile, I shall take you up into the English lines, indeed to the General Headquarters.'

Sophie was by now approaching madness: on one side she was

racked by fear that threatened to submit to hysteria; somewhere else, though, the voice that had told her a faint was in order remained separated from the rest and rational. What could possibly be worse than death, it wondered. Rape? If that's what the reverend meant then he was sadly unaware of how often it occurred in the bedrooms of his congregation.

If the kernel of a farce is a situation where people rush in and out of rooms and cupboards always missing each other by a split second, the men occasionally untrousered, then what was happening down at the Dixon bungalows was farce, black farce indeed, but farce nonetheless. At about six o'clock Captain Craigie of the 3rd galloped up, swung from his saddle and pounded on the door of Dixon Bungalow One.

'James, come out, you old dog, you're needed on our parade ground.'

'Is that you, Henry? What are you on about? I'm just getting ready for church, dammit.'

'Parade ground, James. The regiment are assembling there, they've got the poor chaps out of the prison but it's taking a bit of time to get the shackles off them. God knows what . . . Oh my God . . .'

Dixon had appeared in the doorway, shirt tucked between his thighs, full-dress trousers in his hands. Craigie recovered, went on . . .

'God knows what they'll get up to once they're ready. I'm rounding up as many of our chaps as I can to get down there to persuade them to return to their lines. Don't follow me, get to the parade ground as quick as you can, I'll be there shortly.'

He ran back down the path and into the saddle again.

'The 11th and 20th are coming out of the lines too and there's a mob working their way up from the bazaar, so get a move on.' And he was gone.

Dixon dashed back to his room, swapped the trousers for the undress ones he wore for routine parades, on the march and in battle, hunted round for jacket, scarf, sun helmet, gave up on the scarf, found his revolver and sabre, stopped to load the revolver, a British Adams self-cocking model, bellowed out of the window for his groom to saddle up his big black gelding charger as he did so.

Hardcastle appeared in the doorway.

'What the blazes is going on?' He rubbed his eyes – under the influence of beer and tobacco as well as the heat he had fallen asleep with the *Bombay Times* spread across his face.

Dixon told him, adding that he was going off to the 3rd's parade ground.

'What shall I do? Where shall I go? Where are the ladies, the children?'

'The ladies are up at the church messing about with the flowers. The children should be asleep or anyway in bed in number two. Damn, I've dropped a percussion cap.' They bumped heads looking for it. 'Leave it, I've got plenty. Where the deuce is that groom?'*

But the syce, along with all the other servants, had gone. Hardcastle helped him get the gelding saddled up, Dixon mounted, touched spurs to its flank and jumped the fence into the road where he scattered a dozen or so Natives from the town who were marauding up the avenue with flaring torches above their heads, the flames lighting their dark faces, wide eyes and teeth. Hardcastle dithered for a fatal moment or two then decided that the first priority was the children. He went back into his study and snatched up the one gun he felt confident about using, a long hunting flintlock which he loaded with ball, and ran down the covered way to Bungalow Two. Through these tiny delays he just missed seeing the pale shape of Lavanya disappearing into a small bamboo thicket at the back of the compound. He rushed into the two rooms where the children slept. The beds were empty and neat with their single sheets folded back. He turned into the dining area and small kitchen (the serious cooking was done in the servants' quarters across the yard) and again found no one, just a big saucepan of porridge on the plate of a small wood-fired range. At this moment Bungalow One burst into flames.

He ran across the yard, stumbling in the swinging shadows, through the servants' quarters, calling out for Lavanya and the names he actually knew of two of the other servants, but there was no one there at all. Even in this moment of acute anxiety he could not help

* Revolvers were still loaded by introducing powder and bullet from the front of each chamber in the revolving drum and required percussion caps attached to nipples at the rear of each chamber. The all-in-one cartridge, including its own percussion cap, was not developed until the American Civil War some five years later.

noticing how poor, dirty and ramshackle everything was, to his British eyes anyway. Bare wattle walls, rafters made from undressed timber with the thatch of cane leaves slipping through the cracks, a sickening smell of spices, excrement, rotting vegetables. It was far worse than any country labourer's cabin he had ever had occasion to be in in England, and they had been shocking enough. But no Lavanya, no children, no one at all.

He headed for the stables and even as he did so they too, simple structures made out of hurdles and thatch, caught fire, the flames in the tinder-dry woven branches billowing out like six-foot-high surf, the animals inside thrashing and screaming. The heat drove him back and the presence too of dark figures streaking between him and the flames. Desperate now, holding the gun at waist level so the long muzzle swept the ground in front of him, his finger on the trigger, he broke through six or so rioters – they certainly weren't sepoys or sowars – and began to run up the avenue towards the church and the English lines.

Dixon joined three or four of his fellow officers on the 3rd's parade ground, just below the Abu Nullah and to the west of the bazaar, where they were doing their best to persuade the sowars to return to their duty; but the men knew they had already gone too far and that many of them would face life imprisonment at the very least if they gave in now. They kept their distance from the mounted officers, leaving a dark no-man's-land between them, swept by the long deep shadows thrown by the trees; some of them held flaring torches above their heads, the clouds of black oily smoke deepening the encroaching dusk. Into all this Craigie presently returned. He tried one last appeal and was answered by shots, the balls passing well above his head but bearing an obvious message. He turned, raised his arm and waved his fellow officers back towards the wooden bridge, past the guardhouse and across the nullah, leading them into the European lines. His concern now, and that of Dixon too, was for their wives and children. A few shouted queries directed into the steady stream of white faces heading north for the British barracks and parade grounds established that no one had seen any of them. Among them was Chambers, the adjutant of the 11th.

'Where's Mrs Chambers?' Craigie yelled at him. 'Are our wives with her?'

It had occurred to him that they might have gone to the assistance of the pregnant woman.

'I've no idea, Craigie. I thought she had gone on ahead. Now I'm not so sure, but I pray she has,' and he rushed on into the dark crowd.

'We'll have to go back,' Craigie yelled and pulled his horse's head round. Dixon fell in behind him and a lieutenant called Möller. They cantered back to the bridge, recrossed it into what was now hostile territory, and took the avenue west that led into the cantonments of the British officers of the Native regiments. They found Mrs Craigie quite quickly, and other colleagues and their wives, but no Dixons or Mrs Chambers whose bungalow was almost opposite that of the Craigies. They came under fire, houses around them were burning, and suddenly, though intermittently, it was almost like daylight in shifting pools. But before they could get to the Chambers' place the stables there burst into flames too and they were driven back by mutinous sowars. Again they could hear the screams of the horses, but then, high and cutting the bedlam around like a cheese wire, a scream that was clearly human and female.

A moment earlier Charlotte Chambers, lying in her bed and fearing that the pains in her lower abdomen were more serious than she had supposed them to be, had heard her front door splinter under the blows of what sounded like an axe. There was nowhere to hide, but, driven by instinct rather than reason, she tore down the muslin netting round the bed, wrapped it round herself, threw open the rear verandah door and crouched in its darkest corner, perhaps hoping that the intruder would be looking for loot more valuable than a bundle of cloth. But it was she he was looking for.

The butcher.

He had his cleaver in his hand and his long honed-down butcher's devil in his belt. Seeing a hand clutching a corner of the cotton bundle on the verandah, he threw the cleaver on the bed, stooped over her, searched in the folds for her arm and dragged her out of the muslin curtaining. She began to scream. From behind he wound her hair round his left hand and pinned her head to the floor, drew the knife and neatly, just as he did with pigs, slit her throat, opening the jugular vein. He held her down as the blood spurted, then gushed out, over the decking, until the thrashing of her limbs faded to a last nervous twitching; then he tore open her nightdress from her neck to her knees and, again using almost surgical skill, dissected out from her womb the still living foetus of a tiny girl, cut the umbilical chord and placed the baby on its dead mother's breast.

In spite of the men milling around them Craigie and Lieutenant Möller cut their way into the bungalow. They saw the butcher, briefly but for long enough to be sure who he was, still with the blood-soaked apron of his trade round his waist and clutching the knife he had used. They fired, missed, and he was gone, swallowed into the blanket of shifting smoke.

With their company swollen by a few loyal servants and sowars, and other British officers and their families, they now presented a group formidable enough to keep at bay a mob made up mainly of Natives armed only with old unmanageable matchlocks, knives, or lathies – those iron-bound bludgeons. Their route now took them past the house of Veterinary Surgeon Dawson and his wife. Both were known to be suffering from smallpox and at first the mob had kept its distance, but when Dawson came on to his verandah and fired into the crowd with his shotgun he had fallen, riddled with bullets. The leaders of the mob rushed over his body and into Mrs Dawson's bed-room where they pulled up short, faced with her pox-filled face as she got off the bed. But one of them had a torch and he tossed it so that it landed at her feet, her nightrobe caught fire and for a moment she stood, a pillar of flame, the material and her skin blackening beneath the blaze, the foetid air shivered into shards by her screams. The mob scattered in front of Craigie and his little column, but they could do nothing for her.

Craigie and the other men with their women and children shel-tered in a nearby Hindu temple, while Dixon pushed on to the European lines, catching up with Hardcastle just as he reached the parade ground of the 60th. Hardcastle had stopped at the church where Rotton told him that he had sent Sophie and Catherine to the GHQ in the keeping of his curate, the Reverend Tom Smyth, who had arrived to assist at Evensong. For no reason that he could think of to explain it, Hardcastle assumed the children were with their mothers.

The Commander of Division, Brigadier Archdale Wilson, who wanted nothing more than to retire to a cottage in Norfolk with his old lady, was standing by the flagpole, surrounded by a cluster of staff officers (the flag down as the sunset tattoo had already been sounded). He was struggling against the tide of darkness and poor eyesight to see to what extent the 60th Rifles and 6th Dragoon Guards had assembled. Men were still running in from the barracks and milling round the bells of arms for their weapons, including the new Enfields. Others were falling in by companies and troops, though many of the dragoons were still without horses and some of the younger ones seemed not too certain about where they were meant to be. Whips cracked and the rumble of gun carriage wheels announced the arrival of at least some of the guns.

Dixon briefly shook Hardcastle's hand.

'You see if you can find the women,' he barked. 'I'll be more use helping out the dragoons. There are some out there still don't know their arses from their elbows.' His knees pressed his mount into a canter and he disappeared into the murk.

At this moment Major General Hewitt, Commander of the Station and Wilson's superior, also with some of his staff about him, trotted on to the ground, his fat body swaying and bouncing and with a look of the utmost bewilderment on his red whiskered face. Wilson, who believed Hewitt was an insufferable old dolt, met him in the middle of the ground and saluted.

'Archdale, tell me what the hell's happening, why don't you?' Hewitt gasped.

'It appears, sir, that the town has rioted and the bazaar with it, and entered the Native lines. They've been joined by a large number of the sepoys and are at present burning everything that will burn down there, having first looted the cantonments. We're receiving reports that they are killing people including women and children.'

'My God, they must be stopped.'

'Of course. We are falling in as quickly as we can, and I've sent a couple of my officers to chivvy them along but there are some officers, especially the younger ones, who insist on doing everything according to Queen's Regulations.'

'What the divil do you mean, Archie?'

Wilson pulled himself up even more straightly in his saddle and grimaced.

'The colonel of the dragoons is insisting that the sergeants call a full roll call. Some of the 60th turned up in their white drill; they

154

were expecting to go to church, and were ordered back to change into their green service dress.'

'Archie, I'm too old for this sort of thing.' Hewitt's horse kicked out at this point and threw the general forward so that only his stomach saved his nose from making contact with the horse's neck as its head came up again. 'Far too old. Look, you handle it. I'll stay with you as long as I can and back you, but . . . I don't know what to do. You decide.'

'Is that an order, sir?' Wilson threw a meaningful look back at his nearest ADC. He wanted to be sure that this irregularity had been properly noted.

'Of course it bloody is.'

'Right.' Wilson turned to the men around him. 'Tell officers commanding all units they can start issuing ammunition, immediately. As quickly as it can be done.'

Nevertheless it was gone eight o'clock and pitch-dark apart from the light from the flames of burning buildings when the column reached the Mall and the wooden bridge. The rioters dispersed like shadows, some said like rats, between the houses and into the yards and gardens around them, as soon as the British appeared. There was no wall round the town although the old gates remained, so it was easy for them to filter into the backstreets and lanes and alleys, where it was far too dark to attempt a pursuit. And there was barely a sepoy or sowar among them. A couple of guns and an English rifle company took a more circuitous route which led them to the outer perimeter of the cantonments, and, just as the three-quarter moon was rising, the sergeant gunner thought he saw movement in a tope of mango trees on the far side of a field of sugar cane stubble. The guns unlimbered and fired four rounds of grape into the trees, then the rifles went forward with bayonets fixed. The grove was deserted, or had been deserted, for there were no dead or wounded to be found.

22

Meerut, 10 May 1857, night

Lavanya, a woman now nearly eighteen years old, who had been widowed three years earlier, before her child was born, who had nurtured that child and another not her own, was in many ways mature beyond her years, even in a culture where barely adolescent children were made brides and mothers as a matter of course. This maturity was largely because, emotionally and in most other ways, she had had to fend for herself.

Although among the Hardcastle servants she had relations, extended family, only two of them were women, and anyway she not only worked but lived on the wrong side of the compound, that is, on the Hardcastle side, whether in Simla or Meerut. And of course that world, the one she had been bought into, the one she had sold herself very completely into, her own milk included, was at first utterly alien. She could not speak the language, she was ignorant of every object and its use, she did not know how to behave and, almost worse, could not interpret the behaviour of the only two adults in whose company she passed much of her life. Much of her life? Not really, or only as far as cohabitation under the same roofs went, for most of her life was spent, on their own, with little Deepa and Stephen. And with them she had formed a deep and personal bond.

With no other certainties that bond was her rock, or, more accurately, the tiny craft she manoeuvred through the currents and crosscurrents of a life that remained mysterious to her, a craft that kept her afloat. It alone gave her meaning, purpose and direction.

She could not envisage her life without it, she could not foresee a time when it would not be as it was now. She was hardly even aware of the way its terms had already changed quite fundamentally – for of course she no longer nursed the two babies. She lived with and for them in a continuous present, could scarcely remember a time when they were not as they were now, that is small children three and a half years old, who could walk and run and talk, and certainly she never thought of a time when they might grow up into people.

And now, as the roof of Bungalow One exploded like a Roman candle in a fountain of sparks and the flames licked along the thatch above the covered way that linked it to Bungalow Two, as dark shadowy figures leapt and danced round the blaze, their daggers and tulwars flashing in the light of the flames, some discharging matchlocks into the air, she decided enough was enough, that a burning empty house attacked by a murderous mob was no place for the three of them to be. But also she accepted, and it took an effort of will to do it, that she would have to take the four Dixon children as well.

She didn't mind the girls, but she hated the boys.

She pushed and herded all six children ahead of her, across the deserted compound and into the bamboo patch that separated the Dixon bungalows from fields of wheat and cane stubble and newly ploughed tilth. But even here she decided they were too close; almost all the bungalows along the Mall and the avenues that branched off it were now burning, sending up clouds of sparks and smoke which occasionally parted to reveal the roaring flames within; shots rang out in broken fusillades; there was no indication she could see of white faces let alone of white soldiers coming down from the British lines. Again pushing, chivvying, hustling her flock, she drove them the fifty yards or so that took them to the Abu Nullah, scooping up Deepa when she stumbled, yet finding a free hand to cuff Robert, the younger of the Dixon boys, when he tried to break back.

Remaining always at the back of them, she urged them on to the trees and dried-up pool where Sophie and the other women had gathered their rushes and reeds. Still with a wary eye on what might be happening back in the lines she got among the trees where she attempted to gather the children about her like a feline queen with her cubs or kittens. The girls, Miranda and Emma, were now crying, forcing sobs out on huge gasps of air pulled in, wailing for their mother. Stephen, envious of Deepa's privileged position in Lavanya's arms, clambered over her lap, tangled his arms round her neck. Robert sulked. Adam bit into a fallen mango and then retched and swore as he realised it was full of maggots.

Time passed. An hour or more. Smoke drifted across the fields carrying with it the acrid smell of burnt paint and varnished, polished furniture as well as that of timber and thatch. And occasionally too there was the sour stench of partially roasted meat – horse, for the most part. There was less flame now, fewer swaying columns of sparks, but still shouts, screams and shots. Lavanya contrived to get the children, all of them, Adam even, to huddle more closely about her. Time passed. In front of them, to the east, the sky became nacreous as the moon edged up towards the earth's rim. Then, when the moon was fully up, a new sound: the rattle on stones and gravel of many horses coming at a trot, the rumble of iron-shod wheels, the squeal of metal on metal from an inadequately greased axle, the crack of whips rather than pistol shots, and every now and then a bugle too. She raised herself on to her knees then her feet, peered through the darkness, could make out, piece together rather than actually see, movement, men moving, and horses or mules, on the far side of the field.

A tree, rotten or dry perhaps, surrendering to heat and fortuitous sparks, exploded suddenly into flame just to the side of the bamboo patch they had come through nearly an hour before, and in its light she saw the two cannon, their muzzles black pockets of darkness, pointing at . . . her. She threw herself backwards, reaching out arms for the children around her, and 'Run,' she cried, 'run back, run back into the trees' just as one, two, both guns fired – a brief moment marked by a crescendoing screech, and a hail of grape shredded the leaves and branches above them.

'This way, go this way,' and sent the children off at an angle of less than ninety degrees, which took them both deeper into the wood and back to the dry hollow of the pond. They tumbled, three of them head over heels, down the bank as the cannon cracked again and this time the lead scythed through the very spot they had been in.

Not for one moment did Lavanya consider the possibility that the cannon had been fired by English gunners. Why should she? With no real understanding of what they were talking about she had understood from the gossip both in the servants' quarters and among the British that there was trouble in the air, that the town might rise, that the Native regiments might mutiny. And if they did, then, or so said the servants anyway, all the whites – men, women and children – would be butchered.

To the north and east fires still burnt and shots were fired. Very near and to the east she could see how fifty or so men, whose bayonets gleamed in the moonlight, were moving in open order across the stubble towards her copse. That they were Native troops she had no doubt, and no doubt either that while they might spare herself and Deepa the worst of fates they would kill the others, including Stephen. So she turned away from Meerut and shepherded the children round the copse and on through fields and past woods towards the south-west. Presently the moonlight revealed in front of them the long unbroken line of tall trees that marked the Grand Trunk Road that linked Umballa and Meerut with Calcutta, with, about a mile further off, the junction with the road to Delhi. As they came nearer they could see large numbers of men, some in marching formation but most moving as a broken crowd, gathering at the junction.

Lavanya made the children huddle down in a ditch, told Adam, who was now quite cowed by her and the situation they were in, to keep the rest quiet and together; then, using what cover she could find, she edged her way nearer, near enough to hear a loud voice urging the sepoys to move on as quickly as possible to Delhi where there were no British troops and where Bahadur Shah was ready to assume the mantle of the Mughal Emperors and kill all the feringhees, just as they had already slaughtered all there were in Meerut. That at least was what Lavanya made of the torrent of abuse, hate and triumph that poured from the man's mouth.

She returned to the children and made them wait until all the mutineers had moved off. Emma, Robert, Deepa and Stephen slept uneasily for an hour or so. Miranda, aged ten, darker than her siblings, more like her father, crept up to her and sat close, so Lavanya could feel the warmth of her thigh. A sheen of moonlight filtered through the grasses above them.

Using the family patois of mixed languages Miranda looked up at the Indian girl from large dark eyes.

'Where's our mummy?' she asked.

Lavanya looked down at her, felt the heat of a tear spill on her cheeks, not out of any huge regret for Catherine Dixon, but out of tenderness for the child. She couldn't find anything to say.

'Is she dead?'

A slight but hopeless shrug.

'She's dead,' the child asserted in answer to her own question. 'And Papa too, I daresay.' And after a moment's reflection she added, 'You'll look after us, won't you?'

'If you're good.'

'I'll be good. I'll help you.'

Once the sepoys had moved off, Lavanya got them on the move again, taking the left fork towards Cawnpore and Lucknow. Already, less than a mile away, Sophie was stumbling across the wheat stubble, calling, 'Stephen, Stephen, Stephen' in a hoarse high voice, which, even if they had heard it, the children and Lavanya would have taken to be the cry of a distant owl or even the more liquid call of, say, a curlew, woken by the disturbances of the night and the moon's false dawn.

23

Delhi, May 1857

The city was shaped like a lozenge or irregular oval, its longest axis, from north-west to south-east, being about two miles; the shorter one, from and including the Red Fort high on the eastern side, to the south-west, was about a mile and a half. Its substantial wall was broken by several gates, built of stone and almost as impregnable as the fort itself. The northern sector was slightly higher than the rest and, at nearly its most northern point, was interrupted by the Cashmere Gate. Inside the Cashmere Gate lay the British Civil Lines including the main residencies, administrative offices, treasury, magazine and St James's Church. The southern half of the city, known as Shajehanabad after Shah Jehan who, in 1631, shifted the Mughal capital from Agra to Delhi, was a densely populated warren of narrow alleys filled with shops, the workshops of artisans, and the hovels of the poor, interrupted here and there by larger buildings – mosques and the palaces of dignitaries such as Bahadur's sons.

The River Jumna (Yamuna) ran below the entire length of the eastern walls, a network of waterways separating wide mud flats which would be covered after the summer rains. It was crossed by one bridge only, the Bridge of Boats, which carried the road from Meerut into the city at the northern corner of the Red Fort, through the Calcutta Gate about three-quarters of a mile south-east of the Cashmere Gate. Beyond the Cashmere Gate a narrow ridge of slightly higher ground began a little less than a mile to the north-west of the city and ran for a further two miles towards the north-east, before petering out at about three miles. Known simply as The Ridge, the military lines and cantonments covered much of its north-facing slopes. Its undulating crest was, at its highest points, no higher than the city walls, but that was enough to give it military significance.

There were no British regiments. There were three Company Native regiments and some artillery officered in all but the lowest ranks by British officers, and there was a fairly large British civilian population of Company personnel led by the civilian Commissioner, Simon Fraser, who was *de facto* governor. The King of Delhi's rule did not extend beyond the Red Fort. The city and its surroundings were controlled, following a succession of treaties and enforced agreements made over the previous century, by a British led magistracy, supported by a Native but largely Christian police force and civil service. A middle class of merchants, businessmen, and entrepreneurs supported the British. Many were converts but by no means exclusively Anglican. There were Methodist and allied communities and Roman Catholics as well.

10 MAY, 11.30 P.M.

A Native policeman, well mounted, arrived at the Commissioner's house in the Civil Lines with a letter from the authorities in Meerut. He delivered it to Simon Fraser, the most senior civil official in Delhi. Fraser was about to go to bed. He put the unopened letter in his coat pocket. A sort of excuse presents itself. A message that was truly important would have come by the electric telegraph. How could he know the mutineers had cut the line, since he did not even know there had been a mutiny?

11 MAY, 7.00 A.M.

Twenty sowars, the vanguard of the mutineers, some in the uniform of the 3rd Light Cavalry, some in Native clothes, trotted down the road from Meerut towards the Bridge of Boats above a low cloud of white dust. The road was not as crowded as it had been three hours earlier when day broke but there were still bullock carts laden with

162

vegetables coming in from one of the more distant villages, followed by women pushing handcarts loaded with cages made from withies and filled with white hens. Behind them there was a small herd of bullocks and another of goats, all heading for the city markets. Pariah dogs loped up and snuffled around it all and then began to bark as a distant bugle sounded. Heads turned, and with much shouting and heaving and pushing the entire train was shifted to one side – here and there a wheel slipped over the low embankment and a small cart toppled into the field below.

There was a guardhouse in front of the bridge. Beneath the red walls of the fort the sluggish, muddy river scarcely moved between its paler flats. White marble roofs and towers seemed to float above the battlements; against the now cloudless blue of the vast sky they appeared like carved snow. Beyond them thin smog from the countless cooking fires of the city soiled the air. The sergeant called out the guard. It's not recorded whether he was Native or British. He stood in front of his men, sword in his right hand, pistol in his left, in front of the twenty men drawn up in two files behind him. The leading sowar pulled up in a little flurry of grit and sand and his sabre rasped out of its polished scabbard. There was no room for thought or talk. Head down so that only the top of his sun helmet showed above his horse's ears, he spurred the beast forward and, as the sergeant loosed off his one shot, the sabre flashed and his severed head hit the ground as his body toppled. The guard scattered and the mutinous troopers trotted on, across the gently swaying bridge, to take the left that passed beneath the palace walls. This brought them to a spot below the balcony from which the emperors used to reveal themselves to their people. From behind windows latticed with marble the old King, who had remained up all night, dazed with opium, scribbling snatches of verse, looked down at them. Their leader, still with his bloodied sabre drawn but now lowered, shouted up at the barely distinguishable figure.

'Great King, we have come to make you emperor. Help us fight for our Faith.'

Bahadur Shah turned away, beckoned an aide to his side.

'Get Captain Douglas,' he said.

Captain Douglas commanded the royal bodyguard. He hurried along a passage which took him past the balcony that overlooked the space where the sowars had pulled up. The polished marble floor resonated to the clatter of his boots, fell silent. He shouted down at them.

'Go away. You are annoying the King. These are the private apartments of the ladies of the palace. You are showing disrespect to the King. Go to the Kudsia Garden down by the river. I will hear what you have to say there.'

Waving swords and pistols they ignored him and entered the city by the next gate on the eastern side, to the south of the fort. The King ordered Douglas to close the remaining gates 'lest these men should get in'. But they were in already.

Glancing down into the courts and gardens of the palace Douglas saw that people were pouring out of the apartments and the peripheral shantytown and were gathering into ever growing groups which he sensed would soon coalesce into a crowd, a mob. Many were dressed in white, as if for a festival. There was a susurration of low conversation, of sandals and bare feet on flagstones and grass, punctuated with higher, louder calls and shouts.

7.35 A.M.

When Douglas reached the Calcutta Gate, the nearest, he found Simon Fraser had already closed it. With the Commissioner were a magistrate, John Hutchinson, Fraser's head clerk, Nixon, and the kotwal, the Native Chief of Police. Fraser was ordering the kotwal to see to the closing of the other gates, and as he did so another Native policeman ran up with news that the mutineers were already in the city and plundering the Christian quarter round the Rajghat Gate. At that moment five sowars galloped on to the scene and fired a scattered volley into the group. Hutchinson was hit in the arm but Fraser managed to take cover in a sentry box from which he shot dead one of the sowars. The rest rode off.

Fraser then got into his buggy and drove off towards the palace. Douglas and the others followed on foot but were attacked. Nixon was killed, but Douglas and Hutchinson escaped by leaping down into the ditch beyond the walls. In the fall Douglas injured his feet and back. But they still had loyal servants hanging about within range, trying not to get involved or be identified as such, and these carried the Englishmen to Douglas's apartments in the Lahore Gate, half a mile away on the west side of the city. There they found that the Delhi chaplain, the Reverend Jennings, and his beautiful and recently engaged daughter, accompanied by her friend, a Miss Clifford, had already arrived seeking more protection than their own place could give them. The domed church of St James, a mini St Paul's, was already occupied by the mob who were plundering the plate, hauling out whatever could be moved, taking even the hassocks. But, for whatever reason, they did not set it alight.

Douglas now sent for the King's advisers and told them to see to the safe removal of the women to the Queen's palace. He also asked for troops and cannon to be sent to protect his and Fraser's lodgings. Fraser went with them, heard the King give his assurances that all this would be done, but on his return to Douglas's apartment he was attacked by a small mob including a jeweller who slashed at him with his tulwar. Fraser attempted to defend himself with his still sheathed sabre but on turning his back he was struck in the neck from behind. Three men rushed out from a doorway and finished Fraser off by cutting him up. One of these men was a member of the King's personal bodyguard; the other two were in the service of his chief minister.

Meanwhile, upstairs, the other fugitives had already been slaughtered apart from Douglas who was now bludgeoned to death. Jennings, his daughter and Miss Clifford had already been butchered. The Commissioner and the Commander of the King's Bodyguard were now dead; the only authority remaining was that of the King, and he himself had to some extent been implicated in the murders. He could now assume authority over the whole city: if the rising was successful he would claim to be emperor. If it was not he could claim that he had taken over in order to save the city from lawlessness and looting.

It is not easy to smash a heavy blade into the angle of collarbone and neck. There may even be a moment when one feels the jarring sensation communicated by blade and hilt to your hand, to draw back, soften the blow, allow the blade to do little more than splinter the clavicle. But to press on without diminishing the force at all, into sternum and scapula, lungs and arteries, to see the blood well up and spill and hear the scream of your victim for as long as he can heave the air from his sliced lungs – none of that is easy, not unless you are trained to it, disciplined to do it, the way cavalry troopers are.

The Meerut butcher who slaughtered Charlotte Chambers knew

what he was doing. Already coarsened by his trade, he had killed many animals in a similar way, but above all he had a personal motive – he had been humiliated by a white woman. The sowar who killed the sergeant at the bridge was following a routine, a drill he had been moulded to, and moreover he was well aware of the sergeant's pistol. But this man, this civilian, this artisan and trader, a jeweller from the bazaar, what maddened him to this extreme? And what of the men who cut down Jennings, his daughter and her friend? What about the hundreds who did as much, and, as will be seen, far worse, in the coming weeks across the Oudh, the Doab and much of Rajpootana?

John Stuart Mill's certainty that English rule conferred immeasurable benefits on the peoples of South Asia echoed the views of the English Establishment. It ignored the racism of the occupiers ('racism' was not yet a word included in dictionaries) and the ruthless not to say patronising way in which the reforms had been implemented; it took no account of arrogance, summary trials and confiscations, of harsh punishments and inadequate rewards. It did not comprehend the abyssal divide between the opposed cultures. Above all, it ignored the invasive intrusion perpetrated on a people who in some cases had been conquered and in others bought and sold, the intrusion into their religious lives. It ignored, in short, the fear, not entirely ungrounded, that the central agendum was the conversion of all to an alien faith. It all added up to a psychic rape and the response of many was hate, a hate that could drive a sword edge through muscle and bone, deep into the living flesh and organs of a person you knew nothing about, save that she or he represented for you those who had raped you.

7.00 A.M.

Meanwhile, on the other side of The Ridge, the Delhi Brigade, all three regiments and the bullock-drawn guns, had been paraded on the maidan by the racecourse. It was not a routine parade. The fifteen hundred men were drawn up in close order, with colours uncased, forming three sides of an inward facing square. The senior British officers stood between the jaws around the flagpole from which the Union flag was tossed and turned by a building hot breeze, a gusty affair on which the hooded crows slipped and soared. Dust swirled although the bheesties had been out at daybreak trying to lay it by scattering water from their water bags and jars.

Because the regimental interpreter was off sick it fell to Captain Robert Tytler, a tall, heavily built man in his thirties, fluent in Hindi, to mount the low rostrum and deliver what was the main reason for this full parade, namely a General Order announcing the execution of Subaltern Issuree Pandy who had been hanged three weeks earlier. To his surprise and discomfort the men shuffled their feet so that the dust rose to their knees and through clenched teeth they began to hiss. The noise rose like a head of steam escaping and in the rear files the shuffle became a fast rhythmic stamping. The business of the parade was hurried through and the men dismissed. Inwardly disturbed, Tytler hurried back to his bungalow. On the surface he experienced an angry feeling of affront, which did not quite overlay a deeper, cold apprehension. He burst in on his wife Harriet declaring he'd give the men under his command a morning of drill till they dropped with exhaustion.

Harriet, with two infants to look after and another on the way, busied herself trying to alleviate the effects of the hot wind. She directed and helped her servants to put up dampened tatties at all the windows, bathed the children, saw breakfast served to them and her French maid, then sat down with her husband. Just as they were finishing a dessert of melon their tailor rushed in: 'Sahib, mem, the army has come,' he cried, clasping and wringing his nervous hands. It was not the forerunners of twenty or so sowars he was referring to but the main body of the 3rd Light Cavalry and the vanguard of the Meerut infantry.

9.45 A.M.

Azimullah was, for a time, like a small boy seeing a particularly momentous dare, one which would bring horrendous punishments if it were uncovered, working itself out just as he had planned it. But so far he had not left the Red Fort, finding in the milling throng that filled the grounds enough to keep him there in the way of excitement as news came in of how, regiment by regiment, battery by battery, the army was killing its officers and proclaiming itself the servant of the

167

King-Emperor. Eventually he crossed the courts to the Diwan-I-Khas, the Hall of Private Audiences, to watch how Bahadur, with some skill, prevaricated and dithered.

In the courtyard that lay in front of the Judgement Throne the King was faced with an unruly crowd of sowars and sepoys, about a hundred of them, all shouting and loosing off their muskets. By occupying the magnificent marble seat he was able to get some order, enough to hear how a spokesmen from the 3rd Light Cavalry claimed they were ordered to bite cartridges greased with pork and beef fat and how they had killed all the Europeans in Meerut and that they had come to put themselves under the King's protection. Behind them the area filled up with more and more of the newly arrived Meerut infantry. The King cleared his throat, dabbed at his rheumy eyes, concealed the calculation that was going on behind them.

'I did not call for you,' he rasped; 'what you have done is very wicked.' His voice, though frail, was pitched so that witnesses would hear what he had said and remember it.

'Unless you join us, we are all dead men,' the leader of the sowars replied.

The King said nothing, but with a slight nod encouraged the men to come forward one by one and kneel in front of him and he placed his hand on each bowed head.

Azi admired his skill. 'That was very well done indeed,' he murmured as he turned away.

10.00 A.M.

But now he wanted to be nearer the action if not in the thick of it, and he moved off towards the Lahore Gate.

Making his way west along the Chandni Chouk, the main shopping street of the city, he was almost immediately able to catch the reins of a riderless horse, a white charger that carried him for the rest of the day. He headed north towards the Civil Lines and St James's Church. From the horse's back he saw the litter of bodies between the Main Guard and the church and over to his right how the treasury had already been broken into. But it dawned on him that the magazine, over to his left, was, just then, the more important place. If the mutineers could capture it intact they would put many months' worth of powder, small arms and the rest into Native hands and at the same time deprive the Queen's regiments at Umballa. Pulling his horse round he cantered past the thirty-foot-high brick warehouse with its one big gate, back towards the fort, and soon came on what he was looking for – a section or so of the palace guard looting the house of some departed British nabob.

Azimullah, on his white horse, in his tall Parsee hat called a *khoka* and made of glazed chintz, his neat and spotless dark coat with a small collar, immaculate white baggy trousers tucked into shiny half-boots, was clearly a person of some importance. Some of the men actually recognised him, knew him as someone who moved around the more hidden of the palace apartments, was on familiar terms with all but the grandest officials as well as being the vakil of the putative Peshwa of the Marathas. They mounted, formed up and trotted behind him, lances with fluttering pennants upright. Azimullah reined in in front of the magazine's gate and on his command the havildar in charge of the section unholstered his carbine and banged on it with the butt.

Inside, a garrison had collected in the courtyard under the command of the Commissary of Ordnance, Lieutenant George Willoughby, a shy, hitherto undistinguished officer. He was short, fat, wore his hair parted low on the side providing a combover to conceal his incipient baldness. He also cultivated four moustaches, two on his cheekbones, two above his top lip. With him were two veteran officers, Lieutenants Forrest and Raynor, fifty-one and sixty-one years old respectively, and six British employees of the Ordnance Department. There was also a handful of Native assistants who clearly would have preferred to be elsewhere.

'In the name of the King, who demands it from you, I command you to surrender the magazine.' Azimullah hardly raised his voice – it was more than his dignity would allow, yet those inside heard him well enough.

Raynor clutched Willoughby's sleeve.

'Don't answer him, George,' he hissed.

'I wasn't going to,' Willoughby replied.

Azimullah repeated the order, again received no answer, so he turned his little troop round and trotted back to the Red Fort. It took him some time to get together what he wanted: a couple of companies of Native Infantry, drawn this time from the 11th and 20th, both

Meerut regiments, along with twelve scaling ladders tall enough to reach the outside roofs of the magazine. Once these were up the first people to use them were the Native assistants to the Ordnance Department, who, as soon as they knew they were in place, climbed up on to the sloping thatched roofs that covered a verandah on the inside of the magazine, and, given hands by the sepoys on the outside of the rooftree, clambered up and over and down the ladders. This left just nine British to defend the place. They had two six-pounders loaded with grape covering the double gates and four smaller guns which they trained on the roof. Conductor Buckley of the Ordnance and Lieutenants Forrest and Raynor serviced these, firing grape at the roof in spite of a hail of musket fire that was poured down on them. At some point roundabout then Willoughby went to the main gate and demanded to know who had authorised the attack and who was commanding it.

Azimullah seized the chance.

'The King gave the order and a son and a grandson of the King are in command.' Thus implicating Bahadur.

Convinced that they could not hold out for much longer and that the magazine would most certainly fall into the mutineers' hands – indeed, with the King on their side, it now seemed much more than a mutiny – Willoughby laid powder trails from the main office to the powder stores. A little later Buckley was hit in the arm and Forrest in the hand and were no longer able to service the guns. Willoughby gave the order. Conductor Scully volunteered to carry it out which he did coolly, calmly, without hesitation. The explosion was one of the biggest ever to have occurred.

Forrest, Buckley and Raynor were awarded the Victoria Cross. Scully, who was blown to pieces, and Willoughby, who was murdered that evening by peasants while trying to make his way back to Meerut, were not – at that early time in its history it was not awarded posthumously. An unknown number of sepoys outside the magazine were also blown apart, and many more suffered horrendous burns.

12.00 NOON, OR THEREABOUTS

Forty miles away, outside Meerut, Sophie Hardcastle was still wandering through fields and woods outside the town, calling Stephen's

170

name but with more weariness than before, more a lapwing-like cry than a curlew's. Peee-wit. Steee-phen. The noise, deep and thundery though brief and distant, rolled across the land, assaulted her ears and rolled on. The Day of Judgement? She hoped so. But no angel appeared to sound the last trumpet.

24

The Grand Trunk Road, 11 May 1857

By midday at that time of year the great road was almost deserted. Habitual users, villagers selling and buying in markets in the larger towns, left home at three or four o'clock in the morning, in pitch dark, starlight or moonlight – most knew the way and anyway, once on the road, could hardly lose it. And they aimed to be back by nine or ten, as by then the thermometer (not that any had one) would be nudging a hundred and rising fast, with the hot breeze making the dust storms whirl like dervishes across the fields. Any water that remained in irrigation ditches or the rivulets that fed the broad Ganges ten miles away was brackish and infested with mosquito larvae. In dried-up clumps of reeds or in the shadow of boulders, small black venomous water snakes hid from motionless buzzards that hung on the thermals a thousand feet above them.

Standing in what shade an almost leafless acacia offered, with her three and a half year old child on her left arm, and her saree pulled in a hood over her head, Lavanya and Deepika looked like nothing so much as a Mother and Child by Raphael. Although Deepika was far slighter than any Raphaelesque bambino, she had the same curly black hair above luminous dark eyes. Lavanya's high forehead, the prominent cheekbones, the eyes and mouth that smiled out at you if you were passing, made you want to reward her beauty with a gift.

The effect was somewhat spoiled by the begging bowl she thrust towards passers-by. It was a simple biscuit-fired piece of terracotta with a large triangle knocked out of its rim, no doubt the reason why

172

it had been thrown into the ditch where Lavanya had found it. In it she had a half-anna piece (one thirty-second of a rupee), three dried-up, rock-hard chappatis, and a wrinkled crimson mango with a bite taken out of it.

There were just two other people in sight. A large zebu cow the colour of cheese, with the floppy hump on its neck and spreading horns, was being slowly prodded towards her by an oldish woman, very brown, but the deep reddish colour more the result of the sun beating down out of forty or fifty Doab summer skies than a genetic trait. They, the cow and she, were coming up from the south, from the direction of Cawnpore, still two hundred and thirty miles away. It was the man coming from the other direction, from Meerut, still only fifteen miles back, who would reach Lavanya first. He had a small grubby turban, a very long white beard that set off the darkness of his eye sockets and his thin toothless mouth, wore a dhoti only and carried a thin teak pole, polished at shoulder height by the constant motion of his skeletal right hand. He was clearly no fakir or sadhu but an old man who had entered sannyasa, the last of the ashramas, the state when a man, having performed all household and public duties, turns his back on everything, including even his name, and walks out into the world with nothing, living on what he is given, or, if he chooses to, what he can find in gutters and roadsides, until he dies.

He walked a pace or two past Lavanya, and then turned back.

'I need food, and drink,' she said. 'Not for me.'

She looked down at Deepika.

'Buy some milk from this lady with her cow.'

'I have no money.'

He laughed gently.

'No more have I.'

With a sad smile he set off again, then paused, and shifted the dust at his feet with the end of his pole. A small sun winked back at the big one. A shard of light. He turned again and his smile was less sad. Lavanya put down the bowl and scampered across to it. She almost knelt on one knee as she lowered herself over it, carefully balancing herself to disturb Deepika as little as possible, and scooped it up. One silver rupee, worth nearly a shilling and more than a day's wage for a man.

Presently the sannyasi crossed paths with the old lady and her cow, and perhaps he muttered something to her for when she reached

Lavanya she halted, straightened her back, used the hem of her saree to wipe off sweat and dust, and smiled.

'I can sell you some milk,' she said, glancing down at her cow's small but full udder, 'but I have no vessel to put it in.'

Together they scouted along the roadside ditch until they came to a boarded-up shack with a heap of broken pottery behind it. When open it served masala milk and most of the pottery, some of it whole, was in the shape of the tiny cups that users threw away, but there were some broken jugs that could have held, when in one piece, as much as a pint. The best they could find had lost much of one side, but, tilted so that the other side was underneath, it held a good cupful. Back to the cow. It took only four squirts, one on each teat, to release enough to fill it. Lavanya showed the woman her two coins.

'One half-anna is not enough, and I cannot change your rupee. All right, I'll take the half-anna.'

Lacking the four arms of Durga, the Mother-Goddess in her warrior manifestation, Lavanya now had a problem: how to carry a bowl, a jug and an infant without spilling the milk or waking the child. She found that, with difficulty, she could rather awkwardly carry the bowl in the fingers of her left hand and still keep Deepika comfortable, while holding the full jug in her right in front of her torso and keeping a watchful eye on the tilt of the white liquid so that it remained an eighth of an inch below the rim. I mustn't stumble, she said to herself; I must not stumble, she repeated as the sweat from her forehead began to tip down the bridge of her nose and into her eyes.

A hundred yards back towards Meerut a brook, still with a trickle of water in it, passed under the road through a brickwork vaulted tunnel whose roof at the widest point was nearly three feet above the stream's bed and whose width was about two yards. It had been built by order of the British some five years earlier when the improvements to the Grand Road were carried out under Dalhousie, to ensure that the village a mile away on the other side would continue to enjoy the benefits of the stream as it meandered across the plain towards the Ganges.

But now, dropping down to the riverbed and the tunnel there was a steep bank of stones and rubble to negotiate, partly held together by dried grasses and the roots of weeds. Lavanya managed to sit at the top. A couple of tiny brown moths rose from the grasses and fluttered about her head. She considered a controlled slide on her backside but guessed her saree would slide up, exposing her legs if she did. Maybe worse. In the end she looked as far as was possible all round her, making sure there was no one in sight, and then called out in as gentle a voice as she could manage.

'Adam.'

No response. Louder this time.

'Adam?'

Then, making it an order, a command.

'Adam!'

A high whisper, amplified by the tunnel, answered her at last.

'Who is it?'

'Lavanya.'

'What do you want?'

'Some help, you idiot. Come out.'

A rattle of gravel, a small splashing sound, a cough and a grunt and the eleven-year-old came out on all fours, no hat, hair tousled, sailor suit muddied. He looked up at her, blinked, and as he straightened up shielded his eyes with the flattened palm of his hand, very sailor-like.

'What do you want?'

'Take this milk. And whatever you do, don't spill it.'

He climbed a boulder or two, reached up, took the jug, turned away. Lavanya got to the bottom without any more help and then saw what he was doing: he was drinking the milk.

'You monster,' she cried. 'Stop it. Now.'

He finished it, wiped his white moustache away with the back of his hand, made as if to hand the jug back to her but she still held the bowl in her free hand. His eyes hardened into a wary stare, his mouth became a tight slit. Dare you.

She did. She put the bowl down behind her and fast as a snake strike, so that he really did not see it coming, slapped his face as hard as she could. He hurled himself at her, punching towards her stomach so that she had to swing Deepika around out of harm's way. With her free hand she caught the front of his head and pushed with the force of a blow so that he stumbled back and fell heavily on stones, baked mud and sharp dried grasses. His face crumpled, the defiance and anger melting away, but he did not cry. English boys eleven years of age did not cry, not where they could be seen to do so. But he was sick, vomiting up all the milk he had drunk.

By now Deepika was crying, and the rest of the children had crawled out of the tunnel. Emma aged six and Stephen, a few weeks younger than Deepika, were crying too. Miranda, nine, and Robert, five, held hands and looked on, eyes wide with wonder and terror. Then Miranda shouted.

'You shouldn't have done that. You should not have hit him!'

Lavanya looked down and over them all and screamed.

'Shut up, shut up, shut up!'

They stopped and at that moment the same boom that Sophie was hearing shook the air around them.

25

Calcutta, Delhi, Calcutta, 12–14 May 1857

Draughts, huge draughts of hot air like spectral balls of cotton wool, gusted – no, rolled – down the high corridors of Government House or scurried off into the narrower passages, lifting carpets, playing fey carillons on the chandeliers or swinging on the hanging candelabra. Wherever a writer, or clerk, had forgotten to place a paperweight sheets of paper were launched to float briskly like leaves or snag on the legs of chairs, desks and tables. Here and there, where the currents eddied back into the halls and larger chambers, they performed slow cartwheels across the wider spaces. The governing of India required a lot of paper.

The three storeys of serried floor-to-ceiling windows along every wall and wing could be closed to turn the place into an oven, or left open to make something we might recognise as an oven, but fan-assisted. Water-soaked tatties could lower the temperature by evaporation but required an endless procession of bheesties with ladles and huge water containers to pass through the council chambers and offices, adding a humidity which prefigured the all-pervading dampness, wetness, of the monsoon months which were still to come.

In spite of all this, Lady Canning, very much aware of her duties as the wife of the Governor General of a sub-continent, was receiving five ladies whose husbands belonged to the Society for the Propagation of Christian Knowledge. Two were Eurasian and three were white, and all came from the families who made up an unofficial aristocracy in Calcutta, the ones whose white forebears had been there before 1757, Clive and Plassey. Being women, they had little influence on the running of the Society, yet all were of the opinion that their husbands, pillars of commerce and industry, were wrong not to support the foundation of a hospital for foundlings. The men claimed that such a hospital would, in ways the good ladies found difficult to comprehend, encourage vice. The ladies' view was that starving or diseased foundlings, nursed back to health and then placed with good Christian families, would become exemplars and possibly proselytisers of the Faith that had saved them.

'Thus fulfilling the object of the Society,' declared one magnificently sareed lady with an Aryan 'wheaten' complexion and a noble face lined by several decades of holy living, 'which I am sure your ladyship will recall is "to counteract the growth of vice and immorality ascribed to ignorance of the principles of the Christian religion".'

'Ye-e-es,' Lady Canning replied, 'but surely the SPCK fulfils this worthy aim through the printing and distribution of Christian writings . . .'

Her voice tailed off as she turned her head to one side seeking to capture and interpret sounds hitherto unfamiliar to her within the palace: feet pounding up stairs, across the Throne Room and into Carlo's study on the far side. A shout as a second came behind the first.

'Surely, ma'am, the object is being achieved by any means the good Lord is placing in our hands . . .'

A call, her husband's voice, distant but clear, calling for Tomkins, one of his private secretaries, then a bang like a pistol shot as a big heavy door was flung shut by the hot wind.

'I'm still not entirely convinced that the SPCK is the right channel through which your enterprise might be forwarded. Please don't misunderstand me. I think your idea a very good one. I'll speak to the Bishop of course, but also to the chief medical officer, if you think that would help . . .'

She glanced at the neat little clock, a present from Louis Napoleon, and then the everlasting calendar displayed in a rosewood cylinder which, so long as one remembered to make the adjustment each morning, revealed the date and day of the week. Twenty-five past eleven, Tuesday, 12 May. The ladies took the hint and gathered into themselves their reticules, their skirts and petticoats, and adjusted their hats. Lady Canning rang a small handbell; a Native footman in scarlet livery appeared and led them out.

She followed them to the small landing and stood in the doorway to the Throne Room, looked down it past serried small tables, carved in a clumsy, overdecorated recollection of rococo, the giant fern set in a huge vase of fluted glass, very Great Exhibition in feeling, the plump chairs covered with chintz, the printed cotton reimported from Manchester, and, halfway down the outer wall, the throne itself with its red velvet canopy and curtains, trimmed and tasselled with gold. At the far end was the door to another landing, another staircase, and the corridor to the room where Carlo did all his work. As she stood there she heard more feet on the further stairs and here came her husband's nephew, Lord Dunkellin, the Military Secretary.

'This,' she said to herself as she turned back to her own rooms, 'is serious. Well, no doubt I'll be told what it's all about at tiffin.'

With no further audiences that morning, she turned her attention to the day's post.

Tiffin they took together, usually, apart from a butler and a footman, on their own and unattended. They were an affectionate couple with boundless respect for each other's good qualities. Both had aged well, very well by the standards of the time; she, thirty-eight years old, still quite beautiful in a restrained way, he, even with his baldness, quite handsome, and neither of them, which was unusual, especially in a gentlewoman, at all fat. Physically attractive therefore, both, but nevertheless their relationship was now based on quiet but firm friendship. She had had no children. He probably had, and he was neither particularly discreet nor choosy about whom he had affairs with. These had hurt her to begin with, but, as soon as she realised how quickly one amour would be succeeded by the next, the pain had become a thing resignation could cope with.

'So,' she asked, spreading a napkin across her knees and dipping her spoon into a shallow bowl of mulligatawny soup, 'what was all that about? The commotion this morning?'

'Mutiny,' he replied and sipped from a glass of soda water, 'in Meerut. Sunday evening. The mutineers cut the telegraph wire and it wasn't in place again until this morning. Bad business, very bad. The Native regiments killed their officers and some of their wives and children too, it seems, and went off to Delhi. They didn't attack

179

our lines, and for some reason the Queen's regiments didn't get after them. Don't know much more than that at the moment though I fear strongly it may have spread to Delhi.'

More came out, in the way of speculation than hard fact, during the rest of a meal that was light and short by Victorian standards.

'I confess I'm somewhat bewildered. It's now several months since the cartridge question came up and I felt we had dealt with it. I have no reason to suppose that the orders I issued forbidding the use of animal fats in the making of the cartridges have not been obeyed. The issue of Enfield rifles has been limited to one British regiment so far. The childish rumours that bone meal had been mixed with flour were scotched. So. What's it all about? For the time being we've decided to wait and see . . . What sort of a morning have you had? I trust you saw off the SPCK ladies satisfactorily?'

By tiffin time the same day Delhi had collapsed into anarchy. Looting and arson continued in the areas of the city occupied by Christians, many of them Eurasian, many of them merchants, bankers, money-lenders. There were riots in the poorer sections of the city because the grain merchants had refused to issue grain or flour to the bakers, preferring to keep their premises secure behind locked iron gates. Bahadur, wearing jewelled robes, rode through the streets in a canopied and tasselled howdah on the back of a richly caparisoned elephant, ordering the merchants to open their shops. His commands were ignored but his appearance, a very rare occurrence since the British preferred him to remain behind the walls of the Red Fort, and anyway he had had no inclination to leave the scented halls, kitchens and libraries of his palace, was welcomed by the mob. They hailed him, not just as King of Delhi but as Emperor.

Tucked away in his bare room, with its peeling walls and troupe of performing geckoes, Azimullah stood at the window and watched events unfold. But when the sun, reddened by the smoke of fires to a deep scarlet like the flesh of a pomegranate or watermelon, dipped over the battlements to the west, turning their red silhouettes to black and the marble pavilions to a livid, corpse-like hue, when ser-vants appeared with torches which they fixed to brackets set in the walls, Azimullah slipped out of his room and worked his way through the thinning crowds and into the corridors of the palace. He spoke to ministers, Brahmins, imams and even the Queen. Briefly he even managed to whisper a word or two in the ear of Bahadur himself. Meanwhile, the torches, fuelled with bitumen, spattered sparks and flared beneath plumes of black smoke.

Next day, the thirteenth, the King became an emperor. At about nine o'clock a small crowd drawn from the hangers-on who inhabited the old buildings just inside the wall and the shantytown between them and the palaces, directed by Azimullah and stiffened by hired badmashes, gathered in front of the Throne of Judgement in the colonnade of the Diwan-I-Am. A regiment of Native Infantry was marched in behind the tank and and was later joined by a battery of horse artillery. There followed a half-hour of nothing, broken only by the cawing of hooded crows that wheeled up every now and then from the almost flat roof of the long pavilion. The crowd had to be discouraged from drifting back to their tumbledown dwellings by badmashes wielding bludgeons.

Then, at last, a brass horn note, high and fluking, was joined by others, until at least five had joined in a raucous, barbaric fanfare heralding a troop of ceremoniously dressed horsemen, all mounted on white ponies held into a prancing trot, their riders holding lances with pennants that fluttered above their cockaded turbans. Their slow dance took them to the space below the steps between the throne and the crowd, where, with a little jostling and pushing, they made a line. Bahadur appeared at last, emerging from a group of solemn Brahmins to take his place on the throne. He was now quite high up, beneath the ornately carved white marble baldacchin set against the russet stone of the vaulted colonnade, and from a distance of, say, fifteen paces or more, looked quite imposing, in a doll-like way.

All that could be seen of him, that was really him, were the large eyes, the long, slightly hooked nose between high cheekbones, the thin mouth, the soft white beard, for once neatly trimmed. The rest was a magnificent red robe trimmed with pearls set in small leaf shapes, a sable stole or scarf, and two gold chains set with pearls supporting pendants. The nearer of these to his neck was a large pink diamond which may or may not have been the legendary Agra diamond. On his head he wore a high cap of six arched panels set above a circle, all crusted with diamonds, emeralds, rubies and pendant pearls. On the front of it there was a cockade, but not a feather one: this was a fan of silver wires crusted with diamond chips.

For a moment or two there was silence. Nothing stirred. Then, here and there, some of the crowd again began to edge away as if from a show that was over. Azimullah himself broke the silence. Putting his spread palms to his mouth to make a bell of them, he bellowed: 'Long life to Bahadur Shah, the Mogul, the Emperor of the Trans-Indus.' The badmashes came to as if suddenly reminded why they were there and took up the cry, the trumpets brayed again, and at last the cannon began to fire, bang, bang, bang-bang, bang, a twenty-one-gun salute. The marionette on the throne rose, lifted its right hand and acknowledged the crowd with a small circular wave, then, like an insubstantial vision, faded into shadows the colour of dried blood.

Azimullah turned away. He was pleased, almost ecstatic, at the success of his manipulations though he was intelligent enough to realise that he had done no more than nudge history a little, caused events to include him in them. Now, he thought, he had better get back to Bithur and the Nana. Make sure he too came up to scratch.

The telegrams from Agra continued to arrive through 13 and 14 May but for the most part up to twenty-four hours behind the events they reported.

Yes, Delhi had risen. The British and Christians had been massacred apart from a few who had escaped, some towards Meerut, others more directly north towards Karnal and Umballa. Bahadur Shah – had he been proclaimed Emperor? Canning sat at his desk, sideways on to it as he often did, elbow resting on it, legs crossed, ankle on his knee, cheek supported on his left hand as he read telegrams, commands, reports, and drafted replies. Writers came in with sheafs of more and more papers, more telegrams, lists of troops and *matériel*, positions of ships in ports, estimated positions of those at sea. They were by now supremely careful about how they opened and closed the high panelled doors to minimise the risk of that pestilential, possibly pestilence-bearing, whirlwind from scattering them to kingdom come. They knocked, and waited before entering while a footman behind Canning closed the glazed doors that opened on to the balcony, whose pillars at either end framed the view of the Grand Maidan and Fort William beyond.

The position was becoming clearer. If the mutiny spread then a double daisy chain of stations and cities would be lost for there was hardly a British unit to be found along the cat's cradle of rivers that flowed from the north-west, from Delhi to Barrackpore, or on the Grand Trunk Road that threaded its way through the rivers. Bareilly, Cawnpore, Lucknow, Allahabad, Benares, Dinapore . . . just three European regiments divided into five units, two near Calcutta, one at Dinapore, and one each at Lucknow and Agra. Would it spread? If the King of Delhi allowed himself to be declared Emperor then it would. On the fourteenth the telegram arrived and Canning knew then that the mutiny would become an uprising. He called for a map of north India, the best that could be found, and the decisions he had been considering for forty-eight hours began to flow.

He went through it all with Charlotte over a bedtime pot of tea in the Brown Drawing Room, the position of which corresponded to his study in the opposite wing. They only entertained personal guests in it and for the most part kept it as a private domain for their own use.

He settled himself into the big buttoned cinnamon leather armchair in front of her and, fingertips together, watched her as she poured the tea. She placed his cup on his side of a brown gate-leg table as intricately carved as the one in Mr Mill's room in Leadenhall Street.

'I am considering,' he began, 'that it might be necessary to send you home. With the wives of those members of our staff who have their spouses with them.'

She set down the silver teapot and looked across the table at her husband.

'Do what you like with the others,' she said. 'But I'm staying.'

'I thought you would say that.'

'You'll have to tie me up and put me in a bag before I'll set foot on a boat without you.' She spoke gently, but firmly. 'You have no head for domestic matters or even public events unconnected with what you take to be your real duties. Apart from any other considerations, you need me here.'

Silence for a minute or so. With nightfall the hot wind had dropped at last.

'May the twenty-fifth, for instance.'

'What's special about the twenty-fifth?'

'Carlo, come on! The Queen's Birthday? The State Ball? Invitations must go out tomorrow or the day after at the latest. Or do we cancel?'

Another moment of reflection.

'No. We do not cancel.'

'Good. Leave it to me. I'll see it doesn't get to be a bother for you, though I do think you should put in an appearance.'

A longer pause now as they both sat and felt the enormous weight of the catastrophe upon them.

'You'll use force to crush the whole thing before it spreads,' she asked, summing up everything he had said.

'That's the idea. Earth-shaking force if that's what is needed to restore things to what they were. The first step is to take Delhi and I've ordered Anson and Wilson to combine to do that. If they can manage that, and potential mutineers know that more British troops are arriving from the north, up the Ganges from the east, and from Madras in the south, then I think we can hope the whole thing will subside.'

'What about causes?'

'The cartridges? There are no cartridges with animal grease.'

'Carlo, the cartridges are a symptom only. They believe, they really do believe, we intend to force Christianity on them, one way or another.'

Canning thought this over for a moment, tired head slumped forward, fingers drumming on the arms of the huge chair.

'You are right, of course. But what can I do about that? In the short term?'

'A proclamation declaring it is not your intention to do or even allow anything of the sort.'

He looked up, smiled across the low table at her.

'I'll do just that. Draft the thing tomorrow.'

And that was it, for the moment, as far as the Mutiny was concerned. She told him about the personal mail she had had, news of the London Season getting under way, what cousins and nephews and nieces were getting up to.

'And a very jolly letter from Vicky. Sends her regards.'

'Her Madge . . .' he laughed but there was pride in it, too, that he had a wife who could call Victoria Vicky.

He finished his tea, stood up, as did she, and he kissed her on the cheek.

'God bless you, Lottie. Couldn't manage without you.'

And they went to their separate bedrooms.

The Governor General knows that endeavours are made
to persuade Hindoos and Mussulmans, soldiers and civil

subjects, that their religions are threatened secretly, as well as openly, by the acts of Government and that the government is seeking in various ways to entrap them into a loss of caste for purposes of its own. Some have already been deceived by such tales . . . The government has invariably treated the religious feelings of all its subjects with careful respect . . . and will continue to do so . . . It is the government's earnest hope that all persons of habitual loyalty and orderly conduct will not listen to false guides and traitors, who would lead them into danger and disgrace . . .

PART IV

An Eye for an Eye

26

The Grand Trunk Road, near Meerut to Cawnpore,
11–30 May 1857

The humiliating and painful shove that Lavanya gave Adam in a ditch beside the Grand Trunk Road worked well as a punishment and a warning, but it did more than that. It transmuted Lavanya in Adam's eyes, and in those of Miranda, the elder of his sisters, from being a nigger, a servant, a nuisance, a *thing*, into a person, a human and even, since she was only just eighteen and small for her age by European standards – indeed she was only an inch or so taller than Adam – *one of them*. That is to say, while remaining a Native, she became not only human but a child, older than them, yes, but definitely not a grown-up. Grown-ups arbitrarily tell servants what to do, issuing often irrational, pointless commands and punishing any attempt to question them – but that too is what they do to children. And while they may resort to punishments, quite often physical punishments, from a slap to a more formal whacking with a slipper, grown-ups do not mill with you. And that, most certainly, was what Adam and Lavanya had involved each other in – a mill, what, twenty years later, would be called a scrap.

The distant boom of the exploding magazine, forty miles away, which they took to be thunder, rumbled quickly to nothing and for a moment Adam looked up at Lavanya, blinked away the tears he had not let fall before wiping the last traces of vomited milk from his mouth and chest with his sleeve.

'I'm sorry,' he said. 'Especially about the milk.'

He struggled to his feet and began to brush and pull at the twigs that stuck in the back of the knickerbockers he was wearing beneath his sailor's smock. It was an excuse not to look her in the eye as he summoned up the spirit needed to say what he wanted to say next. At last he looked over his shoulder at her.

'Can we be friends?'

She was still on the bank a little above him. Knuckles on her hips, elbows spread, she looked down at him.

'Yes, but I am the oldest and I am in charge,' she said in her singsong but firm way, mixing Hindi with English. 'If I am telling you to do something, and there is being no time to talk about it, you are doing what I am saying.'

'All right.'

'And the little ones, the two little ones, come first.'

'And Robert too?' he insisted, asserting a say in it all, rather than out of concern for the youngest Dixon who was after all only two years older than Deepa and Stephen.

Lavanya nodded and then ran down the ditch to catch Deepika who was splashing through what water there was and heading out into the fields, but Miranda got there first, took the infant's hand and led her back. Lavanya cradled her in the crook of her arm, her hand supporting the child's thigh, with Deepika's arm round her neck and her head on a level with her mother's, black hair falling halfway down her back. She looked out over her mother's shoulder at the flat plains and the road that seemed to lead to eternity. Stephen and Emma remained below them, but, thumbs in mouths, looked up at them. Adam and Miranda scrambled up to her level. Robert whined.

'I'm hungry.'

'Shut up, Rob,' said Adam.

'Won't.'

But he did.

'Do you think we should go back home?' Adam asked.

Lavanya thought about it. The idea was tempting. But then she reflected on the events of the night. The Natives, her people, had been killing the feringhees, women and children as well as men. If it was a battle it was one that they were winning. And they had fired cannons at her and the children, had come after them with bayonets.

'No,' she said. 'My people will kill us. Kill you anyway.'

'What then?'

'I think we should walk away from Meerut until we come to a place where your people are alive, in charge, can look after you. But first we must be finding something to eat and drink.'

She looked over them, one by one, assessing their chances. Adam and Emma took after Lieutenant Dixon who was fair, fair of skin, had sandy hair. Their mother, Catherine, had black hair, almost as black as her own and a somewhat sallow complexion, quite dark where it had been exposed over several years to the Indian sun, but still very white where it had remained covered. Miranda was like that. Robert was sort of halfway between the two. Miranda alone of the Dixon children might be passed off as a Native. Stephen Hardcastle had the sort of fair hair that would soon be quite dark but because both his mother and Lavanya had allowed him to play out in the sun when they were in Simla, often in only his napkin, his skin was quite brown albeit more red than a Native child's. And, of course, all five of them were wearing European clothes.

They would be safe, she decided, only if they walked at night, away from Meerut, using the road as a guide, or even walking on it. Even without Native clothes they should be all right at night. When it became light, and the road filled with travellers, the fairer children would have to hide up in ditches or topes, groves of mangoes, with Adam looking after them, while she, Deepa and Miranda went looking for food and anything else they might need. And they would go on like that until they found a place where the feringhees were in charge and there they would give themselves up.

She explained all this. When she had finished, Miranda had just one question, one she had already asked.

'Do you think Mummy and Daddy are dead?'

Lavanya thought about it. She remembered her last sight of Stephen's father, standing in the yard between the two burning bungalows, the flame light playing over his frantic face and body, his now useless hunting gun hanging from his right hand, pain and fear and indecision chasing each other across his face, the sepoys and rioters, dancing dark figures against the burning buildings, closing in.

'I think so,' she said at last. Then more hurriedly: 'They may not be. And if they are not then once you are safe with your people, they will find you. Now I am going to try again to find you something to eat and drink. Go back in the pipe and keep very quiet if you hear

191

anyone coming. Adam is in charge and you two must do whatever he says.'

She climbed back on to the road, looked both ways. It was completely deserted, a white arrow narrowing to a vanishing point with almost no shade on it, since, although it was edged with an avenue of acacias, it ran north to south. Out of the ditch the midday heat was now like a blow, but she knew how to arrange her saree and Deepa's gown to minimise its effects. But after a hundred yards Miranda, in her European clothes, began to pant, sweat running down her face.

'I'm too hot,' she gasped.

'All right. Go back to the others. But tell them I will come back. I promise.'

After twenty minutes she could make out, perhaps a further twenty minutes' walk away, a small white bungalow set back from the acacias. She guessed what it was – a dâk bungalow, a stage for the post, probably the last before Meerut, the last of a chain that stretched, one every twenty miles or so, back to Calcutta.

As she got nearer Lavanya realised that nothing was right about the place. Even when she was still ten minutes away she could hear a mule bellowing, possibly in pain. Before she reached it she could see, and smell, a miasma of black haze that hung above the flat roof, and the black soot marks above the front windows and the door.

Having travelled to and from Simla she knew about these bungalows. They were generally manned by a loyal retired sepoy with a good service record or occasionally by a retired British soldier, especially if during a score of years as a sergeant in the Company army he had married or formed a liaison with a Native woman. Such men were often loth to return to England where their pensions would be inadequate and most of their old acquaintance and family dead or moved.

As she approached the bungalow she sensed it was empty of people. There was a picket gate, a short gravel path leading to a small square porch garlanded with a climbing briar rose that had been well watered and still carried some blooms. The door itself had been smashed open taking with it the jamb to which it had been locked. The smell of burnt house was now very strong but undercut with other, nastier odours, and she became aware of a powerful, unvarying buzzing. Flies. She crossed the threshold into a small vestibule. Four doors off it, two on each side, and on the wall facing her a hand-coloured engraving of the still young Queen with a child in her lap. The large heavily lidded eyes set in a softly rounded face, with dark hair pulled back, the generous lips and the fact that the colourist had given her skin a quite dusky shade all gave her the look of, no, not a ranee, a ranee would have been crusted in jewels, but maybe the wife of a prosperous Bombay merchant.

The dakooa was in the first room to the left, clearly his office, with a counter and a broken stool. The impedimenta of his occupation – scales, brass weights, pens and an inkwell, a money box opened and empty – had been swept to the floor around him. As the flies rose from his neck she saw that he had indeed been a feringhee: his sightless blue eyes stared up at her from a red face; white hair, white moustaches, a big man but quite old. His throat had been cut and the rest of his body was marked with sword slashes and stab wounds. Lavanya pulled back and turned to the room opposite. This had been the living room and the scene was even more horrible for here the postman's family had been butchered. Nearest the door, between it and her children, the Native wife and mother lay on a sofa, with arms up protectively across her face, dead by the same means as her husband but mutilated too, with breasts and hands cut off. After a moment Lavanya dared to look behind the sofa and found what she had feared, two children, about six and four years old, one boy, one girl, both clumsily decapitated although they still embraced each other with shattered arms.

She staggered out to the porch again, set Deepa down and sank on to the step beneath the roses; then her body suddenly and uncontrollably heaved from the pit of her stomach up to her throat. She couldn't vomit, only a mouthful of yellow bitter bile – it was eighteen hours since she had eaten – but after that first heave she was racked and twisted with sobs that would not stop for several minutes. Eventually she felt a pull on her shoulder.

'Poor children,' said Deepika. 'Poor, poor children.'

Lavanya got a grip on herself as soon as she realised that what had been unfathomably horrible for the British dakooa and his family might prove to be the saving of her and the six children in her care. In the back room, which had been a bedroom for the entire family, there were a small chest of drawers and a larger tallboy, both smashed, their contents strewn about the floor, as well as two beds. Drapes and broken furniture had been set alight, but were now merely smouldering. The adults' clothes had been taken but there were small sarees for the dead girl and tunics with baggy trousers for the boy. She gathered all she could find that might be of use into one big bundle. In the kitchen, opposite the bedroom, she found a fourteen-pound sack of flour, almost full, and some day-old chappatis, dry and brittle but edible. She stacked all these by the door and then, taking Deepa's hand, went round into the small yard at the back.

The stabling was empty – clearly the murderous looters had taken the two or three horses that might have been there – but tethered to the top rail of the corral a mule and a donkey had been left. This told Lavanya that the intruders had been sowars, sepoys or gujars, rather than local villagers. The mule continued to bellow but it seemed that it was simply thirst that was bothering it. There was a well and she managed to hold the wooden bucket to the animal's muzzle as it butted and pushed at it. She found a saddle for it but it was too heavy for her and she could not get it up on to the beast's back; both animals, however, had rope halters.

At last she was ready to return to the pipe, the tunnel. She looked around, felt driven to have a last look in the bungalow to see what else she might be able to find that would be useful, but finally could not bring herself to go in. Using some rope from the stable she managed to get the clothes and food and a large round narrow-necked clay jar of water on to the back of the mule, but she still had to carry Deepa, who howled when she was put on the bare back of the donkey.

Lavanya kept them all to her original plan: they would go on until they came to a town, or better still a station, with a substantial number of British troops, with people there who would look after the children until they could be returned to their parents. They moved at night, starting at moonrise which was later every night through to the last quarter, taking turns on the animals, two on the mule, one on the donkey. The last week of their journey was made more difficult by darkness, though the nights were generally clear and starlit before the rising of the last fragment of moon. The road became more crowdwd towards dawn and remained busy until late in the morning, and during this period they hid, sometimes in ditches but more often in the thickets on the edge of the jungle when it closed in, or in topes. It was during the late mornings that Lavanya, always with Deepika and occasionally with Miranda, went out looking for food, begging and occasionally taking a chance and stealing. When Miranda was caught with two eggs, Lavanya told the woman who owned them that Miranda was her sister and too frightened to speak, at which the woman let them have the eggs anyway.

At first the children refused much of what she brought: melons which were not melons at all but squashes, sour yellow medlars, and salads put together from spicy leaves like coriander, but after a week or so they took anything. And always there were chappatis either obtained when they went foraging or made from the sack of flour, and often milk as well. Then, after they had eaten there came what was the worst time, the long hours before she said they could walk again, hours when flies and other insects attacked, when she insisted they should be quiet and not run around, right through the night until there was light from one source or another, light enough for them to see the road.

There were adventures on the way. The worst that happened was after they had been on the road for ten days. They were sheltering in a deserted charcoal burners' encampment, a cluster of tiny huts made out of slabs of cow dung (to which Emma objected – 'I'm not sleeping in cow poo', but she did), set back less than fifty yards from the road.

'What if they come back?' Adam asked.

'They won't,' Lavanya asserted. 'They don't work at this time of year – it's too hot.'

Why they had chosen this spot was clear: not only was it on the edge of a forest of teak which their deprivations had pushed back; they had also been able to sink a well, some fifteen feet deep. It had no cover and no parapet, and Stephen came very close to falling in before Miranda spotted him and hauled him back. Towards dusk they heard the steady trotting of some three or four horses and into the circle of huts came two files, four men in all, of British troopers. They gathered round the well, hobbled their horses, fed and watered them, then took out their pipes while one of them got a fire going with a pot of water on it into which he fed dried meat, pemmican or jerk. They spread themselves out on the dry dirt floor and began to relax, while the children crouched together in one hut and watched them through the gathering dusk.

'Why don't we join them?' Adam whispered.

Prompted by premonition or an unconscious awareness that there were more people around than they could see, Lavanya put her hand on his knee.

'Not yet,' she said, and almost immediately they heard what was clearly meant to be the hoot of an owl, but equally clearly was not, and a rustle in the dried-up brush behind the huts. The troopers reached for their carbines and pistols, started to their feet, but too late; a salvo of musket fire crackled round the clearing and two of the troopers fell immediately. The third let off his pistol and winged one of the dacoits who now surrounded them, yelling as they did, before two of them cut him down with their tulwars. The fourth was caught alive. They made him kneel and cut off his head.

There was one final disaster arising from this incident. Although the dacoits failed to discover Lavanya and her charges, they did come across the mule and the donkey browsing off thorn trees nearby. They took them with them.

Later, when the robbers, rebels, whatever they were, had gone Adam was beside himself with partly assumed rage and shame – as an Englishman he should, he cried, almost weeping, have gone to the troopers' aid. Lavanya drew a different moral. It was a lesson to them, she said, that they should not give themselves up to the feringhees until they were present in numbers, and preferably with cannon. It was also clear to her now, though she did not say this out loud, that the mutiny, rebellion, rising, whatever, had gone a long way towards success. In the past an attack of this sort on British troops would have been unthinkable, not only because it might not have succeeded, but because the reprisals would have been too awful to contemplate.

Daybreak, a week later, found them on the banks of a river whose flats and waterways were at least a quarter of a mile wide with the main channel, where they could see fishing boats being poled along and men throwing nets, on the further side. Beyond it lay a small town which climbed gently from three or four ghats, terraced and stepped landing places, towards a rocky outcrop on which stood a palace of brown stone with domes at its corners and crenellated walls between. Some of it, especially the balconies and belvederes, was faced with marble. To an appreciative European the scene would have been the essence of oriental picturesqueness: the immaculate blue sky, the palace on its rock hazed by the vapours from the river, the pavilions above the ghats and the slow, magnificent yet domestic progress of Mother Ganges through yellow and white banks fringed with emerald rushes and reeds, the herons, storks and brightly coloured waders, the fishermen – all adding up to a scene of centuries-old tranquillity. To Lavanya it meant either danger or an end to their three-week walk, and she had to find out which. Following their now established custom she placed four of the children with Adam in charge in a stand of dried but dense sugar cane and took Miranda and Deepika down to the waterside where they asked a fisherman where they were.

'Bithur,' came the reply, 'the palace of the Nana Saheb. But further down the river, fourteen miles away, you will come to a bigger town, called Cawnpore.'

She had heard of the place. Some of the people the Hardcastles had known in Simla were posted there in the so-called winter months. It was a large station, bigger than Meerut.

'Are the British still there?' she asked.

'The British are still there,' he replied.

27

Meerut, 14–22 May 1857

They were distressed and tried not to show it; they grieved and on the whole denied their grief. They had seen horrid sights on the night of the tenth and experienced narrow escapes; many had lost friends and acquaintances whom, generally, speaking they had not felt much for, certainly had not loved, but who, in spite of the transience of military life, the postings, the illnesses (often fatal), the rivalries and promotions which took them out of one caste and into another, had become part of the furniture of their lives, people you could cling on to when you were ready to fall, or who would support you like a chair or a bed when things were really bad.

And then there was the fear, the isolation. India, one had accepted, was uncomfortable, often dangerous (but cholera, no respecter of persons, still swept through London with a virulence that recalled plague in much the same way as it did through Bombay or Madras); there were cobras and jungle fever, which some called 'malaria', believing it to be caused by the exhalations from foetid swamps, and a countryside filled with gujars and dacoits into which one would not venture without a large armed escort. Yet they were protected, they were privileged: an administrator, soldier, civil servant, engineer, lawyer or doctor was better paid than in England and their salaries bought ten times as much in the local markets. And however many white men there were above you in the pecking order you knew there were millions upon millions of darkies below you.

Yes, nearly all were convinced racists but it should be said that there was little to choose between their attitude to Natives and the way they thought of and treated the lowliest in the home country. Particularly the Irish.

And if you were a person of principle you generally believed that the work you and your spouse were engaged in was God's work, its aim to raise the whole sub-continent to a level of civilisation equivalent to that of rural and industrial Britain (the horrors of which, to be fair, they hardly knew) and, above all, eliminate the savage superstition of heathen religions, replacing them with Christianity, which meant, generally speaking, but not exclusively, the evangelical branch of the Anglican brand.

In one night all that had been blown away and the worst of it, in the aftermath, was the terrible uncertainty. Intermittently the electric telegraph was repaired for a few hours before the line was cut again, despatches brought by couriers did get through but were limited to military matters, and yet these gave hope that all might yet be restored – but on the other hand there were rumours spread by Natives, and just occasionally a refugee, a survivor from one of the small sub-district stations, from a railhead or a place where engineers were bridging a river, would arrive with tales to equal their own experience of arson, massacre and destruction.

There were hangings in Meerut but because almost all the mutinous sepoys had escaped to Delhi they were almost entirely of civilians, judged by the civil court, judge and magistrate, and carried out by the kotwal, the Chief of Police. Among the first to go was the butcher – hanged on the evidence of Captain Craigie and Lieutenant Möller, who had seen him leaving the Chambers' bungalow. Sophie and Catherine went to the Civil Lines to see him turned off. They had already, two days earlier, attended the funeral of Charlotte and her baby; they had left behind them but one more tiny hill of raised earth in the cemetery in a row of many similar new ones, waiting for their gravestones.

The butcher was fortunate to have the benefit of a cart to stand on, which, when driven away, dropped him the four feet or so necessary to break or dislocate his neck. In the coming months, when there were thousands of hangings and carts were not always available, the rope was simply thrown over a stout branch and the victim hauled up to it, like a bale hoisted by a derrick. In these cases death by strangulation could be delayed for as much as ten minutes.

The execution of the butcher, four days after the event and one of several, took place just after a dawn with no freshness in it. The air had long been deprived of the moisture that forms dew, and few birds sang. Leaves were dropping from the big fig trees, and drifted on the slight breeze like thin sheets of leather. As soon as the butcher was really gone, his body no longer twitching but simply turning very slowly, the women turned away and walked back to the cantonments.

'It was too quick,' Sophie muttered.

'Yes,' from Catherine, almost a hiss.

Sophie was shaking and very pale, her head filled with a confused storm of conflicting feelings – rage at the man who had so horribly killed Charlotte, frustration that he had not suffered more, but also a great ache of horror and a sort of deep anxious guilt at what she had just seen. And after walking a couple of hundred yards it all showed itself in an almost appalling way – she longed to pee, she had to. With two months left before her second child was due the need could not be denied.

'Sorry,' she said, handed Catherine her parasol, and, glancing over her shoulder, moved off the road and behind a tired hibiscus bush. Though baggy bloomers worn beneath the crinoline-supported skirts were now fashionable, most of the women, on account of the heat, went without. All she had to do was spread her skirts, place her feet apart, splay her knees and let go.

Coming back out on to the road, and, still conscious of dampness between her thighs, she took Catherine's hand, but after a minute or so Catherine disengaged it. No longer the breathlessly talkative woman Sophie had befriended, she hardly spoke at all these days, did almost nothing but stand on the Hardcastles' verandah and look out over the thickets that separated them from India.

The four of them, the Hardcastles and the Dixons, had moved back into the English lines to the Hardcastles' bungalow from which of course most of the contents had already been sent on ahead, back to Simla. Dixon One and Dixon Two were charred ruins. Scavenging around and bidding at auctions of the property of families which had been wiped out, they had managed to put together enough furniture to survive with. Both men now were waiting to see what their futures would be. Tom expected to have to go with what troops could be spared from keeping Meerut secure to retake Delhi. Dixon, whose regiment, the 3rd Light Cavalry, had been the first to mutiny, had no idea what would happen to him.

Sophie and Catherine were very different. Their friendship, (companionship would be a better word), though apparently close was, on Sophie's side, based, like those that often occur at boarding schools or nowadays in the first year at university, on the need to find someone one could talk to and trust rather than on any real affinity. On Catherine's side it happened that Sophie arrived very shortly after her closest companion up to then had returned suddenly to England with a husband who had survived, quite unusually, the amputation of a leg in the Persian war. With no strain between them they had continued to get on well and had even found each other's husbands tolerable. To Catherine it appeared that Thomas Hardcastle was a person of some education and sensitivity compared to James, while Sophie found Dixon's high spirits and easy-going ways congenial. None of this led to even the mildest of flirtations. It was there and it helped to keep the two families close to each other. Now, though, that they were forced to share a house too small, even without the children, and under the strain of their loss, there was a little less readiness to soothe over differences.

Back in the hall of the now shabby bungalow they got in each other's way while unpinning their hats, and then again in the small kitchen as they did their best to put tiffin on the table. They had no servants. The local ones had disappeared; those they had brought from Simla had already gone back with the furniture.

Presently Catherine put down the knife she had been using to butter bread for sandwiches. Her gaze, without real focus, seemed to be fixed on the deserted servants' quarters on the further side of the yard.

'At least you have another on the way,' she murmured, not for the first time.

'I'm not sure I want it,' Sophie replied. 'I'm not sure I shall be able to cope.'

'You don't really mean that.'

This was true. Sophie had said it only to diminish the difference beween them, to mitigate the guilt she felt because her loss, though dreadful, was so much less than Catherine's.

'There'll be no Lavanya this time, no replacement for her. I'll feed this one myself.'

There was guilt here too. Catherine had fed her children and the bond between them had been closer, warmer Sophie suspected, than that between her and Stephen. There had not even been an official ayah as such . . . when Catherine needed someone to look after her brood she had simply called on one or other of the servants and paid her a little extra for the service. She had even undertaken the schooling of Adam and Miranda and done tolerably well at it. They could both read, had some numeracy, knew the major capitals and could place them on a map. Not the least of her problems now was filling days that were empty and endless.

Yet there was room for hope. On the twelfth there came a report that a woman had sold some milk to a strange girl with a baby on the Grand Road, about fifteen miles away, and then another that a girl had been seen with a group of possibly white children moving across fields some miles south of the road, before disappearing into a large tope of mango trees. The colonel of the 6th Dragoon Guards allowed Dixon to take a small detachment out into the plain to follow up these sightings, but of course they found nothing, only sullennness and silence from the villagers and field workers they came across.

'But why doesn't she just bring them back?' Catherine moaned for perhaps the twentieth time as Sophie yet again reminded her of these hints that their children might have survived. 'They've been murdered by gujars. Or . . .' and this was a new fantasy that suddenly occurred to her, 'sold into slavery, sold by gujars to slave-traders.'

This was not entirely fanciful. The gutter press in England had run stories of white slaves, English girls, kidnapped in infancy, and later discovered in the courts of Arab princes on the East African coast and in Malaya. Anything could happen, could already have happened. It was terrible not knowing. If the outcome was to be the unthinkable, then, almost, Sophie wanted to know it now. The uncertainty was unbearable, it crippled everything, made everything seem pointless, even the new life now kicking inside her.

She was learning to hate India. If she was to have children then Dorset was the better place to be.

In silence they continued slicing bread from cob loaves baked the English way in the regimental bakery, spread it with canned butter and potted beef from Fortnum & Mason. Sophie sliced the flesh of five mangoes into a glass bowl while Catherine made custard with a quart of milk, ten eggs and sugar.

'Do you have a fresh lemon?'

'No.'

'It'll be a bit bland without.'

Another accusation? Sophie's lips narrowed into a thin line. The thing of it was she couldn't cook at all, never had been able to, whereas Catherine seemed to know her way around a kitchen. In her mind she sorted through possible retorts but before she could come up with one they heard the clip-clop of a horse in a slow trot and Dixon appeared in the yard. Presently he was with them, leaning against the doorjamb, smoking a cheroot.

'Heard the weirdest stories in the mess,' he began. 'Young Vibart told us it, part of his adventures coming out of Delhi. They were helped by an amazing fakir. Do you want to hear it?'

'Not really,' said Catherine.

'Yes,' said Sophie.

'All right. Cathy, be a love and get me a beer.'

'I'll get it,' Sophie was quite sharp with this, yet another instance of something said or done to make her feel that the Dixons were taking over what was, after all, her home. She put the bottle and a glass on the table in front of James and left him to ease up the wired porcelain cap and pour. He drank, wiped his mouth and moustaches.

'It seems young Vibart, they call him Butcher to distinguish him from his father, Major Vibart . . .' – if the women shuddered at this soubriquet, he did not notice it – 'was leading a group of people, including women and children, out of Delhi, having hidden in old Metcalfe's mansion during the afternoon. Believing there must be a regiment or two heading up from here they took a couple of boats and rowed across the Jumna, heading for Meerut, just as darkness fell. They thought they were safe but almost immediately a horde of gujars jumped on them out of a tope, so suddenly they didn't even have time to draw their revolvers. The gujars set about stripping them, looking for gold and jewellery I suppose, when almost by magic it seemed a fakir appeared among them, in a yellow robe, his face smeared with ashes and paint, and waving a long but stout stick, beating their heads and backs with it . . .'

Catherine looked at Sophie. 'Are you all right,' she said. 'You've gone quite pale.'

'I'm quite all right. Let him get on with it.'

'This fakir was quite an extraordinary chap. First of all the gujars ran off, then he took them to the village ahead where he seemed on good terms with Francis Cohen . . . Do you know about old Cohen? German Jew did us a good turn some years back and the Registrar, old Tom Metcalfe it was then, gave him the rents of several villages thereabouts. Gone native except for religion and kindness of heart. Anyway, he put them safely upstairs, found Native clothes for them for the gujars had left them in nothing but their unmentionables, gave them a good meal and then set about sending a note to General Hewitt here about their predicament. Problem. What to do in case the note fell into the wrong hands? Write it in German, said Cohen. There might not be anyone in Meerut who can read German, said this extraordinary fakir. Try French. No French I am haffing, said Cohen. Well, I'll do it, said this wild fakir. And he did. And next morning what should happen but old Mackenzie turned up with the cavalry and they were safe at last. But who knows what would have happened had that fakir not turned up. A fakir who could write French, would you believe it?'

'I believe it,' Sophie said, quietly, but quite clearly. She was aware of a flush creeping up her neck.

'What was that, Sophie?'

'I said, I believe it. You hear such strange tales about fakirs.'*

---

* This version of Vibart's story (including the 'fakir') is taken, often verbatim, from his *The Sepoy Mutiny, as seen by a Subaltern from Delhi to Lucknow*, London 1898. Several other memoirs and diaries tell similar stories figuring mysterious fakirs.

28

Meerut, 22 May 1857

Another week went by. The troops threw up earth ramparts round the English lines, the civil population, whites and Christians, moved in and used the barracks while the men slept in tents. Then, on the twenty-second, news and orders arrived at last and almost immediately a corporal called with an order that Dixon and Hardcastle should both report to the station headquarters. In an atmosphere that had become stagnant and stale, waiting to find out what was happening was unbearable. Sophie decided to fill in the wait by taking a walk towards the church where she met Victoria Marchant.

'Well,' Victoria began, 'have you heard the news?' and settled herself on the low drystone wall.

'I know despatches have arrived from Umballa, but I don't know what's in them.'

'Nor do I. But I do know who brought them.'

'Does it matter? What's in them is more important, surely.'

'Perhaps so. But in this case, it is of interest.'

'Go on then, tell.' And Sophie settled herself next to the younger girl.

'None other than William Hodson himself. And apparently he did the trip in a day and a night, a hundred and fifty miles.'

'Not so much, surely.'

'Not far off.'

'So they must be urgent. Important. Perhaps things are going to start moving at last.'

'Hodson. I've never met him. What's he like? What's he like, really?'

Sophie, who had met Hodson, briefly, on their way through Umballa from Simla, laid her finger against her cheek, pretended to think.

'Very fair hair. Pale, smooth face, heavy moustache.'

'I do like a good moustache. So manly.'

'Wearing a sort of dun, dust-coloured uniform . . .'

'Khaki. He invented it when he was with the Corps of Guides. Is he really a rogue? Did he steal the Guides' regimental funds?'

'Not proven,' Sophie asserted. 'Hardcastle says he was just a bit careless about the way he kept the accounts.'

'What's he like? Pretty dashing I imagine.'

'And as soon as he dismounted he put on dark glasses. Coloured. Sort of violet colour. Suffers from migraine. Hence his bad temper.'

'He has a bad temper?' Victoria asked.

'Terrible. Won't put up with anyone he considers a fool.'

'But what Marchant says is no one can deny he's the best cavalry officer this army ever had. You'd expect him to make a dash of it, but no, he rides in the front and the centre and controls both wings with his pig-sticking spear and woe betide any trooper that gets in front of him. Just as if he were on a parade ground.'

'And yet,' Sophie interrupted, 'you remember that book our group were all reading last month, *Tom Brown's Schooldays*? About Rugby School under Arnold, written by an ex-pupil, and in it there's a villainous bully called Flashman? Well, I have it on good authority that character is based on William Hodson.'

At that very moment Hodson was sitting at a camping table in the main hall of the headquarters with Dixon, whom Hodson had sent for, standing at ease in front of him. Hodson was wearing his tinted spectacles and had a glass of soda water in front of him. Around them a small bedlam was developing as the despatches and orders were read, dispositions made and so forth. It seemed that the main force in Meerut was to march north-west towards Karnal under Brigadier Wilson and join up with the Umballa force before retaking Delhi. A strong garrison under Hewitt was to stay in Meerut.

206

'I'll put you straight into the picture, Dixon. Up at Umballa we have a couple of hundred Pathan hill tribesmen who came with us out of Afghanistan. All mounted. When this kerfuffle got under way I suggested to Anson that they could be regularised as cavalry for reconnaissance, scouting, distant pickets, that sort of thing, and I volunteered to lead them. He agreed. But I need at least two English officers, one to each troop. Your regiment has disappeared, you have a good record, how would you like to take it on? No promotion at first, but if it works out I'll get my majority and then, if I'm satisfied with you, you'll get your captaincy. Two minutes to make up your mind.'

'I don't need two minutes.' Dixon snapped out a salute. 'I'll come.'

'Good lad. Meet me here in half an hour with your two best mounts and only the gear you'll need. Dismiss.'

Meanwhile, aware of a sudden burst of activity emanating from the Headquarters, and getting the main thrust of it from a corporal who was hurrying by, Sophie and Victoria decided they should make their way back to their homes. Victoria shared Sophie's parasol. Beyond the church and the cemetery they came first to the Hardcastles' reopened bungalow. Victoria declined Sophie's invitation to accompany her, so Sophie went in on her own, removing once more her straw hat and unpinning her silk scarf as she did so. Catherine was sitting on a dusty and threadbare sofa in the sitting room with a small book on her knees.

'What are you reading?'

'Sonnets by Elizabeth Barrett Browning.'

'Any good?'

'She writes well of love and grief. But they are not my love nor my grief.'

Sophie, her head turned away, gritted her teeth, caught between two emotions – guilt that she was unable to maintain conscious sorrow twenty-four hours a day seven days a week, and irritation at what she took to be her friend's pointless moping. Catherine closed the slim volume but kept her finger between the pages.

'What's the news then?'

'The best part of the division marches to join Anson north of Delhi. They'll leave in four days' time.'

'I know as much. James came in a few moments ago. He's actually going back with Hodson. This afternoon. To Umballa.'

'He's what!?'

Catherine shrugged.

'That's what he said. He has to take every opportunity to get on. Though without a family to support "getting on" doesn't seem as important as it did. He's over the moon about it.'

'And you're not.'

'No. I shan't be able to join him until Delhi is taken. And anyway, I want to go south. The children went south. I want to go south.' She put the book to one side and sat up straight. 'He's in our room now. Packing. No more than can be taken on the back of his spare horse, Hodson told him. Tom is helping him.'

Sophie squeezed Catherine's knee, got up and went through to the room the Dixons had been using as a bedroom. Dixon and Hardcastle were both leaning over the bed looking with some dismay at a pile of clothes, books, a revolver, a pistol, a telescope and other impedimenta at one end of his bed and a pair of large soft bags, patently already full, at the other.

'Can I help?' she asked.

'If you are a conjuror and capable of creating spaces where there are none, yes.'

She rooted about in one of the bags and came up with a fairly substantial copy of the Bible.

'You don't need this,' she said firmly.

'Most of the chaps carry one.'

'Then you'll be able to share with them.' Briskly she began sorting through the rest of what he had already packed. 'So, you're off to Umballa with Hodson, and then to Delhi. Well, we'll look after Catherine for you.'

'I'm not sure we'll be able to.' Hardcastle looked across at her, his head pulled back and down as if he were about to admit to some wrongdoing. Indeed, his colour rose a little.

'What do you mean?'

'While you were out I also received a posting, but not to Umballa. They've got the judge advocate general of the whole army there, Colonel Young that is, and he has his staff with him. But a division is being assembled at Benares which will probably move west to Allahabad and they have no proper lawyers. Jungle fever laid them low, apparently. So we have to leave too, tomorrow at the earliest, but we should be on our way tonight, as soon as dusk comes. We're to go via Agra and Cawnpore and we'll have a cavalry escort with a pair of four-pounders most of the way, so we'll be safe enough.'

Sophie looked from one man to the other through the gloom of the tattie-shaded room. Her emotions were mixed. She felt pushed around, that decisions were being made that concerned her and over which she had no control. A long journey ahead, over five hundred miles? At the worst time of year through a countryside in revolt, seven and a half months pregnant?

'We'll take a boat from Cawnpore.' His tone was clearly meant to be mollifying. 'Down the Ganges.'

Sophie heaved in a sigh, clenched her fists.

'No!'

It was almost a shout. Tom's face melted into disbelief and anxiety.

'I've no choice.' It was not much more than a mutter.

'But I have. Listen. Ten days ago I lost my child . . .'

'Our son.'

'My child. I have been blessed with the possibility of having another. I'm not going to lose this one.'

'What will you do?' The question was burdened with suggestion. Part of its baggage seemed to ask 'How can you possibly manage without me, a man, to look after you?'

She turned towards what light there was in the darkened room, her fingers frantically twisting the lace edging to the maternity smock she was wearing above those voluminous skirts. 'We've been told Meerut is as safe as anywhere. I'll stay here with Catherine. She can look after me. It'll give her something to do. Take her mind off . . . things. And she knows as much about midwifery as anyone I'm likely to meet in Allahabad or wherever.'

She took a chance, turned her face towards Dixon.

'What do you think, James?'

Dixon looked about the room as if desperate to find a solution he would not be responsible for. Eventually . . .

'Sounds all right to me. But it's hoped that quite soon we'll be able to get the women and children out of here safely and send them on up to Simla. Where you should have been three weeks ago.'

'So much the better then, if I'm still able to travel. There.

209

That's settled.' She glided across the space between them, stroked her husband's sleeve then kissed his cheek. He turned his head away.

'Sophie, dearest,' it was almost a whisper, 'I'm not at all sure I'll be able to manage without you.'

'Nonsense, Tom. Of course you will.'

29

Howrah (Calcutta), Benares, 19 May–4 June 1857

Did the stationmaster blow the whistle, did the guard wave his green flag, were the last doors slammed? Did the stoker shovel coal, did the driver wipe his hands on a greasy cloth, pull the cord which released the steam that caused the steam whistle to blow with the screech of a giant automaton owl, and then reach for the gleaming brass of the throttle? Was the ritual for setting a steam train in motion the same in India on 19 May 1857 as it was a century later? Sure, the locomotive was smaller, with a tall smokestack, and the coaches still echoed discreetly the lines of a stage coach. At all events the sulphurous smell must have been the same, the sudden cloud of steam through which, striding with as much dignity as a man in a hurry can muster, came the tall, well-built and very authoritative figure of Lieutenant Colonel James Neill, commanding officer of the 1st Madras European Regiment. The first of the reinforcements Canning had ordered had arrived.

'Stop the train,' he ordered, in a deep, bell-like voice.

The guard lowered his green flag to his side, the driver took his hand off the throttle, the stationmaster, in just the way stationmasters used to the world over, pulled a chained watch from his watch-pocket, clicked the lid open, looked at it and . . .

'No,' he said.

And found he was looking down the barrel of an Adams revolver.

The lieutenant colonel thumbed back the hammer, the cylinder turned, a loaded chamber came into the breech, and the sun gleamed on the copper percussion cap perched on the nipple in front of the hammer, poised now like a fighting cock's beak, ready to peck. Behind it, beneath heavy eyebrows, large baggy brown eyelids narrowed above a great shaggy moustache.

'I will blow your brains out if you do not.'

'Oh, I say, sir . . .' came from a much younger subaltern, breathlessly hurrying up behind his superior.

'The man's a traitor if he disobeys me.'

The meaning of life for that ancient and departed breed, the common or garden stationmaster, the whole purpose of their lives, was to ensure that the trains in their charge left their care on time. To have actually to be the means by which one was delayed was as great a betrayal of everything sacred as, well, eating pork was to a devout Mahometan or beef to a Hindoo. A greater man might have stood his ground and taken the bullet, but no doubt the stationmaster of Howrah, the township on the west bank of the Hooghly opposite Calcutta, had a wife who was fond of him and children whose mouths had to be filled out of his stipend, and very reluctantly he signalled to driver and guard that the train would wait.

'How long for?' he asked, looking over his shoulder and hoping none but the officers in front of him had heard a capitulation expressed so humbly.

'Ten minutes,' barked James Neill, carefully lowering the hammer of his revolver and holstering the weapon. 'I have seventy men who have disembarked from their ship and it will take them that long to be here.'

Ten minutes! Seventy men! And not a spare seat on the train!

Neill was big, strong, determined and, to anyone whose status or rank was noticeably below his, a bully. To his equals or superiors he was stern but polite. Most women admired him. In those days many women felt obliged to admire masterful men. And above all, worst of all, he was a stern, relentless, totally convinced Presbyterian.

Although the railway line from Calcutta to Delhi was planned as far as Cawnpore, and for some stretches was in place, in others it was only marked out by embankments and cuttings. It was actually practicable only as far as Raniganj, a mere hundred or so miles north-west of Howrah. From Raniganj to Benares, Neill and his seventy men, followed by a further two companies of his regiment, had to proceed by bullock cart. The carts carried the men, elephants pulled the guns, and the baggage came on as best it could in the rear, mostly on camels, with the officers' servants, the camp followers, and the usual travelling bazaar, including a flock of hens and a herd of goats. Travelling at night and in the first hours of the mornings the first seventy or so were in Benares by 1st June with most of the rest by the third. And Neill found he was on the edge of an abyss.

Benares was a town of massive contradictions. To European visitors it was a long sweep of the Ganges, two miles long, edged with the façades of what appeared to be magnificent, almost Venetian, palaces, bathed in the warm light of sunrise, above gentle flights of wide steps dropping to the Ganges. They attended the solemn evening ceremonies when monks chanted Vedas to the gods and goddesses, and most especially Ganja herself, throwing clouds of incense from their hand-held censers over the darkened river; and went on to indulge in the tranquil ceremony of launching tiny papier mâché saucers, each laden with a flower and a burning wick, to take their place with hundreds of others on the black but glossy water.

But the closer they got the more the vision became frayed from the edges inwards until it fell apart like a curtain rotted by moth and damp to reveal the reality behind it.

First, then as now, there were the Burning Ghats, the fragrance of whose red-hot perfumed branches could not overlay the sickly smell, borne on the black smoke, of roast pork. Those who got close enough to catch this smell, and close enough to see the bodies burning, might not eat roast pork for years, maybe never again. The Burning Ghats were operated by a sizeable population of Untouchables who lived in a network of narrow winding alleys that climbed up from the river to the higher ground behind. It stank of faeces, human as well as animal; cows, pigs and rats fed off the vegetable and animal detritus that lay everywhere, ankle deep, or deeper.

Who knows what authority, if any, rules this teeming wen? Certainly the English in 1857 did not. They lived in cantonments three miles away and rarely ventured into the town at all, and certainly not into the Untouchables' *banlieue*; however, at the beginning of June, the Untouchables were coming out. There were rioting and looting in the main town behind the palaces, preachers on every corner incited rebellion, and at least one of the Native regiments, the 37th Infantry, was believed to be on the point of open mutiny.

The station commander was a Brigadier George Ponsonby, sixty-seven years old, and crumbling. He had arrived only a week or so earlier, and on being told that both the 34th and the 37th were likely to rise he immediately ordered that the regiments should parade on 4 June in the presence of the other troops, both British and Native, to be disarmed and disbanded.

The 34th were the first on the parade ground and submitted to being disarmed without too much in the way of resistance, the first six companies piling their arms in each of their bells of arms. It was between four and five o'clock in the evening, with the shadows lengthening and a breeze, which raised the dust, getting up. An atmosphere of bleak unreality stained the scene as the British officers ordered their men to lay down their arms beneath the immensity of the lowering Indian sky. The monsoon was still some way off but the black clouds were gathering. Then the European regiments, supported by artillery, began to march on to the maidan. There now occurred what had become a feature of disbanding regiments to the extent that it is often supposed it was a prearranged tactic to incite wavering sepoys into open revolt while some at any rate still had their weapons and the bells of arms were still unlocked. Groups of Native officers, commissioned and NCOs, took up the same cry: the British are coming with loaded rifles and guns to massacre us just as soon as we having nothing with which to defend ourselves.

The sepoys quickly retrieved their muskets – their intention was clear though who fired first, the British or the mutineers, is not. Shooting, at first haphazard then organised in volleys, broke out and a Sikh regiment which had arrived with the rest but was at first moving loyally against the 34th got caught in crossfire. They joined the mutineers, and the British guns opened up with grape and round shot.

With the flash of musketry in the clouds of dust and musket balls whistling close, the crack of cannon fire reverberating round the square and the screams of those that were hit and the dusk settling over the whole scene, Ponsonby lost his nerve.

'Neill,' he cried, 'I'm quite unfit for anything . . . you must take over.'

For Neill this was it; this was action with him in command in just the way he had been dreaming of for most of a career spent convalescing from wounds and illness or in administrative posts. He galloped over to the small battery of light guns and got them to fire sharply one after another, as they should; he pulled his own men into a proper two-deep line and directed their volleys; and almost instantly the mutineers scattered and fled.

'After them, lads,' he bellowed, 'after them and string up any man-jack of them you get hold of.'

But this was no easy matter. The mutineers scattered into the alleys and bazaars of the main town and were only seen in small scurrying groups that could turn a corner and disappear. They were heading for the river which they planned to cross by boat and so make their way on to the Grand Trunk Road with the aim of getting to Allahabad fifty miles upstream or even Cawnpore and ultimately Delhi. As darkness fell only a few were left stranded on the ghats. These were rounded up and a few were hanged on the spot, but most were marched back to the English. On their way the English, frustrated by the fact that they had let so many slip through their hands, also rounded up the badmashes and Untouchables who had taken advantage of the evening's chaos to indulge in one of their ever more frequent bouts of mugging, looting and rioting. Normally they were the responsibility of the local kotwali, or civil police force, which was hopelessly inadequate for the job, but now the rioters were at the mercy of roused, fit and ruthless British soldiers. Faced with a British bayonet they went quietly. To their deaths.

Back in the lines and round the maidan the hangings began. There was not enough rope, not enough animals from which the victims could be launched to a relatively quick death by breaking or dislocating their necks. Neill, with his officers about him, a revolver in one hand and a monkey-tail fly whisk in the other, marched from group to group, heard a short statement from a sergeant or corporal on how the victims had been caught and brusquely ordered their execution. A group of boys were brought in.

'What were these up to?'

'Marching about, sir, with the flag of rebellion, sir, and beating tom-toms.'

'Up with them then, and be sharp about it.'

'They were just having a lark, sir.'

'String them up, I say, string them up.'

Understanding what was required of them some officers led their sections out into the surrounding districts and, using elephants for drops and mango trees for gallows, hanged every male they could find. One subaltern boasted of the numbers he had finished off in quite an artistic manner, twisting and binding the victims into figures of eight.

Up the Ganges and the Grand Trunk Road the news travelled as quickly as the mutineers who had got clear. The first told of being deceived by their officers into giving up their arms so they could be mown down, the later ones told of the hangings. The regiments at Allahabad rose, while a few, heading for Cawnpore, passed through Futtehpore. It was Neill's duty now, for he remained in command, to march to the relief of Cawnpore, but as a result of his actions he had these to deal with on the way.

He was thus the cause of his own delay.

30

Strong, knotty, dark legs swung down the long narrow road, carrying the lean figure to the brow of a rise which revealed the city of Jhansi, seven miles away. The dark stone of its fort set on a rock on the edge of the town was softened by the light of the risen sun. It was more than a rock, a sheer isolated lump rising above the land around it, and one of five or six more that dominated the landscape like an archipelago. Between it and the fakir, the rolling hills surrounding these craggy lumps were filled with teak forest, the top boughs of the trees leafless, silvered by drought, draped here and there with the sparse rags of a grey mist. He remained motionless for several minutes, his stick caught in the angle of a raised knee, the sole of that foot set against it, so you might think he was deep in some sort of yogic trance; then, as the sun climbed away from the horizon and what colour it had lent the landscape drained from it, he seemed to shrug, his foot dropped, and on he went, his bare heels puffing up tiny clouds of dust, down the incline until the trees closed around him and he was gone.

Seven months earlier Lieutenant Bruce Farquhar had submitted a report of his meeting and interview with the Ranee of Jhansi to his control in Government House, Calcutta. That personage, hidden away in the corridors of Canning's palace, now decided it might be possible to use him to turn at least one conspirator against the conspiracy. And so it was, in the third week of May, that he, Bruce

217

Farquhar that is, stripped off his uniform and once more daubed his body with his combination of walnut juice and boot polish, tied a money belt round his waist, concealed it under his dhoti, wound on his turban, took up his staff and set off on a long walk of three hundred miles. He might, one supposes, have ridden at least as far as, say, Agra, but to be a white face on a good horse, at that time, in that country, and without an escort of at least a troop of British cavalry, would have courted murder within the first fifty. And there were no cavalry available.

Now, early in June, the road he was on took him out of the teak forest, and into the Jhansi cantonments where the British officers of the Native regiments lived with their families, a hundred yards or so outside the medieval walls of the city. Some of the bungalows had been fired during the night and were now smouldering, and their gardens and even the Mall itself was littered with articles of little value: a broken doll, books with backs broken, paintings with broken frames and shattered glass. One of the latter was a water-colour of Ullswater, executed with the meticulous care of the well-taught amateur. Among the books were Mrs Gaskell's *North and South*.

Sepoys and sowars stood around in small groups, many in a state of undress, their uniforms awry, their trousers replaced with dhotis. The fakir looked up and around, shaded his eyes. The Union flag still flew over the town fort which was big enough to have been rated a small castle had it been in England, and, before he could shift his gaze from it, tiny puffs of white smoke blossomed like cotton flowers against the battlements. They dissipated and vanished as the reports reached his ears. A group of soldiers, cavalry from their accoutrements, idling near what had once been the officers' mess and drinking the officers' beer, caught his attention. He elicited from them that the feringhees had indeed shut themselves up in the fort but would all be dead just as soon as the gunners had finished their beer. Or at any rate by midday.

He moved off towards the gate to the city, passing through a short avenue of market stalls none of which had opened. Pariah dogs nosed through the previous days' litter but, beyond looking up at him briefly, paid no attention to his passing. Then, just as he reached the gate, a small group of men came rushing down the deserted street

218

beyond it, three of them Natives hustling two others along in front of them, all of them apparently Mahometans. The two in front, both rather portly, indeed one of them definitely fat, were not what they seemed at all but like him, though less convincingly, painted to look Native and garbed to appear Moslem. In fact he rather thought he had met one of them some months earlier – a Mr Purcell, working as a surveyor for the electric telegraph.

There now occurred the horror that every spy fears. The three genuine Natives, having got Mr Purcell and his companion beyond the city gate, seized Purcell by the hair and turban and forced him to the ground, wrenched his head back exposing his thick throat from which the colouring had been smeared by his collar, and with great force dragged the blade of a heavy knife across it. Dark blood welled up and spilled, as if from an upturned bucket, across his shoulder and front. His scream became a bubbling gurgle. Held now by only one of the murderers the other European managed to break free, but only for a moment. The guard on the gate, a soldier but not a sepoy, had already drawn his pistol. The percussion cap sparked, the powder took and the ball, smashing into the Englishman's forehead, took off most of the top of what was now revealed to be a bald head. The likeness to a clumsily topped soft-boiled egg was unavoidable.

Lieutenant Bruce Farquhar was forced to look on although every cell of his body that was that of a soldier rebelled. He maintained a look of Olympian disinterest and headed for the palace gate, where it seemed a similar event had taken place. This time, recognising a strawberry mark on the temple of a severed head, he was sure he knew the victim: A. Andrews, Deputy Collector. He had met him and his wife at Simla a year or so earlier. The dogs were already scavenging the body and limbs, which had been hacked into five or six pieces. A sergeant of the palace guard gave one of the dogs a kick – it turned and snarled at him; the sergeant backed off, hand on his pistol butt, and assumed an expression of injured dignity.

Delving beneath the top of his dhoti into his pouched body belt Farquhar now presented him with an English silver sixpence bearing the Queen's head. 'Give your mistress this and tell her an emissary of one great Queen presents his compliments to another and seeks an audience with her.'

'And why should I do such a thing?' the havildar objected.

'Because I will see you beheaded if you don't,' Farquhar replied.

Half an hour passed. Occasional gunfire could be heard from the direction of the fort, but not enough to signify any change in the situation. The sergeant returned. The heat increased and he and Farquhar sought out scraps of shadow under the lintel of the gate, which faced south. The dogs, sated, also sat in what shade there was and licked their genitals. Clouds of black flies settled on what was left of Messrs Purcell and Andrews. The fingers of the hand on the end of one of Mr Andrews' severed arms slowly clenched and then opened out again. At last the gate opened and revealed, attended by a couple of clerks, Farquhar's old acquaintance, the Ranee's vakil.

As they walked across the garden where the tent had been pitched for Farquhar on his previous visit, the vakil inclined his head towards him.

'Lieutenant Farquhar, is it not?' His glance took in the Englishman's appearance. 'Your errand must be one of some importance to your masters.'

'And to the Ranee too.'

The vakil pursed his lips, gave his head a slight shake, as if ready to doubt Farquhar's sincerity. All in all he was no longer the genial old man the Englishman recalled.

'The Ranee will see you when she has finished her customary pistol practice.' Putting his palms together he bowed perfunctorily and left him in the vestibule to the purdah. Carnations and poppies in brass vases flanked the ornately carved doorjambs, echoing the marble slabs which were inlaid with representations of the same flowers. Wondering that such cuttings were available in the second week of June, Farquhar ventured to touch a poppy, half-expecting he would cause a petal to fall, and thereby uncovered its secret: they had been created, most cunningly and realistically, from silk.

Pistols popped some distance off, and then fell silent. Time passed. The door opened and a voice called: 'Lieutenant, come in.'

The room had been transformed. It was no longer purdah. Cushions and low upholstered benches remained, but the curtain had gone; the arched windows were no longer draped, and on a balcony beyond, framed in sunlight, a punkah boy, yes a male, pumped the air across an ornate trough filled with rose-water. At right angles to the arches a large table or desk had been set, covered with papers and the impedimenta a busy writer needs. A British self-cocking Adams revolver did service as a paperweight. Seven or eight of the Ranee's women sat around the room. Two were cleaning and oiling similar handguns; two, their shawled heads bending over what they were doing, were using needle and thread to repair or alter what looked like military uniforms. The Ranee herself looked up from a thin book which lay on the table between her spread hands. Farquhar hardly had to glance at it to recognise it for what it was: *The Rules and Regulations for the Movement of His Majesty's Infantry* by General David Dundas.

Lakshmi Bai, Ranee of Jhansi, removed the spectacles she was wearing and looked up at him.

'Lieutenant! What a transformation. Turn round. There is a patch of pale skin on the back of your left knee. If you can assure me that you will not mark the fabric, you may seat yourself on the bench in front of the window.'

She replaced her spectacles and returned to the book, steel-nibbed pen in hand, drawing a neat line under some of the text. She was thinner. She had made no attempt to diminish the effects of the smallpox marks on her cheeks. Her eyes, which were dark yet glowed with a gem-like light, seemed larger than before though there was none of the kohl she had affected when purdah was being observed. And her voice had lost the slightly irritating feminine whine it had had. She was wearing a soldier's khaki jacket, but undone to reveal a long plain gown of blue silk, the colour not strong. The scarf she wore over her head was a similar blue but deeper, more pronounced. Somewhat incongruously she was wearing a lot of jewellery, gold and precious stones, a necklace with a pendant figurine of Shiva the Destroyer, bangles, many rings.

'Well,' she began, yet again removing the spectacles and placing her pen carefully in an ebony pen-holder, 'why are you here?'

He explained to her that he was an emissary of Lord Canning himself, that the Governor General was concerned that she might not be as ready as he hoped to play her part in quashing the mutiny, and to assure her that he would provide generous recompense of any expense she personally, or the state of Jhansi, might be put to in this cause.

Her complexion darkened.

'Recompense of what it might cost?' she repeated and her voice grated.

'My life?' she added, her voice becoming more acerbic with every syllable. 'Does his excellency's offer include my life, and the lives of my women, should we lose them in his cause?'

He waited. What could he say?

'The sepoys have said they will kill me and plunder the treasury if I do not join them.'

'Why should it come to that? Your highness has the Jhansi Contingency, a thousand strong.'

'Contingencies' were private armies raised locally by princes and rajahs, mainly for ceremonial purposes.

She turned to one of her . . . handmaidens? Subalterns might be a better word.

'Gita. How many of our army turn out on a good day?'

'Three hundred and fifty, Highness.' Gita's eyes and concentration did not lift from her needlework. She appeared to be attaching a bullion epaulette to the shoulder of a British captain of cavalry's blue jacket. Farquhar wondered where it had come from. The woman next to her shifted a little away from him and tweaked her shawl so that her face remained completely hidden from him. There was a moment when Bruce felt a tremor of familiarity prompted by this movement, but he gave it no further thought. Lakshmi Bai had a lot more to say.

'However,' the Ranee continued, 'if I announce that we are about to march to Cawnpore to join the Nana's army there, we should probably muster the full thousand and more.' She put her fingertips together beneath her chin and brought her head forward. 'There is, however, one circumstance under which they might protect me from the sepoys. If Lord Canning were to confirm me as regent until Damodar is of age, and guarantee the continuing independence of—'

Farquhar interrupted.

'Highness,' he said, as gently but as firmly as he could, 'this ground has already been covered. There is absolutely no possibility of what you are suggesting coming about. This is not Lord Canning's decision, although he concurs that it is the correct one – the responsibility lies solely with the Board of Directors, and they will not budge. However, I am permitted to say that Lord Canning might, in return for your help at these times, consider raising your pension,

222

and later that of your adopted son, from sixty thousand rupees a year to a full lakh—'

At this point they were both speaking at once and speech came close to a shout.

'This is insupportable,' came from the Ranee, 'your lord, the jumped-up grandson of an actor and a slut, no better than a nautch, dares insult me with the sort of offer you might make to an aged cook on her retirement from service—'

And from him . . .

'He also wishes you to know that overt support for the mutiny is punishable only by death.'

At this point there was a discreet knocking at the door.

The vakil came an inch or two into the room. A slight but not altogether pleasant smile sat on his lips.

'The three English officials who intruded upon you this morning have been executed.'

The Ranee thought for a moment, biting her lower lip and examining her long and painted fingernails.

'I did not order this,' she said at last, 'but I am not displeased.' She turned to Farquhar. 'They came from the fort which they and their families and the English officers refuse to leave though they have no right to be there. They foolishly attempted to disguise themselves as Mahometans which I, and others, found offensive. Their aim was to arrange a safe conduct to Agra for themselves and their families. I tried to explain to them that I could not guarantee their safety on such a journey and they resorted to both threats and bribery. Eventually I told them to go.'

Gita looked up from her sewing.

'Madam called them pigs,' she said, and smiled.

There was significance here that was not lost on Farquhar. By calling them pigs the Ranee had placed them beyond the protection of law or custom in the eyes of both Mahometans and Hindoos. Silence fell, broken only by the creak of the punkah and the slow running of water from the garden beyond. Farquhar took a breath.

'Why,' he asked, 'was Mr Andrews murdered before the others?'

'He was in dispute with Jharoo Comar, over taxes.' It was the vakil who replied. 'Jharoo's son killed him.'

'Jharoo Comar?'

'He grows opium. The opium inspector knew how much money he made, how much he owed in taxes.'

The Ranee took off her spectacles and her large eyes met his again. Her voice became deeper, almost solemn. 'Mr Farquhar, if I betray the mutineers the people of this city, my people, will force on me the suttee that I escaped when my husband died. They spared me then because they need me to rule until our son is old enough to take my place, for they know that if I do not then the English will. If I support the mutiny and the English win, the English will hang me. I spoke rashly when I used the word "pigs" but I think Shiva the Destroyer put the word on my lips for, by saying it, I placed myself, almost without thinking, on the side of my people. *Main Jhansi nahin dengee* – I will not give up my Jhansi. Not even if I hang for it. But I will do what I can to avoid the shedding of innocent blood.'

Again the silence, then she sighed and stood.

'Mira, Parvati, take him to the baths and get him clean. Then he can eat and drink with us.'

Bruce Farquhar spent the rest of the day in a bewitching ambience of luxury. Bathed, perfumed, robed in cool silks, fed on delicately spiced Persian pastries, sweet dishes flavoured with rose-water or lemon, and sweet but sharp fruits whose names he did not know, he was left free until dusk to wander through the palace rooms and gardens outside the zenana, the women's area, guarded unusually but appropriately enough by armed women. From beyond the walls of palace and town came the sounds of small-arms fire and distant shouts and screams. Smoke, much of it black or grubbily grey, billowed up into the sky and he fancied he could hear the crackle of flames devouring dry wood. The sour smell of burning dried dung occasionally drifted across the hedges of myrtle, the rose bushes and citrus trees, masking the fragrance of their white blossom. Often he returned to a balcony he had found from which he could see the highest part of the fort – the Union flag still flew and he rather thought most of the disturbances were occurring in the town.

After the sun had gone he was taken to a room outside the zenana, where he dined with the vakil and three other officials. They spoke little, but in answer to his questions said that certain badmashes in the town had attacked, looted and set fire to houses belonging to the Bengalese community, most of whom had been employed by the

British as writers or provided services for them. Finally he was taken to a small bedchamber. The privations of his long walk, compounded by this relaxing and unfamiliar experience of comfort and luxury, induced him almost immediately to fall into a deep sleep.

Farquhar was woken in moonlight by the gentle touch of a palm passed across his forehead. In what seemed like a dream, a female figure folded back the fine cotton sheet, embroidered with the likeness of lilies and other flowers, and knelt with her knees on either side of his waist. She was naked apart from rings on her fingers, a jewelled bangle and pearls twined into her black hair. She was perfumed with civet and other, sweeter, odours. Her skin was dark and at first cool, but as her passion grew, became moist. Her movements, her advances and retreats, her final offering of the gift she so urgently wanted to bestow were conducted with a strange mixture of confidence and assertiveness for much of the time, but occasionally with hesitancy and even clumsiness. Her face remained a secret, for she had her back to the window and the night sky was dark.

For all he was a flirt, a philanderer even, Bruce Farquhar, only just twenty-four years old, was, not untypically for his class and background, a virgin. He retained an ignorance supported by fantasies, even a sort of awed fear, of actual sex, of the sexual act itself. Indeed, his brief encounters with Sophie, erotically charged though they had been, were hedged in by his awareness on two occasions of her pregnancies and the sure knowledge, which, in a way, was reassuring, that anything more than a swift embrace was out of the question in a situation where her husband or a servant might intrude.

Transporting him now to a world that even those erotic dreams, actual dreams, that occasionally visited him had not been able to reveal, this houri, or was she a succubus ('the devil hath power t'assume a pleasing shape'), dissolved these doubts. She also revealed to him the secrets of what sexual intimacy can do for a woman; indeed this appeared to be part of her purpose, for when she finally slipped from the bed and resumed a gown she had left beside it, she looked down at him.

'Remember this,' she murmured, 'when you have a wife.'

Which was like slap in the face: for rather longer than he felt should have been the case Uma Blackstock had been entirely absent from his mind. Not that he was actually contemplating marriage with her, though the idea had crossed his mind. However, he was also well aware that marrying a half-caste at this very moment in the story of relations between India and the Raj could be seen as a poor way of advancing his career. None of which presented itself there and then to his mind in so many words: but it did all bang about in his head, in uncomfortable ways. However, his was an unstable and shallow character and he tended always to adapt himself to the immediate situation in which he found himself. He would not have been as good a spy as he was had this not been so.

An hour after sunrise, with his body still tingling and even aching from what had happened, from what had been done to him, with faint bruise marks in his neck and scratches on his back and thighs, conscious of odours about him he had never encountered before, he was taken by the vakil to the room he had seen the Ranee in the day before. This time she was alone but, as before, seated behind her desk and dressed as she had been. She gave no sign that could be interpreted as acknowledgement that anything had happened between them during the night but the possibility brought a surge of embarrassment that quickly faded as he rejected the idea. The woman, girl really, who may or may not have come to him in the night and who was even now taking on all the characteristics of a dream, was not Lakshmi Bai, the Ranee. Beautiful in her way though the Ranee was, there was a steeliness, a spareness about her, not shared by his seductress.

'I need help, Mr Farquhar. I need help.'

'I shall be happy to help you in any way I can.'

'The sepoys want guns and men, and will murder me and my women if they do not get them. They will use them to get into the fort and once they are in and have overcome the score of Englishmen still in there, they will murder the survivors and their women and children. If this happens Lord Canning will hang me. There is only one way out. The English must be persuaded that their only hope lies in giving themselves up in return for a promise of safe passage to Gwalior, if it is still in English hands, or Agra. They will not accept the word of the sepoys for this – there have been too many murders already – but if you go into the fort and assure them that I am the guarantor that they will be spared, they might agree to come out.'

She raised her head and her eyes, perhaps now with some complicity in them, met his. 'I can see no other way of preventing terrible blood-shed both in the fort and . . .' her eyes seemed to wander over the room in a way that somehow included the rest of the palace and its gardens and all who lived in them, 'and here too.'

He left her but the thought went with him that albeit it was certainly not she who had come to him that night, she might very well know who had.

31

Jhansi, 6 June 1857

Most castles have secret exits and entrances – passages through which provisions can be brought to a starving garrison, a way out for escapees or even sorties, and so on. They vary in size and usefulness but generally speaking will accommodate a single man on a horse. The fort at Jhansi had just such a postern at the foot of the north-eastern wall which appeared to drop sheer for forty feet or so to a steep bank that served as a scarp. A turret or tower broke the line of the wall and the gate of the postern was more or less hidden in the angle by etiolated thorn bushes. As the cannonade, provided by two ancient brass guns directed at the great gate on the southern side, commenced, Farquhar, once again 'blacked up', equipped with a large iron key provided by the vakil, opened and slipped through the ancient gate, locking it behind him. A spiral flight of stone stairs took him to a wide platform within the battlements.

He made his way along this to the embrasures that overlooked the gate and was able to see how such a tiny force could hold the fort against a small army. Apart from the postern the only way in was through the gate, for the rest the walls were up to a hundred feet high and almost welded, it seemed, into the rock on which they sat. They were too high and too smooth for climbing or for an escalade. Without a proper siege train the only vulnerable point was the gate and even that was proving too strong for the century-old guns. In an attempt to make them more effective the sepoys were at this moment pushing them closer to the gates but without protective trenches, gabions and so forth the English rifles were picking off the men who serviced them.

As he approached the officers, engineers, Company administrators and their families, all of whose attention was fixed on the enemy outside, Farquhar suddenly heard himself challenged from behind.

'Who goes there? Who are you are? Turn and indent . . . ident, tell me who you are. And prove it.'

He turned, found he was facing a lad of about ten or eleven who was holding a cavalry carbine which was far too big for him to handle safely. The hammer was pulled back and the boy's finger was on the trigger.

Bruce raised his arms.

'Lieutenant Bruce Farquhar of the 75th and your obedient servant. Please take me to your commanding officer.'

'That would be my father,' the boy replied with obvious pride. 'Captain Skene. Please come with me.' And then . . . 'Dad! Daa-ad!'

Skene, a portly bewhiskered gentleman, perspiring heavily, the sweat making runnels in the black of burnt powder on his forehead, holstered his revolver and came over.

'Who the divil are you?'

Bruce did his best to explain and showed him the key to the postern.

'Wouldn't believe a word of it if I hadn't heard gossip about chaps like you. Go about dressed as beggars? Speak the lingo? Jolly useful I'm sure but somehow not the sort of occupation one expects a gentleman to get involved in. Anyway. No offence. What can I do for you?'

The captain's credulity was stretched even further when he was told that Bruce had been in face-to-face contact with the Ranee.

'Deuced fine woman. Nevertheless, a Native, and not to be trusted. What does she want?'

'She's trapped between two impossible choices and is seeking a third way. If she sides with the sepoys she will eventually be caught and tried by the British and she will probably hang for it. Especially if any further harm comes to you and your colleagues. If she sides with us they have promised to assassinate her . . .'

'She has her own army.'

'Which has declared support for the sepoys.'

'So what does she want us to do?'

'Presently they will come to you and offer you escorted passage to Gwalior or Agra. But only if you surrender formally and hand over your arms. She wants you to accept these terms and guarantees your safety if you do.'

Skene chewed his thumb for a moment. Then, 'Let me see what the other officers think.' But hardly on his way, he turned back. 'That key. If there's one there could be two.'

Bruce shrugged.

'It's possible.'

'I should have put a picket on it, but so few people . . . Jamie, go to where you can see the place where the postern stairs arrive and keep an eye on it, there's good fellow.'

And that's how it turned out. The officers were still in deep discussion some ten minutes later when young Jamie gave a shout and ran back to them with musket balls whistling about his head.

'Golly, this is splendid fun,' he said, before spilling out the news that twenty or more sepoys were filling the lower platform.

'Up to the keep then,' shouted Skene. 'Everyone up to the keep.'

'I hit one of them, you know,' cried Jamie, waving the carbine above his head.

'Well done, old chum.'

The women, the children and most of the Native Christians from the town, maybe a hundred in all, were already up there. The twenty or so British males, with a handful of boys like Jamie, now scampered up exposed stairs and ramps between high walls, to an upper level. Skene quickly placed the men at the top where they could cover the approaches and once again a near silence, pregnant with anxiety, fell over them, broken only by the mewling of an infant and the keening of a Bengalese woman whose husband had been beheaded the day before. The Union flag flapped in the hot wind more closely above them, the swifts racketed about the sky above it and even higher Egyptian vultures, white and black, cruised in anticipation.

'Six hours at most,' Skene muttered when he felt sure no one but Bruce could hear him.

'Why so little?'

'No food. No water. When your chap comes we'll have to accept his offer.'

'Not my chap.'

'You know what I mean.'

Towards dusk, with the air becoming just perceptibly cooler, a bugle sounded a parlay and a turbanned sowar appeared at the top of the last ramp with a big white flag, a sheet perhaps or gown, attached to a bamboo pole. Skene ostentatiously laid down his musket and the men behind him followed suit. The ressaldar, the senior Native officer of the cavalry, came forward and saluted Skene, whom of course he knew well.

There was not much to discuss and presently the tiny garrison, escorted by a troop of unmounted sowars, made its way back down all the ramps and stairs that took them through the gate. As they descended their mood lightened. Chatter and even song broke out. Children scampered ahead, two bowled their hoops, and had to be called back.

'We'll take you to the Jokhan Bagh,' the ressaldar said to Skene, naming a small public garden that lay between the fort and the city walls. 'We'll find you some food and you'll be able to sleep there. You can leave before daybreak.'

The garden, when they got to it, turned out to be a dusty piece of ground, longer than it was broad, with dead plants in flowerbeds and acacia trees so dried up in appearance it was impossible to think they would ever bear leaf again. The dying breeze was still strong enough to rattle their long dried-up pods which hung, so one of the children said, like the fingers of dead witches. It also stirred up a fine white ash from what appeared to be the remains of a gardener's bonfire and seeing this it dawned on Bruce that they were in one of the places the Hindoos of the town used for cremations. Indeed behind it all rose the shikharas of a substantial Hindoo temple.

The ressaldar issued orders. The sowars pushed the Europeans and the Christians into three lines separating the men, the women and the children. The sowars drew their tulwars and fell first on the men, hewing where possible their heads from their bodies or simply hacking at them until they fell to pieces. Captain Skene was one of the first.

'It is idle,' he cried, 'for you to hope that by destroying a handful of her men you will denude England of all her bold sons.'

The women were then slaughtered in the same way. Mr Carshore, the chief customs officer, had taught himself Hindi so that he might do his work properly and he had insisted his children should learn Hindi in order to promote a better understanding between the two races. His eldest son now begged that he should be spared as he hoped the mutineers' thirst for vengeance had been assuaged by the blood of his father and mother. Beside him Jamie Skene stood up straight.

'Die like an Englishman,' he said.

Again Bruce Farquhar was forced to watch from under the lengthening shadows of the trees. None of the murderers approached him and he was spared, perhaps on account of his appearance, perhaps because the Ranee had ordered or begged for his survival. Perhaps, though, simply because he was not noticed – he had the gift, when to have it was expedient, of rendering himself almost invisible which is perhaps why the accounts given a year later by Captain Skene's table servant and a Bengalese writer to a court of inquiry describe the massacre more or less as it is set down here, but make no mention of him at all.

And yet his departure, again on foot, did not go unnoticed. He was about three miles down the road to Gwalior and not yet into the teak forest, but passing a grove of giant mulberry trees whose silkworms provided Jhansi's main source of cash, when he heard the hooves of a horse in a slow canter coming up behind him. He turned, waited, poised himself for a sudden dash into a thicket should he catch a glimpse of a drawn tulwar or unholstered pistol. The horse, no more than a pony really, but well bred and in good condition with a well-groomed black coat, slowed to a walk ten yards behind him and the rider threw back the white hood of the gown she was wearing.

Farquhar's heart leapt and he had to grasp his pole tightly to counter a sudden wave of dizziness.

'Uma! Miss Blackstock,' he cried. 'What . . .? Why . . .?'

'I must be quick. I promised Lakshmi Bai I would not speak to you. And it is possible too that you will be pursued by men who do not look on you kindly.'

She leant forward and to the side and ran her long dark fingers through his dyed hair.

'No, say nothing, ask no questions, just listen to me. You have seen terrible things in Jhansi and when the news of them gets out she will be blamed. Please do everything you can to make the truth of what happened, and how she was herself a helpless prisoner in her palace,

232

when they happened, known by everyone of importance, up to the Governor General himself. There. That is all I have to say.'

He sensed she was about to turn her pony back towards Jhansi, and he seized hold of the reins, close to the bit.

'Please let go.'

'No. Wait. Was it you . . .?' He couldn't find the words to say what he wanted to say.

She straightened, looked down at him, and her mouth warmed into a teasing smile though her eyes remained serious.

'Who came to you in the night? Yes. It was.'

'Why?'

'What a question!' She laughed. 'Because I love you and because we are unlikely to meet again. And now, goodbye. Remember what I have said about Lakshmi Bai. That is more important than anything there is between us.'

Brusquely now she turned the pony's head, kicked with her booted heels and she was off again, at a faster gallop this time, back to Jhansi. The fort was still clearly visible above the plain, its dark stone softened to a gentler ochre by the setting sun, but the distance was too great to distinguish the Ranee's standard that now flew from its highest turret.

With his head and heart seething with conflicting emotions, Bruce set his face towards Gwalior, Agra, Delhi, and his regiment.

32

The Grand Trunk Road, Badli-ki-Serai, 6–9 June 1857

Ooooh, we won't know where we're going until we're there
Ooooh, we won't know where we're going until we're there
We won't know where we're going
We won't know where we're going
Ooooh, we won't know where we're going until we're there . . .

Five o'clock in the morning and the rosy sun not quite fingering the distant hilly horizon, the fields and groves still dun-grey or dark with night's retreating shades, and banks of nacreous mist above those tanks that still held water. A black-crested heron planted careful spreading feet along the shallows of a mantled pool and four snow-white egrets launched themselves into the air, their heads and necks four question marks, before settling on the further side.

The rulered road, lined with acacia trees and raised a foot above the fields, was filled with a column two and a half miles long, three thousand strong, swinging along at a steady three and a half miles an hour. A baggage train of bullock carts, elephants and heavy guns, of camp followers and a travelling bazaar, struggled to keep up. The four who had made up the band at Blackstock's reception two and a half years earlier – Nathan (no ts on account of missing front teeth), Sam from Ryde on the Isle of Wight, George with his big black beard, and small dark Taff from Ludlow – made up the third file of the second company of the 75th, the Gordon Highlanders. Nathan and George were Scots, the other two had been recruited as the regiment marched south through the shires to Portsmouth.

Bored with the very much repeated chant, George broke off, spat accurately into the ditch on his right.

'Och, but ye see, doncher, sure as God's my witness, I doos know where we be going.'

'Where would tha' be, Georgie, me ol' mucker?'

'Why, Del-High, mon.'

'Del-Lila, would be better.'

'Not a lot, see,' Taff chipped in. 'She were an a-rab, like as not a nigger, and definitely a Mussulman. Reason she had it in for ol' Samson. It's all in Holy Writ, mark you.'

'Here comes the sun,' cried Sam. Being the left-hand file he felt it first, an immediate warmth as if from an opened stove door on his left cheek, although there was no more than a fingernail, just showing above a low bare rise beyond the mist, almost but not quite the last of the outcrops that climbed behind them back to Umballa, Simla and the Himalaya.

'Shit,' said George and gave his oblong black haversack a hitch then ran a finger of his free left hand inside his collar, making sure that the curtain that hung from the white circular cover which had been pulled over his black pillbox cap was free and hung down to his khaki-clad shoulders. Their previously slate-blue or white jackets and trousers had all been dyed in Umballa in Hodson's khaki while they were waiting to move south. 'How long have we been on this fucking march, then? Black as pitch when we started.'

'Three hours,' said Sam, who had a watch with a gun-metal case that he'd polished until it shone like dull gold, or brownish brass. He thrust it back into an inside pocket he'd made for it.

'Village up ahead. And d' cavalry have been busy already, muss 'av bin 'ere las nigh',' said Nathan who was taller than the others, tall enough to have been in the grenadier company but was reckoned too maverick. Still, he could see over the heads of the file in front of him.

'Hoo d'yer reckon all that oot?'

'Go' eyes in me 'ead, George.'

'Which tell yer what the jockeys have bin up to?'

'*Look*, yer daff bugger, whoi don' yer?'

An overarching bough, half-broken, dipped towards the middle of the road. Eight bodies, six in long white robes, two in dhotis, a couple of them with their turbans coming undone and hanging all awry, dangled from tight nooses. Almost all the faces were suffused, with swollen cheeks and bruise-coloured skin. Their tongues protruded, were also swollen and black, their eyes open and staring except for those that showed only the whites. The lower folds of their robes, and the legs of those that wore dhotis, were streaked with faeces and urine. As the sun struck them the flies reappeared, swarming over their faces and over the ordure. As they passed beneath them Nathan had to use the muzzle of his modified Baker rifle, the P-42, to swing a pair of legs away and behind so the feet wouldn't brush the top of his cap.

'All strangled,' remarked Taff. 'Must have been up twenty minutes or more before they snuffed. Ain't right.'

'Sure an' i' is,' Nathan sounded angry. 'Women an' children there was comin' oo o' Del-High. Oor kin, 'scapin oo Karnal. All hacked oo pieces and wuss. These fuckers go' less than they deserved, believe you me.'

There were another twenty or so bodies hanging from the trees before they got to the village, which was a small one.

'Just about every man Tom of 'em,' commented George, pulling on his beard, 'How they'd know if these niggers were the ones that done it?'

'Doos i' ma'er?'

The village appeared empty though here and there a tattie shifted in a doorway but not with the breeze, because there was none.

'Don't they know they're supposed to come out with jugs of water and garlands of flowers when we march through?'cried Sam.

'Daf bugger y' are, Sam.'

'Was just a joke, Nathan. Just a joke.'

Oooh, we won't know where we're going until we're there . . .

7 JUNE, BADLI-KI-SERAI, ABOUT FIVE MILES NORTH OF DELHI

Evening this time, dusk, the sun on their right, deep yet bright like a blood orange just dipping behind a tope of mangoes that looked like a black silhouette. A tiny owl rose from the top of a telegraph pole and flew above the thin copper wire that glowed like red gold to the next, a hundred yards away.

Hodson, hacking south on reconnaisance with Dixon at his side and some twenty of his irregulars behind him, remarked on its flight.

'*Athene noctua*,' he said.

'I beg your pardon, sir?'

'*Athene noctua*,' he repeated. 'The little owl, James. Don't get them in England, but from Turkey right across to the other side of India, they're common enough. Some ornithologists see a difference in the Indian version and classify it *Athene brama*. Ah! See that? On that rise, to the left of the road. Someone up there's got his eye on us. There. Again! Surely you caught it this time?'

A flash of light winking off glass. Higher than the ground between it and them and still catching the sunlight, the crest of the rise was lined with what looked like a very small settlement of tumbled cabins, their ochre walls of dried cow dung only distinguishable from the rock and soil they stood on by the comparative straightness of their lines. One larger building to the right was whitewashed and stood over the road they were on. Hodson drew his horse to a standstill and an upraised arm brought the others to a halt, then, fumbling in his sabretache, he pulled up a map tightly folded to show the area they were in. His finger traced across it, came to a halt.

'Badli-ki-Serai,' he said. 'Know what a serai is, James?'

'An inn for travellers?'

'Now look along the crest to the left, about three hundred yards. What do you see?'

'A sort of declivity in the slope, as if the earth has been scooped out. Quite large. And a broken chimney, must have been quite tall. Looks like a brick kiln but in ruins.'

'Not so much ruins as ruined. Use your glass and look along the bank at the front of it.'

'Guns, big ones. Three eighteen-pounders and five, six smaller.'

'One of the big ones is actually a twenty-four-pounder. It won't be easy to get past that lot. We'd better see what else they've got here and if there's a way round them.'

Hodson flung out his left arm, urged his horse into a canter and took the ditch that separated the road from the field. They all followed him into the deepening gloaming. A puff of white smoke, a distant thud, then almost immediately the whistling scream of a four-pound round shot shredding the air. It thudded into the road just about where Hodson's horse had been standing and bounded into the field beyond.

'Good shot,' Hodson commented.

Well taught, thought James Dixon, thinking of the artillery range at Meerut.

8 JUNE, BADLI-KI-SERAI

One o'clock in the morning, the moon nearly full again, and the last day's march towards Delhi got under way. First an advance guard of a couple of guns and a squadron of the 9th Lancers with the Irregulars still scouting out in the fields on their flanks, then, General Anson having died of cholera at Karnal, General Sir Henry Barnard now commanding, with his staff, followed by the 75th marching in column of sections, Lt Richard Barter riding alongside the colonel in front. Barter, a handsome almost bullish young man, later wrote up an account of the battle.

By four o'clock or thereabouts it was light enough to see the low rise in front with the white serai on its right. Further to the left the gun emplacements just below the visual crest were still in deep shadow but marked by a large fire, surely more than a cooking fire, from which a column of pale grey smoke climbed against a pearly sky. Perhaps they were burning brush cleared from the slope to give it the function of a scarp or glacis. An officer close to Sir Henry procured a spyglass from a camel orderly and passed it to the general.

'There's no need,' and he waved it aside. 'There they are,' and he gave the orders to deploy ready for an assault. The 75th halted, faced left, and with parade-ground exactitude brought their left shoulders up, the files that had been in the rear swinging out off the road and into the field, the outer end of a radius centred on the stationary files at the other end, forming a line four deep. Barked commands and the front two lines moved forward leaving a ten-yard gap between them and the other two. Thus a column on the march had become the two red lines (khaki now) so celebrated in newspapers and history books.

While this was happening the first round shot from a heavy gun tore through some trees on the right of the road. A second hit the horse of Grant, the 75th's interpreter, in the chest and came out at its tail, giving Grant a nasty fall and a bit of a fright, but no other hurt. The shot, though nearly spent, had not finished its work for it went on to shatter the arm of one of the men just behind Barter and to his right. They were ordered to lie down until the other regiments were in position on their right, leaving them with the enemy guns straight ahead of them. Barter was not sorry to dismount and he made himself as small as possible while the shot went shrieking over their heads with that peculiar sound which, once heard, is never forgotten.

Then came the order: 'The 75th will advance and take that battery.'

In an instant the line was up, Barter remounted and on they went, down a small bank and over a shallow drain. The top of the rise was still a good fifteen hundred yards away. The sun was properly up now and they could see not only the battery near the top but how the enemy had deployed regiments on the plain in front of it with batteries of nine-pounders on their flanks.

Shell and shot fell fast. Men were dropping, some screaming in agony, others staring white-faced and bewildered at limbs smashed to pulp, or body wounds revealing their own intestines. Two ammunition tumbrils were hit by a shell which blew them up killing many more, albeit they had been placed behind an old tomb. Old Dowton, normally a mess servant, fell close to Barter. His hip was crushed to pieces by a round shot and as he rolled over he looked up with a kind of smile on his face and said, 'It's all over with me, Mr Barter.' He was dead at once.

'Ol' Dow'on's gone.'

'Bless me, so 'e 'as.'

'Ain't that little Ali Baba, the bugle boy? Hey, Ali, your turban's slipping. Look, Mr Barter's 'avin a word with him an' he's tying it up. Sweet little bugger, ain't he?'

'Comin' up with the staff and the general we are. See, there they be, on tha' hillock. Wha's tha'? Hal' an' lie down again? Don' mind if I do, squire. Beddy-byes, George, wha' you say, eh?'

'Who's that ol' man on the big grey? Be he deaf or sumthin'?'

'Reckon it's Colonel Chester. Adjutant general.'

'Fuckin' lawyer. Don't know his arse from his elbow in a battle. Christ, I told you so, there he goes.'

'What happened? What happened?'

'Ball hit his holster pipes and set the lot off. Blew his inside outside. Oh shit, you can see the poor bugger's stomach. Next we'll see will be his breakfast.'

'Ain't that young Captain Barnard holdin' 'm? Sir Henry's son?'

'What's he say, Sam, what's he sayin'?'

'He says "Lift me up, Willie, and let me look at my wound . . ." an' then he says, "That will do boy, go to your father."'

'Bless 'im. Died like a gen'leman, an' a soldier.'

'Not dead yet.'

'Good as. Good as – you can't get up and leave your stomach on the floor and live to tell your gran'children.'

'Look at Barter. Reckon he's a lucky sod the number I've seen dropped all round 'im.'

'Hey, Sam, where you goin' then?'

'Never you mind, Nathan . . . I'll come where you are, Mr Barter; I think you're lucky, sir. Shit! Beg pardon, sir, but did you see that shot? Hit the ground just where I was lying, see what I mean?'

'Jammy bastard, that Sam.'

'Always was.'

CHARGING THE GUNS

Brigadier Showers in front, then the colour sergeant, then Barter who was the only officer in the 75th who still had a horse to carry him. Behind him the lads' line was perfectly dressed, the men carrying their arms at the slope, their faces white with determination not to be the first to run for it, the sergeants redressing the line where it wavered or commanding their men to 'close up, close up there' where a man fell or dropped out with a limb shattered or whatever. Then, at about eight hundred yards, the brigadier ordered double time. It was an impressive sight, a frightening one, to see that perfectly dressed line, arms still shouldered, coming up inexorably like a line of khaki surf. At a hundred and fifty yards, which left them still more or less safe from the old Tower muskets the Natives had, they halted and fired a volley from their rifles, which, though not Enfields, were effective at that range.

'How grand fired powder smells,' crowed Nathan, ramming the next round down the muzzle of his rifle. 'Especially in the morning.'

But by now the Native gunners had made the necessary adjustments to their mortars and shells were falling and bursting among them. One burst between their two ensigns, wounding both and

240

shredding the silk of the colours, but somehow they kept them upright. Another blew up in the faces of the company to Barter's right.

'Shit, can't see a fucking thing. Who's that bumping into me? Is it you, Nathan, get the fuck off me, will you?'

'Shrapnel 'ook the skin off the back of me hand. Dropped me fucking rifle. Where the fuck is the fucker?'

'Is that Mr Barter shoutin' at us? What's he say?'

'Tellin' us not to turn, he is. It's all right, Mr Barter, never fear, sir. We ain't agoin' to turn.'

'Cheeky bastard.'

'Come on, lads, let's get in among them while there's any still there.'

'Wait for it, lads, wait for the order.'

'Who's that old Rupert on the 'orse? What's he sayin'? Cain't 'ear nuffin'. Gawn deaf as Lot's wife.'

'Lads of the 75th, you've done frightfully well so far. I'm sure you'll see these blighters home in double-quick time, and God bless you all.'

'Hurrah!'

'Wha' you say?'

'Hurrah.'

'Why?'

'It's what he wanted. Where's Taff?'

'Prepare to charge.'

'About fuckin' time.'

Rasp and click. What was left of three hundred men fixed bayonets as one to become the soft part of that most terrible of weapons – a British soldier with a bayonet. A great shout, and on they came through the swirling smoke, their feet kicking up sparks where the brush had caught fire.

'Aaaaaaah . . . In, twist, and out, gotcha. An' the next please. In, twist, and out. Ah, yer would, would yer? Parry, thrust. You're a well-trained Pandy, ain't yer? Oof. There. Gotcher. Don' worry, my darling, nice clean blade, no fear of gangrene. Who's next?'

Onwards and upwards right up to the guns and beyond, taking them, to the eternal glory of the regiment.

'Ain't that Mr Barter on the ground there? Mr Barter, you all right?'

241

'Not entirely, George. Got a ball in the calf of my leg. Look, you can see the lump down there, couple of inches below where it went in.'

'I'll call for the surgeon, sir.'

'No, George. Others in greater need. I think if I just squeeze up behind it I'll be able to ease it out the way it went in.'

'No, don't do that, sir. You'll make matters worse . . .'

'There we go, George. O-o-out, it comes.'

'Oooh, sir, that's 'orrible, that is.'

'Squeamish, are you, George? Quick, pass me that black handkerchief, let me bind it up . . .'

'Sir, Mr Barter, if you please . . .?'

'Sam?'

'Taff here's bad with grape in his gut. Let me an' George carry him with you to the carts an' we can keep an eye on you like, too.'

'Sounds good, Sam. Pandy seems to have lost his nerve and scarpered so I reckon we can be spared . . .'

The wounded were in carts that looked like nothing so much as horse-drawn London double-deckers knocked together by village carpenters, the walking wounded clinging to each other on the roof, ten to a cart, the inside crammed with the dying and sometimes the dead.

The cart swayed and jogged as the driver whipped his pair of nags into a frenzy, even taking them off the road and into the field to overtake a couple of elephants that were going too slowly for him. Taff mumbled incoherently. All his life as a soldier he had always been in some mess or other, never clean on parade or for guard duty. He was badly hurt having taken a handful of grape in his body and with one arm shattered too, shards of bone and flesh poking through his tattered sleeve. Barter give him some water and tried to cheer him up, but he would beg pardon for all the trouble he had given, saying 'I know, Mr Barter, I have always been a bad soldier.' Barter told him that his wounds and conduct showed he'd been a good soldier in the field where it mattered. They got to talking about his hope in the world to come to which, he said, he knew he was hastening, being mortally wounded.

Barter made it on to The Ridge, a mile or so beyond the serai, having promised Taff he'd send a doolie or stretcher for him as soon as he could.

'George, wassermarrer wiv you?'

'Taff, Nathan. Surgeon took 'is arm off at daybreak an' he died an hour after.'

'Oh bugger. Oh fuck an' bugger. 'Aff. Never 'ave oo check 'is burrons done up ri' before parade again, daff bugger 'e was. Sam? You 'ear tha'?'

'I hear it, Nathan. Heap a shit. Poor ol' Taff. Well. All I want roight now is to get among some pandies and dedicate a few to porr ol' Taff.'

Oooh, we won't know where we're going until we're there . . .

33

Bindki, Futtehpore, 1–10 June 1857

Towards sunset on 1 June, ten Sikh sowars led by a sergeant, or havildar, turned off the Grand Trunk Road and trotted over the raised embankment which would one day be the continuation of the same railway line James Neill had appropriated a fortnight earlier, across the parched fields and dried riverbeds, towards a small and entirely ordinary village. In their midst was a doolie, a stretcher with a back rest and a small awning, supported on two long poles ending in four handles so that the whole affair could be carried by two coolies. Amazingly these maintained, for three hours or more at a stretch, a loping, jogging run that kept up with the slow trot of the troopers' horses. By these means they had carried Tom Hardcastle, a small leather bag containing a spare set of unmentionables and his shaving things, hairbrushes, colognes and so forth all neatly compartmented within, and four of his law books, swaying and bouncing, the three hundred miles from Meerut.

Hardcastle, whose moods had lurched from dull misery through acute anxiety to blind panic throughout the trip called out, 'Why have we left the road?', and bit his tongue just as he had at almost every attempt he had made to communicate with the havildar while they were moving.

'Not to worry, sah, not to worry,' shouted the havildar above the jingle-jangle of harness, the steady cross rhythms of the horses' hooves. *Not to worry* was his mantra, sometimes lengthened to 'Not to worry, no hurry, get the curry . . . sah!'

They are taking me, Hardcastle decided and the cold feeling in the pit of his stomach sank lower and threatened a bout of the flux, they are taking me off the road so they can cut my throat. But no. Presently they passed the nearly empty but still moist pool or small tank where the buffalo heaved and panted and gasped for more liquid than there was, scattered some very scraggy hens, and in a cloud of dust came to a halt in a space among a score of thatched shacks made from slabs of rock-hard cow dung. Silence for a moment as the darkness visibly thickened then tatties shifted, a cough or two were heard and a group of dark men mostly in white and women in a bright rainbow of sarees gathered round them. One taller than the rest, and thinner, with a sad but intelligent face, stood out and engaged with the havildar. Clearly the village zemindar, or headman.

The discussion, which was not heated but on the havildar's side urgent, came to an end and he walked across to Hardcastle who was still sitting in the doolie with his knees up and clasped in his hands which had been gripping the sides for the previous two hours.

'Permission to speak, sah!'

'Of course, Babur. Speak away, only tell me what's happening.'

'We are now fifteen miles or so distant from the district town of Futtehpore. And in the morning my kinsman Jiva, the zemindar of this village which is called Bindki, will take you there.'

'Why can't you take me there?'

The havildar brushed his moustaches upwards, cleared his throat, and then thought better of saying anything at all. A rather odd expression drifted into his eyes and mouth combining a child's plea for forgiveness with a determination not to be shifted from his chosen course. The cold grip returned to Hardcastle's entrails, squeezing them.

'You're going to join the mutiny, aren't you,' he said, trying hard to sound angry rather than wretched. Four thuds behind him; he looked round and down and found his law books on the dusty floor. He began again, trying to give his voice a note of stern authority but it fluked up plaintively before he had finished.

'I'll see you hanged, Babur, I'll see you hanged. Just you wait. You'll be hanged, you know, and all your men with you.'

But Babur pulled his black charger's head round, raised his right arm. All the sowars followed him at a slow canter, back towards the road.

Bastards took his bag, supposing it had more value than his books.

Distributing themselves among relatives, Jiva and his family vacated their home and lent it to Hardcastle for the night. They even, against custom and genuine feeling, killed a chicken for him which they baked in an earthenware pot and served with chickpea dahl and chappatis. He did his best with the chicken, but Jiva's wife was not used to cooking meat – it was almost raw in places and very stringy. Beneath a tiny oil lamp in whose flame flies fried themselves he ate as much as he could and then tried to read from his pocket New Testament, but the light was not good enough and he soon gave up. He had a pee in the chipped enamelled tin bucket, made in Birmingham, that Jiva had indicated might answer such a need, and lowered himself on to the creaky bed. The larger than usual charpoy, a bed made from withies woven to and fro across a simple wooden frame with a very thin mattress and a cotton cover, was not only uncomfortable but richly redolent of the humanity that had used it for forty years.

Whether or not there were bedbugs or other fauna in the mattress he certainly felt that there were. His skin seemed to crawl with them all through the night, on his shoulders, his thighs and in his crotch although he kept on trousers and shirt. He thought of Sophie; he thought of how in circumstances like these she would be practical, would make them comfortable, or at least cheer him up. She should have been with him and, for a time, he could not recall just why it was she had remained in Meerut. But he did think of little Stephen, and now for the first time since the children had disappeared, he began to weep, in the darkness of a hut far down the Doab with, forgetting Futtehpore, not a white man within, what, sixty miles? It must be as much as that to Allahabad.

Cockcrow, and there were several of them. Such a racket hauling him out of the short deep sleep that had fallen on him like a coffin lid an hour before first light. Cows mooed, he could hear people on the move, about their business, greeting each other as if they had been away for months, and a short Vedic chant. And then, just as a horizontal shaft of sunlight struck like an arrow or sword blade between the slabs of cow dung and touched his shoulder, Jiva came in with a tiny cup of thick hot milk, spiced with cinnamon, and the inevitable

246

chappati. But this one was hot and fragrant, soft in the middle, crisp on the outside, straight off the hotplate. So hot he burnt his fingers trying to tear it. At the first mouthful the pain struck, a terrible, clawing crab of cramp in his lower gut, and he knew he needed a latrine more urgently than ever before during his three years in India. And, thank the Lord, and Jiva's wife, there was the bucket.

He knew it was not cholera; cholera he had seen do its work – a few hours of deepening misery, totally liquid effluent, fever, disorientation, delirium and death within forty-eight hours and no pain until the final stages. What he had was dysentery. Almost as likely to be fatal but far more prolonged and painful.

They nursed him, especially Jiva's wife who bathed his face with a cloth soaked in tepid water, gave him rice water, cane syrup, salt. They dosed him with astringent infusions made from field herbs. Day by day, over a week or more, he recovered.

Jiva's English was rudimentary, Hardcastle's Hindi nonexistent.

'Futtehpore?'

That, at any rate, Hardcastle understood. He rather thought it was the administrative centre of a division and so should have a judge, collector, magistrate and so on. Supposing they had not all already been murdered.

'White men?' he asked.

This Jiva ignored.

'Eighteen miles,' he replied.

Speaking slowly, and more loudly, and making gestures like a policeman directing an unruly crowd, Hardcastle attempted to cross the language barrier.

'Can. You. Take. Me. There?'

Jiva could, and, what's more, he found a donkey for the assistant judge advocate. He, however, walked.

J. W. Sherer was the newly appointed, newly arrived Magistrate and Collector at Futtehpore. He kept a diary.

> 7th June: The townspeople now ostracise us almost
> completely. Only the opium addicts still come to the
> station to get their daily allowance from our Opium
> Inspector.

247

9th June: There was much agitation in the fields right from daybreak with the peasantry rushing about like a *jacquerie*, an agricultural *émeute*, with great excitement but no object. My altercation with Judge Robert Tucker continued as before. My point was that we should withdraw across the Jumna and head south as a means of leaving the area most affected by the mutinies and uprisings, while he favoured taking the Grand Road up towards Delhi. We could not agree and parted.

10th June: Last night we were somewhat bothered by the arrival of a Captain Hardcastle, an assistant judge advocate, on the back of a donkey and escorted only by the Zemindar of Bindki. He was on his way, he said, to Allahabad where he hoped to meet up with British and loyal troops, who had lost their legal staff to cholera or fever. He had had an escort, but they had deserted and were, he believed, heading for Delhi, which is why I mention them now – for this surely shows I am right to head south.

This Hardcastle is hardly lucid, very tired, and perhaps not fully in his right mind, for he too rejected my advice to go south and said he would continue at first light towards Allahabad.

Nevertheless he kept out of the way while we made our preparations for leaving. Our Native servants could not have been more helpful. My personal baggage was limited to one small bag but they gave us elaborate instructions as to where the little knick-knacks of the toilet could be found, *viz.*, 'Put your hand in this corner and you will find your comb and here your shoe-horn.' It was more like being sent to school by one's mother than anything else and more so still when our actual departure was accompanied by tearful farewells.

Judge Tucker slept in the guardhouse but set out for his own house early this morning. The gaol had been opened and since many of the occupants had been put there by him, they treated him with contumely.

Certainly he put his rifle to good use and probably injured or killed some of them. On arriving home he ascended to the roof of his office which he had often said was a suitable place for defence.

A group of the lower sort of Mahomedans now approached. They had banners and symbols of the Moslem Faith and a copy of the Koran and they discharged several firearms at the gaunt figure standing against the sky which was leaden on account of the heat. There was a sharp return from the roof. Again a silence, broken only by the monotonously muttered passages from the Koran. Again a discharge and, struck by a bullet in the forehead, Robert Tucker sank to rise no more.

By then Tom Hardcastle, still on the donkey which he bought from Jiva with a sovereign taken from his money belt, but otherwise alone, was five miles down the road towards Allahabad. By noon it was mercilessly hot but he durst not seek shade and rest for fear that while he slept his only friend in the world, the donkey, might be taken from him. Kali, the scarlet and black goddess of death, with her tongue hanging out, pranced in front of him, coming it seemed out of the sun, swinging the rope of skulls round her neck in an antic that recalled Miranda Dixon swinging her hoop in their garden at Christmas three years before. Above it all the voice of the Reverend Rotton denounced the pagan horrors of Hinduism. Then the foul goddess turned her back on him and revealed naked buttocks from between which she let out a thunderous fart. This propelled her ever diminishing image down the perspective of the road until she reached the vanishing point and vanished.

Shame flooded over him – naked female flesh was bad enough, but to desecrate the idea of womanhood by ascribing the ability to fart to the gentle sex (he had of course heard Sophie emit the slightest squeaks of gas in the night while she slept, but what his addled brain had just invented went far, far beyond those) plunged him into a pit of self-abasement so that he felt he had to dismount, and, while still keeping a careful grip on the donkey's halter, and thus on reality, he knelt and banged his head repeatedly on the ground begging that old Prepuce Collector in the Sky to forgive him.

He remounted, kicked the donkey into motion, and, to keep at bay any further horrors the heat might suck from his addled brain, began to sing lustily:

> *The world, the flesh and Satan dwell*
> *Around the path I tread*
> *O save me from the snares of hell*
> *Thou quickener of the dead . . .*

At which point, or maybe an hour and ten hymns later, he was brought to his senses by voices. By then his head and body had slouched forward so that his cheek was on the moke's neck just below its floppy ears and his arms hung down the flanks of its front legs. Flies buzzed around his head but were kept on the move by the donkey's ears which flapped intermittently like a pair of punkahs operated by a lazy wallah.

'I say, this fellow don't seem to me to be a peasant. Look at his boots. Army boots, I'd bet on it.'

'Could have been stolen, sir.'

'Maybe, Williams. But I think we should have a closer look. Either he's one of ours or he's one of theirs, in which case I suppose we shall have to string him up.'

Hardcastle opened his eyes, hauled himself into an upright position, looked around. A dozen or so bay chargers, a lieutenant and a dozen or so troopers, British. White, anyway.

'Can't do that,' he stammered. 'Not without a warrant signed by a legal authority. Mind you, I suppose I could sign my own warrant . . .' And he slipped slowly sideways and hit the ground before any of them could dismount and catch him. They got some water into him, loaded him on to one of the chargers behind the smallest of the troopers, left the donkey to fend for itself and continued on their way at a slow trot towards Allahabad.

They rested up through the hottest part of the day in a mango tope, spent the night in an abandoned serai and arrived in Allahabad at about ten in the morning, having set off before dawn. Over the final ten miles the countryside had been ravaged and raped. Every village had been burnt, and with the proximity of both rivers, the Ganges and the Jumna, whose confluence is at Allahabad, there were many of them. The blackened cabins smouldered, animals lay dead beneath clouds of flies, irrigation channels had been blocked with debris and their small gates that controlled the flow of water smashed or uprooted. And every tree carried a burden of torn and eviscerated bodies hanging from their branches and sated vultures in their crowns. A fog of noisome smoke hung over everything.

Neill, now Brigadier Neill, also kept a diary:

> 17th June. God grant I may have acted with justice. I know I have with severity, but under the circumstances I trust for forgiveness. I have done all for the good of my country, to re-establish its prestige and power, and to put down this most barbarous, inhuman insurrection.

34

'I have a silver rupee,' Lavanya said, and gave Deepika a hitch upwards so that the child could look over her shoulder at the river, the town and the palace on its low hill. 'Take us to Cawnpore. I will see that you get at least one more rupee when we arrive.'

'How will that be?'

She called and Adam and the other four children came out of the sugar cane field.

'See,' she said. 'They are feringhee children. The British will pay to have them back.'

The fisherman's boat was long, and narrow. He shifted his nets, in which small fish twitched for a time and flashed silver in the sun before dying, making room for the children to sit on either side on a narrow ledge that went round the boat just below the gunwale. He stood high up on the stern with his oar and rowed it like a gondolier or poled it over the shallows. Lavanya sat below him, facing the front. She put Adam in the bow but told him always to face the stern so that he could help her to keep an eye on the little ones. The fisherman took them into the middle of the patch of water he had been working and set them going. The current was slow, even when they got into the wide main stream, but running with them.

Lavanya felt her mood lighten. Surely the end of her trial was now in sight. She felt tired, but warm and relaxed, and proud too. She knew she had done well. She smiled at all her charges and then turned and smiled up at the fisherman who smiled back down at her.

He was a young man, lean and strong, with just a turban and a dhoti. She wondered if he was married. Surely he must be, especially since he seemed to be the owner of a boat.

Two hours passed before the first signs of Cawnpore appeared on the right bank. Apart from a thin smog further on these did not amount to much – a riverbank settlement of old buildings above a row of ghats extending for half a mile.

'The old town,' the fisherman remarked, and continued rowing. A strong smell came off the bank – sour, meaty, not unlike the odour you get from kilns where food is smoked, but more rank.

'Tanneries, for leather,' and his nostrils wrinkled. As a good Hindoo he avoided leather. He drew her attention to a large brick building close to the water.

'The magazine for the army.'

Soon, spread across a slight rise, a mile or more inland, a town bigger than Meerut, indeed bigger than any other town she had ever seen, with a long strip of large gardens, parks, bungalows and more substantial buildings with colonnades between it and the river, slipped slowly past.

'The Civil Station,' he remarked. 'Where the English live.'

'You could put us down here.'

'No. They have gone into the cantonments where they are building a fort. They expect trouble.'

The river narrowed and its brown surface was broken by eddies and whirlpools. All he had to do now was steer. At the narrowest point there was a bridge of boats which he guided them under, dropping down on to his haunches as he did so; then, as the river widened again, they passed two or three substantial landing stages. At one of them a steam pinnace was tied up, brass funnel and rails gleaming, dark wood polished, white paintwork. There were two or three similar boats with it, but none quite so grand.

'After the rains large boats come as far as this all the way from Benares, even Calcutta. But at this time of year there is not enough water in the river. The Rajah of Bithur uses that one.'

Another half-mile brought them to a shallow ghat below a temple set among tall trees. Several men were in the water, clothed or part clothed, spooning it up with their hands, letting the water pour over their heads and shoulders, the ritual of bathing in the Ganges. With water opalescent but reflecting the clear sky and some of the freshness of the morning still all over it, it was a peaceful, gentle scene.

'Sati Chaura Ghat.'

A couple of powerful sweeps on his oar brought them around, across the current and then to a crunching halt on river shingle next to a row of boats, some like his, some a little larger and broader with simple frames which supported awnings of thatch. The fisherman hopped into the water which came almost to his knees, took a painter from the bow as he passed and hauled the prow a yard or so further up the gentle slope. He then called to a man sitting on the steps and asked him to keep an eye on it.

'I'll come with you,' he said to Lavanya who was already getting the children on to the land.

'No need,' she answered, 'if you tell me the way.'

He grinned at her again, white teeth in his dark face.

'The second silver rupee?'

There was still a mile to go up avenues of bungalows lined with trees and hibiscus, scarlet, purple and white, all very much like the officers' lines in Meerut, but apparently deserted. Eventually they approached a large parade ground with a group of brick buildings at the far end, two of which were being enclosed by a trench with a parapet. Here at last Lavanya could see European faces, British Army uniforms rather than those of the Native troops, the men actually still digging the trench and throwing up the parapet. There did not seem to be that many of them. There were also an open air kitchen, the box-like sheds over a ditch that she knew would be latrines, and a warehouse. A number of women and children, most of them white, hung about, gossiping, sitting on the ground, or playing listlessly. They kept close to the larger of the two buildings, clinging to the shade.

As they passed over a plank bridge across the trench and through the parapet Lavanya became very much aware that almost everyone near them, soldiers and women, had stopped what they were doing and were looking at them with surprise and curiosity and then suddenly a thin boy of about eight years old, with red hair and freckles, broke away from the rest and ran towards them.

'Adam,' he called, then, turning his head back to the others, 'it's Adam Dixon. Gosh, Adam, we all thought you were dead.'

For a dreadful moment Adam thought he was going to be embraced and to ward off any such calamity he stuck out his hand.

'Hugh Fetherstonhaugh. Good to find you here,' he said, and then, as they shook hands with exaggerated vigour, 'but weren't you about to go back to school in England?'

'Well, I was, but then all this trouble started and Father judged it might not be safe to travel, and the next thing we knew he was posted here. General Sir Hugh Wheeler, he's my godfather, don't you know, wanted a good cavalry man as adjutant of the 2nd Native Cavalry, the one he had died of sunstroke. So, just as soon as we got to Umballa we were told to come here. Father will be made a major when the papers come through. We got here a week ago. We came in a carriage, the whole way. Here's Mama. I'm sure she'll want a word with you.'

'Adam. How nice to see you here. And with all your siblings.' Mrs Fetherstonhaugh, thin, haughty, her hair as red as her son's, wearing a turquoise-blue muslin dress with a shawl round her shoulders and carrying a parasol, loomed over them. 'And the little boy must be Sophie Hardcastle's Stephen. And you are the missing ayah. I forget your name.'

'Lavanya, mem.'

'You have been the cause of much distress and some inconvenience. Children, come with me.' She turned back towards the buildings. 'It doesn't do to stand out in the sun at this time of day.' Then, seeing Lavanya, holding Deepa by the hand and with the fisherman still by her side, was following, 'No need for you to come. You have caused enough trouble already. Be off with you and take your man with you.'

A moment, but only a moment, of confrontation as Lavanya held her ground. Then she picked up Deepa and turned away, back towards the gap in the parapet. Miranda made as if to follow her but Adam caught her elbow and held her back.

'Best do as she says,' he muttered. Already, in that moment or less, Lavanya had been superseded, as far as he was concerned, by the white woman.

Emily sucked her thumb and Robert held her hand. Stephen began to cry then made a break for it but Mrs Fetherstonhaugh grabbed his arm as he passed. He struggled, and she slapped the back of his leg.

Mrs Fetherstonhaugh's behaviour towards Lavanya was not due to racism. Back in Waterford she treated her Irish servants with the same contempt.

*

255

Later that evening, when the air began to grow a degree or two cooler, Adam now wearing a spare set of Hugh Fetherstonhaugh's clothes, too small for him, found Hugh and suggested that the younger boy should take him round what was already known as Wheeler's Entrenchment. They started off on the verandah of the largest building which had been a hospital for the dragoons. It was more than a hundred yards long and twenty wide with a central row of interconnected wards inside and wide verandahs on the outside. It was solidly brick-built, roofed with thatch, and was occupied by the European garrison, a mere seventy invalids from the 32nd Foot with their families and children. With them were sixty gunners, and a nearly complete company of the 84th.

Adam was an object of curiosity to many. As they moved through the hospital he was offered tea and lemonade and asked about their long walk from Meerut with just a Native girl looking after them. This made him feel sad again, thinking of Lavanya and the way the Fetherstonhaugh woman had treated her, and he wondered about the second silver rupee she had promised the fisherman and hoped he wouldn't be a nuisance to her about it. To take his mind off all this he turned to Hugh as they crossed the short distance to the second building.

'Why did your godfather do all this?' he gestured with his arm across the entrenchment. 'There must have been places he could have fortified more readily.' He remembered the big brick building they had passed upstream of the bridge of boats. 'The magazine, for instance.'

A look of deep concentration clouded eight-year-old Hugh's face as he tried to remember what he had been told.

'He was afraid it might blow up,' he said, 'like the one in Delhi. And, um, the cantonments are close by and the Native lines are under our guns so we can bombard them if they mutiny. Something like that. Oh yes, there's another thing. Sir Hugh believes that if they mutiny they'll all go straight to Delhi without bothering us.'

They walked round the second building, a barrack, smaller than the hospital but with a tiled roof. This was where the senior English officers worked and spent their nights, accompanied by their families. Presently they walked back to the point they had come in by. To their right and less than half a mile away the Native lines consisted not of barracks but rows of small huts. Smoke rose from their cooking fires, carrying the smell of curries and cooking chappatis on its breath. They could even hear the Native fifes and drums and occasional snatches of their wailing songs. Three nine-pounders were set into the parapet and directed across the space between. Hugh patted the breech of one of them. There was a guard of four men looking over them but the crews were elsewhere, also having their evening meal. Set back behind them were stacks of round shot and canisters of grape, together with a small tumbril loaded with a couple of powder barrels.

'Plenty of ammunition then,' said Adam. It was what he thought his father might have said had he been there.

'Oh, plenty,' replied Hugh, in the same grown-up way.

They heard a call, turned and found Hugh's mother striding through a patch of dried grass stalks on the edge of one of the small gardens where some of the men had planted vegetables.

'There you are then. Really you should have known better than to come out here on your own. Adam, I have good news.' Up with them now, she tweaked his ear. 'The electric telegraph has been working intermittently and the signallers have managed to get a message through to Meerut to tell your mother you are alive and well. It seems your mother may be able to get down here. There are despatches on their way here under escort coming through Meerut, and she might be able to join them. In which case she should be here in less than a week or so. Now, come on in and have your dinner, and have a word for me with Miranda who, I have to say, does not seem as biddable as a well-brought-up gel should be. Stephen too. He's been crying ever since I sent that girl packing.' She took both of them tightly by the hand, which Adam found offensive. He was no longer a little boy who had to be held on to.

'Come on now,' she said again.

35

Cawnpore, 4–6 June 1857

The Nana had taken a bungalow in a small suburb called Nawabganj close to Old Cawnpore. It was also close to the treasury which he had said he would guard with the Cawnpore Contingency. General Wheeler both believed and trusted him to do just that. The Nana's troops, three hundred superannuated Don Quixotes on skeletal horses armed with lances and tulwars, pikes, bludgeons and ancient matchlocks, were in bivouacs nearby. They were led by Jawala Prasad, a tall old Brahmin with a nasal voice who styled himself a brigadier. Nevertheless, Wheeler paid them: 'They are Marathas and too proud to mix with Bengalese mutineers' was the thinking that lay behind the decision. There was no question of sparing British soldiers from the entrenchment.

That night the Nana used a couple of rowing-boats to get to a secret meeting on his pinnace. He took with him his younger brother, Bala Rao, a tall dark man with a broken nose, no teeth and a temper as foul as his breath. Azimullah, recently returned from Delhi, went too. The meeting took place in a small stateroom with a rosewood table, ormulu lamps, red plush drapes, gilded chairs. Presently they felt a slight bump on the side and heard footsteps on the gangway. A knock and the brigadier ushered in Lieutenant (subadar) Teeka Singh, and Sergeant Major (havildar major) Gopal Singh of the 2nd Native Cavalry. Being cavalry and Sikhs they were more smartly turned out in their military way than anyone else there.

Teeka Singh got the meeting off to an awkward start.

'Highness, you have come to Cawnpore to take charge of the English magazine and treasury and you are using your personal troops to do this.'

'That is correct,' the Nana replied, striving to appear not merely unconcerned by what could be interpreted as an accusation but also to maintain the authority he believed was his by right.

'And this you have done in spite of the fact that all of us, Hindoos, Mahometans and Sikhs, have united for the sake of our religions to break free from the yoke of the British and resist their efforts to make Christians of us. The whole Army of the Bengal Presidency is at one on this matter. What do you say to this?'

The Nana struggled for a moment or two.

'I am, as I am sure you are aware,' he said at last, 'entirely at the disposal of the Bengal Army.'

'Good. In that case we can get down to the details of how you will be able to help us . . . when the moment arrives.'

This took some time. The Nana had his reasons too for mistrusting the putative mutineers. Azimullah put the case for him.

'Many people believe, Teeka Sahib, that when you mutiny you will simply march your regiments to Delhi leaving the British here unharmed in their entrenchment. If that happens there is no possibility that they will give my master any of the rights he claims. How do you answer that?'

'We cannot leave without munitions and money to pay our men. You hold both in the treasury and the magazine. Once we have proclaimed you Peshwa you can release what we need.'

'But you will still go to Delhi?'

'Perhaps so. Perhaps not. We shall stay if there is good reason to.'

'There are English regiments on their way from Calcutta,' Azimullah continued. 'Already they may be as near as Benares. We shall need your regiments to defend what we shall have gained here.'

'Once Nana Saheb,' – and Teeka Singh inclined his head towards him – 'is Peshwa we shall be his to command.'

From then on the meeting became more convivial. The Nana had sent a cook on ahead who now served a Persian-style pilau laced with expensive Afghan apricots and raisins, khormas and dahls, mostly vegetable based, but one with chicken breasts and another with cubed lamb. What had to be resolved was simple enough although everyone there had ideas about the details. They concerned the timing of seizing the treasury and opening the magazine, and the appropriate moment and manner for declaring the Nana the Peshwa of the Marathas. There would be fanfares, a parade, a twenty-one-gun salute.

The Nana was still playing the game both ways. The morning after the meeting on the pinnace Mr Hillersdon, the Collector, turned up at the bungalow next to the treasury. He seemed to know all about the meeting with Teeka and Gopal. The Nana prevaricated with his usual transparency, but Hillersdon had encouraged a friendship between them in the past, partly because he did not get on with the military establishment on his own account, and partly because he knew how the officers treated the Nana with derisive scorn behind his back while making a joke of flattering him to his face. Consequently when, over tea brewed the English way and sweet biscuits, the Nana maintained he had called for the meeting in order to persuade the sowar officers to remain firmly loyal, Hillersdon believed him.

The Native troops at Cawnpore rose on the night of 5 June. During the previous night a drunk British major fired two pistol shots at a regular patrol of the 2nd Native Cavalry. He was swiftly court-martialled but let off on the grounds that he was not in his senses when he committed the offence. During the day that followed the sepoys and sowars felt that the number and seriousness of their grievances were steadily multiplying. They quite rightly objected that if a Native officer had fired on his own troops, drunk or not, he would have been hanged. The case of Mungal Pandy confirmed the point. In response to the unrest Wheeler ordered a lakh of rupees brought into the entrenchment from the treasury with more munitions from the magazine. This deepened the discontent in the Native lines. Those Native troops who might have remained loyal already resented the entrenchment which was, they asserted, an insulting sign that the British no longer trusted them. Finally, a sowar of the 2nd, primed and prompted by Azimullah, declared that a consignment of attar, which had been delivered to the lines and was then discovered to be rotting, had been polluted with ground pig and cow bones. It was part of the British plot to make Christians of them all by making sure that their own religions would reject them and their caste.

The 2nd Cavalry were the first to go. Two Native Infantry regiments wavered, but went over when they were fired upon, on Wheeler's orders. But then the conspirators' plan went awry. The mutineers headed up the Grand Trunk Road, which bypassed the city on its western side, well away from the river, heading for Delhi. At the same time two of their number turned up at the Nana's bungalow.

'You have a kingdom waiting for you if you come to Delhi with us. If you stay here with the British, you die.'

'What have I to do with the British? I am with you,' replied the Nana, taking, as he almost always did, the point of view of those nearest to him at any given time. 'Take the Government Treasure with you.'

As soon as the mutineers had moved on Azimullah argued as reasonably as he could that the Nana was making a great mistake. He must not go to Delhi. He must stay in Cawnpore, declare himself Peshwa there and muster his forces to defeat the British on his own account. Only that way would he get what he wanted. In Delhi he would be lost in the confusion of factions and the necessity of making alliances, and so on. Yet again the Nana gave in to the most immediate pressure, ignoring what he had said an hour or so earlier. He called for his state elephant, and, with his entourage in tow, caught up with the rebels at Kalyanpur, a dâk station eleven miles up the road. It was midnight. More than three thousand mutineers, four regiments and all the usual camp followers, were bivouacked around the bungalow, campfires glowing in the dark.

The Nana's mahout made the elephant kneel and he climbed down out of the once richly decorated howdah, now somewhat tatty, just as Teeka and Gopal came out of the dâk bungalow to greet him. Prompted by Azimullah he began an ill-prepared speech, the delivery of which was soon enough appropriated by his vakil.

'We understand why you want to go to Delhi,' Azimullah began persuasively, 'but think of what you are leaving behind: the treasure, the magazine, and boatloads of ammunition tied up at the ghats. The British are being reinforced but if you strike before the reinforcements arrive you will win easily at the odds . . .' And while this was going on his agents swept through the camp with promises of double pay and free food if they returned to Cawnpore, and a gold bracelet worth a hundred rupees for every soldier once the entrenchment had been taken.

261

Teeka Singh listened to it all, saw the faces gathering among the torches and fires, sensed their mood. As Azimullah closed on a stirring peroration he flung up his arms.

'Long life to the Nana Saheb, the soon to be Peshwa of the Marathas,' he hollered. Two thousand arms went up in response and a thousand muskets or more were fired into the air.

The crowd closed in and the Nana, with his immediate court behind him, was escorted back to his elephant from which he led the mutineers back to Nawabganj where, with horns blaring and much banging of drums, they arrived at first light. There he took over a house near the theatre and began issuing orders – the Rubicon crossed, the die cast, he threw himself at last, and with some fervour, into the role he had aspired to since the death of his adoptive father. He made Jawala Prasad brigadier of his new army, Azimullah Khan Collector, a sign of trust since the position gave him control of the treasury, and his elder brother the Chief Judge. Tatya Tope became commander of the Maratha Contingency. He then sent the 2nd cavalry into the new town to plunder the shops and businesses of Native Christians. Some of these were burnt alive in their own homes, a handful were shot but most were already sheltering in the entrenchment.

The entrenchment was the Nana's first priority and, following the traditions of European warfare, he sent a Declaration of Intent to General Wheeler notifying him that the attack would open at ten in the morning on 6 June but offering him the chance to negotiate terms. The enclosure was by now horribly overcrowded with nearly a thousand people of whom only three hundred were regular soldiers and their officers. The rest were women and children, Christian merchants and civil servants, more than a hundred native servants, a score of loyal sepoys and a number of Christian drummers. Yet Wheeler's reply was defiant.

As the first round shot bounced and rolled across the compound Hugh Fetherstonhaugh turned to Adam.

'At last,' he crowed. 'What a lark, eh?'

Wheeler was becoming aware that he may have blundered. His whole strategy of moving to the entrenchment was much as little Hugh had analysed it for Adam, and it all depended on a speedy

262

relief by British troops from Lucknow, but the garrison at Lucknow was by now in straits as dire as his own. He was sure he could hold out for a week or so and intelligence informed him that there were British troops at Benares, two hundred and fifty miles away, that is within twelve days' march. What he did not know was that the officer commanding them was mad, moving far too slowly up the Grand Trunk Road from Benares to Allahabad, doing God's work by hanging every Native male his army could find.

36

Cawnpore, 10 June 1857

Small bodies of British troops, especially cavalry, continued to move freely across vast tracks of the insurgent countryside. Ten men can see, hear or smell the presence of an army from a considerable distance and if they're well mounted they can keep clear. And not only were the British very well mounted in comparison with the sowars, they were also better armed, with modern rifles and revolvers as well as lances and sabres, and could easily take on and put to flight five times their number if caught in an ambush or if they came on the rebels unexpectedly round a hilly bluff or a patch of jungle.

It was with one such detachment that Catherine Dixon arrived in the outskirts of Cawnpore, three days after the siege of the entrenchment had got properly under way. She was in real danger for the last mile only, which she had to walk, on her own. The young cornet in charge of the eight troopers who had brought her from Naimpur down the Grand Trunk Road had resisted, just, the temptation to fall yet more deeply in love with her, and submitted to the common sense which told them both that she had a far better chance of getting through the sepoy lines on her own.

It was one o'clock in the afternoon, then, when she slipped down from the grey cob she had been riding, handed the reins to the eighteen-year-old man, stepped over the ditch that separated the road from a caked, dried-up field. It was carpeted with the stringy stalks and dry clover-like lentil leaves which were all that remained of a crop harvested two months earlier and which crackled beneath her short riding boots with a sound like that of crisp snow.

'Ah . . . Good luck,' the young man called, and then, 'Goodbye!' and touched the peak of his sun helmet with his crop. His young heart felt intolerably heavy: would he ever see her again?

She half-lifted a hand in reply but did not look round. Her attention now was on the steady, dull concussions repeated every ten seconds or so, coming from behind a windbreak of gaunt acacia trees in front of a line of barracks, just like those in Meerut.

'They are firing at my children,' she said to herself, and a momentary spasm of anxiety as intense as terror gripped her diaphragm as she faced a reality she had only imagined before. She heaved in a huge breath of hot, dusty air, let it out in a long sigh. Perspiration was already coursing down her temples. She set down the soft chintz bag she was carrying which held some toiletries, a change of clothes and English sweets for the children, Harrogate toffees and humbugs. She opened and hoisted her small parasol which had been tucked between the bag's bent bamboo handles and set off again.

The southern edge of the barracks was almost deserted. The few sepoys who lay around outside smoking or chewing betel, many of them sporting dressings patched with almost black dried blood, watched her unblinkingly, intensely, but did not move. She came through an alley between the buildings and the firing of the guns was now loud enough to hurt: she flinched as the explosions came. Immediately in front of her was a gun emplacement; the gun itself, a big one, cased in gabions, fascines and earth, served by six sepoys, crashed out again, filling the emplacement with a cloud of white smoke and dust from the recoil. Then a ball, a round shot, banged into the top of the emplacement, bounced, and skipped like a pebble thrown across flat water, whistled past her and rolled on up the alley into the open ground she had crossed.

She edged up the alley, her back against the wall of the building, until she came to the corner and only fifteen yards or so separated her from the gun emplacement. Looking left and right she could see a shallow curve of similar emplacements linked by an entrenchment much like the one she could see a half-mile away, the differences being that the distant one seemed smaller, more isolated, the rampart lower. There was a low flagpole in front of the larger of the two buildings it enclosed, from which hung a tatter of red, white and blue.

At first the sepoys did not see her, then one looked over his shoulder, muttered something to his neighbour, and like a ripple spreading across a pond every dark face and turban in sight turned her way.

After so many years in India she had some Hindi.

'Take me across,' she called. 'Take me to the feringhees.'

There was some laughter and then a splutter of conversation. A young man unwound his white turban and clambered on to the barrel of the gun, and, with one foot on it and the other on a gabion, he waved it above his head, holding it in both hands. A crackle of rifle fire and he leapt down as three or four balls whistled over his head. Cheekily, he tried again. Silence this time. A minute passed. Then there was a flash of white from the other side. A British gunner had stripped to the waist and was thrashing the air with a white shirt. The sepoys waved her forward and a drummer boy or powder monkey leapt out from a patch of shade he had made his own. His white teeth flashed as he gave her the biggest smile she had seen for a long time. Folding her parasol on to the top of her bag again, Catherine took his hand and carefully but as briskly as they could they squeezed through a gap in the fascines and set off across the space between.

Halfway across she asked the drummer boy his name.

'Ali,' he said. 'What's yours?'

'Catherine Dixon.'

'That's a big name. Why do you want to go there?'

'My children are in there.'

That made sense, and he nodded his head wisely. His hand was small, moist, but she sensed that beneath the moisture the skin was rough, too rough and hard for a ten-year-old, and he could not have been more than that.

As they approached the entrenchment the men behind it began to cheer; when they reached it they took her bag and parasol and helped her over and down. She turned to thank Ali but he was already on his way back. However, he too turned and gave her a wave and as he did so he was shot, blown backwards by the bullet. He twitched and writhed for a moment while blood bubbled from his mouth, and then he died.

Catherine screamed.

'You idiots, you stupid, stupid, stupid idiots.'

But her voice was drowned as the guns roared again from both

266

sides and the balls thudded into the earthen trench or whistled like banshees above her head.

Her first impression of the entrenchment, received even before she was reunited with her children and Stephen, was that it was small and crowded. At first she thought all those in the open were dead or wounded, but just then a bullet plucked at her bag like an impatient child or maybe a bag-snatcher and she too threw herself on to the dusty ground. The fact of the matter was that the rampart was nowhere more than four feet high and a head or torso that appeared above it, soldier, woman or child, immediately attracted rifle fire from the other side of the maidan. Nevertheless, across such a small space news travelled fast and very soon she could see her children, Adam in the front, Miranda with Robert at the back, Emma in the middle, crawling towards her. They looked a sight with Robinson Crusoe hats made of fallen thatch on their heads and she was grinning even before they saw her.

They were, of course, very British about it. Sitting among a litter of rotting mango and plantain peel that already masked far worse – faeces, blood, even dismembered limbs – she embraced each in turn, almost passionately but very quickly, in a way that an observer would have judged perfunctory.

'Are you all all right? Tell me, each in turn, that you are all right. Has Mrs Fetherstonhaugh been looking after you nicely? I'm sure she has—'

'Don't like her,' Robert snuffled.

'Miranda, Robbie has a smudge on his face, could you give him a wipe for me? Listen, see what I have in my bag for you, toffees and butterscotch, no, Emma, no chocolate, it would have melted. Come on, Adam, you must show me how to get to a place where we can talk more easily and you can tell me all about everything. Did Lavanya bring you here, is she here, is she all right?' and on she went, as breathlessly as ever, pouring it all out and behind them the guns crashed out and the muskets cracked like whips and she marvelled that they were all there, and unharmed, though the children looked tired and thin.

37

Cawnpore, 4–10 June 1857

Looking over her mother's shoulder Deepika had cried 'Ishteven, Ishteven', as they walked away from the enclosure across the wide dusty maidan. Lavanya jogged her up and down and told her to hush and then used the edge of her saree to wipe away two tears that spilled down her own high cheekbones.

'The silver rupee,' said the fisherman, falling in beside her. He seized her hand, tried to hold her back, but she shook herself free.

'I'll go back for it,' he threatened.

'No.'

'Why not?'

'They'll beat you if you do.'

Lavanya had lived with the feringhees for nearly four years and she knew very well what happened to Natives, especially the poorer and lower ones, if they became what the English called 'uppish'.

They went back the way they had come to his boat, pulled up on the shingle in front of the temple at Sati Chaura Ghat. There was nowhere else to go. On the way Lavanya thought about it. She had almost no idea at all about money. She had never had any. Her wage was her keep plus the few annas that Sophie gave her each week, when she remembered. She had saved most of these, hidden in the thin mattress of her charpoy, but of course had left them behind when she and the children fled. She supposed a silver rupee, about a shilling, was probably worth a day's work to the fisherman. She was wrong. He was lucky if he made as much in a week.

She sat on the top step, disentangled Deepika's arm from her hair and set her down next to her, shaded her eyes with her palm and looked up at him.

'I don't know what to do,' she said. 'I don't know where to go.'

He hunkered on a step below her so his eyes were on a level with hers.

'There's a market near the river, on the other side of the bridge,' he said. 'I'll sell my fish there and then go back to Bithur. You can come with me if you want.'

The look in his eyes contrived to be pleading, greedy and commanding, all at the same time.

'All right,' she said, and stood, pulling Deepika to her feet as she did so. Innocent in many things Lavanya was wise in others. A deal had been struck.

He only got an anna for his fish since it was late in the day and most shoppers had gone home. Besides, the fish had taken on a stale look in the heat although he had covered them with wet jute sacking and he had to take what was offered. It was much harder work going upstream even though the current was scarcely discernible. He had a paddle in the bottom of the boat, and Lavanya sat in front of him and used it; nevertheless the sun was low by the time they got back. Her dreams that he might be of some consequence since he seemed to be the owner of his boat were quickly dashed. It belonged, he said, to his elder brother who lived on the other side in the tiny town beneath the wall of the Nana's palace, and he had to pay a rupee a month to rent it.

He lived in a low, cow-dung hut, six feet by ten, set in the corner of an opium field. The tall stalks of the poppies, dry now and brittle, some still with seed cases that had been gashed to release the white juice that turned brown to make opium base, rattled in the slightest breeze. Inside there was a charpoy whose legs had broken so the frame sat on the earth floor, three or four earthenware pots and a plate, cracked and chipped, a bag of coarse flour, and a large colony of cockroaches. Falling immediately and almost automatically and without thought into the role her culture prescribed, Lavanya picked up the largest bowl, walked back to the bank of the river and half-filled it with water. Back in the fisherman's cabin she used her palms to scoop the only partially threshed and ground wheat into

269

the water and began to knead it into paste for chappatis. She looked up at him.

'Do you have any milk? The child needs milk.'

He stooped for one of the other bowls.

'I can get some,' he said.

When he was gone she set the dough to rise a little and, taking Deepa by the hand again, went out looking for twigs and branches thin enough to break. These she set in a tiny fireplace made of three large stones that lay just outside the door; then, using skills she had forgotten after three years but which had come back to her during the previous three weeks, she set it going with tinder from the poppy stalks and a spark or two struck from flints she found near the fireplace. The fisherman returned with milk and revealed three small dried fish hidden in the cane thatch of his cabin's roof. They ate well enough.

Darkness fell, there was no lamp, and Deepa slept. Presently they took off their scant clothing and made love as Lavanya had known they would. She was happy to, and at the worst she knew it would be better than rape. It was good. He was happy to make her come, and happy too that she made him come on her tummy when it was his turn. Untrammelled by the hang-ups that afflicted the white race, both male and female, she was pleased. She had not made love since her husband had been killed by his elephant, and it had been an experience that, at fourteen years old, she had been pleased to discover. Nearly four years had gone since then and it was something she often wished for, longed for. But the euphoria soon faded in the darkness and an entirely different sort of longing came over her instead. She had lost a child. She had lost Stephen. She wanted him back, she wanted to know he was all right.

She found she was worrying about Stephen all the time. For much of it it was a nagging anxiety that stained everything she did. Sometimes, when she was really deeply involved in something else, she forgot what it was for, but then it came back like a pain, like a bad tooth that could shoot from a dull ache to a searing pain at a touch. She knew Mrs Fetherstonhaugh, knew what she was like. Had even gossiped with little Hugh's Meerut ayah. She paid very little attention to her son except to criticise him or tell him off or tell off the ayah. Without an ayah, she wouldn't keep Stephen clean, she might even forget to make sure he ate enough. And certainly she would not cuddle him, fuss him. If he fell over, or grazed a knee, she'd scold him, tell him to be a man. Tell a three-year-old to be a man!

On the days when the fisherman caught more fish than he could barter in the little village that lay half a mile away beyond the reach of river floods when the rains came, he'd take his catch down to the Cawnpore market and after she had been there a week Lavanya insisted that she and Deepa would go too. He was quite pleased to accept – at least, using the paddle she made the journey back upriver a great deal easier. This time he tied up at the ghat that served the market, leaving her an even longer walk than before. First, though, she had to reassure him that she would come back.

'Where else could I go?' she asked. 'I just want to see that the little feringhee boy, who is like a son to me and a brother to Deepa, is all right.'

There was no danger of her losing the way – the gunfire, though intermittent, was frequent enough, coming every five minutes or so, to guide her.

She worked her way round the perimeter of the maidan, sticking to trees and using the barracks occupied by the sepoys as cover, until she was standing in a patch of bamboo just short of what had been the Native Infantry lines, but which were now deserted since they came under the guns Hugh had shown Adam on the evening of their arrival. She made Deepa sit down but risked standing herself, almost on tiptoe, so she could easily see over the rampart and into the entrenchment, less than two hundred yards away.

What she saw was awful, though at that time nothing like as bad as it was to become. Tight groups of soldiers in motley uniforms of different units clustered around the guns, some working them, but also because the earth bags and bundles of sticks that protected them provided shelter for the men too. Beyond them the ground seemed almost to be crawling, literally crawling, with prone bodies hugging the ground, making their way to and from the guns or the wells. The besiegers had almost given up attempting to get at them with round shot which either thudded into the low rampart or skipped over their bodies for the most part without doing any harm, but there were at least a pair of howitzers on the far side of the maidan from which shells were lobbed, four or five, one after the other, before the English guns got the range. Then they were pulled

271

back between the buildings only to reappear again and pick up where they had left off.

Sometimes the shells burst in the air and showered the ground with shrapnel, sometimes they fussed and fizzed on the ground for as much as half a minute before exploding. Occasionally some brave soul would try to get to these and extinguish the fuse, but Lavanya saw more than one blown to shreds in the attempt.

A thin pall of smoke and dust hung over everything and the smell was awful.

Lavanya first glanced over it all, saw none of the children, and so then began a slow intense survey of the whole area, square yard by square yard.

She saw the woman first – the red hair and blue dress unmistakeable, standing in what shade there was on the corner of the larger of the buildings and, in the darkness behind her, almost black in contrast to the sunlight, she made out three small figures sitting with their backs against the wall – the three youngest, she was sure, Emma, Robert and Stephen. She almost choked as she smothered the desire to call out.

Then, suddenly, they stood and Emma made as if to break out but the Irish woman caught her wrist and pulled her back. And at the same time Lavanya became aware that an almost complete silence had fallen; the guns on both sides had stopped firing.

On the far side of the maidan a figure had appeared. A woman in white, a woman who was white, carrying a parasol and a cloth bag in one hand, holding in the other the hand of a small dark lad wearing a tunic and a turban, they were picking their way through the debris, out into the sunlight, towards the entrenchment. As she approached it, Lavanya knew who she was. Catherine Dixon. Did that mean Sophie Hardcastle was nearby too? Maybe. At all events, it certainly meant that all the children would now be properly cared for, as far as was possible in the circumstances, by a woman who understood what being a mother meant.

She took hold of Deepika's hand and moved deeper into the bamboo break. Her feelings were very mixed, her relief almost poisoned by a sort of sorrowful bitterness at what she understood was now really the end of the time they had been a little family, a little world of their own together. From now on there would just be Deepika and herself, no longer the threesome they had been.

38

Days merged into a rosary of suffering, marked only by those on which some significant incident occurred or on which something that had been a recurring feature ceased. In the first category there was the day the simple cogged winch over one of the two wells was shot away by a couple of well-placed twelve-pound shots so the bucket that was lowered sixty feet had to be hauled up by hand. Under the second heading one could put the disposal of dead bodies. To begin with they were dumped into the pits already dug for waste food but these were soon filled. Then a length of trench was used and the bodies were covered with earth baked by the sun into rock-like slabs. Finally the second well, marginally shallower by five feet or so than the first, dried up, and the dead were dropped down it, two hundred and fifty of them by the time of the capitulation. The other thing that marked each day's passing was the certainty that each day was noticeably worse than its predecessor.

They were adequately provisioned with food and ammunition for the week or ten days Wheeler expected to be there unrelieved, but too much was eaten in the first few days since much of it came from the officers' messes in the nearby cantonments and was rich, appetising stuff. For a day or two a private soldier could be issued with a bottle of champagne, a tin of preserved herrings and a pot of jam, or tinned salmon, rum and sweetmeats. Food ran short more quickly that it should have done and even before Catherine arrived strict rationing had been enforced.

Catherine, with Mrs Fetherstonhaugh's aid, found a corner for herself and the children in the larger building, the one that had been built as a hospital. This turned out to be less than a blessing although to begin with it was one of the safer places in the whole entrenchment. The social and professional position of husbands decided who had the innermost rooms, for caste dominated the lives of the British almost as much as it did those of the Hindoos, albeit in somewhat subtler ways. The safest places were taken by the families of senior officers or the top echelon of civil administrators. As the wife of a recently promoted cavalry captain, the son of a provincial brewer, it was the fact that she herself was from 'decent' landed gentry that placed Catherine and her children in, if not quite the most inner rooms, ones that seemed safe enough. Further from the middle but still protected by the brick of the walls that had divided the hospital into wards came the civilian families of less senior Company functionaries, while the outer verandahs which, though deep, were exposed to direct fire, were occupied by Eurasian Christians, whose husbands were mostly merchants though some were Company writers.

When night fell, and they had strugggled with a split-pea gruel for supper, the children curled up round her, sucking the last of the toffees and butterscotch, each making a claim on her body, striving to be as close as they could – until the warmth became heat and Adam and Miranda pulled away a little. Sharing the room with fifteen other families, all on the floor since beds or charpoys took up too much room, the air soon became foetid. Children whimpered and occasionally cried, and two of the older women were going mad. One chanted the first verse of Psalm 23 rhythmically and repetitively without break for what seemed like hours; the other had a repertoire of four Yorkshire songs of which 'The Foggy, Foggy Dew' was the least obscene. A single tallow candle lasted an hour or so, then guttered and went out adding its mutton-fat smell to the rest of the brew. Catherine, sleeping in only her innermost petticoat, rested her head on her upper left arm and with her right hand between her thighs thought of James with an almost angry longing. She tried to pray for him – it was what she had been brought up to do – but recollecting that no one now in these awful times could refrain from the pious hope that whatever happened to their loved ones, no matter how awful it was, should be other than their god's will, she soon gave up. It was not her god's will she wanted·but her own. She wanted her husband and lover back, safe, in one piece, and that was it.

On Catherine's third night the thatch caught fire and it was the Native refugees on the outer verandahs who escaped most easily. Those inside had to fend for themselves for the men were under the strictest orders to remain at their posts though some, unable to bear the screams of burning children and women, went to their rescue. And out in the darkness the sepoys were slowly massing, moving through the darkness across the wide maidan. Any noise they made was masked by the bedlam on the other side of the earth wall. At first it was just the thatch, mostly tinder-dry substantial leaves from cane, plantain and so forth, but soon the timber rafters caught and without their tying effect masonry already battered by heavy shot also tumbled into the spaces below. Children suffered crushed limbs while their mothers became pillars of fire as the flames shot up their long gowns and slips.

Catherine got her children and Stephen out from this hell, and, along with many more, sought safety beneath the sheltering wall of the second building, but then, through darkness, swirling smoke and the light from dancing flames, she realised one of them was missing.

'Adam, I'm going back in for Emma.'

'No, Mama, no, I'll go.'

'You'll do no such thing.'

'You mustn't go.' The thought of losing her again after only three days was an agony in itself, and the other two, Miranda and Robert, made up the chorus. Stephen remained silent, sucking his thumb.

'Adam, I'm serious and I mean it. You stay here and look after them. It's my duty to get Emma.'

She found her soon enough, huddled in a corner, dragging in breaths in great gulps, expelling sharp, piercing screams. She was racked with pain, holding her hands out above her bowed head and waving them frantically. The palms were badly burnt from where she had beaten out the flames that had caught on the hem of her dress. And as Catherine half-carried her, half-dragged her back out to the verandahs again, all the cannon along the parapet in front of them roared together, and then again and again. There were not enough emplacements to hold them them all but all had been loaded with grape and canister, and the gunners had to drag the spent ones back,

275

shouldering the others into place while the first were reloaded. Out in the darkness, less than sixty yards away, the massed sepoys broke and fled and left a hundred dead or mortally wounded behind them.

By dawn the vultures, adjutant birds and pariah dogs and the flies had found them and the stench began to build beneath the burning sun.

Lucknow, the capital of the Oudh, was forty miles north-east of Cawnpore. Sir Henry Lawrence had succeeded Coverley Jackson as Chief Commissioner for the Oudh in March. From the middle of May the kingdom, now a Division of the Bengal Presidency, was torn with uprisings and mutinies. Seeing what was to come Sir Henry turned the Residency and the surrounding buildings and parkland into a fortified town within the city. On 30 May the city rose and the Residency and its satellite buildings and palaces were occupied by the British regiments together with some loyal sepoys and the entire European and most of the Christian population. However, the siege did not begin straight away.

Sir Henry was efficient, deeply religious, and, beneath a dour manner, capable of kindness. He had served in India, Burma and the Punjab, preferring to take administrative rather than regimental posts. He hated balls, fashion, and play-acting but was softened very considerably by his marriage in 1837 to his cousin Honoria. She was made for him – a woman of no nonsense, but clever and with a sense of humour. After four children had been born she died in 1854 of rheumatic fever, leaving him a permanently saddened man.

On 16 June he was in his office on the first floor of the Residency with Martin Gubbins, his Financial Commissioner and closest adviser, considering how to answer a letter Gubbins had brought him. It was a piece of folded paper, grubby, and with one quarter hanging loose as if it had been carelessly torn.

'This arrived this morning, Sir Henry. I think you should look at it.'

'What is it?'

'Note from Sir Hugh Wheeler. One of his Indian servants managed to get through with it.'

'Be a good chap and read it for me.'

'Usual greetings and so forth, then "We have been besieged since

276

the sixth by the Nana Saheb joined by the whole of the Native troops who broke out on the morning of the fourth . . ." He goes on to say the Natives have twenty-four-pounders and many other guns while he has only eight nine-pounders still in working order. He says their defence has been noble and wonderful, their loss heavy and cruel. He closes with "We want aid, aid, aid!"'

'That's old Wheeler for you. Never afraid to show his feelings. Why couldn't he just state his position and leave us to draw the conclusion?'

The thought crossed Gubbins's mind: and that's Lawrence for you, hasn't revealed a spark of feeling since his wife died.

'There's a postscript, sir. "If we had two hundred men we could punish the scoundrels and aid you."'

'Could he indeed. What do you think, Martin?'

'I think we should help him.'

'I'm not so sure. Get hold of Inglis, Blackstock and any other of the old hands you can find and we'll see what they think.'

An hour later he sent for Gubbins again.

'I've talked to the colonels. They all say two hundred is more than we can spare and with a smaller force we won't be able to get across the river either here or at Cawnpore. With the guns they've got they'd blow us apart.'

Sir Henry pulled in paper and pen, dipped the pen.

> *I am very sorry indeed to hear of your condition and grieve that I cannot help you. I have consulted with the chief officers about me, and, except Gubbins, they are unanimous in thinking that with the enemy's command of the river, we could not get a single man into your intrenchment. Pray do not think me selfish. I would run much risk could I see a commensurate prospect of success. In the present scheme I see none. God grant you His protection . . .*

Gubbins dared to be angry.

'Sir Henry, there are women and children in the entrenchment.'

'I am aware of that, Martin. And there are women and children here too. They are my responsibility. Those in Cawnpore are Wheeler's.'

*

277

The heat was agony and intolerable to many. Temperatures of 120 degrees were commonplace. A clergyman took off all his clothes and walked around stark naked; an old woman constantly called for her carriage to take her home; others, many of them, sank into a closed-in, shut-off lethargy which drifted into trance and, often enough, death.

Catherine attempted to nurse Emma in a tiny patch of shade against the wall of the smaller building, but she fretted and moaned, and occasionally screamed. Aware of a sudden darkness against the impenetrable blue of the sky, she looked up. A young soldier was bending over her, large dark eyes shining with sympathy or something deeper.

'Try her with this,' he murmured, reaching down with a chipped glass half-filled with a brownish, rather cloudy liquid.

'What is it?'

'Laudanum. The pain will go. She'll sleep.'

'And when she wakes?' reaching up and taking the glass.

He straightened again, stood above them, shrugged.

'The relief will come before she comes to.'

He offered her a gesture of a salute, but she already had the rim of the glass at her daughter's lips and when she looked up he was gone. The relief? From Lucknow? Or led by Henry Havelock, reputed to be on his way from Allahabad? Did it matter? Neither would be there before Emma woke up from the laudanum. Nevertheless, even as she spluttered on it, Catherine urged her to finish what was in the glass.

Twenty yards away Adam and Hugh Fetherstonhaugh crouched beside the bole of a small, shattered acacia and watched the shells, fired from howitzers, giant mortars, come in. They were more fun than the round shot. If you caught sight of one at the zenith of its looped flight you could track the tiny plume of white smoke as it fell, accelerating towards its target.

'The well?' guessed Adam

'The stores' godown.'

But Adam was right.

Bang.

'Got her.'

'Who was it? Looked like a darkie,' Hugh cried.

'Yep. Blew her in half. She was ayah to the Billings family and one of the babies died this morning of thirst. So I suppose one of the others was looking like going the same way.'

'Pretty brave of her.'

Adam shrugged.

'I expect they told her to. I say, I heard some gossip this morning. They say your godfather's cracking up. Can't handle it any more. That Irish chap, Captain Moore, he's running the show now.'

Hugh's turn to shrug.

'His son—'

'Lieutenant Wheeler?'

'That's right. Was brought in this morning wounded. They put him on a sofa in their quarters and almost straight away a round shot came through the window and hit him in the head. Uncle Hughie, that's what we call him, was dreadfully cut up about it, but I'm sure he'll get over it. Meanwhile, Mama says Captain Moore is a fine soldier. Here comes another. This one's definitely heading for the godowns, don't you think?'

General Wheeler sat at a camp table with paper, pen, inkpot, arrayed in front of him. The tears no longer ran but had carved pink channels through the dust on his now hollow cheeks. He looked at the hands on the table. They shook. He clenched his fists, and waited. Behind him two Natives scrubbed at the wall above the sofa, trying to erase the remains of his son's head. Captain Moore stood in front of him and slightly to his side, possibly on a deliberate line between him and the small square window. At last he felt the shaking could be controlled and he picked up the steel-nibbed pen and dipped it. He mouthed the words as he wrote them:

> British spirit alone remains, but it cannot last for ever . . .
> We have no instruments, no medicine, provisions for a few
> days at furthest, and no possibility of getting any. We have
> been cruelly deserted, and left to our fate: we had not 220
> soldiers of all arms at first. The casualties have been
> numerous. Railway gents and merchants have swollen our
> ranks to what they are. Small as that is, they have done
> excellent service, but neither they nor I can last for ever.
> We have lost everything belonging to us, and I have not

279

even a change of linen. Surely we are not to die like rats in
a cage.

Captain Moore allowed himself a wry smirk. Trust an English gent to be worrying about the state of his drawers at a time like this, he thought.

Lawrence to Wheeler, 27 June:

Havelock must be at Cawnpore within two days. I hope therefore you will husband your resources, and not accept any terms from the enemy, as I much fear treachery: you cannot rely on the Nana's promises. Il a tué beaucoup de prisonniers . . .

39

Tell me, Jawala, what happened?
The cleansing goes on, Azimullah bey, the cleansing goes on.
The cleansing, Jawala? What do you mean by cleansing?
Every white-skinned sepulchre.

Two Indian gentlemen, one young, dapper and lean, wearing a long black, high-necked jacket over spotless white trousers, the other thin, old with that cast of features that suggested Maratha roots and in a military uniform whose red flashes indicated in the English way a brigadier but whose accoutrements were definitely Maratha, walked along the top step of the Sati Chaura Ghat towards the bridge of boats.

You've killed them all, Jawala? Every white-skinned sepulchre?
Everyone, all of them, Azi. Men, women and children. Especially the women and children.

Why, Jawala? Why?
They pollute our land and our blood, Azi. They are a disease. Leave them here they'll grow like the weeds they are and choke the beauty of our growth.

Growth, Jawala?

A silver fish rose for a fly and plopped back into the brown turgid waters of the Ganges.

Our religions, our traditions, our race.
Careful, Jawala. There are many races and religions in India and they have not always got on too well with each other. Tell me, Jawala, what did his Effulgent Mightiness decide? What did his Hugely Highness, the soon to be Peshwa of all the Marathas, decree?

281

Jawala, who always had nasal problems, snorted, rather than laughed.

He looked around us with those still, solemn eyes which have nothing behind them. When five of us agree, he nods and says 'So be it'.

So, Jawala, what happened?

To the refugees from Futtehgahr?

To the refugees who came down the Ganges in boats from Futtehgahr. Azi, you know how it started. You saw them arrive at Bithur.

Indeed he had. Azimullah Khan had seen the boats coasting down the river, some with lateen sails, some steered from the stern like Lavanya's fisherman's, maybe a dozen of them, holding in all some one hundred and twenty people of all ages who had two things in common, though in varying degrees: a stain or more of whiteness and a shared religion. He knew this because they were chanting a hymn and the man in the stern of the first boat held a cross taken from a church in one hand, and waved his free hand in time to the tune.

> *Thou whose almighty Word*
> *Chaos and darkness heard*
>   *And took their flight*
> *Hear us we humbly pray*
> *And where the Gospel-day*
> *Sheds not its glorious ray*
>   *Let there be light . . .*

There might be, Azi decided, for those who chose to invent it, a sort of beauty in the way these boats glided out of the morning mist, arrowing the glassy pale water from their prows, with the glint of the not quite risen sun on the gold, or more probably brass, of the cross, and he turned, and ran as fast as he could down winding stairs, across a courtyard to arrive breathless at the guardhouse. There he called out the subadar commanding the troop of cavalry the Nana had left behind to guard his palace.

They made it just in time, with a couple of two-pounders bouncing lightly behind them, just in time to fire a shot across the bows of the leading boat.

*

282

We tied their hands behind their backs and we made a long rope out of several short ones, and put it round their necks so they made a daisy chain . . .

A what?

Never mind, Jawala. And we marched them all the way here and they got here before sunset. Then I came back. So now, tell me what happened to them.

The brigadier made a pointless effort to clear his sinuses by blowing snot through his fingers and into the river.

Well, Azi, the next morning, yesterday, we had them brought to the Savada House and put them in the ballroom there while we all had a little chat about what to do with them . . .

Who were they, Jawala?

Missionaries, Azi. Magistrates and their writers, the Collector, the opium inspector, merchants, indigo planters, Christians all and mostly white though some whitish. His Glorious Effulgence wanted to keep them as hostages but Bala Rao, Teeka Singh and I said they should die, so that was it.

How was it done, Jawala? Was it done well?

We made the men dig a trench, a good deep one, then we had tiffin. Then we got all the soldiers we could spare from the entrenchment, about three hundred of them, and we made them line up between the trench and the soldiers, the men at the back, then the women, the children in front. They all began singing something about walking in the valley and fearing no evil . . .

I know it.

And the head priest man started making a speech about how nothing would be achieved by murdering them, and that England would never be emptied of white people but Bala Rao interrupted . . . did I say there was a big crowd of badmashes and such, and all the butchers of Cawnpore there?

No.

Well, there were. Then Bala Rao interrupted him and said to the crowd that what was happening was all at the Nana's orders and gave the signal.

And?

The soldiers fired, reloaded and fired again, then the butchers went into the ditch and finished them off. When I left they were filling it in.

Azimullah thought about it for a moment, and slowly a grin was born, and grew, and spread, until his whole face was lit up.

Clever of Bala Rao to say that. The Nana must now know that he has no hope of any mercy if the English win. He has to be Peshwa . . . or dead

283

*meat. As dead as the bastards in that ditch. Oh, it was well done. Well
done indeed.*

We need to be sure the British know.

I'll see to that, Jawala. I'll see to that.

They had reached the little temple near the end of the steps, a lonely
spot and silent for it was approaching the hottest part of the day. The
sluggish river drifted by, almost currentless. It was dead low water,
narrow channels with vast sand bars between; and the only living
thing in sight was that grotesque and solemn bald-headed bird, the
adjutant, standing on his six-foot stilts, solitary on a distant bar, with
his head sunk between his shoulders, thinking; thinking of his prize –
a corpse awash at his feet – and whether to eat him alone or invite
his friends. In the distance the guns continued to rumble in fits as if
the planet were suffering from intermittent indigestion.

The two men nodded at each other and went their separate ways –
Jawala Prasad towards Savada House, Azimullah heading for
Duncan's Hotel.

40

Cawnpore, 26 and 27 June 1857

> *The massacre at the Ghat was certainly planned with Satanic genius,
> and by a master mind, which latter the Nana certainly did not
> possess* – Maude, Lt Col. F.C., *Memories of the Mutiny*, with
> which is incorporated the personal narrative of John Walter
> Sherer (London 1894), quoted by Surendranath Sen in *1857*,
> (New Delhi 1957).

26 JUNE, 9.00 A.M.

Dhondu Pant, known as the Nana Saheb, *soi-disant* Maharajah of
Bithur and Peshwa of the Marathas, generally felt slightly awkward,
somewhat insecure, wherever he was. Duncan's Hotel, set back a
couple of hundred yards from the bridge of boats, was no exception.

It was English, very English, especially the drawing room, which
opened out from the vestibule, and had been contrived to create the
illusion that on entering its wide confines the English sahib, after a
journey of some months and many thousands of miles, had been
transported all the way back in a moment, in a twinkling of an eye,
to his club in St James's. The ceiling was coffered with antlered candelabra along its length. The windows were tall and, though filled
with fine muslin rather than glass, were hung with red plush curtains.
The polished floor supported an archipelago of Cashmere rugs which
were, in a sense, Native, but their like could be found in public rooms
throughout London's West End; the same could be said of the polished, black hardwood occasional tables. The seats and sofas were

upholstered in paisley-patterned chintz (the paisley pattern being based on the shape of mango fruits) chosen by Mrs Duncan in preference to the buttoned black leather her husband had favoured. The room was, she said, a drawing room where ladies, as well as gentlemen, must feel at home. So, the sub-continent had penetrated the rulers' culture here in Cawnpore as thoroughly as it had in London, but there remained the paintings of butch stags in Highland scenery (so unlike the fragile and elegant gazelles of Mughal painting) and the polished double wands round which the latest English papers were wound. There was, too, an unobtrusive odour, a mélange of port-wine, Dundee cake, tinned stilton and cigar tobacco picked and rolled at the other end of the Empire.

In these surroundings, then, the Nana, seated on Indian calico printed near Glasgow with an Indian-inspired pattern, could not bring himself to feel at home. He longed to be English or at any rate he longed to be accepted by the English. He despised their brutishness, their lack of any culture, the ugliness of their women, their coarseness, their sour-cream complexions, their very silly religion. But he recognised their competence, their drive, their courage, their individual initiative, an ability to stand alone and survive yet coupled, contradictorily, with an ability en masse to act as one, to make a machine out of a gang of coolies as well as a regiment of foot. He knew they despised him, laughed at him, and what he wanted more than anything was to be recognised by them as one of them.

And so, at ten o'clock in the morning, he sat there, sipping his cold sour lassi, and pretending that he could read a six-week-old copy of *The Times*. He would spend a happy hour ferreting a meaning out of the Court Circular. And presently he noticed that the guns, two miles away, had fallen silent.

'Well,' he said to himself, 'I will remain cucumber-cool like an Englishman. They'll come and tell me what's happening soon enough.'

26 JUNE, 11.20 A.M.

Two hours or so later and two and a half miles away, Ramchandra Panduranga, known as Tatya Tope, at that time in charge of the commissariat, and struggling to amalgamate the Bithur Contingency with

286

the mutineers into a single entity, was sitting at a desk in Savada House, the orphanage, once a palace, which was being converted back into a palace for the Nana's use, and meantime served as a military headquarters for the rebel armies. Looking out between open arches of the loggia where he was sitting he could see a figure in black coat and white trousers hurrying across the park where the children had played and which was now marked by the raised fresh earth of the ditch where the Futtehgahr refugees had been murdered. Azimullah Khan. The youngest of the cabal who ran the show for the Nana, and the only one of them who had not grown up in the court of Baji Rao II, the last Peshwa. Footsteps, a blast of hot air as a door was opened and the papers on his desk lifted, then . . .

'Ramchandra, Tatya, His Ineffable and Wheeler are negotiating a capitulation.'

'They are? Shit. Tell me about it.'

'Wheeler got one of his men, Captain Shepherd I believe his name is, to "black up", as they say, and cross the lines . . .'

'Azi, the terms, the terms, please.'

'When he'd heard what Wheeler was asking for and offering, the Nana sent me and Jawala Prasad to meet their delegates, an Irish captain called Moore, who seemed to be in charge, and two others, on the maidan in front of the barracks . . .'

'Get on, Azi. The terms, the terms,' Tatya Tope cried again.

'Right. On the Nana's instructions I offered the whole garrison a boat trip down the river to Allahabad . . .'

'Have you gone mad, Azi?'

Azimullah ignored him, hurried on, twisting his prayer beads, the thirty-three names of Allah, through his nervous fingers.

'. . . and Wheeler to leave us his guns, ammunition and treasure. Moore agreed but insisted the men should leave with their small arms and sixty cartridges, while the Nana is to provide the women and children and invalids with carriages to get them down to the river. He also asked for flour and other food to be put in the boats.'

'Bastard!'

'We sent a sowar back to the Nana and he returned in an hour. The Nana agreed, but only if they left now, immediately . . .'

'Shit, Azi! They haven't gone, have they?'

'No, Tatya. Wheeler said they won't be ready to leave until evening today at the earliest.'

'And that was that?'

'Just about. Mr Todd, the old dominie who used to read the English newspapers to the Nana, came back with it all written out and Wheeler's signature and so forth, and the Nana signed up, and there we were.'

'So, we've still got time to do something about it.'

'What needs to be done? It's a great victory for the Nana, Tatya.' Azimullah's voice took on a bitter sarcastic tone and his fingers wrestled with his prayer beads even more emphatically. 'And the British will love him for being so magnanimous in victory. That's what he says. And if he changes sides later they'll confirm him as titular but powerless Rajah of Bithur, give him an inadequate pension, and hang us.'

'You think so?'

'If they win back India, yes. And not just us. He'll say he was isolated and forced to do what he did, and that Jawala Prasad, and you and I, and even his brothers, were the real rebels. In order to save his life and remain in a position where he could help the British, which is what he is doing now, he gave the appearance of going along with them, but really he was just biding his time. That's what he'll say.'

'And if they don't? If the British don't win?'

'Tatya, no one is going to make the Nana Peshwa. He has to take it. And it's my belief he won't do that until he's in a position where he's got nothing to lose by doing it. He's still playing both sides.'

'All right. So what do we do?'

'I'll think of something. Hang on. It's coming to me. But you'll have to get Jawala and the brothers in line . . .'

A pause. Azimullah Khan paced up and down the loggia. Those amber prayer beads continued to click across his right index finger as his thumb pulled them through. He avoided Tatya's eye, then turned.

'I think I know what to do. But it will require some planning and organisation and time. Can we delay the evacuation until tomorrow morning? But we must make it seem that it's Wheeler who asks for the extra time . . .'

He turned back, swung a chair to the end of the table, sat down. Elbows on it, he glanced over his shoulder and out into the park, and then leant closer to Tatya.

'Here's what we'll do . . .' he began.

'Sir Hugh!'

'Don't stand on ceremony, Captain Turner. After what we have been through . . .'

Wheeler and his family, his second wife, a Eurasian, and their two surviving almost grown-up daughters, were all crammed together in what had been a small room in the smaller of the two buildings in the entrenchment, the one that had once had a tiled roof. Only three walls and pile of rubble now, dust and dirt everywhere, a tarpaulin rigged up to provide some shelter from the sun and the rains that were daily expected . . . and feared since the earth rampart that surrounded the entrenchment would be washed away.

'We've been down to the ghat and, frankly, we're not happy about what we saw. And heard.'

'Go on.'

'The boats seemed adequate. About forty of those up-river ones used for bringing down produce, cotton, wheat and so forth. You can just about get fifteen passengers in each at a pinch with a couple of watermen to steer them and row them where necessary. Most of them had thatched roofs and those that didn't were having them fixed. They were putting a sack of flour in each . . .'

'It all sounds all right.'

'Yes, sir. But there were a lot of sepoys about, mostly from the 56th, and several times we heard the word *kuttle* used.'

'And what does that mean?'

'Massacre, sir.'

26 JUNE, 4.00 P.M.

The Nana was very pleased with himself, definitely on a high. Outright victories against the British had so far been extremely rare and small affairs, and this was what, in his own estimation, he had signally achieved. He was now in Savada House, head up, doing his best to suppress the smile showing in his eyes, hands clasped behind his back in the manner (he had seen the picture in the *Illustrated London News*) of the Prince Consort. He even tried to hold his stomach in.

The thing was, he had won this victory entirely in accordance with European Rules of Engagement: at the outset he had warned the garrison that the bombardment was about to start, giving them time to surrender; now, he was allowing the whole garrison to march out, bearing arms for their own protection and giving them transport to a safe place; he had, as far as he knew, slain no prisoners although the British had killed the very few sepoys that had fallen into their hands. In short, he had behaved with great magnanimity and though he had been as ruthless in his pursuit of victory as a great general should be, he had been merciful to a defeated enemy. And finally, all those rajahs and self-appointed generals, maulvis and the rest who surrounded Bahadur Shah in Delhi and who had failed to shake the tiny English force off The Ridge, would have to treat him as someone to be reckoned with. He even hoped the English themselves would now look on him as a worthy enemy and a potential friend, should they wish to have him on their side.

Peshwa of the Marathas. Sounded good. But who was this creeping up behind him. Azimullah Khan. What did he want?

'Ah. Azimullah. I take it the British will be leaving shortly? Everything going smoothly under your instructions and directions, I assume? I have a mind, Azi, to go down to the ghat and take my farewell of General Wheeler. What do you think? Perhaps a photographing person could be found.'

'Probably not a good idea, Excellency. The British are not always gracious in defeat. But there is another matter . . . It appears that more of the garrison than we supposed are not able to walk to the ghat, and we have to find more carts and elephants than we had envisaged. The consequence is that they will not be leaving the entrenchment until early morning tomorrow.'

The Nana was not pleased. But in the transcendental state he was in he found in himself the condescension required to suppress the irritation he felt.

'I do want it to go well,' he confided, 'so . . . so be it.'

41

Cawnpore, 27 June 1857

Dawn. Throughout the enclosure the British were up, preparing for their departure, especially the women. There was very little noise and some, revelling in the near silence, even walked as quietly as they could, or shushed their children. Here and there one or two would simply stand, heads in the air, listening to the sparrows in the shattered trees nearby and the caw and cackle of crows and vultures out on the maidan. More than once a woman turned to the neighbour beside her and silently, with tears rolling down through the dirt on their faces, they shared a brief, awkward embrace.

They were not merely dishevelled and dirty; most of them had only just enough in the way of torn petticoats to protect their modesty – the rest of their clothes had gone, torn up to make bandages and dressings. Many of them were wounded, grazed with shot or flying stones and masonry, some wore hideous burn marks on their hands and arms, badges of the courage they had shown trying to save children from fires. A few, generally the older ones, scrabbled through rubble and dust looking for valuables they had hidden and keepsakes of children, husbands or lovers who had been killed.

Then there were those who could not stand or walk, including the men, as many perhaps as two hundred or more, lying on the ground, wrapped, if they were lucky, in one of the few remaining sheets, many of them with hideous wounds exposed, a leg torn off, a shattered jaw held in place by an improvised scarf, a woman who miraculously still breathed hoarsely on one lung, the right side of her body having been caved in by a nine-pound shot. The flies were everywhere. Most of the children huddled in groups, kept close to their mothers or whoever had become a surrogate mother, but there were those, mostly boys, who ran about, played tag, or threw stones towards the Native gun emplacements, then, suddenly aware they had strayed too far and could no longer see the rest of their family, burst into tears.

And, still, there were those who were mad. Some of these continued to move about on all fours, bellies as close as they could be to the ground, staring over their shoulders with large wild eyes, striving to spot the next cannonball or shell coming their way.

Catherine Dixon stood among the families of the more senior officers with what was left of her brood about her, for Emma had died the day after her hands were burnt, passing away on the overdose of laudanum administered by the mysterious medical officer whom she never saw again. The others, Miranda, Robert and little Stephen, clung close to her. She had decided she must not give way to grief for Emma until she could be sure the rest were safe. Adam, hunkered in the dust and filth, played knucklebones with Hugh Fetherstonhaugh, who was apparently not as morose as some adults thought he should be at the death of his mother, in spite of the fact that she had been blown to bits attempting to carry a fused but unexploded shell away from him. His father was still alive. As a member of Wheeler's staff he had spent most of the siege in the tiled building.

Stephen had a problem he could not, at only three and a half, share with anybody. Mrs Dixon kept telling him that he would soon be with his mother again, then, if not soon, that one day this would be so. But who was his mother? That was the problem. Was she a dimly recalled figure in white, a little like the angels in a religious tract 'for very small children' one of the older women had given him, a person who faded in and out of his mind's eye, never quite distinct, but who smelled sweetly of flowers and who seemed always to have music about her? Or did she have long black hair, a dark face, and wear bright colours, usually between orange and red or green? This other mother was warm, soft, held him tight when he was miserable, smelled dusty and often of fresh sweat too. He rather hoped that the second mother was the right one, but felt strangely disturbed at the idea. He felt that the first one might not be too happy if she knew he favoured the second.

Elephants arrived and, with their ears responding to noise the way a sail shifts to catch a breeze, distracted the children. Then hackeries, rough carriages or bullock carts, the waggoneers cracking whips and shouting abuse at the lumbering grey, curly horned beasts. A bugle called and the men in their tattered uniforms, nearly all wounded in one place or another, some supported by a mate or staggering on crutches, fell in in four files facing the shreds of their regimental colours and such of their officers who were still able to stand. General Sir Hugh Wheeler, KCB, staggering a little, and supported by one of his aides when necessary, walked down the ranks.

'Soon be out of it now, eh, Roberts?'

'Yessir.'

'Leg holding up, Edwards?'

'Quite well, sah.'

'You did awfully well, Hustwick. Must see you get acknowledged in the appropriate way.' He paused, looked up and down the rows of men. 'Not the neatest of turnouts I've seen on parade, you'll appreciate that, but you've all done well. Damn well. Thank you.'

He turned away and wiping a tear from the eye further from the men, stumped to the head of the line where Major Vibart helped him on to a broken-down pony. The rest of his staff were similarly mounted. Not far behind him Lady Wheeler and her two daughters were on the first of the elephants. Then came the families of the senior officers, also on elephants, then the bullock carts with the families of junior officers and those of the wounded who could not walk. Catherine and her children, including Stephen and Hugh who had attached himself to her, were in the front of this group. Strict order of precedence was observed. Wives of the NCOs, then of the men, their children and the few Native servants who had remained loyal came last.

The bugle again. Wheeler raised his arm, let it drop in front of him, the mahouts and waggon drivers shouted, poked the pachyderms with their sharp sticks or cracked their whips. At the back of the column a sergeant major in very best and loudest British manner bellowed the order right about turn, quick march, and all moved off at a very slow but steady walking pace. Major Vibart watched them go by and joined the column as the last man.

The route took them down a road of compacted stone for a mile, past St John's Church, very like that in Meerut. As they passed it a large group of smallish boys on the roadside hurled refuse at them, rotten vegetables and some eggs.

Adam took hold of his mother's hand.

'Mama,' he asked, 'why do they hate us so much?'

'We haven't treated them very well. It's their country really and we've taken more than we should.' She thought for a moment. 'And a lot of the time we have been quite rude to them.'

She glanced at the church and Adam's gaze followed hers. Although it had not been fired it was clear it had been looted. The windows were broken, and outside Books of Common Prayer littered the short path between the wicket gate and the door.

'I think too,' she went on, 'we have tried too hard to make Christians of them. They have their own religions which are fine for them. It made them feel bad that we tried to take them away from them.'

'God's fault, then.'

'Adam, what an awful thing to say! He might strike you down with a thunderbolt for saying that. If we had any soap, or indeed water, I'd make you wash your mouth out.'

They swayed on, through the cantonments. The bungalows where many of them had lived had been looted and fired, the gardens trampled.

'The devils!' one old lady on one of the elephants cried. 'They've only gawn and tawn down m' rose arbour!'

No chance of losing their way or taking a wrong turning. The sides of the road were lined with Natives from the town, men, women and children. Pedlars hawked water and chappatis, short lengths of sugar cane, twigs of liquorice, and paan, the small leaf-wrapped packets containing the mildly intoxicant betel nut, to the Hindoo men, and, to the Mahometans, the green flags of jihad. Yet the crowd was quiet, watched with expressionless faces the defeated procession go by.

They took a left, followed the new road for a couple of hundred yards, took a right and almost immediately crossed a bridge over a dried-up nullah and then dropped down a gentle bank into the shallow ravine, on to the bed of the stream itself.

Through the bushes ahead those on the elephants could now see the flat glow of the Ganges, and then the clearing at the top of the wide, shallow steps of the ghat. To the left was a temple, not huge, but bigger than those one saw in the fields or on the outskirts of small villages. And unlike those, which are usually white, this one was a strong but subtle orangey-red, faded saffron. It had a dome shaped like a halved onion supported on pillars and a colonnade that ran along the top step of the ghat. On this, seated in throne-like chairs brought down from Savada House, were Azimullah Khan, Tatya Tope and the Nana's brothers, Bala Rao and Baba Bhutt. Nearby, the pony Jawala Prasad was riding shied and backed as the elephants approached.

They halted at the top of the steps, dismounted, helped their families out of the howdahs of the kneeling elephants. There followed a fifteen-minute wait as the tail of the column was still half a mile away. The senior officers, led by Wheeler, used the time to inspect the boats, which, on account of the lowness of the river, were anchored or tied together ten or fifteen yards out, in two to three feet of water. Watermen, usually two to a boat, sat in them, waiting. There was almost no current. A quarter of a mile away, on the other side of the river, a flock of giant red-headed cranes strutted peacefully along the edge of a sandbank. Just behind Wheeler, Captain Moore leant across to the officer riding next to him.

'Where's the Nana, then?' he asked. 'I should have t'ought he would have wanted to be here to see us off.'

The Nana was pacing the wide, long verandah of Savada House. He knew as well as anybody what was about to happen, though no one had actually told him, which he took to be a source of some comfort and possibly even a safety net.

42

Sati Chaura Ghat, 27 June 1857

Voices drift out across the water.

'I say, Moore, Captain Moore, deuced inconvenient making the ladies wade out to the boats.'

'You're right, sorr. An' if I'd have known it, I'd have organised somet'in' a touch more handy. Jetties or the like maybe.'

'Now we're down here, I'd like to get my son into the boat with us.'

'Of course, Mr Fetherstonhaugh, poor little Hugh, must take care of him now your dear wife has gawn.'

'It's getting the poor souls who can't walk into the boats, that's going to be so bloody difficult. I'll get Sa'ant Major Dowson to organise some of the fitter men to lend a hand.'

General Wheeler and his family took the lead boat, the one furthest downriver, and the boats behind them filled up in fairly strict order of precedence. It was not easy for them to get the wounded and sick from the steps to the boats and it soon became clear that there were not enough boats, not with it being necessary to allow so many of the wounded to remain recumbent. Some of the boats took on as many as twenty children as well as adults and on some children had to be put on the thatched roofs. At last one of the boats at the front, Major Vibart's, began to move and at that moment Jawala Prasad raised his hand and a bugle, high and shrill, sounded from near the temple. The members of the cabal stiffened in their seats. The watermen jumped into the river and made for the shore, some of them firing the thatched roofs of their boats first. Brigadier Jawala Prasad now drew his tulwar and it flashed above his head before he brought it down with a flourish and all along the bank bushes moved or rose up revealing hundreds of sepoys. They loosed off a volley into the boats. There were four nine-pounders too, and more on the far side of the river. The cranes spread their huge crimson wings as one, made a wide circle, formed a broad arrow-like formation, and swept away . . . for a moment Catherine could hear the mournful sawing of their wings, before it was drowned by the cannonade and musketry. In most cases all but the wounded abandoned their boats, some of which were raked from stem to stern by round shot. Most waded further out into the river until only their heads were above water, but at this point the sepoys and sowars on the bank left off shooting and waded in after them, tulwars flashing above their heads. Oddly there was little noise now the shooting had all but stopped. A few children screamed before their screams and lives were cut short. There were creaking bumps as the boats crunched into each other, and some grunts as the weight of the blades crashed home.

Wheeler was chopped down by a blow to the neck. Some of the onlookers joined in with clubs and bludgeons, children were bayoneted and an infant was swung by the leg and hurled out beyond the boats. The water boiled with blood which began to pool across the surface of the river below the boats, drifting downstream with the only one to get clear away. Breaking from the crowd of onlookers a Native girl in a bright green saree ran into the water and seized the hand of a small boy, dragging him up the steps and into the bushes where she had left her own daughter.

The little boy flung his arms around her thighs and buried his head in her stomach, then he looked up at her through the tears.

'*Mata*,' he whimpered. 'Mama!'

The Nana waited on the verandah of Savada House until he heard the first distant rattle of musketry. He then turned to a courier mounted ready on a fast charger and nodded. The courier went off at full gallop and arrived at the ghat within five minutes, dismounted and ran up on to the top flight of steps in front of the temple where he thrust a piece of paper into the hands of Jawala Prasad and made his announcement to the other leaders standing around.

'The Nana Saheb,' he said, 'orders you to cease firing on the English. At all events all women and children are to be spared and brought to Savada House immediately.'

After a moment's consultation with Azimullah and the Nana's brothers, Jawala Prasad issued the order and gradually the guns fell silent. The survivors, just over seventy of them, almost all women and children, waded ashore while the sepoys continued to slaughter any men who were still alive. An occasional musket shot still rang out as a swimmer revealed himself heading for the far side or downriver.

Catherine left Miranda and Robert in the care of Adam while she wandered through the small gathering, calling for Stephen. She even waded into the water but quickly sickened at the sight of maimed bodies and even limbs drifting like discarded rubbish on the red surface of the river. A body, on its back, bumped past her, the face twisted in fury as much as pain. She recognised Captain Moore. For a second or so she was surprised by a wave of euphoria. It was not James, James Dixon, her husband, how could it be? And then the euphoria dissolved into bitter longing for him. There were children too, babies even, but none was Stephen. She clambered back up the steps, the ruched fabric of her only garment, a petticoat, clinging to her knees with water that seemed thicker and darker than even Ganges water usually was.

'Excuse me. I do beg your pardon.'

She squeezed through the gathering crowd of surviving women and children. Many were hurt, wounded. One woman crouched over a small girl, wringing her hands. Her child was bleeding from a gaping slash across her thigh. Catherine knelt beside them, pulled out a couple of hairpins that still miraculously remained above the nape of her neck where they had been holding up the ruin of her bun, and, gritting her teeth, trying desperately to control the shaking of her hands, pinched the sides of the wound together and forced the ends of the pins through the skin and flesh and wound the ends together. The child let out a single fearsome scream and then appeared to faint. Catherine tore off the bottom tier of her petticoat, wrung it out, and tied it as a tourniquet above the wound.

'Jemima, isn't it?' she said, recalling the snotty kid of a sergeant major whom she had once caught pushing Robert from behind so that he fell over on his face.

She returned to her remaining three children. Apart from scratches and a nasty graze on Miranda's cheek, they seemed unharmed. She couldn't remember what had happened between the firing of the first shots from the bank and getting back to the steps. To be honest she didn't want to. Would she ever meet Sophie again? Would she be able to tell her how she had lost Sophie's firstborn?

'Bastard's done it again,' Azimullah muttered to Tatya Tope as they mounted their ponies. '"Look," he'll tell the Brits, if he has to, "we shot the soldiers but they had rifles and they fired first. But at some risk to my men I saved the women and children. And anyway I wasn't there."'

'Right,' replied Tatya Tope, shaking his reins and the pony into a trot, and then looking over his shoulder and calling out since Azimullah was having less success in getting his mount to move; indeed, back legs splayed, it had stopped to have a piss. 'Think of something. You usually do. You're supposed to stand up in the stirrups when they do that.'

'How about a coronation?' yelled Azimullah.

Behind them, in the space at the top of the steps beside the temple, responding haphazardly to orders barked by the brigadier, the sepoys disentangled themselves from the bushes; then, using the butts of their matchlocks and, those that had them, prodding with the bayonets of their rifles, they herded the seventy-odd survivors into a huddle which, as they made their way back up the ravine, lengthened into a column again but only about a quarter of the length of the one that had come down. No elephants this time or hackeries, and many of them had lost their shoes. On the way their captors pushed in among them inspecting fingers for rings, ripping from their necks any lockets or whatever that remained, tearing off earrings often with the flesh of the ear lobes too. It took an hour to get them there but eventually they were herded on to the dried-up grass of the park round Savada House and from there drifted into the shade of a big tamarind tree.

> *Abide with me, fast falls the eventide.*
> *The darkness deepens, Lord with me abide*
> *When other helpers fail and comforts flee.*
> *Help of the helpless, O abide with me.*

What makes them sing that? thought Catherine. It's not yet even midday.

From the tamarind tree they watched through the afternoon the slow assembly of all the Native regiments. The heat built, the sky filled with clouds, there was a heavy humidity in the air and distant thunder rumbled. Some said it was the cannon of Havelock from Allahabad or Lawrence from Lucknow on their way to relieve them, but they were wrong. Thirst became a problem. A couple of the more elderly women, old hands with the Natives, asked for water in the tones they and their mothers had been using for a century, and the sepoys who had been obeying them for as long brought them water, chappatis too, and a three-foot-high cooking vessel filled with dahl from one of the Mahometan regiment's kitchens. The Hindoos always cooked their own food, often individually, so as not to break caste.

At five o'clock the Nana appeared on the verandah of the house. For the occasion he had adopted a set of clothes that was military in tone, and, apart from an ostrich-plumed hat and bullion epaulettes, not too showy. The troops marched past, still with their old colours, still with bands playing what they had always played: 'Prince Albert', 'The Keel Row', and so forth, but avoiding the more overtly patriotic numbers like 'The British Grenadiers' or 'Hearts of Oak'. When that was done the Nana made a short speech congratulating them on their courage and skill and especially praising Azimullah Khan and Jawala Prasad who, he intimated, had initiated and organised every-thing. At last came the climax, one of the moments he had been waiting for, it seemed, almost his entire life, certainly since the death of Baji Rao, his adoptive father – his artillery fired off a twenty-one-gun salute, the prerogative of a reigning king or prince.

'That went well,' Tatya Tope remarked.

'We'll do better on Wednesday at Bithur,' Azimullah replied.

Tatya went on, gestured towards the huddled crowd under the tamarind tree. 'What are we going to do with them? They can't stay here.'

'I'll find a place in town. There's a sort of bungalow with a couple of good-sized rooms not far from the bridge. Old Sir George Parker built it for his mistress, his *bibi*.'

'I know the one you mean. The Bibigarh, they call it.'

'That's the one.'

*

On 1 July the Grand Throne of the Peshwas of the Marathas was placed on a dais in the courtyard of the palace of Bithur beneath a huge canopy hung with tarnished silver tassles and fringes. Trumpeters with curly brass horns resembling rams' horns blew barbaric fanfares while horsemen banged kettledrums slung on both sides of their saddles. The Nana took his place on the throne. A priest applied sacred marks indicating royalty on his forehead and the crowd, as many as could be brought in, chanted 'Peshwa, Peshwa, Peshwa, *Zindabad Peshwa*, long life to the Peshwa . . .!' As night fell both Bithur and its palace and Cawnpore were illuminated with thousands of lamps, torches and candles hung from every arch and roof, placed in every window. The townspeople feasted off goodies bought with the largesse the Peshwa had distributed from the British treasury and all agreed it was a great occasion and the beginning of a new era or a return to the old one. The troops paraded through the town, led by richly harnessed elephants.

Though Cawnpore had never been part of the Maratha Confederation, the new Peshwa announced himself in a proclamation as its ruler.

The yellow-faced and narrow-minded people have been sent to hell and Cawnpore has been conquered so it is necessary that all the subjects and landholders should be as obedient to the present government as they have been to the former one.

The rain held off through most of all this, which was a blessing, especially as this was also the day on which the survivors of the ghat massacre, now increased to two hundred and six in number by the addition of a further one hundred and twenty-six lately arrived refugees from Futtehgahr, all women and children, were made to walk nearly four miles from Savada House to the Bibigarh.

The Peshwa remained in his palace. The sepoys began to complain that he had gone off with what remained of the British treasure, which had been promised to them, and that if he didn't come back they would replace him with the Mahometan Nawab of Cawnpore, known as the Nunny Nawab. There was news too from Allahabad. The British and Sikh army, nearly two thousand strong, with six guns, was ready to move under its new commander, General

43

**The Grand Trunk Road through Futtehpore, Bindki,
1–16 July 1857**

Havelock was later spun by the London press and the near adulation of some of his juniors into a hero of the Mutiny, though this was not at first the general opinion. One journalist, attuned to the current craze in Britain for dinosaurs, described him as an old fossil. Lady Canning took a kinder view. 'General Havelock is not in fashion. No doubt he is fussy and tiresome but his little, old, stiff figure looks as active and fit for use as if he were made of steel.' The process of beatification was made easier by the fact that, like Nelson, he died on the job, but that was later. He was sixty-two years old, just five feet tall, and affected an old-fashioned goatee beard, Disraeli-style. When he dressed for dinner he always put on his medals, of which he had quite a clutch, even if the occasion was only a simple family affair. But one of the things the papers liked about him in that strange period between the glamour of the opening of the Queen's reign, sealed by the Great Exhibition of 1851, and the bloated opulence of its closing decades, was his religiosity. He married the daughter of a famous baptist missionary and devoted himself to taking care of his men's spiritual welfare, holding bible classes and preaching sermons.

On this occasion he was late.

Not entirely his fault. He arrived in Allahabad on 30 June having taken only five days to get from Calcutta, but Wheeler had capitulated on the twenty-sixth. The news arrived the next day: it seemed to take the urgency out of the situation and Havelock made his final preparations for the march on Cawnpore and Lucknow more carefully than he might otherwise have done. Indeed he must have considered bypassing Cawnpore and taking the long side of a triangle by marching straight to Lucknow, leaving a force under a Major Renaud, which had already gone on ahead to relieve Wheeler, to march on Cawnpore and protect his left flank. However, the next news was that a very large army of insurgents had left Cawnpore and was marching down the Grand Road towards Futtehpore. Havelock ordered Renaud to halt four miles south-east of Futtehpore and set out in a torrential downpour on 7th July, leaving Neill behind to look after Allahabad. Neill was furious.

Havelock's column, led by the pipes of the 78th, came up with Renaud on the Grand Road. After resting for some hours he sent volunteer cavalry to reconnoitre ahead; they came up with the rebel vanguard in the outskirts of the town. The rebels believed they had only Renaud's small force in front of them and attacked. As Renaud fell back Havelock waited for them with the 64th armed with Enfields in a copse on one advanced flank and his artillery across the road. It was the Enfields and guns that won the day against a force at least twice as large. Cannon in the hands of expert gunners and the rifles were both deadly accurate and lethal at more than eight hundred yards. The rebel army broke and was pursued through Futtehpore until the exhausted British could go no further. Behind them came the walking sick, a reserve and the baggage wallahs, all of whom took time out to trash and burn the towns and villages they passed through, as they had every other village, right back to Allahabad.

And behind them came the lawyers.

Shocked by what he had seen of Neill's slaughter of guilty and innocent alike, Havelock had insisted that appropriate formalities should be carried out before any further executions took place. There should be trials, even if they only lasted a half-minute or so, and Hardcastle was one of those qualified to conduct them.

Assistant Judge Advocate Tom Hardcastle, heading into the sun on the back of a halfway decent horse for once, glanced over his shoulder to make sure that the raggle-taggle two score of men and boys he had been put in charge of were still with him and behaving reasonably well. All were soldiers deemed unfit to be in the ranks of their proper regiments: they were the lame and the halt, the deaf, blind and shell-shocked; recidivist thieves and drunks; five men who were clearly mad, and six Christian Native drummer boys.

There was a village to his left, about a mile away, with a low railway embankment between it and the road. He raised his arm and the tiny column followed him down the bank and into the field below, and as they went, slish-slosh, plip-plop through the mud, it occurred to him he might be making a mistake, that this might be Bindki where the village headman and his wife had probably saved his life. Well, so be it.

Tom Hardcastle had become an automaton. Off his horse he moved with the jerky, slightly uncoordinated gait of a marionette whose master has not quite mastered the art. On one occasion he became aware, but at a distance as it were, that when walking or marching he moved his arm forward and back in time with the leg on the same side. He tried, tried very hard, to correct this, but found he could not.

For most of the time he was unburdened by emotion of any sort at all – he felt nothing. He had been like this for a week ever since waking up on the third morning out of Allahabad and realising that it was beyond Tom Hardcastle's ability to continue doing what he had done over the first two days. So someone else, more akin to the living dead, would have to do it for him.

A small crowd of women and children gathered round him like pilot fish and went with him into the circle of huts that framed the centre of the village and its meeting place. Without being told his men and boys set about their usual business of stacking a pile of drums to be used as a table, putting a camping chair behind it, and raising a short flagpole with the Union flag nailed to it. Then Sergeant McCartney, a malingerer from Toxteth, set a ledger, an inkwell and a pen on the drums.

They brought three men in front of Hardcastle and one of them, as he knew it would be, was Jiva. Jiva would not run away. He stood in front of him, tall, thin, deep lines etched in his dark cheeks, a polished stick held in his knobbly hands. Hardcastle looked at the bare feet. They were long, narrow, brown, well-shaped as those belonging to people who have spent most of their lives unshod often are. He avoided Jiva's eye. He filled in his ledger: name, crime – aiding the enemy; defence – none, and Sergeant McCartney took Jiva and the two men away to the outskirts of the village where one large mango tree had been left. There was no cart. Jiva's wife, who had nursed Hardcastle, went with them. Hardcastle stayed where he was. Presently he heard first the rattle of the two drums that had not been used to make his table, then her voice raised in a wild keening cry that broke on a convulsive sob.

The sun sank. His men refused to move on. They slept under what cover they could find. The moon rose behind gathering clouds but gave some light. Thunder rumbled. Hardcastle got up, gathered up the folding chair and a rope that had not been used and walked to the tree, his gait as awkward as before. Jiva's body and those of the other two men had gone: they were already burning nearby on and under a pile of branches which an Untouchable tended. As Hardcastle approached the Untouchable stirred the red-hot embers and a cloud of sparks floated beneath a cloud of the evil-smelling smoke towards the moonlit clouds. At dawn or shortly after the ashes would be gathered up and taken the ten miles or so to be scattered on the Ganges.

Hardcastle placed the chair, slung the rope over a branch, made the end fast round the trunk and the noose round his neck, stood on the chair and stepped off it. His feet hit the ground. He managed to loosen the noose and get it off. He then went back to his horse and took from the saddlebags his four law books which he placed on the seat of the chair. With some difficulty he got his foot on to the top book and the whole structure collapsed. On the third attempt he managed to stand upright on the top book. He stepped off but the drop was still not enough to do more than dislocate his neck and ten minutes passed before he was properly dead. Quite early in the process of dying he realised he should have used his horse. Too late by then.

The Untouchable went on with the task in hand. What the yellow face did to himself was not his problem. Rain began to fall, heavy drops but not yet a downpour.

Havelock fought two smaller engagements on the Pandu Nadi River which brought him within twenty-two miles of Cawnpore and, on 16 July, after a day's rest and a morning march of sixteen miles, a more major one four miles from the river and the city. With one twenty-four-pounder and several other guns the Nana, now personally leading his troops, made a last stand along a line of villages which might just have succeeded had not the third decisive weapon Havelock had at his disposal, the British infantryman with his bayonet, come to his rescue. Regiments charging in close-disciplined order drove the rebel infantry out of strong positions and finally the 64th charged and captured the twenty-four-pounder. The rebel army melted away, heading for the bridge, which they blew behind them while the British gave way to exhaustion and heat sickness within sight of the roofless and now deserted barracks of Wheeler's Entrenchment. They were a day too late.

44

The Bibigarh, Cawnpore, 1–17 July 1857

The Bibigarh was a bungalow set in a small enclosure which once must have been a garden. From the outside it looked plain, squat even, and poky, but was blessed with a proper roof, not thatch but tiles. It consisted of two main rooms, set parallel, each about ten by twenty-four feet. One inside wall with square pillars supporting semi-circular arches opened on to facing verandahs with a small courtyard between them. At one end there were four small bedrooms, at the other the servants' quarters, occupied by the sepoy guard. It was not suitable accommodation for the two hundred and fifty-odd women and children and five men who were held there for sixteen days. There were no beds or punkas. Most of the prisoners were suffering from wounds from the ghat, some of them serious, indeed fatal. Their guards were abusive and rough with them, but did not, in spite of what the British press asserted later, threaten or commit any sexual violence.

Over more than a fortnight social dynamics must have occurred. Things must have changed. Forceful characters – and there have been perhaps few of our species so forceful as a British middle-aged or elderly upper-middle-class lady used to be – would have emerged and asserted themselves. Once some recovery had been made from the shock at what had happened at the ghat, women who had managed substantial households of extended family and many servants, and, moreover, had survived in Wheeler's Entrenchment, would have insisted on some order and regulation. They would have put the

308

severely hurt or ill in one place, probably one airier and cooler than the rest, and organised a rota of care for them. Nevertheless, one in ten died of cholera during the first week.

Their next care would have been the children, seeing to it that they were properly fed and watered before the adults got their share; regulating behaviour, suppressing bullying on one side and uncalled-for whingeing on the other. They might even have organised some simple schooling to keep them occupied. A piece of charcoal on a plastered wall would do for blackboard and chalk; without books they would rely on the memory of books. It is not perhaps beyond possibility that there was a story-telling corner, perhaps another where a little history and geography were passed on. And certainly, there would have been bible classes, for there were indeed bibles. And the singing of familiar hymns. Nothing like a rousing verse or more of the Old Hundredth – 'All people that on earth do dwell, Sing to the Lord with cheerful voice' – to lift the heart.

At the outset the diet was watery dahl and chappatis, but after only a few days milk and a little meat were added and also clean clothes. It would not have occured to their captives to provide these, and when asked they might well have turned a deaf ear, but those women . . . They even managed to get a Native doctor to visit regularly and presumably treat the most severely wounded and those suffering from cholera with what was for the Victorians a universal nostrum – laudanum, opium dissolved in alcohol. Their link with the outside world was Hosseini Khan. When little more than a child she had been the Nana's adoptive father's favourite slave-girl. Now in her thirties and a servant of the Nana's favourite mistress, she was tall with grey streaks in what had been oddly blonde hair. Her bossiness had earned her the nickname the Begum, the Queen. To begin with she showed little interest in the prisoners' welfare, but she was essentially a servant and those ladies were used to managing servants, especially those who were excessively uppity.

Asiatic cholera took hold with the coming of the rainy season. The first stage is a day or two of painless diarrhoea, no vomiting. This is followed by violent diarrhoea of a whey-like or rice-water appearance with large quantities of disintegrated mucous membrane, and vomiting of similar material, accompanied by intense thirst and pain. During the final stage, which lasts no more than a day, the skin becomes cold and blueish purple, features pinched, eyes sunken, pulse imperceptible, voice (*vox cholerica*) a hoarse whisper. The pain, abdominal cramps and cramps of legs and feet, is now severe. Remission can occur but is usually followed by relapses and weakening, leading to death after all. Among those who do not contract the disease the effluent, the smell, the distress of seeing people suffer must add considerably to the temptation to give way to despair.

Catherine Dixon was like a she-wolf with her cubs. She found a corner, a real corner, an angle where two walls met, and made it their den. Here she fought to maintain a viable space in which the three children could lie down while she placed herself across them, between them and all the others; her body language, an expressionless thinning of her mouth and narrowing of her eyes at any intrusion on that space, even occasionally a firm resistance, a push, or a straight verbal assertion, 'I'm sorry, but that is my child's place, please move,' taking the place of the wolf-mother's baring of fangs accompanied by a snarl. But then, as things settled and most accepted the limitations of what they had and ceased squabbling for more, she began, able-bodied and virtually unhurt as she was, to help those more helpless than herself or her family. Accompanied by Adam she took bowls of the watered-down dahl or ground gram with milk to those who could not fend for themselves, kneeling over them to spoon food into old or shaking mouths, sending Adam for water or a clean cloth.

One old lady, a Scot who had been employed at the Free School for twenty years, caught Adam's wrist in her knobbly almost skeletal hand.

'You're a good wee bairn, and Jesus has a place waiting for you by his side.'

He looked down at her and his eyes, deadly serious, filled with tears.

'God let this happen,' he muttered, and his gaze flitted over the gloomy, filthy room. 'I don't like God any more.'

The ancient dominie released her clasp as her eyes filled with anger and hate, but she was not strong enough to put what she felt into words. She turned her head away and flapped her hand in dismissal. Adam stood up.

'You shouldn't have said that,' his mother whispered.

He shrugged dismissively.

'What do you think, then, Mummy?'

She put her arm round his shoulder and smiled down at him.

'I'll have time to think when we're out of this.'

Miranda succumbed to the water-borne cholera and died.

'What made Lavanya bring you here?' Catherine, angry, through tears.

Adam had almost forgotten Lavanya. It required an effort of memory to bring back her image. At first, on their three-hundred-mile walk, he had hated her, then he had begun to respect her. Finally, he knew they all depended on her and now he felt a sudden wave of gratitude mixed with an odd sort of nostalgia.

'She did her best,' he said.

'She could have, should have, taken you to Agra.'

'I don't suppose she knew where Agra is. I'm not sure I do.'

'Ignorant, you see?' Catherine's hands twisted and tore at the tassles of a shawl she had picked up from another of the dead. 'Pig-ignorant peasant girl. I never did like her.'

'Mama!'

She glanced down at him, eyes still wide and wild.

'Oh come on, I'll take you to the geography corner and show you where Agra is.'

Early in the afternoon of Wednesday, 15 July, they heard gunfire, and it was close enough to be sure that it was indeed gunfire, not distant thunder. Presently the Begum arrived. She was laconic, to the point.

'The British are here,' she announced. 'Their horse are ten miles away, coming up the big road.'

But the main army was still more than sixteen miles away.

They sat along the sides of the long table in the hotel dining room: the Nana's brothers, one of whom, Bala Rao, had been wounded in the shoulder during the morning and had his arm in a sling, Jawala Prasad, Azimullah, Tatya Tope, Teeka Singh. Nana, the Peshwa, sat at the head.

Tatya Tope, who was emerging as the least incompetent soldier, presented the military position.

'The British are exhausted. They have fought four battles in just over a week. They have marched nearly one hundred and thirty miles. They have to rest. They have to wait for their baggage train, with ammunition and field hospitals and so forth, to catch up before they'll move on. There's a good position four miles out where the Grand Trunk Road forks with the road to the cantonments. Line of villages. I reckon we can hold them up there until we are reinforced.'

'Maybe we should get out while we can,' muttered his Magnificent Majesty.

'Where to?' asked Teeka Singh, once a sergeant major, now a general. He stroked his glossy Sikh's beard, held in place by a black cloth chin strap beneath his turban.

'North-west towards Agra,' suggested the Peshwa's younger brother.

'Or south-west towards Gwalior and Jhansi. That way the Ranee will join us,' the elder brother countered. The Ranee of Jhansi had shared her childhood with him. They were close.

The Nana-Peshwa sighed deeply, looked at the ceiling. His podgy hands twisted on the table top in front of him.

'We'll fight them here, on the ground Tatya Tope suggested,' he said. 'And, if we have to, we'll pull back to Bithur and see what the English do, before we make up our minds.' He didn't want to give up his palace, his home.

Tatya Tope whispered so only Azimullah heard him.

'Go on, bring up the women in the Bibigarh.'

Azimullah cleared his throat.

'Which, your highness, leaves the question of the women and children in the Bibigarh.'

The Nana-Peshwa waved a dismissive hand.

'They are not important,' he said. 'The English can look after them.'

All round the table there was subdued consternation. Apart from anything else it now seemed the Nana was resigned to accepting yet another defeat. But they had other concerns too. They looked at each other, fingers drummed briefly on the teak surface. Bala Rao spoke first.

'No,' he barked. 'We know what the British are doing. Indiscriminately they are hanging every male they have found between here and Allahabad. The Sikh regiments who have stayed with them are

312

raping Hindoo women. They have burnt every village they have passed through. We should teach them a lesson. Those women shall be executed.'

Teeka Singh was now furious too.

'It is not Sikhs who rape the Hindoos. It is the Muslims who have been doing so for centuries . . .'

'And no doubt the Scots and Irish,' Azimullah quietly suggested.

'Well, we could keep them as hostages.' The Nana Peshwa contrived to sound rational. 'They could turn out to be very useful.'

But Tatya Tope, whose main function was still the running of the commissariat, pointed out the snags.

'They are ill and weak. They cannot walk. If we take them with us we shall have to put elephants and hackeries we cannot spare at their disposal. We shall have to feed them and guard them.'

A moment's silence, then the Nana-Peshwa stood up.

'Decide it among yourselves. They are a problem you yourselves created.'

Which was unfair, as Azimullah pointed out when His Effulgence had left them: after all it was the Nana who had sent orders to the ghat that the women and children should be spared. Then he looked up and down the table.

'Raise a hand if you think they should be killed.'

Silence. No one moved. Then Jawala Prasad, in his whining, nasal Brahminical voice, intervened at last.

'We were all at the ghat. We were seen at the ghat. If these women survive they will tell the English, this General Havelock, just which of us was there.'

One by one, all hands were raised.

Tatya Tope stood.

'I'll do it now,' he said. 'Tomorrow will be too late.'

Tatya Tope passed the order on to the Begum. She called out the sepoy guard who went into the bungalow and came out with the handful of males who had trickled in during the previous few days: three survivors from Futtehgahr, two colonels and a magistrate, Robert Thornhill, son of a director of the Company. They were followed by an indigo planter and two fourteen-year-old boys. All were shot by a firing squad of sepoys. The Begum then told the women that they would be next. Three formidable ladies, led by Mrs Moore,

313

the widow of Captain John Moore, walked briskly over to the other end of the building and found the young jemadar – lieutenant – who commanded the guard.

'Young man, Hosseini has just told us we are about to be slaughtered. Is this true?'

'Of course not, mem.' He was no less in awe of these English memsahibs, or in this case Anglo-Irish, than he had been before the Mutiny began.

'You have not received orders to that effect?'

'Certainly not, mem.' He turned to his corporal. 'Fetch me the Begum.'

She came from round the corner of the building where she had hidden when she saw the ladies leaving it. The lieutenant, whose name was Yusuf Khan, was brisk with her.

'There is no question of killing these women. And you are certainly not the person to give this order, or indeed any other.' He knew her caste and history.

Haughty and paranoid, proud but conscious of how she was looked down on and even laughed at behind her back, she strode across the short space to the hotel. She returned twenty minutes later, walking behind Tatya Tope, and wearing a smug, fulfilled look on her face.

Tatya Tope told Yusuf Khan to call out the guard and have them fall in. The man whom the white officers of the Cawnpore garrison had called 'Bennie' and had mocked for his wild features, snub nose and bad teeth, which gave him what they called a 'negroid' look, spoke quietly.

'If you do not kill them all, women and children, I'll see you blown from guns before dusk.'

He was referring to a form of execution common under the Mughals, and occasionally used by the British, of tying condemned men over the muzzles of large guns charged with powder only and blowing them to pieces.

In spite of this threat the sepoys remained less than enthusiastic. First they tried to pull the women out into the yard, but, hand to hand, they fought back. The ones in front clung to the doorjambs, they punched like men, scratched like cats and spat in the men's faces. Meanwhile the Nana's women in the hotel had heard what was happening and, from the first-floor balconies, they too screamed abuse at the sepoys and encouragement to their sisters. Tatya Tope

314

then ordered the sepoys to fire through the windows. They did, but aimed just one volley at the ceilings and then refused to reload.

Meanwhile, Hosseini had gone to fetch the man she most frequently consorted with, one of the Nana's bodyguard. His name was Sarvur Khan: he was a big man, a bully, and had a deep grudge against the British for his mother had been a prostitute and had often been abused by British officers and NCOs. He turned up, just as the sun was setting, with two Muslim butchers and two of the Nana's Hindoo kitchen servants. They were all armed with tulwars or the cleavers butchers use.

It was a battle and its logic was that of a battle. When the sepoys had tried to drag them out the women were defending a narrow doorway and their children were not under immediate threat. But once these new and far more committed arrivals had carved their way into the room each woman's first concern became her children. Had they combined against the five murderers they might have disarmed them. A handful of them remained together and hurled themselves on their attackers but these were no longer concerned to get the women out: they were there to kill, nothing else, and they cut them down, severing heads and limbs, gashing torsos, necks, shoulders, breasts and waists with great sweeps of their heavy curved swords. The amount of blood was appalling, spouting, gushing, pouring over everybody, everything. The noise too was hellish: screams of pain, grunts of rage, terrible anguish cut off with gasping, bubbling sobs, the clang of metal when a blade hit a doorway or pillar. What made it yet more awful was the density of the crowd – one hundred and ninety-seven victims, of whom one hundred and twenty-four were children or babies, crushed into less than five hundred square feet. There was nowhere to go, no hiding place, no way out.

It was dark though, those rooms were always gloomy, with little light getting round or through the tatties or blinds, and outside the dusk was thickening. Catherine held her corner, one of the furthest from the doors, pushed Adam and Robert into it and managed to lie across them before the killers reached them. She feigned dead, aware that the blood that had already splashed over her might serve to look like her own. Robert screamed that he couldn't breathe and writhed to get out from under her. She pinned his arms to his side, got her mouth over his and almost choked him in a last wretched embrace.

She might, one could suppose, have thought at this moment of her husband and her eldest son, of how what now could have seemed a selfish desire to have them both in India had contributed to their being trapped in this awfulness. Perhaps her mind was more emotionally occupied with love for Dixon in these last moments, or, like many there, dwelt on the sufferings of Christ and how hers were a sacrifice for Him. On the other hand her feelings may have been entirely preoccupied with the physical experience she was enduring, the warmth of her surviving children's bodies beneath her own, the way Robert disengaged his mouth from hers to draw breath and then fastened on her again just as she had fastened on him, the numbing noise, the iron stench of blood, even the roughness of stone flags beneath her lower thighs and legs, the awkwardness of the way she was lying. Then Sarvur Khan himself smashed his tulwar into her back, repeating the stroke two more times before moving on to the next.

But Adam, heaving and pulling himself out from under his mother's body, with her hot blood sliding down over his shirt, managed to drag himself to his feet and hurl himself on to the big man's back, where he clung like a monkey, tearing at his turban and hair. To get rid of him Sarvur turned and smashed his back against a wall but still Adam hung on, feeling round the murderer's head now, seaching for his eyes. But one of the Muslim butchers got there, and with a swiftly calculated swing managed a slice across Adam's torso, beneath his ribs. The blade almost cut him in half but did not touch Sarvur's back. Adam's dying body dropped to the ground. Sarvur stamped on his head and then kicked it.

The five men came out after only half an hour during which Sarvur had twice run back to the hotel for another blade, having broken the ones he had. It seems that a berserk rage had taken hold of him and that his wild slashes had caught the masonry of angles and doorways. Although they clearly believed they had finished what they had come to do, low cries of pain, sometimes sharpening to a scream, went on all through the night from behind the locked doors. Perhaps to smother this disturbance, perhaps even in celebration of the victory he still hoped for, the Nana-Peshwa ordered a nautch, that is a performance of erotic dancing, after supper, in the hotel.

*

Early the following morning, while the British began their final march on Cawnpore from sixteen miles away and the Nana-Peshwa and Jawala Prasad drew up their army in a defensive crescent four miles from the city, four Untouchables, cleaners from the hotel, dragged the bodies from the bungalow and dropped them down a dry well nearby. Six were still alive, three women and three small boys; the women, severely hurt, were propped against a bank while the three boys ran madly round and round the well. The cleaners did not know what to do with them. A message was sent and a reply came from the hotel: 'Dispose of them'. First the women and then the boys were tossed into the well. There were still enough naked or near naked corpses available to cover them. When the well was full the remaining bodies were dropped in the river which was not more than a couple of hundred yards away.

Havelock entered Cawnpore on 17 July. The remnants of the Nana's army deserted him and made their way upriver to Futtehgahr. He and his entourage abandoned the palace at Bithur which was taken and looted by a small detachment of British soldiers. From then on, Havelock was occupied with the business of relieving Lucknow, forty miles away. First he had to get his army across the Ganges. The Nana had destroyed the bridge of boats behind him and the only available means was the Nana's small steamer, the larger riverboats having been destroyed at the Sati Chaura Ghat. Once on his way he found the opposition to his tired and depleted force too strong and he had to return.

Meanwhile, James Neill was promoted and put in charge of the Cawnpore Station. He and Havelock did not get on: 'Now, General Neill, let us understand each other; you have no power or authority whilst I am here, and you are not to issue a single order.' But Havelock was not there for much of the time and Neill displayed his usual almost bestial ruthlessness in hunting down and punishing the perpetrators of the two massacres. Those who were deemed to have played leading roles were forced to eat pork and beef before being hanged. The Bibigarh murderers were made to lick up at least a square foot each of the blood on the floor of the building before they too were hanged on a large banyan tree nearby. A century later this was revered as a memorial to the Martyrs of Cawnpore, that is the murderers. It was blown down quite recently in a storm and remains

45

The cockroaches were as big as mice, the black mildew climbed up the walls, at meal times the choice was between placing smouldering fumigators burning insecticidal sulphur-based proprietory compounds along the tables or enduring assault by fifty varieties of bug, beetle, fly and moth. Charlotte Canning tried penny-royal plants as she did in England but they were of course ineffective beyond eighteen inches or so as were burning oils of citron which the old hands recommended. The latter were expensive too. A thin layer of dirt appeared over everything, in part made up of fungal spores, in part of the tarnish or rust that spread over everything metal, and in part of the mud which any number of precautions could not hold back. From the Brown Drawing Room windows the maidan appeared to be a sheet of water pockmarked with the rain, but the sludge it produced was mixed with that of the rising Ganges which backed up the drains and stank of raw sewage. It got trodden into everything.

The dirt and the damp. No fabric, clothes, curtains, carpets, sheets whatever, were ever dry; all were always damp. Even the pages of *The Warden*, which Charlotte read in bed to encourage a good night's sleep, were floppy, flaccid. The heat of June seemed not to have dissipated at all, but came now on the back of 100 per cent humidity (four ounces of water vapour per cubic yard). Through it Canning worked a twenty-hour day, covering every aspect of the daily running of the British possessions as well as attempting to contain and ultimately suppress what was variously called a mutiny, an insurgence, a rising and a rebellion. The only thing no one, on either side, thought of calling it at the time was a War of Independence. From four o'clock in the morning to midnight he sat at his desk almost without a break, going through one departmental box after another (labelled 'military', 'political', 'revenue', 'shipping' 'transport', to name a few), responding to telegraph messages landing on his desk only minutes after they had been sent and to despatches which had taken a month to arrive by steamship, and fending off pressure or requests to allocate dwindling resources from bishops and regimental veterinary surgeons, from merchants and schoolteachers, from railway engineers and the men in charge of the post, from his generals and a deputation of over-worked writers.

Lady Canning was beyond fearing for her husband's health – it was too late for that. What she feared was breakdown.

And, as if all that were not enough, there were the reactions to the crisis of the people she had to entertain: the women who came to tea and soirées, the men and women who attended the big dinners custom demanded she and her husband should give on a more than weekly basis. These varied from barely concealed panic (the lady who announced, as she unfolded her napkin, that she wondered if they would rise again from their seats and on being asked why she should expect otherwise declared she had heard of a plot to poison them all) to demands for immediate vengeance on the niggers even if it required the annihilation of whole townships or Districts, let alone armies. Nevertheless the ball for the Queen's Birthday had gone off as it should. To show it was business as usual they even kept the usual Indian guard of honour, and refused to have European soldiers hidden in the basement.

Day by day the news was bad or worse. Reports, despatches, telegrams told first of massacres then of the consequences. She pored over them endlessly. Charles encouraged her to, hoping for help and advice from a quarter he had always trusted, and it was when she came to the reports of the Bibigarh murderers being made to lick congealed blood from the floor that her hand came down sharply on the table the report was on and she looked up and around her. There was no sound but that of the rain and the relentless buzzing of some creature caught in the folds of a drape it could not escape. Then, from somewhere upriver, a steam whistle blew: train or boat, she wasn't sure, something that was going somewhere.

'This will not do.'

She said it again.

'This will not do.'

She stood, gathered up the report and the others that had come with it and set off to the wing where Charles was working.

They talked about it and he wrote to the Queen:

There is a rabid and indiscriminate vindictiveness abroad, even among many who ought to set a better example, which it is impossible to contemplate without a feeling of shame for one's own countrymen.

Her Majesty replied:

Lord Canning will easily believe how entirely the Queen shares his feelings of sorrow and indignation at the unchristian spirit shown – alas! also to a great extent here – by the public towards Indians in general and towards Sepoys without discrimination . . .

and added, with her usual good sense

. . . It is however not likely to last and comes from the horror produced *by the* unspeakable atrocities *perpetrated against the innocent women and children which really makes one's blood run cold. For the perpetrators of these awful horrors no punishment can be severe enough & sad as it is, stern justice must be dealt out to all the guilty ones . . .*

But to the native at large, to the peaceable inhabitants, to the many kind & friendly ones who have assisted us, sheltered the fugitives & been faithful and true – these should be shown the greatest kindness. They should know there is no hatred of brown skin.

To Charlotte Canning, when she came to him with reports of Neill's activities, Charles exclaimed 'I will NOT govern in anger', a sentiment he repeated in a letter to Lord Granville, the Lord President of the Council. To another correspondent who had recommended fiercest vengeance:

*You are entirely and most dangerously wrong. The one difficulty
which of all the others is the most difficult to meet, is that the
regiments which have not yet fallen away are mad with fear – fear
for their caste and religion, fear of disgrace in the eyes of their
comrades, fear that the European troops are being collected to
crush and decimate them as well as their already guilty comrades.
Your bloody, off-hand measures are not the cure for this sort of
disease . . . Don't mistake violence for vigour.*

What emerged from all this was expressed in an official resolution,
issued by Canning, which became known as the Clemency Order. It
was hardly clement at all in its insistence that punishments meted
out should be harsh, though deserved and just. It earned him the
soubriquet 'Clemency Canning'. Applied originally derisively by the
press in Calcutta and London, it had become an honorific by the
time he died in 1862.

The Queen struck a prophetic note. In a letter to her friend
Charlotte Canning she wrote:

*I think that the greatest care ought to be taken not to interfere with
their religion as once a cry of that kind is raised among a fanatical
people – very strictly attached to their religion – there is no
knowing what it may lead to and where it may end.*

PART V

Things Can Only Get Better

46

The Ridge, Delhi, August 1857

Below The Ridge lay the parade ground and the blackened cantonment bungalows. A canal protected the north side of the lines. Above it the newly pitched tents in uniform rows, row upon row, lay across the hillside. White boards with neatly painted black numbers indicated which company, troop, regiment or battery each belonged to. Above, The Ridge itself, covered with scrub and occasional copses, netted with tracks, climbed quite steeply to a broken crest, overlooking the walls of the Red Fort and the Cashmere Gate, a mile and a half away, glowing in the last of the sunlight. The smoke of thousands of cooking fires filled the air above the city. Kites and crows wheeled in hundreds above the rubbish pits and the disputed ground between, which was littered with bodies. Sam was sitting there with the rest of his section, his hand resting on the hand of their new mucker Alec, son of a crofter driven off his grazing by Highland enclosures. Alec, who had been moved forward to take Taff's place in their file, was lean, Viking red-blond, and only seventeen years old so his beard was no more than a soft haze of yellow.

Sam released Alec's hand but did not break the silence that had fallen between them as they sat on the turf, knees up, arms round them now, their thighs almost touching. For a moment or two they watched the puffs of white smoke from the sepoy batteries on the ramparts that rose above a broken wilderness of cottages, tumbledown walls, the stones too hot to touch, orange groves and brambles. They were just below the top of The Ridge, the setting sun behind them, and part of the thin red, or rather khaki, line, the whole regiment, what was left of it, behind a breastwork the engineers had thrown up. It was high enough to give cover, but not so high as to impede a bayonet charge over it should Pandy get so close.

Bang.

Bang-bang. A crackle of rifle shots. One of the men down the line had stood up, had leapt across the breastwork. 'Sod this for a game of soldiers,' he shouted, high and wild, and went hurtling down the slope into the little wilderness at the bottom. He shot one Pandy hiding there and bayoneted two more as they tried to run from him, climbed one of those burning walls and as he straightened on top was hurled backwards by a hail of ball that shredded his body.

'Berserk with the heat,' muttered Alec.

'Or fed up of waiting to die of cholera or sunstroke. Maybe he had the symptoms already.' The faces of other men dead passed in front of Sam's eyes. He sighed.

'Fucking hell, this place is,' muttered Nathan. 'Scorpions as big as small lobs'ers.'

'And snakes four yards long.'

A bugle call, high and clear, and in response the 75th began to stir, hauled themselves to their feet, hoisting knapsacks on to their backs, dusting down the fronts of their khaki jackets, sun-bleached almost to white.

'Supper-time soon.' Sam reached down a hand, pulled Alec to his feet. Another brief squeeze, then Alec stooped to pick up his rifle.

Next day.

'Ya'ta'ta't't't' . . . That's Warning for Parade, ain't it'? Where's it comin' from, George?'

'The fuck should I know, Sam. Deaf in one ear I've been since that tumbril blew at Badly Kiss My Arse.'

'There 'e goes agin. Y'da'da, ya'da'da . . . Fall in A, Fall in B, Fall in ev'ry company. Come on lads, ge' yer gear oogitherr.'

'Don' be daff, Nathan, it's coming from down below. Over there. The Cashmere Gate, I reckon.'

'Fuckin' Pandy bugler, 'avin us on.'

'Look back there, to your right. The old 'ouse. The Ruperts of the 68th are lookin' for 'im, got their glasses out.'

'Ya'ta'ta'ta'ta'taa 'taa . . . Come to the cookhouse door boys. I wish.

326

But there doos be two of them now, innit? One like answerin' the other.'

'Aye, bu' both down there. One in each of those bastions each side of the gate.'

'Yer richt, Alec, m'bhoy. Two o' them. Hark'ee!'

'Aye, bu' look o'er there. Down by they ruined cabins. Where the orange drees are. Pair o' laddies from the 68th. Wi' yon Enfields.'

'Jasus, Nathan, I reckon they be stalkin' the poor buggers.'

'Wha they playin' noo, wha they playin' the noo?'

'General Salute, the cheeky bastards. Only get that for top brass.'

'Ain't it Revally?'

'' 'Tis now. But it wor the General Salute.'

'And now it's Lights Out. Shit.'

'Wha' were tha'?'

'They stopped. Just like that. Two shots like cut them right off.'

'They Enfields.'

'Fuckers.'

'When do we get them?'

'When the siege train arrives, I reckon.'

'Fuckers. They Pandies was only 'avin a laugh. Didna mean noo 'arm.'

After the fall of Delhi both buglers were found to have been killed. Their bugles became trophies in the mess of the 68th.

'Fucking flies.'

'Can't get away from them, Sam.'

The inside of the tent roof black with them at dawn, then as soon as the two lads moved apart, down they came.

'Can't eat without getting them in your mouth no matter what you do.'

'Nathan an' George blowing them up did no good neither.'

'Laugh, though. Nearly pissed myself.'

First Nathan had put sugar on a flat stone, then a ring of powder round it, then when the sugar was covered with flies, tossed a taper in and whhooomph. They all rose up and the flame with them and they sizzled in the air above the stone.

47

The Ridge, the Road to Rohtak, 15–16 August 1857

A silhouette filled the triangle of the tent's opening.

'No news, James?'

'We know the worst. We just lack the last awful evidences. Their bodies are either at the bottom of the Ganges or in that dreadful well. And, please, do not repeat to me they may have escaped, and be wandering the countryside looking for a safe haven. I must learn to accept the truth and find what consolation I can in the sympathy of my friends and between the covers of this.' Dixon lifted a bible from the camp table.

'I'll make us a pot of tea, if you like,' Hodson offered.

Dixon looked up gratefully. 'Please do. But I can ask my kitmutgar . . .'

'I'll do it.'

Hodson tipped most of the water from one tin copper camp kettle into another, set the near empty one on a camp stove with an argand wick, and lit it with a lucifer.

'Take a few minutes,' he said, adjusting the wick so it burnt more brightly, without smoking. 'Good stuff, this new paraffin oil. And does the holy book live up to your expectations?'

Dixon hardly knew what to make of this.

'Of course. And dear old Rotton calls by every now and then to persuade me it is all part of the Divine Will.'

'You don't sound too convinced.'

A long silence in which the distant exchange of artillery fire became insistent, a burden to the ceaseless buzz and whine of flies and mosquitoes.

'I take it you are not.'

'No. I'll spare you the full sermon but let me just say that it needed religion for all this to come about. If the Pandies hadn't got it into their heads that we are trying to make Christians of them, which on the whole we are, then none of this would have happened . . .' He paused, suddenly aware that Dixon was not taking this too well. 'While I see to the doings you might care to cast an eye over this.'

He pulled a dozen or so sheets of octavo printed paper, loosely bound between marbled boards, from the side pocket of his jacket.

'What's this?' Opening it. Five of what appeared to be quatrains on each page.

'Where's the teapot? There we are. First draft of a translation of an eleventh-century Persian poet. Friend of mine back home is translating it and he asks my opinion on each new version that he makes. He hopes to present it to the general reader in a year's time.'

'Two teaspoons are enough. Let's look at it then. Damn fine print. Can hardly read it.' Dixon carried the pages to the tent flaps, held them so the last of the daylight fell across them:

> 'Awake! For morning in the Bowl of Night
> Has flung the Stone that puts the stars to flight:
>   And Lo! The Hunter of the East has caught
> The Sultán's Turret in a Noose of light . . .'

'Turn towards the end. Verse fifty-one or thereabouts.'

> 'Turn not to that inverted Bowl we call the Sky,
> Whereunder crawling coop't we live and die,
>   Lift not thy hands to It for help – for it
> Rolls impotently on as Thou or I.'

'I'm not sure he's got that last verse as neat as can be. Go to the very end. He reverses your situation and imagines the love of his life surviving him. But it doesn't signify. It's all one, whichever.'

'You mean this bit? Ah, Moon of my Delight . . .'

'That's the one. And the stanza that follows.'

> *'And when Thyself with shining Foot shall pass*
> *Among the Guests Star-scatter'd on the Grass,*
>   *And in thy joyous Errand reach the Spot*
> *Where I made one – turn down an empty Glass!'*

'Jesus wept! I didn't mean to make you cry. Here. Blow your nose while I make the tea.'

In silence they let it brew; then they drank it, English fashion with milk and sugar. Presently, a figure in a turban and the uniform of an employee of the dâk filled the triangle of darkening sky,

Dixon tore at the envelope, his heart pounding. Good news? Or tragic, confirming what he already knew?

Dear James

  I am reluctant to add to your woe with news that may burden you further but I have to tell you that it seems certain that Tom's body has been found in a shallow grave in a village called Bindki, not far from Futtehpore, where it is presumed he was carrying out his duties. What he died from is uncertain, I am told, but doubtless it was the cholera or dysentery.

  I should also tell you, though the news sits uneasily with what I have just reported, that three days ago I was delivered of a baby girl. She is healthy and thrives while I am as well as can be expected. I have it in mind to have her christened Miranda Emma but will not do so until I am assured you would in the event be pleased.

  Please take care of yourself. Too many of our little circle have gone already and it will not survive further loss.

  Yours in sorrow

Sophie Hardcastle

Hodson glanced down at him. Oh dear, he thought, poor fellow's taking another blow, but I haven't got time to spare playing the nursemaid any more than I already have. He finished his tea, stood up.

'What I came to tell you, James, is that a detachment of Pandy cavalry left the city this evening, heading north-west, and Wilson wants us to go after them, see what they're up to. He's given us a hundred of the Guides to fill out our lot and we ought to be on the move at least two hours before sun-up. All right? Best to have something practical to do when things get you down, eh? Keep the verses for now. Thanks for the tea.'

Pre-dawn, very first light – the trees black against the luminescent blackness of the sky, the featureless flat of the ground enclosed by the racecourse lighter, just taking on the dun ochre of mud and grass churned up into a trampled miry mess. Horses whinnied, slip-slopped in the mud, harness jangled, havildars shouted commands and abuse as the two hundred or so men of Hodson's Horse contrived to get themselves into something like a column.

They were hill tribesmen, still trying to maintain a nomadic lifestyle in spite of the encroaching settlement of their grasslands in the Himalayan foothills. Some were mounted on big blundering English carthorses but most had brought their own ponies, scrawny looking ungroomed animals, much mocked by the English cavalry, but possessing unexpected stamina and speed. They had been bred to herd semi-wild ponies of their own stock and goats and sheep up and down stony valleys, were able to leap mountain streams and carry their riders in intertribal skirmishes.

Dixon slapped his chestnut mare's withers, reached forward and pulled her ear, then hacked up to Hodson, saluted him with his switch. Hodson nodded, turned back to watch how his Irregulars were getting on, and the smile on his thin lips lengthened beneath his pale moustache.

'All right, so we are an aggregate of untutored horsemen, ill-equipped, only half-uniformed, quite unfit for service, and only here because . . . because I have willed them into existence. But, by God they're ready for a fight, I can tell you.'

A fight was what they had not yet had, their duties so far being limited to reconnaissance out in the fields beyond Delhi, keeping an eye out for what Wilson most feared, a threat to his rear that could leave him hemmed in on The Ridge, the besieged instead of the besiegers. Wilson? General Barnard had died of cholera and Archdale Wilson from Meerut had stepped into his shoes. Four generals, four commanding officers of the little army that marched to Delhi and retook it, died within just over four months.

Hodson gave a nod to his bugler who sounded a rough version of the command to walk and then trot on. The havildars guessed what was required and interpreted the signal to the turbanned and swathed villains who moved restlessly around them, finding it hard to remain stationary in a column, and all moved off.

'Well, James, this all should be fun. Shake you out of the doldrums.'

'It's not doldrums that afflict me, William. It's grief.'

'Of course, dear chap.'

The landscape became clearer, the sun rose and shone through the gathering clouds, bleeding colour into the landscape, turning the cumulus nimbus to the west into great palaces of domed but evanescent marble. Already the fields were greening up with shoots of rice and other crops, flowers were abundant again, but the waterways were swollen, fords often too deep and bridges unsafe in the steady flow of water. The heat built, a heavy humid heat which made the pools, the backs of the horses, even the men's jackets, steam gently. After a time stony rises broke out of the flat cultivated plain, wildernesses of gravelly slopes dotted with bushes or occasional patches of forest, not dense, more like parkland. Dixon felt his mood lighten, in spite of himself, and he fancied he heard a voice in his head, though no doubt he willed it to be there.

'Come on, James. There's nothing where I am to enjoy or suffer, there is nothing, so make the most of this while you have it.'

Perhaps Omar Khayyam had as much to do with it as poor dead Catherine.

Nevertheless, when a group of rebel horsemen, identifiable through Hodson's glass as such by their Company uniforms, were seen a half-mile or so in front of the column, a different sort of vitality surged through his veins. Hodson told him to take twenty men and go after them. This time it was anger transmuting into hate, as they galloped down the straight road at full tilt and the hooves of their mounts whipped the mud into a storm behind them, that energised him. But the rebels' horses were fresher. They were off and away, all except one trooper whose mount was lamed. At a hundred yards he reined in, turned and faced the onslaught, empty hands raised. Dixon, twenty yards in front of his men already, slashed at him, a backhand textbook cut, caught a glimpse under the flashing blade of a face twisted with shock and fear. He brought his mare up short, turned. The rebel trooper was clutching his right shoulder in his left hand, actually holding his right arm to prevent it from dropping off. Blood spurted between his fingers and as Dixon came back his head dropped to his chest and Dixon's second blow took it off.

His troopers reined in around him, milling about, cheering English fashion, making their ponies rear up to salute their commanding officer's prowess, and Dixon felt the hate and anger shift into elation. He raised his sabre above his head and letting out a huge halloo made the mare pivot on her back legs. He would kill, again. And again. For the well outside the Bibigarh and the lover and children whose bodies rotted in it.

Hodson was not pleased.

'Get that far in front of your men again and I'll see you made officer in charge of latrines.'

Later in the day they came up with, pursued and caught another party of rebel cavalry. This time the Irregulars managed to circle the enemy on an open patch of land and enforce the surrender of a dozen or so. They were made to dismount and their horses were taken from them. Most were still wearing the uniforms, in part at least, of the 1st Punjab Cavalry, one of the few regiments from the north-west who had not remained loyal. Hodson walked his horse through them, his face pale and set, until he was looking down on the man who had been the senior Native officer, ressaldar, of the renegades. His countenance became even paler, the set of his mouth thinner.

'Bisharat Ali. Although I never liked you, I am sorry to see you here.'

The Punjabi looked up, a sort of half smile creasing his face.

'I am sorry to be here, sahib.'

Hodson turned his horse away.

'Hang him,' he said. 'Hang all of them.'

Back by Dixon's side, as the preparations were made, he grunted: 'Hanging is too good for him. I'd rather have roasted him in front of a slow fire.'

Was this Flashman speaking? Dixon would have liked to ask him, but did not quite dare to.

48

Delhi, the assault, 14–16 September 1857

The siege train arrived at last. From The Ridge they could see it, coming in from the north, even when it was still five miles away, a column eight miles long. There were guns and howitzers pulled by elephants, dozens of them, then mortars on carts pulled by buffalo and more and more carts, tumbrils for ammunition, for the most part pulled by oxen, loaded with shot and shell and the Enfield rifles many of the men were still short of. And such a din, you could hear it from that distance, swelling, getting louder, the crack of whips, the mahouts and bullock drivers yelling at their beasts, and the clatter of the cavalry escorting them, bugles blowing. They must have heard it in the city, indeed from the highest turrets they could probably see it. Half of the sepoys in the town packed up and left. And then at the back of it all, it was always the same, the camp followers, the travelling bazaars, the servants of the officers, the herds of goats and sheep, and hens in coops or even waddling along in a flock . . . any column on the march, unless it was designated a 'flying column', was doubled in size by those who reckoned they could squeeze a rupee or an anna for services their masters did not need.

It was like that even up on The Ridge. The Native hangers-on were paid two annas for every shot they could collect from what was fired from the town – they took them down to the English guns for many happy returns. And what was comical was to see three or four of them run for the same ball and maybe the first would catch it up while it was still hot so he had to drop it or burn his hands, and maybe his mate got it instead . . .

During the first night the guns were wheeled down the slopes and into the emplacements the engineers had been preparing for some days before, some only two hundred yards from the walls and gates, and, came the daylight, whooomph, it all started, the twenty-four-pounders blasting all together so the full weight of the metal hit at once and in the same place and soon it all began to crumble and tumble down the glacis and into the ditch . . .

The night before the assault, just after midnight, they assembled behind The Ridge. By the light of lanterns the officers read out the orders for the assault. *The wounded, officers or men, to be left where they fall, no one to step out of our ranks to help them as we have no men to spare. If we are successful they will be picked up by the doolies and taken to wherever medical assistance is available. If we fail then all, wounded and sound alike, can expect only the worst. No plundering but all prize taken to be put into a common stock for fair division by the prize agents. We take no prisoners as we have no one to guard them, but no women or children to be harmed.* To this last they answered, 'No fear, sir', and promised to follow their officers' example.

Then, as often happens in military operations, just when every-thing was ready and their minds set to do the business, came the delay. This time because an outlying picket had to be waited on. There was light in the sky, beyond the river, before they moved off. The 75th were at the front of the first column, leading regiment of the first brigade, under Brigadier Nicholson himself. The 75th had already lost more than half its men. They had left Umballa back at the end of May more than a thousand strong. Now, on 14 September, there were barely four hundred fit to turn out. And 'fit' meant able to walk or, like Lieutenant Barter who still suffered from the wound left by the ball he took in his shin back at Badli-ki-Serai, hobble. As many had fallen to cholera, sunstroke, dysentery and even snakebite as to the direct action of the enemy.

Just past what they called Ludlow Castle they took the left lane into an enclosure, an orchard that brought them behind the heavy gun batteries. More waiting, so that by the time they went in it was not far off full daylight.

This second delay was caused by the fact that during the night the sepoys had filled in much of the breach with gabions and these had to be blown out by a half-hour of continuous bombardment, the firing as rapid as possible.

And then, as suddenly as it had started, this final bombardment stopped. Lieutenant Fitzgerald, standing on an old Muslim tomb with a handkerchief held above his head and his eyes on the Headquarter Staff halfway up the hill behind, took the signal from them, dropped his handkerchief and they were off, through an archway, at the double, into the garden.

Beyond the archway there were roses, heavily perfumed in the dawn, and songbirds, some brightly coloured. At the end of the garden, lining a bank which closed it off, the 60th with their Enfields rose and poured aimed volleys into the breach, as the 75th came through, in column of fours, so the rifles could keep up their fire over their heads until they were on the glacis. Their colonel, Lieutenant Colonel Herbert, and Lieutenant Barter were in the front leading the grenadier company, Mr Barter having been made adjutant to the regiment. Leading the second company Lieutenant Fitzgerald was supported by Lieutenant Farquhar, who was thought of as a wily cove since he had not been around until a fortnight earlier and was rumoured to have been out in the country as a spy, blacked up even, pretending to be a beggar.

The breach was in and close to the gate itself, the gate being two pointed arches, the right-hand one as they faced it blown in. In front of it there was the glacis, which the storming party had to climb, then drop into the ditch, then up the other side into the rubble in front of the breach. This bank of rubble was high and loose, and needed scaling ladders.

They climbed the glacis through a hail of grape and musket balls and many did not get further than the top. Three times the ladder party was swept away by this fire, including the colonel with a ball in his leg. Mr Barter and Mr Fitzgerald got into the ditch and called for the ladders to be thrown down to them which was done and they hoisted them and began to climb. Mr Barter had to make a go of it with his sword under his arm, for the officers wore no scabbards in a fight like this one, and his revolver in the other, which left him one hand and one leg to climb with. He would have been like a clown in a circus, getting in a muddle on a ladder, had it not all been so awful.

Meanwhile, still on the glacis, down went Nathan. He was on his back in front of Sam who stooped to see if he could help, but he managed a shake of his head as if to remind Sam what the orders were. Then his face, what was left of it, convulsed into a horrible rictus which Sam recalled in nightmares for years. He'd taken a ball in his chin and the blood and bone were already all over his throat and jacket; he'd lost his front teeth some years before and now his lower teeth and his life had gone the same way. Sam moved in to his place and signalled to Alec to take the place behind. Down they went at last into the ditch, treading over the fallen and wounded, some of whom screamed for help, but all they could say was, 'Later, my friend, we'll be back for you later.'

That was the worst of it done, for the men were now climbing up nineteen to the dozen behind and some of the Natives, Punjaubs they were, were so eager they didn't wait for places on the ladders but climbed up on each other's shoulders. The enemy, seeing their numbers ever increasing, took fright and fled into the alleyways of the town beyond. And there on the breach Mr Barter and Mr Fitzgerald shook hands as if they were the first two in Delhi which afterwards Barter claimed though it was disputed by an officer of the 52nd. Mr Fitzgerald then turned right along the walls and into a discharge of grape from the street below which killed him. A few minutes later the Cashmere Gate itself was blown and all could get in any way they wanted. Brigadier Nicholson himself died later of wounds caused by the explosion.

49

Delhi, 16–20 September 1857

It is a fact that British troops, especially the professionals, have a history of behaving badly following the storming of a city. There were instances as far back as the Hundred Years War, one recalls Drogheda in 1649, Ciudad Rodrigo and Badajoz in 1812, and no doubt there were many more. One may offer reasons if not excuses for the bloodlust, destructiveness, drunkenness and greed that over-took the victors on these occasions. First and foremost were the traditions that governed siege warfare. A fortified town was initially offered the chance of honourable surrender. If this was refused unconditional surrender was offered once viable breaches had been made in the fortifications.

If unconditional surrender was refused then it was considered all right to hand the city over to the victors. This was because the troops in the final assault would be exposed to unacceptable casualties: the units directly involved in the assault of Delhi lost between a third and a half of their men; moreover, they had been on The Ridge for more than three months in appalling heat, under constant if not overaccurate bombardment, plagued with cholera, heatstroke and fever. Finally it needs to be said that much of the slaughter took place during the week after the assault and before the final capitulation and was the consequence of bitter hand-to-hand street fighting, house by house, through the streets and alleys of the city. That every inch was disputed is borne out by the fact that General Wilson at one time felt he could not hold what had been won and contemplated withdrawal.

Only the insistence of his juniors, led by Nicholson from the bed where he was dying, kept the old man up to the mark.

Nevertheless . . .

A pariah kite, *Milvus migrans*, swooped on angled wings and long forked tail with graceful and acrobatic skill across roofs and domes, along narrow high twisting alleys, and wider throughfares. There were thousands of these scavengers – some in flocks spiralling above places where a skirmish or exploding shell had left several cadavers, many singly hunting out bodies lying half-buried in the rubble, or swinging from a tree in a courtyard or a window lintel. Sated as they were by the end of the first day they thrashed their wings to get from one corpse to the next, scorning those that had already been visited by their sisters and brothers, for now all they were interested in were the softer, richer, tastier parts, the livers especially, the eyes and the testicles and, if they had already been torn out, then on they'd go looking for the one the others had missed, leaving torso and limbs to the pariah dogs and jackals that had sneaked in from the countryside.

The one we've fixed on, a female, perches on a windowsill for a moment and watches the general scribbling a letter with a spattering pen to his wife back in Simla . . . *I have not a Queen's officer under me worth a pin . . . this street fighting is frightful work and pandy is as good a soldier at that as our men . . . The fact is our men have a great dislike of street-fighting. They do not see their enemy, and find their comrades falling and get in a panic and will not advance. The only good officers I had are killed or wounded, and such a set left, no head, no control over the men . . . It has been a hard task imposed upon me, dearest, harder than I can bear. Both mind and body are giving way . . . I am knocked up . . . cannot sleep . . . unequal to any exertion.* Our kite flies on, takes a left, and then another one that takes her back past the Cashmere Gate towards the Mori Gate, and what have we here . . .?

A Mussulman butcher at the back of his shop, cleaver in one hand and a freakish grin exposing rotten teeth, facing a squaddie of the 75th, with a big black beard, who levels his rifle and fires, taking the top off the butcher's head. Well, she'll wait and have a look at that butcher when the Brits have moved on but now the squaddie is being bawled out by his officer, Lieutenant Farquhar . . .

'What the fuck, George, what the fuck did you do that for? That was simply fucking murder.'

And George laughs in his face and replies, 'Well, you see, sorr, I was seeing if my firelock would go off all right after being loaded so long, but faith it didn't miss and I bowled him over right there in his little shop.'

A bit further on she gets a fright. She's flapping along at the height of the upstairs casements when she's suddenly aware of a small shell with a fizzing fuse soaring and then dropping in a parabola above her head from the roof on one side to the roof on the other, left to right. A bang and a flash and the tatties in the windows on her right billow out in front of her on a cloud of smoke and flame. She flies up above it all pretty sharpish and there on the roof of the left-hand house, but hidden from anyone lower, a group of Brits with their officer are working a couple of small brass mortars, the sort that actually look like oversized kitchen mortars, lobbing five and a half inch shells, not much bigger than a cricket ball, on to the roof over the road. They have already made a hole in the roof and the shells are now dropping down into the floors below, and, judging from the high-pitched screams, have got through to the harem. Well, that too may repay a later visit, she thinks, the flesh of women and children being more tender than that of the males. As for the males, they run out of the now burning house and into the street where they are picked off by riflemen at the windows opposite.

And so it goes on, day after day, for six days, and gradually the streets fill with the bodies of the dead and soon the kites find they can hardly fly at all so sated are they, and the dogs lie about, not able to walk but still crunching at bones to get the marrows, and night by night the city becomes quieter and quieter and on the sixth night a sort of deep silence falls over it since the last of the gates where resistance continued longest have been taken and all the fighting has ceased. Only the smell remains, the lazy thrashing of tired wings, and the crunching of bones. The smell is truly awful for no bodies have been moved or collected and in the heat and the damp, for there is heavy rain every now and then, and coated by the flies that blacken them, they swell up so they look like huge bladders, straining their clothes and often bursting with noisy flatulent sighs.

50

Delhi, 19–20 September 1857; February 1858

The Tomb of Humayun, the second of the Mughal Emperors, lies five miles south of the Red Fort, three beyond the old walled city. It is a magnificent construction, built of red sandstone and white marble, symmetrical, domed, huge, as big as a medium-sized cathedral. Gardens surround it and a wall with an arched and imposing entrance encloses them. It was there, after the city had fallen, that Bahadur Shah, the last of the Mughals, sought refuge and sanctuary with two of his sons. Hodson, accompanied by the Begum, and Bahadur's youngest son and their physician Hakim Ashanullah Khan, arrived at about ten o'clock in the morning with fifty troopers of Hodson's Horse under the direct command of Captain Dixon and a Lieutenant Macdowell. They stopped at the entrance to the gardens over which milled several thousand men who had followed the old man they still thought of as their ruler, like swarming bees in the wake of their queen.

Hodson sent in the Begum, accompanied by Hakim Ashanullah Khan. Inside there were no separate rooms on the main floor in which negotiations could be satisfactorily carried out, just the big spaces separated by columns supporting the dome above the tomb itself and open spaces at the corners. If there were rooms above or below then they were inaccessible to the old man who refused to be carried up or down narrow winding staircases. The Begum and Hakim found him sitting in piles of cushions, beneath a big ceremonial umbrella. Sherbert-filled jugs remained untouched at his side,

341

but his nargileh bubbled away filling the air with the rich, vegetable smell of apple and molasses cut with opium. His older sons and a handful of courtiers of no particular note stood around. Dappled sunlight shone through the fine marble lattice work behind him, but, since the sun was already high, did not penetrate more than a few feet from the outer walls.

The Begum went across to him, made the humblest of obeisances and did her best to get through to him. To no avail. Hakim took it upon himself to speak for the Mughal though he was constantly interrupted by the sons who clearly began to suspect that they had no place in the proceedings but would be treated as a separate problem. What with their interventions and increasingly frequent interjections from the Mughal as bit by bit he recovered his wits, Hakim found it increasingly difficult to maintain any direction or momentum in the discussion. Eventually, after nearly two hours of wrangling, they were interrupted by James Dixon who came, spurs and accoutrements jangling, up the steps and into the chamber. The negotiators were scandalised and horrified, but took the point. By sending an armed man into the presence, Hodson had shown he was serious. Dixon returned with the message that the King-Emperor would surrender if Hodson himself would personally come up and repeat the Government's guarantee that his life and that of his Queen and youngest son would be spared.

Hodson, suffering from migraine, was short-fused. He walked, sword in hand, to the bottom of the flight of steps that led up into the tomb and bellowed out that if the King came out he would repeat the promise he had already made and that was enough. In a few moments the King appeared and was helped by the Begum into a covered waggon, maintained for women in purdah, which she had left at the foot of the steps. Together with their son they were drawn back to Delhi by bullocks, to the palace, where General Wilson immediately incarcerated them, pending the King's trial.

As they left the garden Hodson turned to Dixon and, with a thin, almost bitter smile, recited:

> 'Think, in this batter'd caravanserai
> Whose Doorways are alternate Night and Day,
>   How Sultán after Sultán with his Pomp
> Abode his Hour or two, and went his way.'

The two older sons and a grandson were thus deprived of the protection of the aura of history and royalty that still emanated from their father, though between two and three thousand armed followers, committed by vows to fight for them, continued to occupy the tomb's gardens.

They could not be allowed to remain there. They had been far more active leading the Mutiny than their father had ever been, occasionally riding into battle albeit some way behind their armies. It was now highly possible that they would flee south to the largest concentrations of rebels and allow themselves to be declared emperors in place of their senile parent, providing the movement with the legitimating figureheads it needed.

The following morning Hodson left Delhi at eight o'clock and this time he took a hundred of his troopers rather than the fifty of the day before. He was confronted again with a crowd of armed men, perhaps bigger than that of the previous day.

'Hakim,' he called, 'go into the tomb and tell the bastards they are to give themselves up unconditionally.'

It was a full half-hour before he was back. The princes would come out but only if certain conditions ensuring their safety were fulfilled. Hodson put on his tinted spectacles.

'Unconditional,' he repeated. 'Or we come in for them.'

Back went Hakim, remembering all he had ever been told concerning the fates of bearers of bad news. He laid it on a bit this time, telling the brothers to consider the fact that the King had been spared so they might be as well. And anyway, if they were not taken by force now, they soon would be. At last they agreed to come out. Hakim got the message back to Hodson who had a cart pulled to the bottom of the steps with an escort of ten troopers while the rest were drawn up across the road that led up to the arched entrance to the gardens. The princes came down the steps of the tomb and got into the cart which, with its escort, arrived safely outside, at which point the mob surged forward. Moving hastily Hodson manoeuvred the cart and its escort through the line of troopers and then turned to face the mob. He unholstered his carbine and raised it above his head.

'I'll drop the first man who moves,' he shouted, and Hakim put it into Hindi for him. The message was clear enough anyway.

Nevertheless the odds stacked against him were still of the order of thirty to one.

'Right. Now I want every man-jack of you to lay down his weapons.'

He was answered by an angry murmur, but not loud and only from a handful.

'I told you, gentlemen, to lay down your weapons.'

And they did. First those who had looked down the barrel of Hodson's carbine, then bit by bit the ones behind came forward to do likewise.

'Great Scot,' declared Lieutenant Macdowell. 'Who'd have thought it?'

Hodson turned.

'Macdowell, find us a couple of hackeries to put this lot in, there's a good chap.'

It took two hours, time Hodson had been playing for. The bullock cart with the princes was moving at a man's walking pace – those carts always did – and he wanted to hold back the mob until it was back in Delhi. Nevertheless they, Hodson's Horse and the now more or less disarmed mob, caught up with them just short of the city walls and here the mob began to look nasty again. They closed in round the troopers and the cart, and from somewhere at the back of them a matchlock that had not been handed in was fired, fortunately into the air.

Hodson turned to Dixon and Macdowell.

'What are we going to do with them?' he asked; and he took off his spectacles, gave them a wipe. He meant the princes. He looked down at them and you would have been hard put to it to decipher the smile that was on his lips again. 'We'll never get them in. Best shoot them here, don't you think?'

He put his specs back on and issued three or four brusque commands. The troopers moved in round the cart, facing the crowd. The princes were pulled out of the cart and made to strip off their outer clothes. Hodson then denounced them, in a loud, clear, penetrating voice.

'These men,' he called, 'are going to die because they have massacred British women and children and committed many other lesser though capital crimes, such as treason, breaking faith with us, leading armies against us. Enough!'

Firing his carbine from the waist, with the muzzle touching the brow of the eldest prince, he blew his brains out, handed down the empty gun, and thrust out his hand. Without having to be told the nearest trooper placed his own carbine in it and down went the second prince, and then the third, the grandson. Hodson looked down at their bodies.

'Malcolm, they're still wearing rings and other jewellery. Collect it for me, there's a good chap.'

At this point the Sikhs in Hodson's Horse, and there were a good few of them, burst into rapturous cheers.

'What's that for?' Dixon asked.

Hakim knew the answer.

'The grandfather, I believe, of the present King, being Grand Mughal, commanded the death of a great Sikh guru, who was put to death on this very spot. Needless to say the guru prophesied that the descendants of the man who condemned him would also die on this very spot, in exactly one hundred years' time. The odds are they've got the date wrong, but it's good enough for them.'

Hodson was made to put the jewellery into the common prize but he kept one of the prisoners' swords saying he would give it up to Queen Victoria only. He believed he had done a difficult job well, at very considerable risk, and expected to be made a Companion of the Bath for it. After he had shot the princes he again confided to Dixon that he would have preferred to roast them over a slow fire.

The nightmare continued. Delhi remained under martial law until February the following year. The pariah kite fed well and saw plenty that amused her. Several factors were at work. In the assault Wilson had lost most of his senior officers, that is, young men in their twenties with a few old hands in their fifties. What were left were subalterns in their late teens, many of them replacements, who had less control over their men than they should have done and who, in any case, were as eager as they for loot and revenge.

Revenge? Revenge for the massacre of women and children, including Native Christians, on 11 May and the looting of their houses, shops and churches. Much of the hate was directed specifically at Muslims and Islam.

And here she is again, hopping around the tent of one officer, who has left the letter he is writing on his table while he saunters off to

345

the latrines for his morning shit, taking his pipe and an old newspaper with him.

> There has been nothing but shooting these villains for the past three days. Some 300 or 400 were shot yesterday . . . There are several mosques in the city most beautiful to look at. But I should like to see them all destroyed. The rascally brutes desecrated our churches and graveyards, and I do not think we should have any regard for their stinking religion. One was always supposed to take off one's shoes on going to visit one of these mosques, or to have an interview with the king. But these little affairs we drop now. I have seen the old Pig of a King. He is a very old man and just like an old kitmutgar . . .

And another . . .

> Lots of blackguards are hanged every morning. The more the merrier. I am delighted to see that the good folks at home hate the Pandies almost as much as we do. You say Delhi ought to be thoroughly destroyed. We all say the same.

The looting continued. It became quite the thing, a treasure hunt, a family outing. The very few European women who had survived the May massacre and returned took part; and then there were the wives, who, now it was winter again in Simla and the other hill stations, came down to share their husbands' tents or requisition a town house while the bungalows were rebuilt in the cantonments.

One set off after breakfast, found the town house of a rich merchant and, if it had not already been broken into, one's servants broke down the doors and locks. Everything of any value that had been left out in view would have gone, and the floors would be littered with broken furniture, especially glass, for what Anglo-Saxon does not enjoy breaking glass, whether chandelier droplets or pier mirrors? Now, methodically, but with little squeals of anticipation, one's bheestie, whom one would have brought along with one, would empty his big bag or skin of water over the ground-level floors, and all in the party would watch carefully to see how and where the water seeped away. A sudden glugging, draining between cracks, indicated a space below, a hiding place, and now the picks and crowbars would come into play. By such means substantial sums of money were found, as much as seventy thousand sacked rupees, in one instance.

Meanwhile, upstairs, the men would be carefully measuring the rooms' dimensions, the depths of floors, and where discrepancies were found the picks and crowbars and heavy hammers were again called for, and this time, in the smaller spaces, jewellery or fine fabrics might be 'recovered'.

In truth, and it is bootless for either side to disagree, both sides in the Mutiny behaved appallingly. The scars, the anger and the guilt remain to this day and vitiate all but a novelist's attempts to portray the truth.

Neither the remnant of the 75th nor Hodson's Horse remained in Delhi for long. On 24 September both units were drafted into a flying column, two and a half thousand-strong, and marched out of the city under a Colonel Edward Greathead en route to the relief of Lucknow. Captain James Dixon took a twenty-four hour furlough from the column to make the detour to Meerut.

51

Meerut, 25 September 1857

An enquiry at the mess revealed that Sophie Hardcastle had moved back to the Hardcastle bungalow in the British lines. A servant, could have been Lavanya's younger sister, showed him into the drawing room, explained that her mistress would be 'half-hour, sahib, half-hour'. He looked around. Most of the furniture, including the Broadwood piano, was back from Simla and the Spode Chinese Rose was displayed as it had been before in a glass-fronted cabinet. The music on the piano was a passacaglia by Handel. He moved about awkwardly for a moment or two, tried an upright chair, felt absurdly like a small boy waiting to see his headmaster, tried the sofa but it was low and his knees seemed to be on a level with his chin. He stood at the window instead from which he could at least keep an eye on his horse and the syce who had ridden with him on his mountain pony.

'Captain Dixon, I am honoured, indeed grateful, that you have felt able to make me a visit. Have you come from Delhi? How are things there . . .?'

She stood in the doorway, very upright, fair hair parted in the middle and scraped back, a black ribbon round her neck, black dress, fastened high, her white fingers fiddling gently with the top button under her chin. The formal, polite greeting that was on his lips died on an indrawn breath and he strode across to her, spurs snagging on a rucked fold of carpet, and reaching out, partly to recover from the stumble he did not take but mainly because he wanted to. She caught both his hands and pulled herself briefly into him, then pulled back

348

and the sudden tears spilled down her cheeks. He saw them and drew her in again so her head rested on the top of his tunic. Suddenly his heart was beating much faster than it had been and he felt his palms prickle with sweat.

Presently the sobs and sighs were controlled and her breathing came back to something closer to normal. Then she spoke, murmured, but still without pulling back to face him.

'Please, Dixon – James – don't just now say anything about any of it. We both know how we feel. I shall only cry and cry if we talk about our loss, and believe me I feel the loss of Catherine and your dear ones as strongly as I do the death of Mr Hardcastle and that of dear Stephen. There. There, then.'

Now she did move away. She sat on the sofa and her black silks rustled around her. He picked up the chair and placed it so he could sit quite close to her, facing her.

'I'm sorry I was not able to come as soon as you arrived,' she began, then her head came up in a challenging sort of way. 'I was feeding her. Nursing her. You know what I mean.'

Poor man. He looked quite confused. She went on.

'I was wrong not to do the same for Stephen. He, poor baby, became attached to Lavanya and she perhaps to him.'

'There's still no news of them?'

'No. Believe me if there had been you, dear friend, would have been the first to hear it from me.'

'There is still hope then.'

'I think not. It is now nearly twenty weeks and I have no reason to suppose that little Stephen did not die with . . . your . . . I'm sorry. I said we must not talk about such things.'

He stood up, walked to the window this time and waited until he felt she had recovered. Then he turned.

'May I ask what your plans are now? I only ask because I would wish to assist you in them in any way I can. I am no longer paying rent on three houses, so I have money to spare if you are short . . .'

'You are so kind.' She laughed a little at last. 'Oh, James, it is quite comical to hear you, who were always complaining how strapped you were, making such a generous offer. But no. I am temporarily on half Tom's pay and in any case my father is more than tolerably well off and as soon as he heard . . . about it all, he sent me a substantial banker's draft.'

'And, of course, you will go back to England?'

'Yes. But not until travel is entirely safe again nor until I am sure Miranda has a sufficient hold on life to be able to sustain the ardours of the journey.'

'She is all right though?'

'Oh yes. Quite all right. Flourishing indeed.' A gentle flush rose in her cheeks. 'My . . . um, my feeding her seems to suit her.'

'May I see her?'

'Of course. I was about to suggest you should.'

She rose, walked to the door and he followed. They moved to a room at the back of the bungalow and presently he found himself looking down at a chubby but pretty ten-week-old baby in a wicker crib, fast asleep with a contented smile on her face, blowing a tiny milky bubble. The room was shady and a small punkah, operated from the outside by a six- or seven-year-old boy, creaked at the window.

'I think the noise soothes her.' Sophie reached into the cot and still in her sleep the baby's tiny fist closed on her finger. 'We won't wake her, if you don't mind.'

Dixon took her other hand in his – he could not really help himself, overcome by the warmest sentiments as he was. Sophie seemed about to release herself but then she answered his palm with the slightest of squeezes. In the shady quiet of the room they both felt the flow of emotions that were not easy to name, for to give them a name would have seemed to both an act of betrayal of Catherine. Indeed the feeling was so intense that Sophie felt she had to give it expression, however obliquely.

'I do so miss her,' she said. 'Her liveliness, her flow of talk, the way she . . . embraced life before the bad things began to happen. It must be so much worse for you.'

His head dropped at this and she reached up, held his face in her hands and did not move away even when he came closer, as close as he could. Then she let him put his cheek against hers and she felt the warmth of his tears. At last he straightened and sighed as deeply as a man can sigh.

'I have to go soon,' he said. 'Almost straight away actually. But you must excuse me. Your loss has been as great as mine, perhaps greater. For a woman to lose a loving husband is . . .'

She cut him off with a finger placed firmly on his lips.

'No. I do not wish to speak of Tom. In truth I did not love him as

350

much as I should, and perhaps, after all, my duty lay with him and I should have gone with him.'

'You have absolutely nothing to blame yourself for. Your duty was with your unborn child.'

He sighed again, perhaps thinking of his own easy acceptance of Hodson's offer, then shrugged it off. The Reverend Rotton had told him a dozen times that a career officer cannot refuse the prospect of promotion, nor, in the field, withdraw from danger on account of an undue preoccupation with his loved ones.

'I'm with a column heading to the relief of Lucknow and I must not let them get too far ahead of me.'

'But you will have tiffin with me first.'

'I should not,' he laughed, 'but I will.'

'I'm afraid it will be pretty poor commons. An omelette perhaps, some salad. The salads, following the rains, are very good. And chappatis, of course.'

'Chappatis, of course,' he laughed.

'As I am on my own,' she went on, 'I eat very simply and I think healthily. I'm afraid we memsahibs overeat dreadfully. I had become decidedly plump.'

They managed to talk about mostly neutral things while they ate – who had gone where, survived this or that, how the tide had turned against the Mutiny, how British troops were arriving almost every day in Calcutta and had only to move west, or north up from Bombay or Madras, for all to be over.

When they had finished she led him back to the front door.

'Will you pass through Cawnpore?'

'I think so.'

'Will you visit . . .?' She meant the Bibigarh, the well, but left the words unsaid. He knew what she meant.

'I think I must.'

'Well, do so. And speak to them for me when you do.'

'I will say a prayer on your behalf.'

'No. Do not do that.' Her voice became quite harsh. 'I am not on good terms with the deity, under any of his names. Jehovah, Allah nor Brahma.'

He thought about this.

'I can understand that,' he said at last. 'Indeed, I find myself unable to pray much, but I feel I should try.'

Turn not to that inverted Bowl . . . was that how it went?

'Give it up, James. Give up on God. He has forgotten you, why should you not forget him? You will feel lonely, unsupported, but somehow stronger if you do.'

These words confused him, even though they echoed those of Hodson, and he did not reply. Only later, as he was hacking down the Grand Trunk Road towards Cawnpore, did he feel a sort of lightening of his soul, as if a burden had turned to water and run off his back.

But before that, at the door she took his hand again.

'I want to thank you for letting me call my baby Miranda. But you would not allow Miranda Emma. Why not?'

'I'm not sure. I think it occurred to me that I might have occasion to use the name again some day, much in the spirit that made you want to call your daughter Miranda.'

'Of course. How silly of me. I should have thought of that. If I had I should not have used "Miranda".'

'I'm glad you did. No . . . what's the word? Copyright. No copyright exists on names.'

Then he kissed her, lightly on the lips, the way very intimate friends were permitted to do, none of your double '*baisers*' on the cheek in those days, far too French a fashion.

He went through the gate, swung into the saddle and his groom did so too, and with a final salute he was off.

'Be careful!' Sophie called after him. And then surprised herself by adding, almost beneath her breath, 'Come back. One day.'

trees that had fallen into the water, or sauntered through the shallows dredging for frogs and small snakes; the egrets, the cranes, the pelicans as well. And other animals too emerged from whatever cool tunnels and recesses they had used as shelter from the sun: voles, many varieties of mice, ground squirrels, wild dogs and wild boar. Then there were the reptiles, the Bengal monitor, a yard long, a coppery brown with fine tiny scales, and the smaller more colourful of the lizards; and the snakes, the green python with dark almost black patches like a giraffe's, sunning itself along the branch of a flame of the forest tree, the hooded cobra and the wicked slimline krait.

Of all the animals Lavanya's favourite by far was the jungle cat with its hooped tail, black on russet, its ghostly body markings, high black-tipped ears, the intelligent eyes and the clearer markings on its front legs. On one occasion a pregnant female found them camping under an evergreen neem tree and stroked their ankles with its face and head and lapped at the porridge of milk and chappati Lavanya had begged or occasionally stolen. Though wild and entirely able to cope with the wilderness, these cats can be friendly to humans, especially female humans, and will accept domestication when it suits.

With the rain the fields filled with people again: women in sarees stooped to plant rice and other crops in the shallow tanks marked off by low ridges of turfy soil; men in dhotis often with capes flung over their shoulders beneath their turbans, prodded and whistled at granite-coloured bullocks as they heaved their ploughs, turning the muddy soil so the water could glug below. Within days, a week or so at most, the green shoots began to appear, wild flowers in the ditches, and blossom buds grew plump on the orchard trees. Humped, dewlapped white zebu cows, proper cattle and therefore holy symbols of the gifts the goddess pours on mankind, swiftly lost their skeletal look and browsed along the edges of the wider lanes. And with the first flowers came the butterflies and moths and jewel-like dragonflies that flitted and darted across the sheets of water beneath clouds of tiny gnats. Small fish leapt, flashed silver, caught them.

Lavanya headed south, walking with a child on each side of her, held by the hand, or carried one at a time, turn and turn about. South? She had started by going north towards Lucknow, but found that spur of the Grand Trunk Road too occupied by military units and *matériel*. She retraced their footsteps, almost the whole way back to Cawnpore, crossed the Ganges and headed south and east towards

Futtehpore, which they reached in the middle of the battle. And it was here, three weeks after the Sati Chaura Massacre, that she at last chose to head south. And soon she felt she had it right. There were fewer and fewer soldiers, sepoys, sowars or troopers on the road, almost no burnt villages, no bodies left to hang over the roads.

Because their requirements were minimal Lavanya and the children lived adequately off what she could beg. On the worst of days three chappatis and a bowl of milk would get them through, and usually they scored some lentil or chickpea dahl as well, or a couple of raw eggs that she could beat into the milk. The worst was the cold that came, after some weeks, with the wet at night, but Lavanya still had the sacking she had taken from the fisherman's hut to wrap round the children. She had already learnt how to make a tiny cave out of the stones of a tumbled wall or hollow out a hole in the undergrowth and in many of the fields there were tiny tent-like structures made from thatch where, when the crops ripened, a farmer would spend the night to protect his grain or rice from wild pigs. In these ways, as darkness came on, she would improvise or find shelter; the three of them would take off their clothes and spread them to dry a little and then cuddle up as closely as they could on straw or grass beneath the more or less dry sacking and soon create there a little Dutch oven of warmth and comfort.

There were problems, of course, minor calamities, which seemed dreadful when they occurred, such as the parting of the sole from the upper on one of Stephen's English sandals, or Deepika's dress torn as she leapt too eagerly through some thorns to regain the road after relieving herself in a thicket. In the first instance Lavanya improvised soles out of newly sprouting sugar cane leaves and bound them on Stephen's feet with a periwinkle-like creeper strong as twine. But these were uncomfortable and within a few weeks he went barefoot like the others. She used the same tough stems to make a girdle into which Deepika could tuck her skirts so the tear did not show.

They sang songs in Lavanya's Hindi-based dialect as they walked, nursery rhymes telling of incidents from the Ramayana, the story of Rama and Sita, and because they were songs Stephen picked them up. That was just a step from learning what they meant. Gradually he used more and more of the language they spoke, eked out with the English Lavanya knew and bit by bit the English became less and less necessary. Deepika and he had always got on well together, especially

355

back in Meerut when they had been faced with Adam's bullying during the time when the older boy was still typically English, typical, that is, of his class and his peers within it.

The intimacy grew. They played games – hide and seek and tag, and those that belonged, with only minor differences, to both cultures, like tossing small stones off the backs of their hands and catching as many as they could. He made a little straw doll for her, and she made a better one for him, and by the time they reached the hills they spoke as freely to each other as any infants just three years and nine months old or less may, though anyone outside their tiny circle might have had difficulty in understanding them.

They took their time. With no particular place to go there was no hurry to be anywhere other than where they were. Sometimes they did not manage more than five miles or so in a day. Sometimes, where the villagers had been particularly kind, they'd stay for a day or two. But as soon as Lavanya felt the presence of even the slightest threat – a muttered suggestion that Stephen could be pale enough to be European, or an overly flirtatious youth paying attention to her, Lavanya moved them on. What shifted her most quickly was any suggestion that she, they, might be institutionalised into the fabric of the village – she as a servant or concubine, the children adopted by people older than her.

The hills. Gradually the great plain broke up into low rises which they had to climb, the reverse downhill slopes of which were never as steep as the climbs. The vegetation became sparser in spite of the rain which, though less heavy already, still coursed down towards them through widening clefts that were occasionally deep and wide enough to be thought of as valleys. Outcrops of rock broke through, especially near the crests, and took the form of fissured cliffs often carved by the weather into fantastic shapes, like the heads of giants whose eyes were caves. And some were balanced on hill tops where millennia of erosion had deposited them. There was less cultivation in these areas, though flocks of sheep and goats, guarded and guided by dogs like small mastiffs, drifted over wide patches which had greened up with a thin cloth of grass. Birds of prey cruised at great heights above them, chips of jet against the blue depths or the gathering clouds.

These ranges whose foothills they were threading a way through ran basically east–west, and, as we have seen, climbed. For a week or so they followed the course of a river that tumbled out of the hills and down to the plain they had left. Near the top it issued out of a valley filled with boulders. Lavanya took them up and away from it so they were walking along the crest above it, and, quite suddenly, a very different view opened in front of them.

The land below them still undulated but less sharply and it was green again but not with cultivation, or only in patches round villages – the rest, most of it, was jungle. Do not be misled. In both Hindi and Marata the word is *jungal* and refers to any wilderness, uncultivated land, wild forest or scrub. What was in front of them was teak forest for the most part, greening up with the rains, but not intensely so. However, basins where the vegetation looked richer, heavier, darker, greener, and the blue of what might be lakes, small lakes, linked like turquoises on a silver necklace by the river below them, nestled in the forest. To their left, to the east, a higher range of forested hills rose above the rest, bounded by the river whose course they had followed up from the plain.

They dropped back down to the river and soon they were walking along the bank where a narrow strip of turf separated the great grey boulders that lay in it from the jungle. There were kingfishers now, herons again, and, basking on the shingle on the far side, a huge crocodile. Lavanya tightened her grip on the children's hands and pulled them in closer to her. A sudden chattering above their heads broke the quietness and a troop of monkeys, black-faced, silvery white, langurs perhaps, swung through the highest branches above them, making miraculously acrobatic leaps, close to flight, from one branch to another. And then, a hundred yards ahead of them, there was a more serious crashing and crunching in the undergrowth and a small herd of elephants broke out of the trees and trundled down to the water. Bath-time. Two young ones, very young, not much taller at the shoulder than Stephen, were dowsed, squirted on, gently pushed into the water where they instantly caught on to what was expected of them, and began, clumsily, and not very efficiently, to drag their own water up in their trunks and squirt it over their anvil-shaped heads. They disturbed a shoal of fish and a fish eagle dropped out of the sky, its screech like an ungreased cartwheel.

Opposite them at this point, on the further bank, there was a tiny village, just seven or eight huts, surrounded by small fields hacked out of the jungle, which then closed round it. Lavanya wondered if a

357

crossing was possible, if there was a way to be picked through the boulders and patches of shingle, but in between there were channels of brown foam-capped rushing water and, remembering the crocodile too, she decided against it for the time being.

The forest closed in more densely now with rises on both sides dropping down to the riverbank. Lavanya was beginning to think she had made a mistake, that she should go back to the village and maybe call out for help to get across, but decided to take one more turn round the next bluff, which was really a small crag faced with another opposite as the river narrowed even more and ran yet faster. They pushed on round the corner, threaded a low, short gorge at the end of which they glimpsed bright sunlight, rich greens, flat water, and what looked like a brown rocky prominence rising out of the water to a height well above that of the surrounding trees. Taking a chance they paddled, and in Deepika's case waded, round the last boulder.

Lavanya's heart lurched, the sort of apprehension one feels when faced with the apparently numinous flooded her veins; she felt a wave of dizziness. The children, as small children do when faced with the preposterous, the unknown, fell silent, turned away, faced each other, excluding what they could not understand.

The river had opened out into a lake about a mile long and three quarters wide, swampy inshore and dotted with islands. Each of these islands supported a temple, some the size of English churches, five or six of them as big as cathedrals or bigger and all built to the same pattern, huge clusters of pointed domes or shikharas piled above gated entrances in narrowing tiers to the largest and highest of all, built and carved from warm glowing russet sandstone, set on massive plinths made from blocks of some harder, greyer rock. Every surface and pillar was crusted with decorations which at that distance she could not decipher.

The water, the lake, was clearly not deep, or at least not in places, for it supported water lily pads, lotus, with lotus buds not yet ready to burst. There were patches of rushes and reeds round the edges which in places thrust out towards the islands. The scalloped edges of both river or lake and islands were filled with trees and bushes, many in flower – the peachy coloured and white of the rain tree, the tiny yellow pompoms of the amaltas acacia on leafless branches above the white, waxy curling elfin trumpets of the temple tree, the larger

358

brilliant carrara-white of dhatura horns, poisonous even to touch. Brightly plumaged ducks cruised across the open patches of water, ruffling the perfect reflections of the temples and here and there small clouds of tiny flies celebrated their day-long lives in swirling dances through three dimensions above the surface, attracting swooping sweeps from white-bummed temple-haunting martlets. A rich sweet smell filled the air, subtly almondish, frangipanean.

There were no humans, none at all. But there were monkeys possibly in hundreds, mostly the langurs they had seen before, whose dominant males looked like wise old men with their heavy fringes of fine white hair circling their black faces. They swung through the trees, they sat in the crotches where branch grew out of branch and groomed each other; they fed their babies. There were some on the islands, in the temples or climbing up the crusted walls, but not many since there was no food there to attract them.

Lavanya sat on a grassy bank beneath a huge spreading mango tree, a perfectly formed hemisphere above its massy trunk, as big as an oak, whose clustered flowers were in bud, not yet burst, and made the children sit beside her.

'Where are we?' Stephen presently asked. 'Are we in heaven?'

He was a bright lad though not yet four.

Behind them a cat growled. A big cat.

53

Lucknow, 30 June–25 September 1857

A letter from Mrs Pamela Courteney to her mother.

The Residency
Lucknow

Dear Mama

I do not suppose you will ever receive this letter and,
recalling as I do the circumstances under which we parted
from each other four years ago, I doubt you are expecting one.
About those circumstances I have little to say. I do not think
I did wrong in marrying Courteney. I have been happy
enough with him which is no less than I hoped for. Our
union, as I am sure you must have heard, was blessed with two
children who were christened Alexander and Jane for Papa
and you. Both died from the dysentery just over a month ago.
As to the wisdom of accompanying Courteney to the Crimea
and then India all I can do is repeat what I said before we left:
with no income of my own, I had no say in the matter and for
at least three years it all worked out quite tolerably well, until
the present awfulness that afflicts us broke about our ears.

Mama, I have been very close to death both from illness
and the sort of events which occur when one is in the very
thick of a war, and I am very lucky to have survived for as
long as I have. Very many of my acquaintance have gone
before me and I now have the strongest presentiments that

my turn is about to come. If you were here you would tell me I am a prey to irrational fears; however, it is a fact of this dreadful conflict that many caught up in it have foreseen their passing only hours or days before their predestined fate occurred. With this in mind I find myself desirous of communicating with you as perhaps a daughter should. I also have a wish to put on paper a memoir of what we have all been through in this place and describe some of the events that have taken place. With my children gone I am perhaps a little too aware that my own passing will write *finis* to an existence too unimportant to be remarkable in any way and if there is to be a memorial of it, then I must write it myself.

I can, I suppose, be a little more frank about why I am putting pen to paper. The fact is that since the children were taken from us there is very little to do here. Boredom is bad enough. But boredom clouded, indeed cloaked in mourning, in perpetual fear and anxiety about which there is nothing to be done, is quite another.

June the thirtieth marked the turning point, and Sir Henry Lawrence was the instrument. He was a tall man, thin, melancholic, pointed chin supporting what would have been a goatee had he not let it bush out a bit. He started out a soldier but always chose to take administrative posts, so he was suited to the job of Chief Commissioner. The rebellion here in Lucknow broke out at the end of May when most of the sepoy regiments rose and kicked out their English officers. They murdered some, including General Handscomb, but not all. They then marched out of the city, some towards Delhi, some remaining in the hinterland. Sir Henry opened up the Residency which is a big building in its own grounds, surrounded by houses almost as large, used by senior English officials; there are also a treasury, a hospital, a church, and smaller buildings. Into this compound Sir Henry welcomed the Europeans of the city and many of the Christian Natives too, and set the troops he had to fortifying it, building gun emplacements and so on. It is all on a low eminence above the River Gumti, and on the other three sides closely surrounded by Native buildings, some large, some small, with wide streets and narrow alleys. Along or near the Gumti there are several palaces, and the now abandoned British cantonments.

By 30 June there were upwards of three thousand of us inside the fortifications, of whom seventeen hundred could fight though only seven hundred were trained soldiers. The rest were men from the city, of all colours, who were quickly trained in the rudiments of the art. Half of all the fighting men were Natives, mostly loyal sepoys. Thirteen hundred of us were women and children. Sir Henry saw to it that a huge amount of food was brought in, and of course ball, shot and powder and we were all allocated places to live in. He even had a swimming bath filled with grain without telling anyone, thereby ensuring our survival after the first relief which considerably enlarged our garrison with fighting men.

We, myself and the children, were put in Doctor Fayrer's house, a dozen or so of us to one room. Courteney visited us there when he could but was mostly occupied in the Residency where he was artillery officer on the staff. On 30 June there was a battle.

News was received that a force of mutineers was coming in from the east and had reached a town called Chinhut, eight miles away. Sir Henry inadvisedly decided to take them on though, considering the extent and nature of our defences, there was no good reason to. That, at any rate, was Courteney's opinion. However, Sir Lawrence's military ability had been called in question and he felt that a battle under his belt would improve morale greatly; he wanted to test the loyalty of his Native troops; it was generally believed that British soldiers always won against Native armies, however bad the odds, on account of our steadiness under fire, our superior arms, and having well-trained officers who know what to do.

Quite a crowd of us, women and children, gathered on the rise above the Iron Bridge and watched our troops assemble including a large howitzer pulled by an elephant. The children loved her. No matter how many elephants they saw, and they saw many, they always loved an elephant.

It occurs to me, Mama, that you might not know what a howitzer is. It is a short-barrelled cannon that fires large shells high into the air fused to explode as they land. They are the

362

best instrument for discharging large shells since the shell, or bomb, lies near the mouth and its fuse can be adjusted and lit after it has been loaded. They are also best for short-range work, say under half a mile, when the object is to kill people rather than knock things down. Courteney, as you are aware, is a gunnery officer, so I know about these things.

There was a delay and who should come down to us but Colonel Charles Blackstock. He is a dear old buffer, but on this occasion was positively fulminating. 'The devil's in this, you know,' he declared. 'It's a confounded trap, I'm sure, to lure us out and destroy in the field what should be a garrison. We know how many mutineers left the town; if half of them are out there waiting for us they'll chew us to rags and spit us out. Then what will happen to all you lot . . .?'

Colonel Blackstock was right in every particular. First of all the delays meant that they didn't move off until the morning was well advanced, and they had assembled early, without a proper breakfast. I recall, Mama, how often Nurse used to tell us that breakfast is the most important meal of the day. And you cannot imagine the debilitating heat on the last day of June. Our fellows were literally dropping dead from sunstroke before a shot was fired.

I wasn't there, of course, but we heard all about it later. The mutineers outflanked our little army using tall crops and mango groves as cover. Then their guns stopped firing and Sir Henry supposed they were retreating and moved forward into the jaws of the trap. Their infantry now revealed itself and came on at us in quarter-distance columns as if it were a parade or a field day. Most of our Native troops broke and ran for it. Sir Henry ordered the retreat but none of them would have got back had it not been for the bravery of our British cavalry. Thirty-five of them charged and drove off five hundred of theirs and in the face of two nine-pounders at that! We lost three hundred and fifty men and a lot of our Native troops who, having fled, didn't come back. Worst of all, the poor elephant, which had also missed out on its midday meal, just didn't have the strength to pull the howitzer up a slope of wet ground so that was lost too.

The evil consequences of this fiasco were made manifest

the very next day. Sir Henry and his secretary were working in his apartment in the Residency when a shell from that awful howitzer landed between them. The fuse was a shade long and they were able to shelter behind the furniture before it went off and neither was hurt. Courteney and the rest tried to persuade him to move to another room. Sir Henry replied that sailors say the safest place in a ship is where the last shot landed. Which is idiotic. Ships are on the move in a battle, buildings are not. Set the same charge, the same elevation and direction and you stand a good chance of getting your projectile to land where the last one did. Every gunnery officer knows that. Anyway, he agreed to move in the morning. Next morning, about eight-thirty, Captain Wilson of the commissariat reminded him of his promise.

To which Sir Henry replied: 'Damn it, Wilson, I've been up since four o'clock. I'll have a lie-down for a couple of hours and then we'll get my things moved. Meanwhile carry on with your report, there's a good chap.'

Captain Wilson continued his report: 'Sugar, just over two tons, so I calculate if we keep use down to half a cup a day per person it'll last for . . .' and at that moment the second shell exploded.

'Sir Henry. Sir Henry? Are you hurt?'

'Killed, more like. Oh my God it hurts!'

A piece of the shell had smashed into his upper pelvis, shattering the bone and his thighbone too. They got him over to Doctor Fayrer's house and put him in a room on the ground floor which was obscured from the rebel artillery by the buildings outside the compound, but was exposed to musket and rifle fire which rattled continuously off the walls and shuttered windows. On account I had had some nursing experience with Miss Nightingale at Scutari I was next door in the hospital which was close to being the centre of our hell. There were never fewer than two hundred in there, lying on the floor so close you could hardly get between them, and most of them amputees who were virtually bound to die.

It was almost a relief to be asked to go to Sir Henry's bedside. I was allowed to assist and was present almost all the time until he died. My special duty was to change the

364

tourniquet. The placing of each fresh one was a matter of the nicest judgement considering the position of the wound at the very top of his leg, but I am satisfied I managed without undue immodesty. Doctor Fayrer gave him forty-eight hours, but he managed an hour or so more than that. During those two days he put his affairs in order. He left Brigadier Inglis in charge, issuing a memorandum of some fifteen points for his guidance. The last concerned his epitaph. *Here lies Henry Lawrence, who tried to do his duty. May God have mercy on him.* As to family matters, he spoke often of his departed wife and recited their favourite passages from the Bible. He also left advice and counsel for his children and sent them his love. His expression as he died was a happy one, expressing relief and joy perhaps that the pain was over. His last words were to the brigadier:

'Dear Inglis, ask the poor fellows whom I exposed at Chinhut to forgive me. Bid them remember Cawnpore and never surrender. God bless you all.'

It was a lovely passing.

The following day or a day or two later, the self-appointed governors of the city, mullahs, rajahs, senior Brahmins, whoever, proclaimed Birjis Qadr, the nine-year-old presumed son of Wajid Ali Shah, the King who had chosen exile in Calcutta, ruler of Lucknow. The boy, that is. For ten minutes or so we thought the commotion signalled the arrival of Havelock from Cawnpore. Such a disappointment.

What followed has been four months of hopeless hell. The monsoon broke. In July Lucknow can have two and a half feet of rainfall in the month. The temperature remains in the high eighties. There is no amelioration until well into September, it is not bearable until October. Under normal circumstances no European women or children remain in the city during these months; normally we are all in the hill stations by the end of May at the latest.

We have been under unremitting bombardment. They are entirely indiscriminate about whom they shoot at: women and other noncombatants are mown down as readily as fighting men, almost more so since the men are behind fortifications or in entrenchments while we have to move about, in order to fulfil our duties and obligations of childcare, giving temporary care and comfort to the wounded, lining up for the daily rations, and so forth. One of the first of my friends to go was Mrs Dorin, from the station at Sitapur, where we spent some time in '56. She was billeted in Martin Gubbins's house and very early on was killed by a bullet through a window which hit her in the head. Mr Gubbins has a large library which he values highly, but he values the welfare of his guests even more. So after Mrs Dorin's demise he had all the windows blocked up with books. A volume of Lardner's *Cabinet Cyclopedia* stopped a musket ball at page one hundred and twenty. Findon's *Illustrations to Byron* was shattered by a three-pound round shot, but rendered it harmless.

I could go on all night listing those of my acquaintance who were shot or hit by cannonballs. One felt it was in God's hands whether we were hit or not and He knew what was best for us. Major Francis was hit while sitting in his chair in the officer's mess. More than once, while sitting at cards, bullets passed across the table between us and on one occasion my partner, a Mrs Tredonnick from Cornwall, took a two-pound shot in her chest (I felt the wind and heat of it pass under my arm which was raised to make the first play) which, being spent, merely shattered her ribs without penetrating beyond them so, poor woman, she lingered on for three days in quite remorseless pain. I could not resist looking at the cards she held and to my chagrin found she had six spades to the king ace, while I had four to the jack.

There are many cattle in the park round the Residency, bullocks belonging to the artillery, cows, goats, some sheep. We need the latter for milk for the young children and babies. It is extraordinary how frequently those who have been recently blessed with motherhood dry up because of the strains they are under. Well, these barbarous shooters, when there are no easy targets presented by the human part of the garrison, take to shooting the animals instead. A dead or wounded person can be pulled in by one man or two at the most, and the dead buried, but a large bullock requires four or even six men and possibly the services of a mule, and no one will risk their lives for the sake of a dead bullock. So they are left to fester out in the open, in the mud. In the presence of

366

heat and wet the carcases swell with gases and an awful stench hangs over the whole fort. A fatal attack of dysentery can be brought on by the exhalation alone.

There are only two dhobi wallahs and they charge inordinate sums to do our washing, and do it badly, without soap. We mothers wash for our children, but generally speaking, while we are prepared to cook and nurse, I am sure, Mama, you will agree, ladies who have been called to our station in life do not do washing.

Alexander and Jane died. Of dysentery.

We have to do our own cooking, and I must tell you our early efforts were not distinguished. The basics are beef and chupattees. The beef is tough and only by trial and experiment did we learn that very slow and gentle cooking tenderises the meat. And as for chupattees I learnt to respect those women who have served us in the past who could bring to table a hot chupattee which was neither charred to black nor at the other extreme, scarcely cooked at all. It is quite an art, believe me. Many of us are a lot less junoesque than we used to be and our clothes hang from us as if from clothes horses.

Collecting the very limited firewood that was available we left to men too old to fight. Occupied thus, three from our house alone were killed.

The surgeons are in two or more minds about anaesthetics. They have æther available I believe and chloroform too but are loth to use them. Surgery is confined to amputation of limbs, and death almost invariably follows amputation. Mr Rees, a Swiss trader, remarked that it is a law in medical science, as practised by the garrison surgeons, that death follows amputation as sure as night follows day. This naturally bothered the surgeons and one came up with the idea that the enforced lethargy that follows administration of æther so weakens a man's mind and body that he is unable to withstand the shock of amputation, especially of a leg. Moreover æther and chloroform are in short supply and since both alleviate toothache when applied to the gums there was a strong move made by many mothers that they should be reserved for the children.

Opium seems not to have been on Sir Henry's shopping

list. And this has caused a lot of misery. Opium eating is very common indeed in Lucknow, the poppy being grown extensively in the area, indeed some say the habit is as rife as it is in China whither most of our crop is exported. There are very many addicts both in the town and in the Residency and not a few of these are Europeans and almost all the loyal sepoys. Many of the sepoy addicts slip away into the city at night, leaving messages scrawled on walls . . . 'Gone for opium, back soon', and so on. Others buy from dealers on the other side, and considerable fortunes are made. But the many who lack the courage to go out into the city or the wherewithal to buy within the walls suffer terrible agonies of withdrawal and some even cut their throats to end their suffering.

Throughout all this we have been waiting on General Havelock and General Sir James Outram to come to our relief, Sir James having recovered from the illness that kept him from being Chief Commissioner. Many times our hopes were raised and then dashed. Havelock would lead his tiny army out of Cawnpore for a few leagues and was then forced to return, either because he was faced by a vastly superior force, superior in numbers, you understand, or he received reports that Cawnpore was again threatened and he had to return to defend it.

You may wonder how we know all this, cut off as we are, but there are at least four exceedingly brave men who find ways of getting through the enemy's lines, crossing the hostile fifty miles that separate us from Cawnpore, and return with the latest news. Two are Natives. Two are British: a Mr Kavanagh and a Lieutenant Farquhar.

Havelock and Outram at last got through to Lucknow, and, after bitter fighting, into the Residency. Problem. They cannot get out. However, a second relief force is on the way under Sir Colin Campbell. Campbell is the new Commander in Chief. Courteney served under him at Sebastopol and says he is the best general officer we have. He has assembled a large force of European troops at Cawnpore as well as loyal Natives and we have high hopes that a final relief is on the way.

Dear Mama, I do not think I can continue with this letter for much longer. I am very tired and somewhat distressed. News has just been brought to me that Courteney has been killed by a shell while laying one of our guns in the churchyard.

If I do not survive and yet this letter does reach you, I do hope you will believe me when I say that I remain, in spite of everything, your devoted and affectionate daughter.

Pamela Courteney

Pamela Courteney, in pursuit of a small child who had run out of Dr Fayrer's house, was killed by a shell on 27 September in the grounds of the Residency. Two days earlier, on the twenty-fifth, the Residency was entered by a force led by Major General James Outram and General Henry Havelock. This force, however, was not strong enough to effect an evacuation and remained in the Residency.

54

Lucknow, 9 November 1857

No one knew where the fakir appeared from. He was not there and suddenly he was, walking round the baobab tree in front of the main entrance to the Residency itself. The corporal of the Quarter Guard at the top of the big colonnaded steps later supposed that he had used one of the many tunnels made by the sappers of both sides. The garrison dug outwards towards the buildings or batteries that were causing them most nuisance; the besiegers strove to get under one or other of the fortified buildings inside.

Whatever. There the fakir was, a lean dark figure in dhoti and turban, holding a thin teak staff, striding past poor mad Sergeant Atkinson, an ex-tunneller and now a paraplegic who had, miraculously one must suppose, survived double amputation with one leg taken off below the knee, the other between knee and pelvis. The consequence was that when he knuckled himself along the ground like a malformed ape, he was forced to lurch from side to side, from stump to stump. It was the laughter provoked by this that drove him mad.

The fakir offered him a most informal salute.

'Take me to your leaders. I have a message for them from General Hope Grant.'

Hope Grant had succeeded Colonel Greathead as commander of the Flying Column from Delhi.

The actual delivery of the message to Generals Havelock and Outram was the cause of some embarrassment. It took place in the billiard room. The baize from the full-size table had been used for bandages and the thick slate was upended to cover the window. There was no closet nor even a cupboard Bruce Farquhar could withdraw into or behind.

'Excuse me,' he said, 'but I shall have to remove my dhoti and then . . .'

The generals and their staff politely turned their backs on him.

'Thank you most kindly. You may turn yourselves around now.'

The dhoti was back in place. Farquhar held out his right palm across which lay three inches of goose quill. The open end was plugged. He squeezed the plug out and then, borrowing a pin from Havelock's desk, extracted a tightly rolled sheet of onion-skin paper. The message on it was written in ancient Greek. None of them could understand it.

'Hodson wrote it,' supplied Farquhar. 'He was sure Simon Gascoigne, Simple Simon we used to call him, would be able to read it for you.'

'Captain Gascoigne was killed three weeks ago. Do you know the contents of the message?' asked Havelock.

'More or less. Hope's column are at Banna but there are only five hundred of us so we are to remain there until Sir Colin Campbell comes up with the main army. Campbell expects to mount an assault on Lucknow within a week, give or take a day or two. His purpose will not be to take Lucknow, but simply to effect a complete evacuation of your position here. Sir Colin trusts you will be able to hold out until then. That's about it.'

He put the quill on Havelock's desk where it remained since all that saw it guessed where it had been and none would touch it.

That evening the Blackstocks made a great effort to entertain Bruce. They saw to it that he had what he needed, including a Native servant's help, to make him presentable in mixed company – that is, down in the basement of the building, in a tiny improvised bathhouse, the blacking was scrubbed off with the aid of the last sliver of soap they had, and a uniform was found for him that more or less fitted. No one asked where it came from, and no one needed to ask since there was a bloodstained hole below the shoulder of the jacket. Perhaps it had been Simon Gascoigne's. While all this was being done Sir Charles went to the expense of three stale chappatis to provide a meal that was better than bullock beef. He scattered the crumbled chappatis on the ruined lawn between the Residency and the churchyard and, using his fowling piece, demolished about forty sparrows. He had the opportunity of taking a very handsome peacock but it displayed while he was taking aim and its beauty saved it from the table.

Meanwhile, Farquhar presented himself to Lady Blackstock. The Blackstocks had been billeted in a tiny attic room at the top of the Residency building. It was lit by a small square window, had a deal table, a couple of simple chairs and two charpoys. Most of the plaster had fallen from the walls revealing the laths beneath, a result of the outside wall being hit by shot from without, and there was a thickish coat of dust over everything.

Lady Blackstock was not herself. For a start there was a lot less of her. Her hair had thinned (or possibly she no longer bothered with the hairpieces she had affected) and what there was hung no longer in ringlets but lank; shadowy eye sockets and sunken cheeks exaggerated the size of her nose; the sinews in her neck stood out like taut cord; her once magnificent breasts had shrunk and flopped droopily within her now oversized dress. Her spirits had suffered too: she was melancholic where she had been cheery and complaining where forcefully expressed contempt had been her style.

'Mr Farquhar, this is not the life I had in mind when I allied myself with Sir Charles. Incessantly I dream of dear Dorset and the house I shared with my first husband in Dorchester High Street. Would that I had stayed there but the attractions of marrying into the aristocracy got the better of me, those and the life of ease and comfort Sir Charles promised me. All vanity, you see? I have a little bramble cordial left and I believe there is a bottle of gin somewhere. If you'd care to join me . . .?'

She drifted to the tallboy that had so far escaped being split for firewood and rummaged about in the big drawer at its base. Bruce caught a glimpse of bundled unmentionables, glass chinked on glass beneath them; when she straightened she was holding a bottle of Gordon's Export. She found two small glasses in which, holding them to the light, she measured one large measure of gin and one smaller, and then added a purple liquid from a stoppered flask. Bruce was handed the glass with the lesser amount of gin.

'Cheers. Here's to better times.' She sat down and began to reminisce, following an unstated train of thought. 'For a time we shared this tiny room with a lady of mixed blood, Rosemary Patel. She is large, fat, and wears more in the way of gold and jewellery than is strictly nice. Bangles, anklets, necklaces, pearls in her headdress, would you believe? Charles says it all amounts to her life savings, but, really, I don't know . . .' Her voice faded and then picked up again. 'She would talk of nothing but her husband's business in the indigo and cotton trade and insisted on their very superior standing in the city. Her main claim to preeminence among her acquaintance is that Patel is at least three-quarters white. "Why," she'd say, "he may look dark but it's all sun-burn. Push his sleeve above his elbow and you'll find skin as white as yours, Lady Blackstock . . ." She had to go. Not because she was a blackie, Mr Farquhar, far from it. Charles's first wife was a blackie. But Mrs Patel was plain unbearable and that was that. Ah, Uma, my dear, no doubt you have been told about our visitor and have come to see him for yourself . . .'

Bruce turned to the door and his heart leapt as conflicting emotions swept through him and then the questions: why was she here? Five months earlier she had been in Jhansi, apparently a member of the Ranee's personal entourage, even bodyguard, more concerned, it had seemed, with protecting her mistress's reputation, at that last meeting on the roadside, than allying herself with him in spite of the world-shattering ecstasy she had shared with him and which had left him almost broken by an agonised longing for her that was all the more exquisite for being almost certainly unassuageable.

She was even more lovely than he remembered. She too was thinner – the healthy bloom of late adolescence was now touched with an ethereal quality which a romantic might have described as spiritual. Her countenance looked tired and perhaps even greyish but was at that moment lit with excitement and, possibly, happiness. She took his hands but resisted the pressure which sought to draw her into an embrace.

'Mr Farquhar, I must thank heaven that you have come through the terrible vicissitudes of the last months unscathed. You look well, yet you were first in the assault at Delhi, what, less than two months ago?'

'To say I was first through the breach is an exaggeration. But I was not far behind those that were. But, dearest Uma, I trust you too are well . . .'

Lady Blackstock emitted a strange barking cough.

'These are difficult times and difficult circumstances,' she began, 'I am going to leave you and go downstairs to see what Charles has managed to find for dinner. I warn you, though, that if I run into Mrs Patel I shall come back.' She finished her gin and cordial in one quick gulp and was gone.

Left to themselves the lovers' embrace was long and passionate but ended, in spite of the charpoys, with them chastely seated on the two chairs. There followed a long and murmured conversation, broken only by the occasional thud of round shot on the masonry outside, sometimes near enough to make the room shake, while each described to the other the dangers and horrors they had been through. But at last Uma came to a point she must have had in mind the entire time. Taking his hands again she pulled Bruce closer, and held his eyes with hers, dark wells of dark amber.

'You will have to go soon?'

'Tonight. I promised General Havelock that I would carry messages back to Sir Colin Campbell.'

'I want you to take me with you.'

'No, it is far too dangerous.'

'Surely we will both be taken for Natives if we are apprehended.'

'Perhaps. But that would not necessarily save us. They are mercilesss to those Natives they believe support the English.'

She sighed, chewed her bottom lip, turned her head away to conceal what might have been a tear of frustration. Then back again.

'How long before Lucknow is taken?'

He shrugged.

'Months at least. But the immediate plan is to take and hold the Residency, effect an evacuation and withdraw. And that could happen very soon indeed.'

'I suppose that will do.'

'Uma, what's on your mind? What are you suggesting?'

'I am a Native, Bruce. Should I call myself Indian, whatever that is? Among the English I shall always be the Native. Among Indians I am an Indian.'

'This is absurd, Uma. You are Uma, no one, nothing else—'

'Not to the English.' Her voice hardened and he felt the grip of her hands in his palms tighten. 'You have no idea how I have been treated here. Spat upon, pushed and pinched, denied food when we have lined up for rations, ostracised, and all this by women of the highest breeding. It has been as if they blamed me for their condition and situation. They call me nigger and tell me to get back into the city with the other niggers. It would be different, of course, if I declared myself a Christian and, like that Mrs Patel, wore a cross, but I am not and I won't.'

'Surely all this, regrettable though it is, arises from—'

'Let me finish. My mother was a cousin of Lakshmi Bai, the Ranee of Jhansi. We visited her often when I was a child and much later, after my mother died, I stayed with her when Sir Charles went back to England. Now, I want to be with her, with my people. After all that has happened, the Blackstocks, kind, and, on Sir Charles's side, loving though they are, are not my people. They talk of returning to England and settling there once this is all over. I will not go to England. There. Help me, if you can or will, to get back to Jhansi. I shall not blame you if you do not.'

Farquhar let her hands drop and his head fell forward over his chest. Where there had been doubt earlier, now there was turmoil. The whole business was far too difficult for a young man to handle. Why the Ranee, of all people? He knew she had been ruling Jhansi for some months with the apparent collusion of the British, but he also knew that she was generally held to be responsible for the massacre back in June, at least could have prevented it . . . he had been there himself, and, when pressed, was ready to admit she might have done more than she did, had indeed said so in his report. At last he looked up again.

'I must go back. I have men to command as well as a message to deliver. Please do not think of trying to leave here on your own. When the attack comes I shall find you and look after you, I promise.'

'And after?'

'I don't know. I really don't know.'

He stood, he stood with the table between them.

'I'll go now. I think it best if I do not dine with you. Please convey my apologies to your . . . parents.'

She rose and turned away from him back to the tallboy and opened the left-hand top drawer.

'At least take this with you,' she said, and handed him a holstered revolver on its belt with a small cartridge case hanging above it. She came round the chairs and helped him buckle it on, the shoulder strap and the belt.

'Your father won't be pleased to find it gone.'

'He has his pistols and his hunting gun. And anyway, he is not my natural father. He knew my mother was pregnant when he married her. I have no white ancestors. Go now, but come back for me if you can.'

He embraced her properly, once, shared one long and passionate kiss, but already as he clattered down the long flight of stairs the questions rushed back: why was she here, why had she left Jhansi, and why was it now so important for her to return?

Lady Blackstock could see that she had been crying.

'He left,' Uma managed to say, 'on account of something I said. And it cannot now be unsaid.'

Lady Blackstock looked round the room, at the undisturbed bedding on the charpoys.

'You should have given him what he wanted,' she said. 'At times like these men deserve everything we women can offer.'

55

Farquhar returned to the lower floor of the Residency. Havelock looked up from the spiced broth he was drinking with a spoon and waved the inevitable chappati at him with the other hand.

'You are too late, young man. Mr Kavanagh left a half-hour ago, wouldn't you say, James?'

'At least half an hour, Henry.' Sir James looked up from chewing at a mutton bone which had been through the pot three times, his intelligent, enquiring eyes narrowing as he took in Farquhar. 'Got up in a turban and so forth, blacked up to the manner born. A disguise quite as good as yours when you appeared before us. Quite took us in, did he not, Henry? Took a map for Sir Colin and other details.'

Farquhar persisted.

'He might not get through, sir.'

'Indeed he might not. All right, you can back him up. But the gist of what we said is plain enough, no need to make out another map. Give the show away if you're caught. We were wrong a month ago to attack across the river from the south. Got badly caught up in the streets of the city. Campbell will do better to come in from the south-east, take the Martinière College which gives him a good vantage point, covers the canal, you see? Cross the canal, and come in through the palaces and parks and the old cantonments, along the riverbank, cut out the street fighting. More space to fight properly. That's about it, eh, Henry?'

'Yes, James.' A weariness in Henry Havelock's voice. Who, in

377

God's name, was in charge, after all? On his arrival Outram had quite gallantly declared he would leave military matters in Havelock's care – but in the event he would interfere. 'But he should also be told to give us plenty of warning so we can clear a way through the Baillie Guard and get the wounded, the women and the children ready to move. It would help a lot if he brings bullock carts with him.'

'How will he do that? Send Kavanagh or young Farquhar here back?'

'Semaphore perhaps, James?'

Bruce saluted and left. After some thought he decided to remain in the uniform that had been found for him – with the main army now on the other side of the canal and only four miles away there was no open country to cross.

He wandered round the grounds for twenty minutes or so as the darkness deepened and a light rain began to fall. The buildings, once splendid or domestic, now holed and battered, stood against the encroaching darkness and the last glimmer of light in the west. A few men moved about like the living dead; one, propped against a tree stump, sang a garbled version of 'Molly Malone'. Sergeant Atkinson swung close by on his clenched fists, paused in front of him, attempted a salute and nearly keeled over. Farquhar righted him, just in time. Muskets cracked, the flashes ruby tongues from the windows they were fired from, and a ball whistled past his head.

'Well, Sergeant, I'll be off, I think. No, no, please don't try to salute again. Take it as read.'

He headed past what had been the hospital and was now a ruin above an exposed cellarage, to the Baillie Guard, the main gate. A high bank of earth and rock had been piled against it on the inside, and as he approached he saw there was a guard on duty, but one who appeared to be asleep though still on his feet. The rest of the picket certainly were asleep, lying down and snoring. Thinking that an assertion of authority would help him to get past more easily he shouted at the man.

'What the hell do you think you're doing, soldier?'

'Ah, sorr. I was just deep in t'ought over a matter that has been trobling me these nights.'

'And what might that be?'

'That if all men onnerstood that suffrin' is our destiny, we might be less anxious to inflict worse on one another.'

There seemed to be no answer to that. Bruce began to climb the embankment.

'Forgive me, sorr, but I take it as you know where you're going?'

'I do. And it's none of your business.'

'Indeed not, sorr. My job is to keep the boggers out, not in.'

By now Farquhar was at the top of the banked-up debris, held in by the shattered remnants of the gate itself, and looking down over a short drop to a similar ramp on the other side. No hail of musket balls greeted him. The rebel commanders knew very well that Campbell had arrived and had pulled most of their troops back to the bridges over the canal to the south, aware that an assault might come as early as dawn. Threading his way past the Kaiserbagh, the other palaces, and, on his left, the deserted and looted English barracks and bungalows, Bruce headed south-east and then south through the narrow streets and alleys of the city. In less than an hour he had covered the four miles and was on the bank of the canal and close to the point where the Cawnpore road crossed it. It was held by a company of sepoys.

He scouted along the bank and, among bigger craft used to carry produce in from the surrounding countryside, quite quickly found a small flat-bottomed boat. There was a man fast asleep on the planks in the bottom. Using the sporadic gun and musket fire from both sides of the bridge, catching it as it reached a more intense climax, he put the muzzle of Colonel Blackstock's revolver against the man's temple and fired. He slid the body into the black water, found a punting pole, untied the painter, and got across. Twenty minutes later he was outside Sir Colin's tent, behind the Alambagh. In all this he was well aware that he was taking very great risks but it did not matter. He felt Uma was slipping away from him and if she did, well, there was not a lot of point in being overprotective of himself.

The Alambagh was a summer palace with what had been a pleasant garden in front of it and fields behind. The British had maintained a small but well-equipped garrison in it during the weeks since the first relief, and Sir Colin had made it his headquarters, pitching his tent among those of his troops behind it. The only thing that distinguished it from the rest was the Union flag on a not very tall flagpole; that and the presence of a couple of tall sentries from a grenadier company.

'Is the General up?' Farquhar asked.

'Not yet, sir. He won't stir until first light. But I can wake him.'

'No, no. The message I have for him is not that urgent. It can wait until then. Do you think you could find me a spare blanket?'

They could and presently he was lying on his back underneath it. It was the coldest part of the night and the sky was clear. The stars wheeled above him, thousands upon thousands. Each one a sun, so the astronomers said. Some not just suns but whole galaxies of suns, each a pinprick but as big, maybe, as the Milky Way that flowed like a river acoss the northern quadrant. The stars, and the overpowering sense that he would never have Uma, left him feeling unbearably sad and lonely.

'Bruce? I say, Bruce, wake up, there's a good chap.'

The face of the man who was leaning over him and shaking his shoulder in the cold grey light of early morning was familiar, though distorted by uneven blacking and a turban which had slipped to the point of revealing the fair hair underneath. Farquhar heaved himself up into a sitting position. The man came into sharper focus as his eyes and brain cleared. He was tall, had sharp but very self-aware bright blue eyes. There were a couple of Sikh troopers standing behind him.

'Tom, you're too late. I got here first.'

'Absolutely, old boy, but could I have a word or two with you about that before you see his nibs?'

Tom Henry Kavanagh, clerk in the Deputy Commissioner's office in the Residency, a notoriously unlucky but compulsive gambler, was likely to face an inquiry, if any of his accusers survived the siege, into allegations that he had been dealing in laudanum.

Farquhar sighed wearily.

'Go on then, Tom.'

'Well, I'm in a bit of a hole one way or another, and it seemed to me that if I could pull off an act of great derring-do I might be let off the hook. And frankly, old chap, I did set off first, before you, and, well, my need is greater than yours. I might say too we've had a hell of a night. Might not have made it if these two fine fellows' – he indicated the Sikhs behind him – 'hadn't picked us up.'

'We? Us?'

'Kanuji Lal came with me. He deserves to make something out of this too, and these two are hoping for a handout at least.'

At this moment an elderly gentleman in a red nightshirt appeared in the doorway to the tent. He had dark hair with silver streaks clinging in curls to his scalp, a heavily lined forehead above bushy eyebrows, dark eyes that often seemed to be fixed on the middle distance, or perhaps on some preoccupying inner reality. But when they did focus on you they were like a surgeon's probe. Kavanagh did not recognise him.

'Oh, I say, could I possibly have a word with Sir Colin Campbell if he's awake? I've just come from the Residency with messages from General Havelock and Sir James Outram.'

'I am Colin Campbell. You'd better come in.'

Kavanagh followed the Commander in Chief into his tent but as he went managed an apologetic if cheeky smile at Bruce.

Bruce got himself to his feet, looked around, nodded to the grenadier sentry, and made his way back across the fields, through the rising mists, to the two hundred or so who still remained of the 75th. The first cannon of the day was fired from the other side and a nine-pound shot whistled overhead. Within seconds the bombardment, more or less futile, began on both sides.

Kavanagh was awarded the Victoria Cross, one of the very few civilians to be so honoured. He also received a cash reward of twenty thousand rupees, and was made an Assistant Commissioner.

56

Sir Colin Campbell, the son of a Glasgow carpenter, though capable in a crisis of extreme bravery and notorious for a fearsome temper when crossed, was a cautious and meticulous general. His thoroughness in preparation had even caused his younger officers to label him, out of impatience, 'Sir Crawling Camel'. It was in character therefore for him to parade his men in the fields behind the Alambagh and subject them to a thorough inspection.

Some had been fighting for six months; others had been travelling vast distances at very short notice, frequently getting ahead of their baggage. The Madras Fusiliers had patched their uniforms with curtain fabric and some were wearing silk pyjamas. The artillery batteries were made up from the crew and guns of HMS *Shannon*, now designated the Naval Brigade. The men were still in their naval uniforms, among them Captain William Peel, son of the erstwhile Prime Minister, in his fore-and-aft hat. They were great keepers of pets, these sailors, with monkeys, parrots, guinea pigs and mongooses jumping from shoulder to shoulder and the cadets, lads as young as fourteen years old, sitting astride the barrels of their huge guns.

The 8th and 75th in their patched uniforms, khaki faded almost to white, looked weary, even miserable. In front of them the 75th's replacement commanding officer, Colonel Gordon, sat on a reddish-brown brute of a Native horse. He wore a basin-like hat made out of an old shako, a khaki jacket and baggy trousers thrust into jackboots furnished with enormous brass hunting spurs. The sword knot on his sabre was made out of green and pink silk pyjama cord. Everything about him was dirty; indeed, he was known as 'Dirty Gordon'.

The only complete regiment was the 93rd Highlanders and they, at least, looked capable of doing the business. Wearing full Highland dress with cockaded bearskins skirted over the nape of the neck and the forehead to ward off the sun, brown tunics with red facings, kilts in the Sutherland tartan, they were a solid mass of brawny-limbed men, most of whom wore Crimean medals on their chests. As Sir Colin approached them they broke out into a loud rolling cheer and at last his face, which had grown increasingly worn and haggard as he went through the ranks, split into a broad and genial smile. So chuffed was he, he broke into a rousing address delivered in a strong Glaswegian accent.

'When we mek an attack y' must come to closhe quartersh uz quuckly uz pawsible. Keep well togither and use the bayonet. Remember that yon cowardly sepoys, who are eager to murther women and bairrns, cannay look a Eurupean sholjer in the face when it is accompanied by cauld shteel. 93rd! Ye are my lads. I rely on yous to do the wurrk!'

Turning away he barked at his nearest aide: 'Keep yon 75th back in reserve. They've had the fight knocked oot o' them.'

This was terrible news for Bruce Farquhar since he had committed himself to getting Uma out of the Residency, and he had very little time indeed to do anything about it. He spent twenty minutes with Colonel Gordon, Captain Barter and his colleague Lieutenant Brookes arguing that it was a smear on the reputation of the regiment that had led the assault on Delhi to be excluded. He also went among the NCOs and pointed out that they had so far not received any of the prize money due to them from Delhi and that getting into Lucknow could be an opportunity for some privatised prize gathering.

'I tek it, sor, y' mean lootin',' commented one Corporal George MacGregor, a big man with a big black beard.

'You may think what you like, Corporal. But it would be an honest gesture to return to our private common pool whatever you get here.'

This advice drew a quiet ripple of sardonic laughter and someone audibly growled 'wind-fucker!', a soubriquet which possibly supplies the derivation of 'wanker'.

The upshot of it all was that Colonel Gordon sent a request to Sir

Colin that a detachment, fifty-strong, of the 75th might be included in the attack. An answer was returned: 'Permission granted'.

That afternoon Sir Colin led out all of his army bar three hundred left to guard the Alambagh. The main body of them occupied the Dilkusha, a hunting lodge surrounded by wilderness; the Naval Brigade, its big guns drawn by elephants, climbed to higher ground, to La Martinière. The Martinière was a huge and extravagantly decorated mansion built in 1800 by a French general, Claude Martin, who left it to be turned into a school for the children of well-to-do Indians – which is what it still is today, though it also offers scholarships to bright lads from poorer backgrounds. From there Campbell's big guns could shell, albeit at the range of a mile or more, the main buildings occupied by the defenders, principally the palaces that lay on the far side of the canal and across his proposed route.

There was almost no resistance. The rebels withdrew in good order across the canal, their first line of defence, leaving the British with the Dilkusha and its deer, many of which, butchered and skewered on bayonets, were roasted over open fires. They spent the next two days reconnoitring and skirmishing across the canal to the west, thus masking that their attack at dawn on the sixteenth would be launched at the south-east corner of the city close to the junction of the canal with the river. The nights were made musical by nightingales punctuated by less lyrical nightjars, the yips of small owls and a smattering of rifle fire as detachments continued to probe the south-west of the city.

On the morning of the sixteenth every man was issued with three pounds of salt beef, and twelve big biscuits (bread cooked twice), half of which they put in their knapsacks. The beef was cooked in big Soyer stoves which were becoming a feature of the campaign as more troops arrived from the Crimea and Britain: standing nearly five feet high, and looking like oil barrels with stove-type chimneys, each could cook for fifty men. The top half was where the food went, usually stewing beef with whatever vegetables the locality provided; it was separated from the lower half by a circular watertight plate below which a wood, charcoal or even coal fire was lit.

With full stomachs and in good heart they set off shortly after sun-up, marching north from the Dilkusha instead of west, through fields with high crops and past woods, only revealing themselves fully to the defenders when they reached the junction of canal and river. A bridge of boats the sappers had spent the three intervening days building was pushed across the canal and the 93rd and 53rd, with the 4th Punjab Infantry (all Sikhs) in support, marched across in quarter distance columns of companies, headed by light guns and followed by the fifty men of the 75th led by Farquhar and Brookes with George, Sam and Alec in the first file. To begin with there was little resistance but as they approached the palaces and their gardens that lay between them and the Residency they came under increasingly heavy fire, especially from a small palace, the Sikanderbagh, oddly neo-classical in style, that stood at the back of a high-walled garden with circular bastions at the corners. Sir Colin went forward to have a look and was hit, but the ball, having already passed through and killed a British gunner, was spent and he suffered nothing worse than a badly bruised thigh.

Not far behind him, and barely noticed as the noise and smoke increased, a naked man, apparently a mendicant, sat in a doorway on a leopard skin, and clicked his beads through his fingers. He was streaked with ashes and red paint and had a shaven head.

'Jasus, but I'd like to try out me bayonet on the hide of that heathen varmint,' one of the men called out.

A nearby officer replied.

'Don't touch him, he's a harmless Hindoo jogee [by which he meant holy man or conjuror], he won't hurt us, it's the Mahometans who are to blame for this mutiny.'

He was wrong and the prayer beads should have told him so, and the leopard skin too. Hindu holy men do not easily touch anything dead. The man was a Muslim and he was also a suicidal fanatic. With a movement as sharp and quick as a cobra's he pulled a short brass blunderbuss, from under the leopard skin and shot the officer dead. The soldier who had drawn attention to him quickly made sure that his bayonet was indeed as sharp as it needed to be.

385

57

As the musket balls clattered off the walls around him, Sir Colin saw
that the Sikanderbagh could not be ignored. He issued the order
that it should be taken. But first he ordered the engineers to throw a low
mud wall, no more than a couple of feet high, across the street.

'Lie down, 93rd, lie down,' he bellowed. 'Every man of you is
worth his weight in gold today!'

He watched as the two- and three-pounders he had brought with
him thumped their shot uselessly into the wall two hundred yards
away, and noted how the crews were falling to the musket fire. Then
in a sheltering doorway he scribbled a note, an aide galloped back the
way they had come to the pontoon bridge where the Naval Brigade
was hauling its heavy guns, two twenty-four-pounders, on to the left-
hand bank of the canal. Twenty minutes for them to get within sight
of the Sikanderbagh, another five to get the great guns unlimbered,
and forty-five while huge blocks of brick and mortar tumbled back
into the gardens beyond.

A sergeant of the 53rd, Joe Lee, known as Dobbin, called out, his
voice cutting the air above the pandemonium caused by the huge
guns in a confined street, 'Sir Colin, let the infantry storm and we'll
soon make short work of the murderous bastards.'

'Do you think you can, Dobbin?'

'Some of us'll get through and we'll hold the space while the
pioneers pull it wider with their crowbars.'

The soldiers crowded forward, the Sikhs in front. A few more rounds then Sir Colin let them go, but the Sikhs wavered as two of their European officers were shot down after only a yard or two had been covered.

Sir Colin turned to Colonel Ewart of the 93rd.

'Bring on the tartan, Colonel Ewart. Let my own lads at them.'

All seven companies leapt up with a shout of pent-up rage that drowned the bugle that sounded the charge and surged forward, their faces twisted with the ecstasy of battle and hate. The Sikhs, who had endured centuries of persecution and even massacre from the Mahometans, bellowed their war cry '*Jai Khalsa Jeet* – Victory to the Khalsa'; the Highlanders came on with 'Cawnpore, you bloody murderers!' Ewart, his bonnet shot away, took out six with six shots from his revolver; a man called Wallace, known as 'Quaker' though clearly he was not, slew twenty with his bayonet while chanting Psalm 116, metrified thus: '*Dear in God's sight is his saints' death, Thy servant, Lord, am I,* Take that y'heathen múrtherer, take that from me . . . *Thy servant sure, thine handmaid's son: my hands thou didst untie* so I can send the next black bastard straight to hell . . .'

There were at least two thousand sepoys in the garden and palace of the Sikanderbagh and there was no way out, no escape. And no possibility either of taking prisoners: first because these were mutineers, criminals in the eyes of the British, secondly because there were no men to spare to secure prisoners, and thirdly because they were now ineradicably established in the minds of the men as the perpetrators of the horrors of Delhi, Cawnpore, Jhansi, Futtehgahr and countless lesser places.

And how was it that a few hundred could so easily overcome two thousand in hand-to-hand conflict? Again it was the bayonet and the efficiency with which it was used. Real resistance was soon at an end, and it was kill, kill, kill. The bodies began to pile up, some still living, and the attackers had to clamber over them to get into the palace itself where they found women and children, women who were simply servants of whatever princes had been using the palace. A British ensign tried to hold back a Highlander from bayoneting women but the man turned on him, his face a grimace of anger and bloodlust so fierce that the ensign expected for a moment to be bayoneted himself.

Covered with blood and black with powder fumes, eyes flashing like a lunatic's or those of a man wildly drunk, clutching the colours of a rebel regiment, young Colonel Ewart rushed through the gate near the front of the palace and grabbed the bit and reins of Sir Colin's grey charger.

'I have killed the last two of the enemy with my own hands and here are their colours.'

'Damn your colours, sir, it's not your place to be taking colours. Get back to your regiment this instant, sir!'

The sergeant major called the roll call of the 93rd and found they had lost ninety men and nine officers. Meanwhile, fires were started, some among the bodies, and within the piles the screams of the half-buried wounded rang out.

At last the tide of hysteria receded and exhaustion, physical and psychic, set in. A group of men from the 53rd gathered beneath a big pipal tree among the bodies of their comrades. Casting an eye over these an officer noted that many bore wounds that had clearly been inflicted from above. He called for Quaker Wallace to see if there wasn't someone high up in the thick foliage of the tree.

'I see him,' he cried, 'I'll pay my vows now to the Lord before His people all', raised his rifle and fired.

The body that tumbled down, branch by branch, was wearing a red coat and rose-coloured silk trousers. Two heavy cavalry pistols, decades old, came with it. The body was that of a woman and when Quaker Wallace saw that he had killed a woman, he burst into tears.

It was still some hours short of midday. Exhausted, sated, many suffered a generalised depressed reaction or, more specifically, mourned, albeit with forced jocularity, the absence of familiar faces: 'Puir auld Jock, ees gawn at last and still owes me a shulling.' Maybe they ate their saved beef and biscuit, and maybe drank tea from the Soyer stoves which had entered the city not far behind them. They smoked their pipes and maybe some slept a little.

Later the garden and palace were cleared of most of the bodies, dragged away by Captain Peel's elephants. They were counted into a mass grave, one thousand eight hundred and fifty-seven of them, and that was not all, for a photograph taken some time later shows skeletons still lying on the open ground in front of the palace.

Three major obstacles still stood between them and the Residency and the first of these was a tomb, the Shah Najaf. This, like the

Tomb of Humayun in Delhi was, though smaller, more than what we understand by the word tomb, being as big as a large church with a white dome, surrounded by a garden overgrown with brambles behind a high wall. Sir Colin walked among his Highlanders.

'I was hoping to tell you you have done enough for one day, but if the Residency garrison are not to perish that tomb over there must be taken.'

'And you're telling us it's us as has to do it, Sir Colin. Is that it?'

'Aye, lads.'

'Will us get medals?

'That's not for me to say, laddie, it's up to the Queen's Government. All I can say is you already deserve one better than any troops I've seen under fire.'

They dragged the guns into place, Peel's guns, and a Royal Artillery battery with lighter cannon came up at a trot, the drivers waving their whips and the gunners their caps. A scream and a curse: one of the sailors had lost a leg, taken clean off above the knee.

'Here goes a shilling a day, a shilling a day,' he gasped, as the blood gushed as if pumped from a well, 'Pitch into them, boys, pitch into them. Remember Cawnpore', and he died before anyone could get a tourniquet on him.

Again the garden wall was too strong and it became clear it would take hours to breach. They tried to get over by climbing on each other's backs and were driven back – the rebels' fire from loopholes, from the tomb itself, from trees and bushes, was intense and accurate; they even used arrows to great effect. These were loosed by a group of women whose leader, young and beautiful, was never identified, though a statue to her has since been erected on the spot. The crews of the big guns were being picked off, men were falling everywhere including the staff around Sir Colin.

'This won't do,' he announced. 'We'll pull back and see if we can't work our way round . . .' But they'd need covering fire as they pulled back. 'Captain Peel? You have rockets?'

And at that moment someone spotted a narrow gap in the wall at the furthest corner, and as the rockets whooshed overhead the first men got through. The sepoys were already fleeing. They had not seen or faced rockets before. These swung and swooped above them trailing fire and clouds of smoke and exploded noisily when they hit an obstacle. It seemed they were guided by djinns. In almost no time Sir

Colin was able to ride into the grounds while the Highlanders, including what was left of the fifty men of the 75th, cleared them.

Those that were left.

'Mr Pidgeley, we are leaving for Balmoral tomorrow.'

'Yes, Ma'am.'

'But of course you will stay. There is a lot of work to be done outside in the autumn, is there not?'

Twenty years later. Sam Pidgeley had been an under-gardener at Osborne House, on the Isle of Wight, the Queen's favourite home, for ten of them. Snip, snip, and another one hits the dust. Dead-heading the roses; the proper pruning would come later. Sweeping up the leaves on the far edge of the big lawn that sloped from the house and the parterres in front of it, towards the sea a mile or so away. A column of white smoke rose into the chill air from a bonfire on the edge of the woods.

'Yes, Ma'am.'

Sam was not any more surprised by visitations like this, not even greatly in awe. Her Majesty walked out on her own in the grounds quite often, chatting silently, it was said, with the long-departed, dear Albert. But if she came across one of the garden staff she'd pause for a chat out loud.

'Walk with me across the grass until we can see the sea properly. I miss much of Osborne House when I go away but I think the sight of the sea is what I miss most. Does it seem very empty when we have all gone?'

Sam thought about it. They drew the blinds and drapes in the house and it looked not dead, but blind. Asleep anyway. Hibernating.

'The house itself, perhaps, Ma'am. But I am not often in it anyway and out here, well, as you say, there's a lot to be done before winter settles in properly.'

Their footsteps left a trail across the grass – a heavy dew still clung like flashing diamonds to tiny cobwebs where the grass was longer.

The Queen murmured. Two syllables.

'Beg pardon, Ma'am? My hearing is not as good as it should be.'

'I beg *your* pardon. So often the case with people who have served. I remember Arthur was the same. The old Duke, you know?'

'Yes, Ma'am.'

'His hearing was seriously impaired by the cannonade at Waterloo. What I said was,' raising her voice, '"Lucknow".'

It was still, even after all that time, a blow in his diaphragm, followed by a surge of coldness.

'My maid tells me you lost a special friend at Lucknow. Twenty years ago, is it not?'

'To the month, Ma'am. The day even.'

They walked on, in silence. She looked up at his pale lined face, head high, staring at nothing beyond and above the trees, and regretted that she had spoken.

'It is not my business. I'm sorry.'

'It is your business, Your Majesty, if you choose to make it so.'

She felt a touch nettled by this. Just once let a commoner do something for Vicky rather than for her majesty.

'All right, then. Tell me. Tell me about it.'

He looked down at her. A small woman, and, it was not to be denied, fat, dressed as she nearly always was in widow's black, sixty years old. But, for all that, regal, firm, not to be denied. She was looking ahead, but sensing the movement of his head, she looked up again. A complicated sort of a smile teased her lips. He read sympathy there but more too. This was a woman who was accustomed, very accustomed, to getting her own way, and not always by crude exploitation of her position. What he did not know was that she had recently begun to interest herself in India, the jewel in her crown; indeed, Disraeli, her new Prime Minister, had suggested she take the title Empress of India. If that happened then *Ind. Imp.* would appear on all the coinage. Queen, by the Grace of God, Defender of the Faith, Empress of India. She liked it.

Sam took a deep breath, felt sweat break out in his palms, but nevertheless took up the challenge.

'Alec, his name was. He was young. Younger than me. And . . . and, well,' the word had to come out, 'perfect.'

Like Achilles, he thought, a frequent thought. Or Patroclus. The Greek Love.

If the Queen was surprised she managed to conceal it. But perhaps she was not. Romantic love between young men was not unheard of. Across the island lived her Poet Laureate who had written so movingly about the death of his dear friend Arthur Hallam. It was even enviable, this love, and something men seemed to be able to share, but not women. That such relationships could have a physical dimension was something she chose not even to consider. Anyway, all *that* was far from her mind as she placed her next question.

'How did he die?'

'He was shot by our sergeant.'

'By accident, surely.'

'No, Ma'am. We were storming the Sikanderbagh. It was a massacre. Terrible things were done. And in the middle of it all Alec just sat down. When the sergeant asked why, this is what he said. "This is bad. This is wrong. I will have no more to do with this."'

For a blinding moment the lawns, trees, the sea and the Queen were wiped out by the relived nightmare: the screams, the crash of cannon, the crack of pistols, the smoke, the smell of blood, faeces and vomit, the faces twisted in savage anger and pain, the rasp of metal on sinew and bone. The sergeant who had tormented both of them for weeks, flushed with bloodlust and triumph, teeth exposed in a wolfish snarl . . .

'And the sergeant, who had a pistol as well as his rifle, pulled it out and shot him in the head. For mutiny.'

As he pulled the trigger he had yelled: 'Bad cess to ye, ye bleeding nancy bhoy, ye filthy angelina, go back to hell where you belong,' but that was something Sam did not wish to repeat.

They walked on. The Queen knew very well that there are times, moments, which are so mixed up and confused that no sense can be easily made of them, so she said nothing. The view slowly opened into wide spaces of sky above a calm white sea which stretched below them to the distant horizon. There were a couple of fishing boats in the bay and a steam packet inched away from them along the coast. On the far side of Gosport, Portsmouth and Spithead were shrouded in mist.

'*Calm on the seas,*' she murmured again but this time he heard her, '*and silver sleep, And waves that sway themselves in rest, And dead calm in that noble breast Which heaves but with the heaving deep.*'

58

The street-fighting, the fortified palaces had already cost too many men. The right thing to do was to get every soul out of the Residency and then make an orderly withdrawal back to Cawnpore, and the striplings who called him Sir Crawling Camel could go to hell. But first, there was work to be done. Two major buildings, fortified and occupied, still stood between him and the Residency.

Once they were taken Havelock and Outram made their way down the narrow alleys to meet him. On the way a shell landed at Havelock's feet and blew up – the explosion knocked him flat on his back. But he got up unharmed and moments later entered the Khoorsheyd Munzil where Sir Colin raised his cap and held out his hand. All very British: 'How do you do, Sir James' and then 'How do you do, *Sir* Henry' for the news had just come in that Havelock had been made a Knight Commander of the Bath. Which pleased him a lot.

But Sir Henry was not well. He already had dysentery and had to be carried down to the Dilkusha where he was given the only tent available in the garden. He died a week later. As he weakened he kept repeating, 'I die happy and contented.' His son Harry sat with him and soon after dawn on the twenty-fourth his father called for him and murmured, 'Harry, see how a Christian can die.' Harry held him and he died without a sound.

It was decided that the final evacuation of the Residency would take place on the nineteenth. Sir Colin had naturally expected them to move at least the day before but the women insisted they needed a day to prepare themselves for departure.

This left Bruce Farquhar in a quandary. He had begged Uma not to leave the Residency without him. And, he now realised, in the light of her determination to join the Ranee of Jhansi, she might well attempt to leave ahead of the main body. She could be gone before he got to her. She might even cross the lines and throw herself on the mercy of Begum Hazrat. He struggled to make sense of what she had said, of what she was planning to do. Was she motivated simply by a desire to be among her own people, or was she in fact contemplating espousing their cause? The former he could countenance and possibly even help her to achieve, the latter was, in the face of her upbringing and the life she had led, nothing short of the rankest treachery. But through all this he was haunted, possessed even, by the recollection of her now wan beauty, carried with a triste air of vulnerability. Whatever else, he had to see her.

Four hundred and fifty men and eighty officers had been killed in the previous twenty-four hours or so. If he could get away unseen he could rely on being written up as missing, presumed dead, and one thing Bruce was good at was remaining unseen. To Lieutenant Brookes, who was preoccupied anyway with a broken arm, he muttered the usual stuff about needing a dump, back in a minute, and climbed over a heap of rubble into the gathering gloom. There was a moment of sheer fright as he approached the Baillie Guard gate ten minutes later and drew a shot from the same sentry who had seen him out two nights earlier. The streets around the Residency had already been occupied by pickets of the relief force but that didn't stop the sentry from taking a crack at him. The ball ricocheted off a wall inches from his ear and a shard of masonry sliced his cheek, but not deeply. He came into the open, clutching his cap to the wound.

'Born to suffer we may be,' he growled as he approached the man, 'but there's no need to be so ready to add to the sum.'

'Jasus, your honour, you should have spoke first and then moved instead of the other way about.'

The heap of stones and debris on the inside of the gate was already part cleared away in preparation for the evacuation and he was able to negotiate it with only one hand. Eventually, and with a slight burning sensation in his side, he made it to the attic door at the top of the Residency itself.

'Who's there?' The voice hoarse, riding on a crackling phlegmy breath.

'Bruce Farquhar, sir.'

'Oh come in, lad, come in. Can't say how pleased we are to see you.'

Sir Charles let him in. The strangest of sights met his eyes. Betty Blackstock, wearing only her shift, what was left of her hair tumbling about her face and down her back, was standing in the middle of the tiny room. Behind her all of the drawers in the tallboy were open and two were on the floor at her feet. Clothes of all sorts surrounded her and the table was piled with jewellery, some loose, some in cases, fans, handbags, shoes, hats, one with black ostrich feathers, bottles of perfume and at least three of gin, cordials, and pills in pillboxes.

'Don't mind me,' she cried, 'I am merely the victim of that Pict carpenter who has told us to be out by tomorrow nightfall. As if he were a landlord and his men nothing better than the bailiffs . . .'

The colonel puffed and spluttered back at her. 'Sir Colin is a very fine soldier and but for his strength of purpose and adherence to good military practice, we'd be in a well by now or the river, like those poor souls in Cawnpore.'

'Charlie, if he bloody knew his arse from his elbow he'd have driven that whore and her son out of this town by now and we'd be back in our old quarters. Bruce. How am I going to get this lot out of here? No more than we can carry is what that mean bastard has said. I've no doubt he'll let his men in after us to loot what we couldn't take. Charlie? My wedding dress! Do you think I can still get into it? Bruce, if you're looking for Uma, the girl's gawn.'

'Gone!'

'Don't know where. Half an hour ago.'

'I'll go and look for her.'

'Do that, why don't you? But don't let her fill your hands with all her stuff, such a lot of nonsense she has with her. She even brought her archery things with her. You'll need both hands to help me carry my things. What's the matter with your face? You're bleeding like a pig.'

He searched for Uma for nearly twenty-four hours, all through the Residency, the outbuildings, the walls, even the mine tunnels. Every hour or so he laboured back up the stairs to the Blackstocks' attic to see if she had returned in his absence. Again and again he questioned them. What had she taken with her? Just a purse and the clothes she was standing up in. What had she said before she went? We told you. Back in half an hour. And on each visit Lady Blackstock's apparent bulk was different. Sometimes she looked like one of the huge sacks the peasants used to collect and move cotton; at other times she was as thin as Lady Blackstock could ever be, having dismantled herself so she could begin again.

'Buggered if I'm going to leave my wedding dress behind, it's trimmed with Honiton lace, class stuff, not leaving that for some nigger to swank about in. Trouble is, I doubt I can get into it, and with the train it's too big to carry.'

'Cut the train awf m' dear. I'll carry it. Wind it round my stomach. Could do with a stomacher these cold nights.'

When, in the early afternoon, bugle calls announced that the evacuation was about to start she looked like a barrel again. She was wearing, she proclaimed, three sets of undergarments, a pink flannel dressing gown, a plaid jacket and then over all this a cloth dress and another jacket. She tied her cashmere shawl round her waist with Sir Charles's silver mug wrapped in it. On her head she pulled a worsted cap and a hat above it. 'That was my mother's last present to me, God bless her soul.' Her pockets were filled with jewellery, and valuable papers regarding her marriage settlement. Getting her down four flights of stairs was an adventure in itself and when she was at the bottom, she looked about her.

'Charlie, I've left m' travelling escritwah behind. You'll have to get it for me.'

'I'll go,' volunteered Bruce, and was on his way before they could stop him.

Again the pain in his side as he reached the top. Gasping for breath he looked down through the tiny window. A huge crowd was gathering between the churchyard and the Residency, mostly women and children, and many of them almost as overdressed as Lady Blackstock. Dresses and coats made for them when they were fat were now stuffed to breaking seams with silks, satin and lace. He scanned them all, at first at speed, then more meticulously in the way he had taught himself when spying on troops on the march, sector by imaginary sector, and there she was, he was certain, almost certain, moving towards the head of what was slowly forming into a column, her silver-grey saree beneath a black cape, lifting the hem of the saree to step out when she saw a gap in the crowd that might take her nearer the front. He shouted, shouted until he was hoarse but in the bedlam below there was no chance of her hearing him.

He caught up Lady Blackstock's escritoire which was a walnut-veneered box with a sloping lid containing three bottles of ink, troughs for pens and pencils, marbled notepaper, sealing wax with a wick and a small brass seal. He tucked it under one arm and raced downstairs again, still clutching his cap to his cheek – in moments of exertion the wound tended to open and bleed a little – and earning a heap of abuse from an angry ayah when he pushed a small child who tumbled down three steps to the last landing. From halfway down the last flight he picked out Blackstock, rushed across to him and thrust the escritoire into his arms.

'Oh, here I say, dash it, I can't manage this.'

'Please take it. I just now saw your daughter outside and I'm going after her.'

'Good man! I told Betty to go on ahead. If you see her, tell her I'll catch up sooner or later. You should be able to find her: she'll be riding the donkey I bought for her. Cost me what I'd have paid for a thoroughbred at Eltham sales.'

The column, ragged at the edges, crowded and pushing in the middle, and occasionally subject to musket fire from the streets beyond where rebels still held rooms in some upper storeys, shambled towards the Baillie Guard gate. Here and there the luckier women were mounted on asses, ponies and in one case, or rather six cases, an elephant. Farquhar attempted to weave a way through it, but found his way constantly blocked by these oversize women who resisted his efforts to squeeze between them.

'Young man, mind where you're pushing me.'

'No point in behaving like that, take your turn like everyone else.' And so forth.

He caught up with Betty Blackstock just as they were passing the Sikanderbagh. The smell was appalling. He fell in beside her for a moment or two, clutching for breath as he did so, and then explained that he was pretty sure he had seen Uma up ahead. She struggled to finish a mouthful of a tinned-ham sandwich she was eating.

'Can't say I've seen her, but she may be up there. Did you find my escritwah?'

'Gave it to Sir Charles. He's coming up behind. No, nothing to eat, thank you.'

'Mrs Germon here,' she indicated a large woman on a pony on her further side, 'has an inexhaustible supply.'

Mrs Germon leant across towards him.

'My husband's breakfast, but he was called away before I could give them to him,' she cried. 'Dreadful smell, don't you think? They say they killed two thousand niggers in the garden. Bad place to be caught.'

She did not mean the garden was a bad place for the rebels to be caught, but was referring to the fact the column had come to a stand-still. Soldiers of the 93rd in kilts and bonnets were attempting to keep them moving but the problem was a convoy of munitions and guns attempting to get through on the other side of the Sikanderbagh while on the town side the interference from the rebels was becoming moment by moment more dangerous and, making matters even worse, darkness was falling. Within twenty minutes the daylight was gone. Farquhar, with increased desperation, did his best to move on but got no further than twenty yards in front of them before everything came to an impassable deadlock.

'Worse than the Strand when the theatres come out,' a voice near him called out.

'Worse than the old Duke's funeral,' someone else answered.

'He should have been here. He'd have sorted this lot out.'

Did she mean Lucknow on that night, or the whole Mutiny?

'Anyone know where we're going?'

'Dilkusha. Whoops, we're moving again.'

But not for long, not for far. It took three hours for the head of the column to get to the Dilkusha, having taken a circuitous route down a sandy track near the river to keep away from the rebels' fire. Camels fell into the ditches, the darkness became impenetrable; no one had thought of supplying torches for no one had foreseen how long it would take to get them out of the Residency. It became cold, then bitterly cold. And when they got to the palace they found it was full, and they were left to stumble through guy ropes they could not see attached to the tents packed together in the gardens. Children separated from their parents and their ayahs screamed in the darkness: many of their mothers simply keeled over and lay where they fell. A few soldiers with lanterns tried to pick their way through, distributing bottles of wine and cold mutton sandwiches.

Farquhar stumbled back towards the river and finally curled up behind a fallen tree near the water. He was exhausted, utterly worn out, and still bothered by the stitch-like pain on his right side, just below his ribcage. Musketry crackled on the further side. There were fires burning back near the Residency. Acrid, poisoned smoke drifted across the black water. Behind him a bagpipe wailed and then marched. 'The Campbells Are Coming'. Hurrah. At times he longed to die, at others Uma's face swam in front of him. He tried to consider his situation: if he went back to his regiment, what was left of it, could he be arraigned for desertion in the face of the enemy? Probably yes, and if the charge stuck he'd end up in front of a firing squad. Exhaustion produced a fitful doze towards dawn.

He woke shivering with cold, yet thought he was in heaven. Uma's face really was above his, her hand on his shoulder. Her dark eyes glowed with a smile that grew as she realised he was alive and awake. Holding her tumbling hair back with one hand she brought her lips down to his and kissed him briefly but gently on the lips.

'Did you come looking for me?' she asked.

'Yes.'

'Will you come with me to Jhansi?'

In a flash he sensed she would be lost to him if he even hesitated.

'Yes.'

They moved out together, often hand in hand, into the wilderness and presently came to a village where Uma bought trousers, a tunic and a turban for Bruce. That night they made love under a huge mango tree, lying in the long fresh grass beneath its bright fresh foliage, and for a time after that they were happy as they moved south and west; but, inevitably, he had to find out why she had been in Lucknow.

She made no attempt to deceive him.

'The Ranee sent me. I had already told her that my stepfather had been sent there as military adviser to the Chief Commissioner. I was . . .' she laughed a little, 'I am a spy. Like you. You know all about that.'

So. He was aiding, protecting, a spy. What did that make him? A traitor?

'What did you find out?' They were walking along a narrow raised path between fields of sprouting green wheat.

'Just recently my stepfather told me that the end of the Mutiny was in sight. That as soon as all the reinforcements are in Sir Colin Campbell will divide the army into columns and reconquer the Oudh. Meanwhile, an Army of Central India is being formed in Bombay. In the spring it will move north on Jhansi, Gwalior, and finally to the relief of Agra.'

Bruce stumbled, snatched at the pain that fastened on his lower right abdomen. She caught him by the elbow, steadied him, looked into his eyes, held them with hers, dark, unflinching, serious.

'You have to decide. Stay with me, be one of us. Or turn round now and go back.'

He could not go back: desertion, consorting with the enemy . . . and the only way forward was to go with her to Jhansi where, perhaps, he might find a way of redeeming himself, his honour, his past by doing for the British what she had done for the Ranee. If, that is, the will to do so remained.

59

Meerut, Khajuraho, November 1857

Standing in the church of St John with her father singing lustily beside her, Sophie Hardcastle felt a lightening of the heart, a sense that the worst was over. The despair that had led to rejection of the deity had lifted a little: at any rate to the point where she found she could enjoy church, if not God. And it was 'Stir-up Sunday' again.

> *O worship the king, all glorious above;*
> *O gratefully sing His power and His love:*
>   *Our shield and defender* (All very well, but where was He when we needed Him?), *the ancient of days,*
> *Pavilioned in splendour and girded with praise* . . .

Her father? Of all people, this portly, red-faced gent from Dorset, well-to-do and highly respected, who rode to hounds with the Portman, had braved the enormous distances, the storms of Biscay, the heat of Suez (a canal was now spoken of, there was talk of City involvement in the financing, he thought he might take the opportunity on the trip to take a look for himself), the tedious trip round the Indian peninsula and up to Calcutta, the railway, the steamboat up the Ganges, the camel from Cawnpore to Meerut. Through it all he had lost a stone and felt much better for it; moreover, as he frequently remarked: 'It's all been very interesting . . .'

But the purpose of the trip was to bring Sophie and her new

daughter Miranda, his granddaughter, home in safety and tolerable comfort, as soon as could be managed. Meanwhile, he stayed in the best Meerut hotel, was a frequent guest at the Officers' Mess (he was, after all, a captain in the Dorset Yeomanry), drank India Pale Ale and learnt to like the milder, creamier, more fruity curries. The lost stone was already on its way back. And in between times he called on Sophie, let Miranda hold his finger, and tried very hard not to object when Sophie fed her in front of him.

Meanwhile, she put her affairs in order, had what had been sent to Simla brought back, disputed by post what in the way of a widow's pension she was owed by the Queen's Paymaster General back in Calcutta.

'We can sort it out on our way back,' her father insisted, but she knew he would only bluster and lose his temper and probably thereby lose her ten pounds per annum out of what she believed she was due.

> O tell of his might, O sing of his grace,
> Whose robe is the light, Whose canopy space.
> His chariots of wrath the deep thunderclouds form,
> And dark is his path on the wings of the storm.

Sounds more like Jove than Jehovah, she thought. Then, distracted by a glance from a young cornet in khaki on the other side of the aisle (You're a pretty boy, but I'm too old for you, all of twenty-two as I am) her mind drifted to thoughts of James, Captain (as he was now) James Dixon. He had been writing letters to her, quite long and entertaining letters, which, she thought, was kind of him, and she had answered them in much the same way, chatty notes about mutual acquaintance in Meerut, an account of her father's doings, and so forth. She presumed his aim was to keep her spirits up and she adopted a similar tone. And if, almost but not quite unconsciously, she avoided any expression of deeper feelings, then this was out of consciousness that he was still riding with Hodson's Horse, continuously scouting round Lucknow, and was as subject to risk as any other cavalry officer. In short, she resisted giving her heart to someone the next news of whom could be those of his death.

> O measureless Might, Ineffable Love,
> While angels delight to hymn thee above,

Thy humbler creation, though feeble their lays,
With true adoration shall sing to thy praise. A-a-a-amen.

Her father, bless him, hit the G at the bottom of the bass clef, two octaves beneath her, holding it until the rest of the congregation had fallen silent.

She left the pew and joined the queue of families heading for the door, with her father behind her, but as they turned left she had, for a moment, a sight of the vestry door immediately in front of her beyond the font, and she remembered Bruce Farquhar, standing by the pump, washing off the blacking, the streaks of it down his back, his tight buttocks, and then as he turned . . . Was she blushing at the memory? She rather thought she might be, and she thought of James and the way he had loved Catherine, and how it was silly to think she might take her place, and, well, what about Bruce Farquhar anyway? Stir up, we beseech thee, O Lord, the wills of thy people, indeed. Was not this the fourth anniversary of the evening she had met him in the cemetery? No doubt his heart was still Uma Blackstock's, wherever she was, but, well, she could still dream a little, could she not? Feeling a touch confused, but not entirely uncomfortable with it, she took her father's hand and went out into the gloaming with him.

'They've got a couple of good-sized turkeys roasting down at the hotel,' Mr Chapman remarked. 'Would you care to join me?'

'Only if you'll allow me to bring Miranda.'

'Well, you must promise not to, um, feed her in the public rooms.'

The cat was a young female black panther. She was about ten yards away lying in the shade, or out of the rain, beneath the huge horizontal boughs of the mango. For a moment Lavanya felt terror, then realised the body of a small deer, a chital with a spotted back, lay between her paws. The cat was slowly, lazily, eviscerating it, paying no attention to Lavanya and the infants, though she had probably been woken out of a catnap by their presence.

Nevertheless Lavanya saw no reason to take chances. Although she knew largish cats were not averse to wading through water, even swimming, and would take fish, she suspected this one would prefer to remain on land, especially since she had no immediate reason to go hunting. She gathered Deepa under one arm, and reached out only just in time for Stephen, who, on his knees now, was crawling towards the beast, uttering sibilant chirpy noises. Moving carefully into the water she felt an immediate surge of irritation as the cotton of her saree clung to her shins.

The water, flood water from the swollen river, was, just as she had expected, nowhere more than three feet deep except where the riverbed ran. Where it did was obvious for there there was a current and the surface was broken into eddies and ripples. She ignored the first island temple in their path – it was smaller than the others and its porch was almost filled with a big bronze-coloured statue of a boar, an avatar of Vishnu, rather ugly, though richly decorated in shallow relief. Instead she pushed on to the first of the bigger ones. It was approached by a flight of big steps, too high to climb easily while carrying two children, so she set them down on the first whose surface was clear of the water, and sat with them there, their feet kicking up a storm while she got her breath back.

'Keep away from the water.' She half-lay down, supported on her elbows, felt the warmth of the sun, then leant forward to squeeze out the bottom half of her saree, threw a glance back towards where they had come from, checking that panther was still satisfied with the kill she had already made. A big dragonfly whirred by between them, and the sun glittered on the surface of the water. She knew they'd feel hungry before long and that three stale chappatis would not be enough, but that could all wait. She stood up, bent to smooth out the wrinkles in her garment, made when she had tried to wring it.

'Come on. Let's see what there is here.'

Clambering up the big steps, each with a drop of at least two feet, was not easy, and she had to lift and swing the children up each one. At the top, on the base of the actual temple, she looked up and around, first at the diminishing tiers rising above them, then at the lake around them. From this height she could get a better idea of the extent of it all, thirty or more temples rising out of the water, the big sub-tropical trees round the edges, the stillness of most of the mirrored reflections. It all had a sort of tranquillity that comforted her mind, allowed muscles and anxieties to relax, yet it was by no means lifeless: indeed the birds both above and on the water, the monkeys, the occasional drift of blossom on the warm scented breeze, gave it a natural, unfussy busyness.

She turned and began to take in the rich profusion of sculpted stone that encrusted the walls, rows above rows of figures, the lower ones near life-size, placed in very deep relief, almost freestanding on shelves and plinths which zigzagged in and out, creating corners and niches, bright light and deep shade. They figured, she supposed, gods and goddesses in human, animal and monstrous forms – indeed some of them she instantly recognised: an elephant-headed Ganesha, rounded, robust, jolly and almost comical, the god of welcome; and monkey-headed Hanuman. Others she lacked knowledge of the iconography to give a name to, but that was almost better, not having to remember stories, myths, but being left to marvel at the generously bosomed lady, decked with beads, bangles, a belt, necklaces, a head-dress and little else, holding on one arm what might have been a doll and in the other . . . well, was it a baby, a monkey, or what? Then there were the ladies whose almost naked bodies were given delicious curves by what they were doing – extracting a thorn from a foot; applying vermilion to a forehead with an arm curved above the head while the other hand held a mirror to her face; the lady writing a letter.

And then, done smaller, there were dividing friezes showing soldiers on the march, animals, and couples coupling in more ways than you could think of, and having much more fun (she giggled at the thought) than she had ever had with her mahout whose incompetence went beyond his lack of ability with elephants, and who never showed the tenderness (her eyes now returning to the larger figures) of this god who fondled his goddess's breast while she caressed his rising prick.

A cry – Stephen, of course, had got his feet on a shelf a foot from the floor, with one hand round the foot of a baby elephant, and was stuck. She helped him down and wiped his cheeks with her saree.

'Let's go and see the god inside,' she said, and hoisted them up another shorter flight of steps.

The first antechamber was occupied by the house martins, swooping in and out of their tiny nests made from pellets of mud clinging to the undersides of architraves. The chamber was filled with and amplified their high-pitched chirping, their droppings streaked the walls with white guano. The next was darker and appeared empty; the third was taller, higher, even darker. Lavanya made the children stand and stay quiet while her eyes grew accustomed to the darkness. Soon the space seemed almost filled by the sculpted icon of a god in

PART VI

The Beginning of the End

60

Most of the Naval Brigade had gone with Campbell to the relief of the Lucknow Residency but a detachment was left behind at Cawnpore as part of General Windham's tiny garrison of only five hundred. A second entrenchment was dug out close to the bridge of boats which was once again in place and functioning. At the end of November they were attacked by a force at least thirty thousand-strong comprising the Gwalior Contingent and what was left of the Nana's army.

Edward Spencer Watson was fifteen years old, a midshipman on HMS *Shannon* and a cadet in the Naval Brigade. He kept a journal, and wrote letters.

> *Naval Brigade*
> *Camp near Cawnpore*
> *3rd December 1857*

Dear—

> *On the 28th and 29th we were being pounded into like fun. The artillery officer gave me charge of a gun and we did just let fly at them. The only thing was we fired away almost all our ammunition. On the 29th Lascelles and I were looking over a parapet when we saw a round shot kick up the dust just outside and it came just over us. Lascelles slipped and I bobbed to avoid*

409

it and over we went both of us together; such a jolly lark we had and everyone laughing at us.

On the 30th Sir Colin Campbell, having heard the news of our being shut up, arrived from Lucknow with a large force to our rescue with good old Captain Peel. We were so glad to see him, and he delighted at our being in action, but ordered Lascelles and me to resume our old duties as his aides, to put it bluntly his messenger boys.

The day before yesterday we had tremendous fighting but thank God I have not yet got a touch. I always say a little prayer to myself before going under heavy fire and then I never lose my pluck. It is quite a sight to see the captain under fire, he is so cool. He was leaning under a gun one morning, looking through his telescope, when a shell came and burst close to us, and he never even lifted his head. When a man behind us exclaimed that the shrapnel was coming down like rain he said 'Nonsense, nonsense, it is only the dust and dirt!' I am getting used to the twang of bullets now and I hardly care about them at all, but the round shot I have a great dislike to.

Most of the ladies from Lucknow are here now and the brutes have found the place and fire into them tremendously and into the hospital. It is a fearful thing to see the wounded coming in, some with legs and others with arms off, and some in the agonies of death. When once we get hold of these fellows won't we just drive them out of it . . .

Getting on all right.

Naval Brigade
Camp near Cawnpore
December 11th, 1857.

Dear—

6th December. Early that morning we had just woke up in our tent when an order came to strike tents immediately. Up we all got, put our things in the hackeray and everything ready. The Captain called Lascelles and me up privately and said that we were not to run and blow and go head over heels and to get out of breath, but to take it coolly. Captain Peel went galloping all over the place so I *could but run after him like a groom. We blazed away for some time as hard as we could, they giving us shot for shot, and bursting their shells beautifully. But this did not last long. Our marines and the 53rd charged and at the same time we gave them two rockets slap into the middle of them and then with three good cheers we advanced our guns and they actually ran. Didn't we just yell and shout!*

On came our infantry and we fairly set them running. I can't tell you how jolly it was seeing the brutes run. I felt perfectly mad, and our men got on top of the guns waving their hats and cheering and yelling like fun; it was most awfully exciting. We pursued them to the camp, found it all deserted; tents, horses, ponies, baggage, bedding, swords, muskets, everything lying about. I got fairly out of breath and the only way I could keep up when I was on a message from the captain, was to say to myself 'Hoiks over, hoiks over, fox ahead!' and I used to go along double the pace. We chased them for about ten miles along the road to Calpee before we got ordered to halt.

When Captain Peel joined us that night in the tent where we were messing he was very pleased with us, with himself, and all things in general.

'Mark my words,' he said, 'it's just about all over now. We've broken the back of it. Mind, there will be a lot more fighting, a lot more to do, but they can't win, they won't win.'

The Gwalior Contingent, led by Tatya Tope, withdrew in disorder to Calpee, some sixty miles south-west of Cawnpore, but the rest of the rebel army fled north with the Nana, his brothers and Azimullah.

Canning moved the seat of government to Allahabad where he lived and worked from what William Russell, who had arrived somewhat late in the day, thought was almost too grand a complex of huge tents, divided into rooms by glass doors. In the public areas the Persian carpets were strewn with rose petals 'ankle-deep'; the offices, however, where Canning worked from a desk, were efficient and more spartan. Here, in January, he met Campbell and together they sorted out the order in which what was left to be done should be tackled.

The Oudh and Lucknow were the first priorities. North and west of Lucknow the rebel rajahs and maulvis, reinforced by the Nana and what was left of his troops, more or less held the country, but continued to bicker with each other so that no united command or army emerged that could stand up to the now increasingly reinforced British. They suffered successive defeats from British columns while more and more British troops arrived in Cawnpore where they prepared to undertake the final siege of Lucknow. One hundred thousand men, of whom thirty thousand were sepoys, while many of the rest were competent soldiers recruited from what had been the King's army, still held the city under the Begum.

The final assault on Lucknow was held back until the second week of March 1858 in order to allow three thousand goorkhas under the charismatic Nepalese Jung Bahadur time to arrive and join in. William Hodson was at Campbell's headquarters when the signal gun was fired. Calling up any of his squadron who happened to be around, and with Captain Dixon right behind him, he galloped into the city, determined to play his part. Or, maybe to get as much booty as he could. At all events, with Dixon at his back, he was working his way through a dark house near the Kaiserbagh when they came across a locked door. 'Let's see what we can get out out this,' he exclaimed.

'Hang aboot a munnit,' cried a Highlander who was behind him. 'I'll get a bag o' powder', for that was the method they were using, tossing fused bags of powder through doorways and bayoneting any survivors who came out. But Hodson wanted to keep things moving and kicked the door in.

The sepoy who was hiding there loosed off his musket. The ball went through Hodson's liver, out of his back, and, having lost much of its force, hit Dixon in the groin. The Highlanders who were behind them killed the sepoy, found a doolie and rushed Hodson to Bank's house outside the Residency, with Dixon limping behind. The regimental surgeon, Dr Anderson, lay next to Hodson on the floor all night holding his hand, trying to soothe the very severe pain he was in. Eventually the brandy he had given him took effect and he slept for a couple of hours before dawn. He seemed stronger but then, at about ten o'clock, the bleeding started again and he sank quite rapidly. Anderson told him he was dying. He sent for Colonel Napier and gave instructions about his property and business matters, and a message to his wife. Then he grabbed Dixon's hand. 'I came like Water, and like Wind I go,' he murmured.

And that was how the real Harry Flashman died.

61

Called by the watchman on the tower of the castle above the city, Lakshmi Bai paced the battlements, shaded her eyes to watch how five, six miles away a cloud of dust, a mile long, moved, but only just perceptibly, through low rocky hills and then on to the plain, marking the presence of an English column under General Sir Hugh Rose. The cavalry and artillery had arrived the night before and were bivouacked beyond the cantonments, Civil Lines and bungalows, all reduced now by pillage, heat and the rains, to piles of rubble. Near them, the Jokhan Bagh, the garden where the massacre had taken place beneath the city wall and the shikharas of the temples, was still marked by a short ridge in the earth, now not more than a foot high above the mass grave.

Sir Hugh Rose. Another Hugh, another general. This one had seen very little action, had indeed spent most of his career in diplomatic posts, the most recent of which was as liaison officer between the French and British in the Crimea. Fifty-eight years old, of poor health, one doctor described him as effeminate. What could he possibly have meant?

The Ranee felt almost sick with anxiety and chagrin. She knew the British were there because they had confected for themselves a myth that she had ordered the massacre whereas, in her mind, she had done what she could to prevent it, giving way only when she, her adopted son and her father too, were threatened with death, and her

413

city with pillaging by the mutinous sepoys. And since then, as the region sank back into the anarchy of competing warlords which had been the state of things before the British came, she had defended her town against neighbouring princelings, including the Ranee of Orccha, just down the road. In short, she had done everything the Governor General could expect of her.

Anxiety and chagrin, yes. But there were other emotions too as her gaze moved over the battlements of the fort and along the wall of the city: pride, anticipation. Nine months before, the city had had no more than the two brass cannon the mutineers had blackmailed out of her. Since then she had set up a foundry, and tens, dozens, maybe a hundred cannon had been cast, powder and ball made and stored, shells put together. She had personally directed and financed the rebuilding and improvement of the walls, organised and supervised the training of her own troops, the Jhansi Contingent, and those mutineers who had stayed, into a disciplined fighting force, and now she had no doubt at all that the castle and city could hold out for as long as was needed to bring Tatya Tope and his army, still re-forming at Calpee, to her rescue. The British Army would be caught between the town and the field army and they would be annihilated. It was possible too that many of them would change sides before that happened: for half of them were sepoys, from Madras and the south.

Her head lifted, she pushed back a lock of hair that had been dislodged by a gust of hot air, and her dark face flushed a little with, after all, excitement. She looked back over her shoulder at the high white tower above her, where her standard, depicting Durga, the goddess in her warrior form, straightened in the first hot breeze of the day.

She looked around at the seven or eight women who went with her everywhere.

'Courage, my darlings. What you see is nothing more than we have expected and prepared for. We'll deal with them.'

Down in the plain the British Army was feeling the heat and the effects of the scorched earth within a radius of several miles with which the Ranee had circled her city. The roads were dusty, the wells almost dry, the grass bleached and withered. In the jungle the dry yellow leaves rustled and fell, leaving naked boughs, and the cattle crept in vain beneath them searching for shade. The winds began to blow as though they had just escaped through the gates of Pandemonium. They swept through the ranks, scorching up every pore, making the eyes feel as if they had been blistered. Nothing was cool – once the camp was established the chairs the officers sat on felt as if they had been baked, tables and tent poles were too hot to touch. Getting cold beer became a great and momentous object. Each bottle was wrapped in a wet cloth and punkah'ed for an hour before it was drunk. The heat indeed was so great that many officers placed themselves in the hands of the barber and came out cropped to the scalp.

For ten days they banged away at each other. There were few casualties on either side: that was not the point. The British guns were directed at creating practicable breaches in the city walls, those of Jhansi at stopping them. In fact the British gunners were the more successful – not because those of Jhansi were incompetent, but because the Brits most definitely were not. Their gun emplacements, their use of fascines and sandbags and all the other techniques developed over centuries of European warfare, left the gunners and the guns virtually untouchable, and stone by stone, brick by brick the walls began to crumble in the two places Rose had designated. But the Ranee and her garrison were not dismayed. Tatya Tope was on his way.

In a cool room close to what had been the purdah in the Ranee's palace, Bruce Farquhar was dying from a burst appendix. He was lying on an ornate and mattressed chowdah, naked apart from a clout thrown across his genitals. The large hard and discoloured swelling, to the right of his navel and above his groin, had subsided when the infected appendix burst, allowing the poisonous pus inside it to escape through the peritoneum. This had brought transitory relief, but now the toxins were streaming through his blood vessels and he was sinking under the effects of acute blood poisoning. Uma sat at his bedside and bathed his forehead, his neck and chest with tinctures of aromatics which certainly improved the foetid atmosphere but did little or nothing for Bruce.

Uma was distressed but nevertheless preoccupied. Wearing a red scarf, decorated with tiny pearls tied back behind her ears like a bandanna, a buff-coloured military jacket and baggy cotton trousers, she had assumed the uniform of the Ranee's bodyguard of women and part of her wished to be with them. She had told Bruce that marriage was out of the question at least until the Ranee's position had been acknowledged and ratified by the British; if that did not happen then possibly it might even be postponed until they were driven right out of India for ever.

Neither condition was likely to be fulfilled, and now this handsome if slight, charming if ultimately rather shallow, Anglo-Irishman was dying beneath her ministering hands.

Bruce Farquhar fell into a fatal coma on the day after the British arrived. He did it well, modelling his posture on Henry Wallis's *Death of Chatterton* which had been exhibited the previous year. Engravings of this lugubrious painting had been very popular among the memsahibs. He was cremated, Hindoo-style, in front of the small temple dedicated to Ganesha that still stands near the top of the steep ramp above the main gate of the fort. The Untouchable in charge put his torch to the sandalwood pyre and sparks and smoke gusted out over the plain below, unblemished by the smell of burnt grease that often accompanies these occasions. Bruce's body had hardly an ounce of fat on it. The Ranee took Uma's hand.

'You are lucky not to have married him,' she said, her eyes meeting those of the younger woman's. 'If you had there are people here, priests, Brahmins, who might have insisted that you joined him in the flames, as much as an act of defiance to the British interdiction against suttee as out of any desire to celebrate your fidelity.' Then her eyes lightened into a smile that was almost mischievous. 'You'll have as good a time without him as you would have had with him.'

With his jaunting about as a fakir, his easy ability to change sides, and a certain wild romanticism in his make-up, she doubted he would have made a good husband.

By the time Tatya Tope arrived Uma was a lot less heartbroken. This did not mean that her feelings for Bruce had been anything less than sincere and passionate. Simply that they had been subsumed by an overwhelming and indeed joyful commitment to the Ranee and her cause.

One of the first things Rose did was raise a telegraph mast on the highest eminence to the east of the city which communicated to him what his cavalry pickets could see beyond his range of vision. This was nothing to do with the electric telegraph, but was made on the lines of a man-of-war's mainmast and equipped with a moveable yardarm. From it signal flags could be flown following a code adapted from the one the Royal Navy used. It did not occur to him that there would be anyone in Jhansi able to read these signals, but Uma could. Colonel Blackstock had of course wanted a boy (what Englishman of a military cast of mind does not?) and had encouraged her to play boyish games as a child. They had spent many a happy hour, well, quarter of an hour or so, signalling to each other with models across their lawn in Simla. Thus it was when, on the evening of 31 March, a line of fluttering flags appeared on the mast, and the Ranee, taking the air along the battlements with her women, expressed a wish to know what they meant, Uma was able to tell her.

'The enemy,' she said, 'that is their enemy, our friends, are some five or six miles off to the north, approaching the Betwa River.'

'How many, Uma, tell me how many?'

'It says . . . twenty thousand.'

Lakshmi Bai gave several little jumps in the air and smacked her jewelled hands together.

'We've got him,' she cried. 'He's between us like a nut in the jaws of a nutcracker.'

'What will the British general do?' cried her chief aide.

'What can he do? There is nothing he can do except pull out at night, as fast as he can.'

'Gentlemen, I have made up my mind what to do.'

They, that is Rose, his staff, and his brigade commanders, had had a better dinner than usual. On this occasion they did well because a flock of partridges had flown into a picket just before sundown and the subaltern in command had allowed his riflemen to bag as many as they could. Then, much to the annoyance of his men, he had had them sent with his compliments to the general's cook.

With the birds reduced to little heaps of bone on their plates, and the lamps above their heads casting a cosy glow over the interior of the big tent, a bell tent of military design, the lean, dapper, if rather elderly gentleman lit a cigar, poured himself a glass of port, and cleared his throat.

'The crux of the matter,' he continued, and picked a shred of leaf from his lip, 'is the Ranee. We must not allow her the opportunity of making a sortie and attacking us while we are fighting the Gwalior

417

62

The Battle of Betwa, the fall of Jhansi, Gwalior, 1 April–17 June 1858

Sir Hugh Rose's despatch, edited.

> FROM
>   MAJOR GENL. SIR HUGH ROSE, K.C.B.,
>   *Comd. Central India Field Force.*
> TO
>   THE CHIEF OF STAFF

SIR,
For some time past, Tantia Toopee, a relative and Agent of Nanna Sahib, has been collecting and organizing a large body of troops and displayed the standard of that abolished authority. Towards the end of last month, I received constantly reports that this Force, estimated at 20 or 25,000 men, with 20 or 30 guns, was advancing against me. On the 30th ultimo, I was informed that its main body was about three miles from the Betwa and would cross that river during the night and attack me the next morning or the day after.

At sunset, the Enemy lit an immense bonfire on a rising ground this side of the Betwa, as a signal to Jhansie of their arrival: it was answered by salvos from all the batteries of the Fort and City, and shouts of joy from the defenders.

I drew up my force across the road from the Betwa, half a mile from my camp. My force was not in position till long after dark.

The silent regularity with which it was effected, did credit to their discipline. Both ourselves and the Enemy slept on our arms, opposite each other . . .

In his account of the battle, Thomas Lowe, medical officer with the Madras Sappers and Engineers, quotes *Henry V*:

> *From camp to camp, through the foul womb of night*
> *The hum of either army stilly sounds,*
> *That the fixed sentinels almost receive*
> *The secret whispers of each other's watch:*
> *Fire answers fire; and through their paly flames*
> *Each battle sees the other's umbered face:*
> *Steed threatens steed, in high and boastful neighs,*
> *Piercing the night's dull ear.*

Not only boastful neighs. The Native soldiers on both sides exchanged insults and threats throughout the night.

> *I had intended to commence the attack at daylight, advance in line, pour into the Rebels all the fire of my Guns and then turn and double up their left flank, but the enemy, before daybreak, covered by a cloud of skirmishers, advanced against me.*
>
> *I ordered my front line of Infantry to lie down, the Troop of Horse Artillery to take ground diagonally to the right, and enfilade the enemy's left flank.*

Bombarding a line of infantry full on means no round shot can hurt more than two soldiers at once, but if the fire can be directed down the line then each shot might kill or disable up to ten men.

> *Whilst the Enemy were suffering from the fire of the Troop and Battery I directed the Dragoons to charge and I charged myself their left. Both attacks succeeded, throwing the whole of the Enemy's first line into confusion and forcing them to retire. I ordered a general advance of the whole line, when the retreat of the Rebels became a rout. A cloud of dust about a mile and a half to our right pointed out the line of retreat of another large body, the second line of the Rebels, which by a singular arrangement of the*

Rebel General, Tantia Topee, must have been three miles in rear of his first line.

In this Tatya Tope was adopting an arrangement which had already cost him the Battle of Cawnpore. The thinking behind it was that if the first line were successful, the victory would be made doubly certain when the second line was launched. However, if the first line failed then the second could be brought off unharmed and able to fight another day. In both cases it was the disciplined but ferocious British cavalry that wrecked the plan. Following up on the enfiladed cannonade, they broke and scattered the first line, driving it back so quickly that it tangled with the second line at just the point the cavalry arrived. Dub a dum dum dub a dub, indeed.

The whole Force again went in immediate pursuit and came up with the skirmishers in rocky and difficult ground, covering the retreat of the second line. Driven in they closed to their right and uncovered the main body which cannonaded the troops in pursuit. Colonel Turnbull answered with a few rounds, which told. The enemy did not wait for the attack [from the cavalry], but retired with precipitation by the high road to the Rajpore Ford. Neither the Jungle which was set on fire to stop the pursuit, nor difficult ground, could check the ardour of the pursuing troops. The Enemy kept up a heavy fire on us as we crossed the ford, and ascended the steep road leading up the opposite bank. The cavalry gallantly surmounted all opposition, and sabred the Rebels who still held their ground.

Horses and men being completely exhausted by incessant marching and fighting and being nine miles now from Jhansie, I marched the troops back to Camp. I beg leave to bring to the favourable notice of the Commander in Chief the conduct of the Force under my command which fought, with the few numbers left in the Camp, a grand action with a relieving Army; beat and pursued them nine miles, killing 1,500 of them, and taking from them all their Artillery, Stores, and Ammunition . . .

I have, etc.,
(Signed) HUGH ROSE, Major Genl.,
Comdg. Central India Field Force.

The British and allied losses amounted to less than a hundred killed.

The Ranee would not allow despondency. She spent the next day and most of two nights, with her women in a cloud behind her, storming through the city, attempting to put things in order, repairing breaches, exhorting those who were ready to give up. Hugh Rose himself, his glass to his eye, remarked on how work went on on the walls, much of it carried out by women in spite of unremitting bombardment. When anyone appeared slow or lacking in will, Lakshmi Bai herself went down into the breaches and hefted fallen pieces of the wall or bags filled with sand into place. She issued a proclamation: *We fight for independence. In the words of Lord Krishna, we will, if we are victorious, enjoy the fruits of victory; if defeated and killed on the field of battle, we shall surely earn eternal glory and salvation.*

Rose himself was no slouch either. Lowe reports how he looked to the ladders that were being prepared for escalation on the left, went closer than he should to the breach that had been made on the right. He visited the sick and cheered them up and never failed to notice any good conduct. Men were rewarded on the spot and he often distributed money from his own purse among them when they pleased him by accuracy of fire or other gallant acts. He expected much of them, but never failed to show them that he too could bear the hard and harassing duties of the field.

The nights were brilliantly moonlit, so there was no chance of stealing to the walls unobserved; the hour was nigh at hand, one more dinner together, one more 'good night', a few short hours' sleep, and then to the fearful work of the 'storm'. Thomas Lowe again. He was in the very thick of it. Why? Because division of labour within the army made the sappers not only responsible for making the scaling ladders, but for bringing them forward and holding them while the storming party climbed them.

> *No sooner did we turn into the road leading towards the gate than the enemy's bugles sounded and a fire of indescribable fierceness opened upon us from the whole line of the wall, and from the towers of the fort overlooking this site. For a time it appeared like a sheet of fire, out of which burst a*

storm of bullets, round shot, and rockets, destined for our annihilation. We had upwards of two hundred yards to march through this fiendish fire, and we did it, and the sappers planted the ladders against the wall in three places for the stormers to ascend, but the fire of the enemy waxed stronger, and amid the chaos of sounds of vollies [sic] of musketry and roaring of cannon, and hissing and bursting of rockets, stink-pots, infernal machines, huge stones, blocks of wood and trees – all hurled upon their devoted heads – the men wavered for a moment, and sheltered themselves behind stones. But the ladders were there, and there the sappers, animated by the heroism of their officers, kept firm hold until a wound or death struck them down beneath the walls. It seemed as though Pluto and the furies had been loosed upon us; and inside bugles were sounding, and tom-toms beating madly, while the cannon and the musket were booming and rattling, and carrying death among us fast . . . In a few moments Lieut. Dick, Bombay Engineers, was at the top, in a few seconds more he fell from the wall, bayoneted and shot dead; Lieut. Bonus was hurled down, struck by a log of wood or a stone in the face, and Lieut. Fox, Madras Sappers, was shot through the neck; but the British soldiery pushed on, and in streams from some eight ladders at length gained a footing upon the ramparts, dealing death among the enemy . . .

Both storming parties were now flooding into the city and when this happens a city is generally lost. One reason for this is that the attackers will keep together; if things have been properly organised there will be communication between them, they will be able to call up assistance when they need it. Meanwhile, the defenders are being steadily fragmented, chains of command break down, they become isolated and can be destroyed piecemeal. Hugh Rose's despatch after the event makes clear by implication that he was well aware of this. He had divided the city into sections, briefed his brigadiers and colonels thoroughly about where their particular responsibilities lay, and they took the town methodically, step by step, thus avoiding the expensive chaos which faced Archdale Wilson's army once they were inside Delhi. The only area where this broke down was the Ranee's palace itself. The English destroyed everything: doors inlaid with plate glass, mirrors, chandeliers, again it was the mindless release of breaking glass that grabbed them. But among everything else they found a silk Union flag that had been presented to the Ranee's husband's grandfather fifty years earlier in recognition of loyal service to the Empire-builders. With Rose's permission it was hoisted on the palace roof where the Ranee saw it from the battlements of the fort.

And what of Lakshmi Bai herself? She had personally led a counterattack manned by Afghan troops, which at least sent the Brits scurrying for cover, but only until the grape-firing guns could be brought up. At that point an old tribal chief, seventy-five years old, told her: 'To be killed by their bullets is as useless as dying an ignoble death. Return to the fort and do whatever God wills you to do.' Gripped by the strange exhilaration that comes with knowing one has fought to one's utmost – and lost – she did just that, and her bodyguard of women including a newly invigorated Uma, all thoughts of Farquhar now forgotten in the excitement and desperation, went with her.

As darkness fell the Ranee stood on the battlements of the fort and wept. Below her the city, her city, burned, or seemed to. Already thousands of corpses were being hauled into heaps and set on fire. The smoke, carrying its hideous stench, blocked out the setting sun.

She turned away.

'Bring me gunpowder,' she said. 'It is time I made the sacrifice my enemies wished upon me when my husband died.'

The same tribal chief intervened.

'Go to Calpee,' he said. 'With you by his side Tatya Tope might yet contrive to win a battle.'

As long as she was in the fort, resistance would continue. Rose pondered the problem that evening, dining again in his tent.

'How can we get her out without further loss of life?' He smoked for a minute and then answered himself. 'She must know she'll die if she stays there. We must leave her a way out.' He gave orders that one of the pickets ringing the fort should be conspicuously withdrawn leaving a gap four hundred yards long in the ring that now contained it.

She took the bait, and called horses up to the hidden postern from the stabling that lay outside the fort. Legend has it that she jumped from the battlements and was borne up by the gods she worshipped, but no doubt she used the stairs and gate Farquhar had used nine months earlier. She swung into the saddle and her eight-year-old adopted son was hoisted up behind and secured with a silk sash. Then, clad in a breastplate, armed with her sword and two revolvers, she led her party down the hill and through the gap. The party included her father who had been wounded in the leg, and also an elephant with her baggage. They were fired upon but got clear, and then were pursued by a squadron of dragoons under a Lieutenant Dowker.

He got close enough to her chestnut horse to make a grab for her cape. In tandem they hurtled across the plain, pumping dust from behind their horses' hooves, but he was hit by a ball from a matchlock and forced to let go. The dragoons stuck with her for some time but their horses were blown and soon fell behind. Later in the day they came up to a mango grove where the fugitives had been having breakfast. Again they had got away but this time left the elephant and their baggage.

Twelve miles from Jhansi her father could go no further and she left him and her paymaster in the care of the zemindar of a village. He betrayed them and sold them to the dragoons who took them back to Jhansi where they were both immediately hanged from a tree in the Jokhan Bagh, above the mass grave.

The Ranee reached Calpee, a hundred miles away, within twenty-four hours. Rose had not thought she would get away. He had assumed that the women were not used to riding and would easily be captured by the dragoons.

Tatya still kept his front lines too far apart and did not sufficiently protect his flanks. The British guns, the dragoons, the Enfields and the infantryman with his bayonet were still too much for the massed ranks oppposed to them. After two defeats the rebels, with the Gwalior Contingent still intact and still their most effective corps, withdrew to the Maratha town of Gwalior itself.

The situation here was confused. Maharajah Scindia of Gwalior maintained throughout the war a pro-British stance, only apparently wavering when his life was threatened. However his private army, the Contingent, remained one of the most steadfastly rebellious of all the formations ranged against the Raj. The Maharajah lived in a fortified palace on top of a large flat-topped rock, almost a mountain, which was virtually impregnable for as long as its garrison remained loyal. This it did not do. When the Contingent turned up late in May the Maharajah had to flee up the road to Agra. On 3 June, Rao Sahib occupied the palace and held a magnificent durbar. Clad in the family's royal robes and masses of jewellery he was proclaimed viceroy to the Peshwa and the Maratha Confederacy was declared restored. The Ranee stayed away. With the British virtually knocking at the door she believed there were less frivolous things to be done.

Early in June, Sir Hugh had a mild hissy when Sir Colin dissolved the Central India Field Force and put him in command of a mere division; however, he returned to duty after a short spell of 'ill health' and on the sixteenth was four miles east of Gwalior driving the rebels out of the old cantonments. The town and its rock lay to the west, there were rocky hills spreading between them and a plain in front of them. Standing between the plain and the hills was a serai, the Kotah-ki-Serai. It is still there – a circular compound with a gate high enough to let in camels and elephants. What were the stables and rooms for travellers are now small shops.

The Ranee, with her bodyguard of women about her, was outside the serai, watching from the back of her chestnut charger the effect of the British bombardment on positions further down the line. She was wearing a red jacket, red trousers with a white silk scarf round her head, a pearl necklace taken from Scindia's treasury and heavy gold anklets. Uma Blackstock was at her side.

Suddenly, a troop of the 8th Hussars came cantering through smallholdings and small orchards to her left, an area which she supposed was held by the rebels and from which she was not expecting an attack. The hussars burst out on to the space in front of the serai and one of them went straight for her, and shot her in the back with his carbine. She was able to turn and fire a shot at him, but missed and he then cut her down with his sabre. He was never identified and never claimed the very large price that was on her head. She fell as both sides skirmished around her. The British were driven off but not before Uma too had been sabred and lay dying next to her mistress. Still alive, they were carried into a nearby mango grove. There Lakshmi Bai's last act was to distribute the necklace and anklets among her closest women. The bodies were then taken a short distance and a pyre was built beneath a tamarind tree and lit. General

Rose himself was later shown the ashes and bones. There is today a large and handsome equestrian statue of her close to the spot where she and Uma were burnt.

A mean-minded reluctance to give way once a position has been taken prevented the British, from Lord Canning down, to consider her case, first for the succession of her adopted son, then for whether or not she could have prevented the massacre. Had he done so she might well have been and remained an ally. But there were others who took a different view of her. Here is John Latimer, an officer in the Central India Field Force, on 9 July 1858:

> *The cruelties attributed to her at Jhansi have since been officially contradicted . . . Seeing her army broken and defeated, with rage in her heart and tears in her eyes, she mounted her horse and made her course towards Gwalior. Here the last stand was made, she disdained further flight, and died, with a heroism worthy of a better cause. Her courage shines pre-eminent and can only be equalled but not eclipsed by that of Joan of Arc.*

63

The River Ken, November 1857; Cawnpore, May 1858

The black panther appeared to have gone back to sleep but Lavanya was taking no chances. With a child under each arm again she stepped down into the lake and waded away from the temple, heading for the bank some one hundred yards or so above the point where her ladyship snoozed in the sun. Occasionally her tail beat the warm air around her, but more to move on the flies that were settling on what was left of her kill than to express hostility.

Stephen wriggled.

'Put me down!' he demanded.

'Wait until we're out of the water.'

'No. I can walk. Put me down.' He wriggled again.

She let him go. Splash. A squawk. Tears. She took his hand and held tight when he tried to pull it away until, hoisting him so that he dangled for a moment, she swung him on to the grassy verge. Immediately he ran between the aerial roots of a banyan tree, hid behind the trunk.

'Can't catch me.'

'Don't want to.'

'Bad Stephen,' said Deepika.

'I'm all wet.'

'Come out into the sun, then. You'll soon dry off.'

'Shan't. I'm hungry.'

'The sooner you come out and the sooner we get going again, the sooner we'll get something to eat.'

She sat down, put her hands round her raised knees. Deepika played between her long brown feet for a minute or so, counting her toes, then she too got up and wandered between the rooted pillars Lavanya sighed.

'Well, I'm going anyway,' she stood up again. 'Mind panther doesn't come for you.'

But they wouldn't come out and she had to get them. Giggling and then screaming with mock fear, they ran round her until finally she caught them and gave them a shake.

'Come o-o-on!'

The lake narrowed into a river again, quite wide, and the exposed boulders and shingle showed how in the rainy season it had been much wider. After a mile or so the land on their side began to break up and rise, soon becoming steep rocky slopes covered in trees. Monkeys, macaques, chattered and swung high above them. Kingfishers flashed emerald and lapis lazuli along the bank below. On the far side where the land was flat and cultivated in places, she could see, set back from the river, an ornate and fairly substantial sort of a palace. Though Lavanya wasn't aware of this it was the hunting lodge of the local rajah. Presently the path they were on narrowed and virtually disappeared into smoothed-over rubble left by the river. She took the children's hands again and headed away from it up the slopes, hoping that they might at least find some fruit. The only alternative was to cross the river but she guessed that the lack of a ford or a village anywhere near where they were indicated that there were hidden dangers. And some not so hidden. On the far side, quite far below them now, basking on the shingle there was another croc, even bigger than the first one they had seen. She put on speed, dragged them even more quickly up the slopes.

They followed a crest between two ravines for a time and saw a herd of six elephants walking in the shallow stream that ran down the bottom of one of them. A flock of parakeets played tag above, shrieking with pleasure at the fun of it. A pair of russet dhole dogs with bushy black tails loped by but paid no attention. Presently the slope began to level out somewhat, the trees were not so high or luxuriant, with far fewer of them. Among etiolated teak there were some tall and spreading trees with few or no leaves and almost white branches and trunks. To Lavanya they looked like the ghosts of trees. The ground was drier, more gravelly, supporting tall coarse grasses rather than thickets or shrubberies. Without the denser shade the heat became almost unsupportable. Views opened up. Looking west and south the ground was hilly, almost mountainous, thickly forested with deep, wide shaded valleys; but to the east and north, back where they had come from, she could still see the ox-bowing river and beyond it the land opening out into a plain or plateau. She began to realise she had got it wrong, made a mistake; they would have to retrace their steps, go back down and look for villages on the further side, crocodiles or no. Stephen sulked; Deepa whined. Lavanya wondered if there were an easier way down and made them walk another half-mile or so towards what looked like the edge of a ravine.

It opened out in front of them, a big semicircle of cliff, red, ochreish, dropping three hundred feet or more in what looked like quarried faces and blocks from the level they were on to a widening valley below. More monkeys sat along the lip, grooming themselves and pestering each other, but a more remarkable feature was the presence of many big birds, vultures of some sort, she supposed, perched in pairs on the many ledges by untidy nests made of small stacked branches and twigs. And beneath each nest the rock was heavily streaked white with their droppings, the droppings maybe of many seasons, right down to the scree below. And at the top of the scree a man with a small shovel was scraping the guano off the rock and spading it into a large sack. The acoustic was such that, although he was a half-mile away and far below her, she could hear the rasp of the shovel's blade.

She hallo'ed and waved her arms almost frantically above her head. Her shouts echoed back off the rock faces, bounced once, twice, three times between them. And then he looked up.

'It is so demned hot, I don't think I can stand another day like this. How long now?'

'You know very well, Papa. Just ten days. Where have you been?'

'Having tiffin with Mr Sherer. Decent feller. Got his head screwed on. Says it's daft of us to hang about waiting for a boat. Do you mind if I take my jacket off?'

'Not in the least, Papa. But as for Mr Sherer, we've been all over that several times. I'm not taking Miranda down to Allahabad by road in a palanquin or whatever and that's that. Not even with a whole troop of cavalry.'

Sophie's father took off his coat and slung it over the back of a chair, glanced round the lounge of Duncan's Hotel to see who else was there, pulled a handkerchief from his trouser pocket and wiped his face and neck. To be honest, albeit he was suffering, he looked a lot fitter than he had, had once again lost the stone he had put back on in Meerut.

'Morning, Fitz. Missed you at cards last night.'

'Morning, Chapman. Touch of the flux, took some Dr Collis, went to bed early.'

'Better now?'

'Yes, thanks.'

A rattle of old newspaper signified the subject was closed.

'Dreadful chap, talking about the state of his bowels in mixed company,' Chapman rasped at his daughter in what he thought was a whisper. 'You'll never guess who I saw coming out of the reading room. Must say they've done a good job on that; it was practically a ruin when we arrived here.'

'No, Papa, I won't.'

'Won't what?'

'Guess who you met there.'

'Ah, yes. That fellow Dixon. Captain Dixon. Hodson's Horse. Poor old Hoddy, wonder what they'll call that lot now.'

Lucky I am sitting down, thought Sophie, and fought like mad to keep her left hand from going to her left breast. Her heart rate had doubled, she was sure. Why? This was stupid. She had no reason at all to feel like this just because an old friend was virtually round the corner.

'How was . . . Captain Dixon?'

'Not good. Walking with a stick. Said the wound was still causing him gyp.'

Be still my beating heart.

'Wound?'

'Thought you knew. The ball that killed Hoddy ended up in Dixon's groin. Well, not exactly. Had enough force to scrape the skin with the cloth of what he was wearing, left a nasty bruise and it all became infected. Asked him to have dinner with us tonight. Hope that's all right with you?'

431

It turned out to be an awkward meal. Dixon and Sophie found little they could talk to each other about that was not too painfully serious to be discussed in the public rooms. However, when Dixon took his leave he offered to wait on Sophie in the morning, before it got too hot to be out. Her father surprisingly discovered enough tact to say he would not accompany them since he had an engagement to see his new friend Sherer who was now established in Cawnpore as the senior magistrate. They met at seven o'clock in the hall of the hotel. Outside Sophie hoisted her parasol and took his elbow with her free hand.

'I don't know where to go,' she said. 'I hate this place. There are horrors in every direction.'

'The church?'

'If you like. At least we can sit outside. I'd rather not go in.'

'I understand that. At least I think I do.'

'I wonder if you do. Church, the services and all that, can be very beautiful, and even a consolation, but, well . . .'

'A whited sepulchre?'

'Something like that.'

They did indeed find a bench outside the west door and spread themselves on it.

'I was not aware you knew my father?'

'Oh, only slightly. He comes over to Sherborne occasionally to do business with my father. My father owns the major, um, brewery there and bought barley from Mr Chapman.'

Sophie laughed a little.

'Nothing wrong with brewing. A very respectable occupation these days. Think of Mr Whitbread.'

'Our nation has a great desire to find respectability in any occupation that makes money.'

'Indeed, yes. Now tell me why you are in Cawnpore.'

'My wound, though not life threatening, is deemed to be sufficiently at risk of becoming worse in this climate for it to be recommended to me that I take some months off at home until it is properly healed. Since I cannot ride I am engaged to be on the same boat to Allahabad as you.'

'Indeed we may then share the whole voyage home.'

'It's possible,' he agreed.

*

They spent many hours over the next few days in each other's company and found, albeit they proceeded with delicacy and mutual awareness of their departed spouses, much pleasure therein, to the extent that Mr Chapman began to make sly remarks about a possible romance which Sophie was at pains to discountenance. However, on boarding the steam pinnace, waiting for its departure, they realised that Dixon was not in the company: a bellboy from the hotel was, and he thrust a note in her hands just as a short poop from the boat's whistle announced their imminent departure.

Dearest Sophie

I write to say that I am not after all able to accompany you and your father on your journey home. The fact of the matter is that over the last few days, and indeed, if you want to know the truth, for sometime before that, I have entertained feelings for you that go beyond those of normal friendship and I fear that if we had remained in each other's company I should have been forced to make a declaration and ask you to make me the happiest man alive.

However, this is not to be. Why not is a matter of some delicacy, but I see no recourse except to be blunt about it. The nature of the hurt I suffered in the siege of Lucknow is such that it may very possibly circumscribe my ability to perform those marital duties that should be the delight of every married couple. And indeed medical opinion has declared that our union would not be blessed with children. I have no right to suggest to you a relationship which would deny you the greatest happiness any woman can hope for, that of having children whose father holds you in the highest esteem heaven allows.

I remain, dear Sophie your humble, most devoted and unhappy admirer,
Yours etc.

James Dixon. (Capt.)

The young guano collector – he was about Lavanya's age – lived with his mother on a smallholding, one of the very few on that side of the river. He was friendly and kind: although he was carrying a quite heavy sack of guano (which, he explained, did wonders for a new crop they were growing, called maize) he took Stephen on his shoulders, allowing

Lavanya to carry Deepika the whole way. Both children were naturally delighted with this arrangement. He talked incessantly on the way down, perhaps to conceal his shyness, perhaps to spare Lavanya the possible embarrassment of explaining her situation and the fact that one of her children was European and the other clearly Native. He pointed out and named the birds they saw, far more than she had noticed on the way up, but then he seemed to have the knack of noticing what someone less interested would have missed: two hoopoes, cinnamon, black and white, raising their crests at each other in the grass; bee-eaters, green and dark red; purple sunbirds, a black shouldered kite in the top of a tree, a fish-owl, ditto; a drongo, like a blackbird but with a long forked tail, and, now they were by the river again, a small cormorant and a great egret. In the sand on the edge of the water he showed them the paw prints of a civet and then a jungle cat, and wild boar diggings. There was a dead pariah dog too which he said was not one of his, and had possibly been killed by a leopard. He knew the trees too: a lantana tree with orange flowers, a variety of plum they used in pickles and the elephant apple, ditto, both in bloom.

They climbed the bank and she found they were now in small fields or plots with crops whose plants, her background, being limited to a family in service to the sahibs, had left her ignorant of: lentils, chickpeas, peppers, wheat, and a stand of maize, just then about waist-high, but which he said would grow as high as an elephant's eye. And then the farmhouse – that's far too grand a word, the hut – where he and his mother lived, a squared-off building about twelve feet by twelve feet made from baked cow dung with a thatched roof sloping down each side from a roof tree. It stood in the shade of a large tamarind, and was set on a raised bank, so, he said, it would be above the controlled flood they let spread over all the land in July. A cock and six white hens waddled away from them, leading them in, and a small pet monkey on the end of a light chain swung up a pear tree. There was a well with a bucket.

Out in the wheat field there was a small domed temple, sacred to Parvati, the goddess, with two saffron pennants on bending bamboo poles.

His name was Gulam. Because of his harelip and the fact that he and his mother lived on the wrong side of the river, he did not expect ever to have a wife.

And he was wrong.

434

64

Last Words

Tatya Tope was hanged after losing the Battle of Gwalior. His stoic behaviour on the gallows earned the admiration of onlookers.

In 1860 Colin Campbell, now Lord Clyde, retired to Chatham in Kent with a pension of £2000 a year. He died three years later.

Bahadur Shah, the last of the Mughals, was exiled to Rangoon where he died in 1862.

Lord Canning, exhausted and heartbroken at Charlotte's death in India from malaria, also died in 1862. Before he retired, the East India Company was wound up and India came under direct British rule: Canning was the first Viceroy.

The Nana escaped to Nepal where he remained until Jung Bahadur threw him out. No one knows what happened to him after that.

Azimullah Khan possibly got away with an Englishwoman known as Miss Clayton. He settled in Istanbul as emissary of the Sherif of Mecca and was believed to have been assassinated many years later.

Captain William Peel, VC, was knighted but died from smallpox in 1858.

I cannot entirely make up my mind about what happened to the fictional characters.

Maybe Dixon recovered the use of his balls and eventually married Sophie. Maybe he did not.

However, I am certain that Lavanya had six more children and yet found time to expand Gulam's smallholding into a prosperous little estate growing cash crops like indigo, cotton and opium. Stephen was accepted as an Indian lad with a wheaten complexion and soon forgot that he had ever been anything else, though very occasionally, when stressed, he dreamed of an angel in white. Under the new dispensations he became a lawyer. By the time he died, in 1935 (the year I was born, so close in time are we still to 1857), he was a retired high court judge. His father would have been pleased.

Notes and Reflections

Very extensive reforms were made following the Mutiny, both to the Indian Army and the governance of India. Most notable of the latter was the creation of a Native civil service, educated in Western ways in universities in the four major cities, which created an influential middle class. No doubt the aim was, in part at any rate, the restoration of the social conditions of profitability. It was from this class that later leaders of the independence movement came, people like Mahatma Gandhi himself.

The building of railways and roads, hospitals and schools was accelerated creating the infrastructure of the modern nation-state India eventually became. Only 1 per cent of the taxes collected in India went into the British treasury. The rest was spent on the improvements described above.

Abuses remained, but these were mostly the result not so much of direct rule as the promotion of free trade under the *laissez faire* economic policies of successive British governments. These led to horrific famines when harvests failed, due to the El Niño phenomenon, because the reserve grain was held by independent, mostly Asian, traders who used the shortages to make huge fortunes. Later, protectionism and imperial preferences also held back investment and industrialisation. Britain undoubtedly benefited from, in Ruskin's phrase, the loot of empires, but through investment and accumulation of capital rather than direct taxation. India became India, the largest democracy in the world.

It should not be forgotten that in 1757 a state of anarchy existed in India in which rajahs and princes fought each other, failed to maintain order and law, and indulged in massive conspicuous consumption that benefited no one but the moneylenders and tax farmers.

The Mutiny, A Novel necessarily concentrates on the English experience of the Mutiny. I cannot presume to have any more than the most minimal and superficial understanding of Indian culture in the mid-nineteenth century in any of its manifestations. However, I hope I have been even-handed in showing how both sides were guilty of the most appalling atrocities while remaining capable of extreme gallantry and self-sacrifice. Both nations failed to learn some of the appropriate lessons. For instance during the Mau Mau rising in Kenya in the 1950s the English hanged seven hundred and forty-four insurgents in the very last decade of Empire. Since 1947 the Indian record with minorities seeking a measure of independence within its borders has been less than unblemished.

Mutiny, conspiracy, popular uprising, or a War of Independence? Certainly it was a mutiny: the sepoys and sowars of the Company army had many causes for serious discontent, of which the real or imagined issue of cartridges greased with pork or cow fat was the last straw. Apart from matters of pay and conditions of service there was the very real and justified perception that a main plank in the British project was the conversion of South Asia to Christianity. The evidence that there was a conspiracy involving the King of Delhi and various rajahs and princes is almost entirely circumstantial but very convincing. There was a popular rising, involving the peasantry and villages, in the Oudh and to a lesser extent the Doab, but not to any great or significant extent anywhere else. Much of South Asia, including the Native army, remained loyal to the British or at any rate uninvolved. A War of Independence? No. India was a multifarious collection of ethnicities, religions (which persecuted each other mercilessly when stirred up to do so), kingdoms, principalities, and enclaves: a war of independence could not be a reality until it had been shaped into the nation-state which was the supreme achievement of the Raj between 1857 and 1947.

I have often used the word 'English' rather than 'British', for two reasons. Even the histories use these terms as if they were interchangeable. My own feeling is that the word 'British' has very little if any real meaning, and is merely shorthand for the United

Kingdoms, Principality and Province that make up Great Britain. It has administrative usefulness, and it allows us to play rugby football against the Kiwis with a reasonable chance of winning. We go to the Olympics as the United Kingdom and so presumably as the British; however, we send three separate nations to the Commonwealth Games and the World Cups for football and rugby. The present Prince of Wales frequently uses the words England and English when he means Britain and British.

The spelling of Indian names and occasionally vocabulary has been a problem. I have reverted almost always to forms and spellings current in English texts during the 1850s, though these are by no means consistent. My use of the spelling 'Hindoo' is a case in point and is not intended in any way to be derogatory. I have used 'Hindu' when the context requires general or twenty-first-century usage.

Sources

The list that follows is presented in a spirit of gratitude rather than as a demonstration that I have done some homework; it is also here to provide a partial guide to those readers who have been moved or interested by my story to find out more. It is not intended to be a sort of proof that I have got the history right. I'm sure I have not, and in one or two places I know I have not. *Mutiny, A Novel*, is just that – a novel, and that is how it should be read and, if necessary, judged. It is the story of fictional characters presented against a re-imagined historical background: in short a historical novel.

There are two popular histories of the Mutiny readily available and I have read both and used both extensively. Particularly I have found their bibliographies enormously useful. They are: *The Great Mutiny: India 1857* by Christopher Hibbert, published by Allen Lane and Penguin in 1978 and 1980; and *The Indian Mutiny 1857* by Saul David, published by Viking Penguin in 2002. For the Cawnpore massacres and Lucknow particularly I used *Angels of Albion: Women of the Indian Mutiny* by Jane Robinson, published by Viking Penguin in 1996. I also read and used *The Indian Mutiny of 1857* by Colonel G. B Malleson (London, 1892); *1857* by Surendranath Sen (New Delhi, 1957); *Awadh in Revolt 1857–1858* by Rudrangshu Mukherjee (New Delhi, 1984); and used *Selections from the Despatches and other State Papers 1857–58, edited by George W. Forrest, Volume IV* (Calcutta, 1912), for the official English accounts of the Battle of Betwa, the Siege of Jhansi and the death of the Ranee of Jhansi.

Guided by these books I also read numerous collections of contemporary letters, diaries and memoirs, many of them published by the Naval and Military Press, and I found much useful and stimulating material in the collections in the National Army Museum, Chelsea, the staff of which I would particularly like to thank for their unwavering helpfulness and courtesy. One of my main regrets regarding *Mutiny, A Novel* is that there has not been room to quote more extensively from these contemporary sources. Almost without exception they are wonderfully well written: vivid, detailed and often stylistically terse in a way the novelists of the period are not.

The use I made of these contemporary sources is exemplified in Pamela Courteney's letter from Lucknow. This is an amalgam of selections taken from several collections of letters and memoirs. Pamela Courteney herself is a fiction. However, passages purporting to have been written by historical persons such as J. W. Sherer, Edward Spencer Watson and Major General Henry Rose are edited versions of actual documents.

Although both describe India thirty years or more after the Mutiny I returned to Rudyard Kipling and discovered Mark Twain's *Following the Equator*.

And of course there was the Web. I was amazed at the amount of relevant material there was there: nineteenth century maps, the uniforms of all the regiments involved, the income of an infantry officer and how it was disposed, numerous contemporary paintings, photographs and drawings, many of specific incidents, a life of Lakshmi Bai with a detailed account of her English lawyer's visit, a detailed account of a journalist's visit to the Enfield factory, and so on and so on.

But best and most exciting of all was a tailor-made tour by car, train and plane of all the main sites mentioned in this book, organised by Nina Barua at Excel Travel who understood what I was up to and where we should go. It all worked out perfectly. And I should also mention with gratitude Nasir Abid, our guide in Lucknow, who not only knew in detail the events and places I needed to know about, but also checked the Lucknow chapters for topographical or historical errors. He even arranged for us to spend a rewarding couple of hours with a very real rajah, one of whose ancestors was a leader in the Lucknow rising.

Characters

The main purpose of this list, which may not be complete, though I have tried to make it so, is to inform the interested reader which characters are fictional and which historical. Thus, 'f' signifies 'fictional', 'h' historical.

Ahmed Ahmadullah Shah, the Maulvi of Faizabad, conspirator and preacher h
Alec, Pte, of the 75th f
Anderson, Dr, regimental surgeon of the 93rd h
Andrews, A., Deputy Collector at Jhansi h
Andrews, Rose, wife of Mr Andrews h
Anson, Mrs, guest of the Blackstocks h
Ashanullah Khan, Hakim, physician and adviser to Bahadur Shah h
Atkinson, Sgt, paraplegic in the Residency garrison f
Babur, havildar, accompanying Hardcastle as far as Bindki f
Bahadur Shah II, King of Delhi, proclaimed Emperor h
Balachandra, leader of Meerut badmashes h
Barnard, Maj. Gen. Sir Henry, o/c briefly at Badli-ki-Serai, died of cholera at Delhi h
Barter, Lt (later Capt.) Richard, of the 75th, author of *Mutiny Memoirs*, published by The Folio Society as *The Siege of Delhi* (1984) h
Baugh, Lt Henry, 31st N.I. h
Bhutt, Baba, the elder of the Nana's brothers h
Blackstock, Col (rtd) Sir Charles, KB, later military adviser to the Chief Commissioner for the Oudh f

Blackstock, Lady Betty, wife of Col (rtd) Sir Charles, KB f

Blackstock, Uma, putative daughter of Col Blackstock, stepdaughter of Lady Blackstock, f , but in part based on more than one anonymous h characters

Bonus, Lt, Bombay Engineers, killed in the storming of Jhansi h

Buckley, John, VC, Conductor of Ordnance, Delhi h

Butcher, the, of Meerut Bazaar h

Campbell, Gen. Sir Colin, later Lord Clyde, C in C India h

Canning, Lady Charlotte, wife of Lord Canning h

Canning, Viscount Charles, Governor General of India 1856–8, later Earl, GCB, first Viceroy h

Carmichael-Smyth, Col George, of the 3rd Light (Native) Cavalry h

Carshore, Mr, chief customs officer, Jhansi, killed with his wife and son h

Chambers, Capt., adjutant, of 11th Light Cavalry, Meerut h

Chambers, Charlotte, wife of Capt. Chambers h

Charlie, aka Joseph Charles Edward Bosham, central character in *Joseph, A Very English Agent* and *Birth of a Nation* f

Cohen, Francis, German Jew, owner of villages between Delhi and Meerut h

Courteney, Pamela, wife of Capt. Courteney, based in Lucknow f

Craigie, Capt., 3rd Light Cavalry, Meerut h

Dalhousie, James Ramsay, 10th Earl of, later Marquess, Governor General of India 1848–1856 h

Dawson, Capt. and veterinary surgeon to the Meerut Station h

Dawson, Mrs, wife of the Meerut veterinary surgeon h

Deepa (Deepika), daughter of Lavanya f

Dick, Lt, Bombay Engineers, killed in the storming of Jhansi h

Dixon, Capt. James of the 3rd Light (Native) Cavalry f

Dixon, Catherine, wife of James f

Dixon, Adam, Miranda, Emma, Robert, children of Catherine and James f

Dorin, Mrs, killed in Gubbins's house, Lucknow h

Douglas, Capt., i/c the King of Delhi's bodyguard h

Dowker, Lt, Dragoons, pursued Lakshmi Bai from Jhansi h

Dunkellin, Lord, nephew of Canning, Military Secretary h

Edwards, Capt., Paymaster to the 75th h

Ewart, Col, of the 93rd at Lucknow h

Farquhar, Lt Bruce, of the 75th (Gordon Highlanders) f

Fetherstonhaugh Capt., Arthur, f

Fetherstonhaugh, Hugh, eight-year-old son of Mrs Fetherstonhaugh f

Fetherstonhaugh, Mrs, née Beresford, wife of Captain Fetherstonhaugh f

Fisherman from Bithur f

Fitzgerald, Lt, 75th, killed in the storming of Delhi h

Forrest, Lt, George, VC, Ordnance Dept, Delhi h

Fox, Lt, Madras Sappers, killed in the storming of Jhansi h

Fraser, Simon, Commissioner of Delhi h

Gascoigne, Capt. Simon, killed at Lucknow f

George, Cpl, of the 75th f

Germon, Mrs Maria, author of *A Journal of the Siege of Lucknow* h

Gordon, Col h

Greathead, Col Edward, first commander of the Delhi Flying Column h

Gubbins, Martin, Financial Commissioner in the Oudh h

Hardcastle, Capt. Tom, assistant judge advocate f

Hardcastle, Miranda, daughter of Sophie and Tom, born July 1857 f

Hardcastle, Sophie, née Chapman, wife of Tom f

Hardcastle, Stephen, son of Sophie and Tom, born 26 December 1854 f

Havelock, Brig. Gen. Henry, later Sir, KCB h

Hearsey, Maj. Gen. Sir John h

Hewitt, Maj. Gen., Commander of the Meerut Station h

Hewson, Sgt Maj. James, 31st N.I., attempted to arrest Mungal Pandy h

Hillersdon, Charles, Collector at Cawnpore f

Hodson, Lt, later Maj., William Raikes, of Hodson's Horse, reputed model for Harry Flashman of *Tom Brown's Schooldays* h

Hutchinson, John, magistrate in Delhi h

Jackson, Coverley, Chief Commissioner of the Oudh, 1856 h

James, Lt of Engineers, guest of the Blackstocks f

Kavanagh, Tom Henry, VC, clerk in the Deputy Commissioner's office, Lucknow h

Khan, Azimullah, vakil to the Nana Saheb h

Khan, Housseini, member of the Nana's household, the woman in charge of the Bibigarh h

Khan, Sarvur, consort of Housseini Khan, member of the Nana's bodyguard h

Khan, Yusuf, sepoy lt in charge of the guard on the Bibigarh h

Lakshmi Bai, the Ranee of Jhansi, the Joan of Arc of India h

Lascelles, Henry, naval cadet from HMS *Shannon*, with the Naval Brigade h

Lavanya, wet nurse and later ayah to Stephen Hardcastle f

Lawrence, Gen. Sir Henry Montgomery, Chief Commissioner of the Oudh, 1857 h

Lowe, Thomas, medical officer of the Madras Sappers and Engineers, author of *Central India during the Rebellion* h

McCartney, Sgt, a malingerer from Toxteth f

Macdowell, Lt Malcolm, of Hodson's Horse h

Marchant, Mrs Victoria, guest of the Blackstocks, later at Meerut f

McGuinness, Mrs Dolly, madame of the Meerut brothel h

Micklewight, Arnold, Superintendent at the Enfield Ordnance Factory h (though I have invented the name)

Mill, John Stuart, Examiner of India Correspondence, East India Company, author of *On Liberty* etc. h

Möller, Lt, Meerut h

Moore, Capt. John, became stand-in commander at Cawnpore h

Moore, Mrs, wife of Captain Moore h

Nana Saheb, aka Govinda Dhondu Pant, *soi-disant* Maharajah of Bithur and Peshwa of the Marathas h

Nanak, accountant for the village of Bindki f

Nathan, Pvt., of the 75th f

Neill, Lt Col. James, later Gen., 1st Madras European Regiment, later Commander at Cawnpore, killed during final assault on Lucknow h

Nicholson, Brig. John, died following the storming of Delhi h

Nixon, Fraser's head clerk, Delhi h

Outram, Maj. Gen. Sir James, Chief Commissioner of the Oudh following the first relief h

Pandy, Lt Issuree, possibly Mungal's brother, also hanged h

Pandy, Mungal, the first sepoy to be executed for mutiny h

Patel, Mrs Rosemary, wife of a Lucknow merchant f (but based on h)

Peel, Capt. Sir William, VC, of HMS *Shannon*, commanding the Naval Brigade h

Prasad, Jawala, commander of the Nana's troops h

Prasad, Jiva, headman of Bindki village f

Purcell, surveyor for the electric telegraph, killed at Jhansi h

Rao, Bala, younger brother of the Nana h

Rathbone, Philip Henry, Liverpudlian businessman, philanthropist, patron of the arts, great-grandfather of the author h

Raynor, Lt, VC, Ordnance Dept, Delhi h

Rose, Maj. Gen. Sir Hugh, commander of the Central India Field Force h

Rossiter, the Very Rev. Canon, guest of the Blackstocks f

Rotton, the Rev. John Ewart, chaplain of St John's, Meerut, later of Delhi h

Russell, William, journalist, war reporter for *The Times* h

Sam, Pvt., of the 75th f

Saunders, Reginald, railway surveyor f

Saunders, Elizabeth h

Scindia, Maharajah of Gwalior h

Scully, conductor of ordnance, Delhi h

Sherer, John Walter, Magistrate and Collector at Futtehpore, later Chief Magistrate at Cawnpore, author of *Daily Life during the Indian Mutiny*, etc. h

Singh, Gopal h

Singh, Ranjit, butler to the Blackstocks f

Singh, Teeka, Cawnpore mutineer, later commander of the Nana's cavalry h

Skene, Capt. Alexander, Superintendant of Jhansi fort and town, killed in massacre h

Skene, Jamie, Capt. Skene's ten-year-old son, killed in Jhansi massacre h

Smyth, the Rev. Tom, curate and later chaplain of St John's, Meerut h

Taff, Pte., of the 75th f

Tatya Tope, also known as 'Bennie', real name Ramchandra Panduranga, follower of the Nana, later commander of the Gwalior Contingency h

Thornhill, Robert, son of a director of the East India Company, murdered at the Bibigarh h

Tredonnick, Mrs, killed while playing cards, Lucknow f

Tucker, Robert T., District Judge in Futtehpore h

Tytler, Capt. Robert h

Unnamed philosophical picket at the Baillie Guard, Lucknow h

Vakil, the, unnamed, of the Ranee of Jhansi h

Vibart, Maj. Edward, escaped from Cawnpore, was captured and died of wounds h

THE LAST ENGLISH KING

Julian Rathbone

In 1066 a 'jumped-up little Norman and his bunch of psychopaths' cross the water and alter the course of English history. Three years later and Walt, King Harold's only surviving bodyguard, is still emotionally and physically scarred by the loss of his king and country. Wandering through Asia Minor, headed vaguely for the Holy Land, he tells his extraordinary story.

'Embroidering fact with fiction, rather as the makers of the Bayeux tapestry did, Rathbone has Walt expand on the confessions of Edward the Confessor, on the megalomaniac notions of Canute's descendants, the ambitions of the Saxon thanes, and the savage empire building of William the Conqueror . . . powerful'
Sunday Telegraph

'Fascinating'
Guardian

'There are scenes of such solidity that no reader will easily forget them'
The Times

'Gripping . . . a rattling good story, told in strong, clear prose . . . unforgettable'
Spectator

Abacus
978-0-349-10943-5

Now you can order superb titles directly from Abacus

☐	The Last English King	Julian Rathbone	£7.99
☐	A Very English Agent	Julian Rathbone	£7.99
☐	Kings of Albion	Julian Rathbone	£7.99
☐	Joseph	Julian Rathbone	£8.99

The prices shown above are correct at time of going to press. However, the publishers reserve the right to increase prices on covers from those previously advertised, without further notice.

──────────────── ⟨ABACUS⟩ ────────────────

Please allow for postage and packing: **Free UK delivery.**
Europe; add 25% of retail price; Rest of World; 45% of retail price.

To order any of the above or any other Abacus titles, please call our credit card orderline or fill in this coupon and send/fax it to:

Abacus, P.O. Box 121, Kettering, Northants NN14 4ZQ
Fax: 01832 733076   Tel: 01832 737526
Email: aspenhouse@FSBDial.co.uk

☐ I enclose a UK bank cheque made payable to Abacus for £ . . . .
☐ Please charge £ . . . . . . to my Visa, Delta, Maestro.

Expiry Date ☐☐☐☐   Maestro Issue No. ☐☐

NAME (BLOCK LETTERS please) . . . .

ADDRESS . . . .

. . . .

. . . .

Postcode . . . . Telephone . . . .

Signature . . . .

Please allow 28 days for delivery within the UK. Offer subject to price and availability.